FAKE
SKATING

Also by Lynn Painter

Better Than the Movies
The Do-Over
Betting on You
Nothing Like the Movies

FAKE SKATING

LYNN PAINTER

SIMON & SCHUSTER

London New York Amsterdam/Antwerp Sydney/Melbourne Toronto New Delhi

First published in Great Britain in 2025 by Simon & Schuster UK Ltd

First published in the USA in 2025 by Simon & Schuster Books for Young Readers,
an imprint of Simon & Schuster Children's Publishing Division,
1230 Avenue of the Americas, New York, New York 10020

1 3 5 7 9 10 8 6 4 2

Simon & Schuster UK Ltd
1st Floor, 222 Gray's Inn Road
London WC1X 8H

www.simonandschuster.co.uk
www.simonandschuster.com.au
www.simonandschuster.co.in

Simon & Schuster Australia, Sydney
Simon & Schuster India, New Delhi

The authorised representative in the EEA is Simon & Schuster Netherlands BV, Herculesplein 96,
3584 AA Utrecht, Netherlands. info@simonandschuster.nl

A CIP catalogue record for this book is available from the British Library.

PB ISBN 978-1-3985-3786-6
eBook ISBN 978-1-3985-3788-0
eAudio ISBN 978-1-3985-3787-3

Printed and Bound in India by Thomson Press India Ltd.

MIX
Paper | Supporting
responsible forestry
FSC® C010615

The way you are doesn't have to make sense to anyone else.
You are *exactly* how you're supposed to be.
YOU ARE PERFECT.

And you might not have met them yet,
but there are people who are going to love you
BECAUSE
of the way you are.

FAKE SKATING

PROLOGUE
Alec

There was no way it was actually happening.

Dani Collins was moving to Southview.

"Impossible," I muttered to myself as I stomped on the gas pedal.

An hour ago life had been normal. I'd walked through the front door after practice, inhaled a few bowls of goulash while my dad talked about his buddy's new duck boat, and I'd been just about to leave the table when my mom gave me the news.

She'd excitedly filled me in on the details of how Dani's parents were getting divorced and now Dani and her mom were going to move in with her grandpa. She squealed about how incredible it was going to be to finally have them close by.

Just imagine how often we can see them now!

I smiled and nodded like a good boy while trying not to lose my ever-loving shit at the thought of having to see her every day.

Dani Collins.

Was moving.

To fucking. Southview.

I made up an excuse to get out of the house as soon as possible, because I needed air—and music—while I tried to wrap my head around this unexpected turn of events. I had a cousin who neurotically made playlists for every waking moment of her life, and that slightly obsessive habit had rubbed off on me to the point that I couldn't deal with the harshness of reality anymore unless I rolled it around in music first.

So I got in Burrito (my piece-of-shit '03 Olds Alero) and just drove, cranking "Escorpião," the Brazilian song that I didn't understand but fucking loved. I knew the translation was something along the lines of "'I love you' is bullshit," so that seemed good enough for me.

But almost as if Burrito had a mind of his own, I found myself turning down the barely there dirt road that wound through the woods next to the pond. I drove over the snow-packed path until I saw the old, abandoned shed that had once been "our spot."

What the fuck am I doing?

The night was quiet, the deep snow insulating the world so all I could hear was the crunch of snow under my shoes as I got out of the car and walked toward the structure. It'd always looked like it was five minutes from collapsing, and that hadn't changed since the last time I'd been there.

The summer after seventh grade.

I pushed in the door of the abandoned shed and stepped inside, half expecting a pack of raccoons to fly at my face. It was darker than dark, but when I turned on my phone's flashlight, it felt like I'd taken a puck to the chest because how could it still look the same?

The actual chairs we'd stolen from my dad's shop to furnish our ridiculous little shed were still there, and so was the massive hole in the roof that we called our skylight.

Holy shit.

I swallowed and looked up at the moon. Everything about "our spot" remained the same. And, who was I kidding, so was the memory of her. Of Dani.

And the last time I saw her.

Five-ish Years Ago

"I don't want to go home."

I looked at Dani's profile as she stared up at the moon and couldn't believe she was already leaving. We were sitting side by side on a blanket in the pond shed and I uttered the understatement of the century when I said, "This sucks."

Dani and her mom came for one month every summer, one month where our mothers (best friends) hung out twenty-four seven and we got to do whatever we wanted, every single day. We rode bikes, went fishing, walked endless miles while debating *everything*, hung out at the pool . . . it was summer perfection.

It'd been an annual event for longer than I could remember.

Literally.

The reason for their annual visit was to see Dani's grandparents, but since she spent most of her time with me at our house (or in our shed hangout), it always felt like *our* vacation.

And it was hands down the best part of summer break.

Because for one month of the year, she was my best friend.

We screwed around and laughed our asses off for thirty days, and then she went back to whatever Air Force base her dad was stationed at until the next season of the fireflies.

But now they were leaving after only two days. This time their visit had been for her grandma's funeral, and this time her prickish dad—*the colonel*—had come with them.

Which was a big mistake, because his presence made everything blow way the hell up.

It was epic in the worst way.

3

Mick—Dani's grandpa—lost his shit on her dad after the funeral, saying it was Mr. Collins's fault that her grandma died of a broken heart because he took Dani's mom away and moved her all over the country.

Then Mick told them—in front of everyone—to go back to "wherever the hell you're stationed now" and get out of his sight.

Yep—nightmare.

And now they were leaving in the morning.

Which meant we wouldn't be walking to Kriz's Bakery, where we were supposed to sit at a sticky table outside and try to guess which donuts the customers were going to order by what they were wearing.

One of our (many) annual traditions.

"I know it makes me a garbage person," she said, looking at me with brown eyes that were too sad, "but I think I'm more bummed about not getting my month here than I am about the whole family-fight thing."

And then I saw it.

She had tears in her eyes.

Seeing anyone with tears in their eyes made me uncomfortable; I wasn't good with serious. But seeing the most sarcastic person I'd ever met, looking sad?

It was a little gutting, to be honest.

"Collins," I said, bumping her shoulder with mine, needing to nudge her back to a comfortable spot. "If you cry, I swear to God I will toss you out of this shed and into the pond."

She coughed out a laugh, and her voice was thick when she said, "Such a little badass, threatening me when we both know you couldn't, come on."

"You're so mean," I teased.

"And you're so short," she teased back, a painless joke because I wasn't short; she was just taller than everyone else.

"You're not a garbage person, by the way," I said, noticing that her eyes still had that emotional shimmer that made me want to kick her grandpa's ass for being a dick. "You're allowed to be sad that you don't get to stay."

She swallowed and bit down on her lower lip, like she was trying to hold it together.

"I mean, *I'm* sad," I admitted, my voice cracking because I *was* sad. How was I supposed to summer without running all over town with Dani?

"You are?" she asked, her voice so quiet it was almost a whisper. Her eyes moved all over my face. "Really?"

I nodded and felt a stabbing pain in my chest when I watched a tear escape, because Dani Collins couldn't be crying.

She *couldn't*.

Suddenly everything in the universe shifted, and I just needed her to stop. Immediately.

Everything was wrong if she wasn't happy.

Because Dani was sparkling eyes and contagious laughter. Dani was happiness.

Before I knew it, my thumbs were on her cheeks, brushing away the tears, and I struggled to swallow as she stared at me like she was trying to figure out what was happening.

"I don't know either," I admitted, because we'd always been able to read each other's minds, and I had no idea why I suddenly wanted to kiss her. "I don't know what this is."

"Same," she said, nodding. Her eyes went down to my mouth, and in an instant my pulse was pounding.

"Should we?" I asked—no, *breathed*—as I realized my thumbs were still sliding over her soft skin.

Did I seriously just ask (without saying it) if we should kiss?

What the hell is happening?

"I mean, we have to have our firsts *some*time," she said, reading my mind about the kiss and getting that look of resolve in her eyes that meant she was all in on something.

No one committed to scheming like Dani. She was game to do nearly anything. I always wondered if that was just the "vacation" version of Dani, or if she was like that at home, too.

"So maybe we . . . should?"

She said it with a question in her voice, and I had no idea how we'd gotten here.

Holy *shit*.

"Are you serious?" I managed, my voice coming out a tiny bit strangled. *Should my hands still be on her face?*

What the hell?

Why did this sound like a great idea when it was *Dani*?

"I think I am," she said, her eyes dancing, pushing away the sadness.

I might've been able to reverse it, to pretend for the sake of our friendship that we hadn't contemplated it, but then she looked at me like *that*, and it was over.

She looked at me like she wanted me to kiss her. Like she was *waiting* for me to lean in.

And, God help me, I'd dreamed of kissing her far too long for me to be strong.

"Then come closer, Collins."

I inhaled through my nose as my brain rewound crystal-clear memories of lying back on that blanket and losing my mind with her. The smell of the shed—a mix of dirt and cedar and nostalgic longing—wasn't helping, either. The scents were so fucking familiar that it felt like I should follow the walls over to the tiny section in the corner where we'd written nonsensical bullshit with paint markers, just to see if our long-forgotten artwork remained.

But the second that popped into my head, I remembered the rest.

And then I didn't want to remember at all anymore.

Because even though it'd been years, I was still pissed. Logically, it should've been water under the bridge by now. *I should be over it.*

But as I drove home, I realized that I wasn't.

Like, at all.

We might be older, and it might be illogical, but I still hated Dani Collins for what she did after the night we kissed.

"Te quero bem" é o caralho
Eu vou acabar contigo

Or, in English:

"I love you" is bullshit
I'm going to end you

CHAPTER ONE
February—Senior Year

Dani

"Wake up—we're here."

I opened my eyes, but instead of seeing my bedroom, I saw snow and gray skies through the cold window that my forehead was resting on.

The same things I'd stared at for countless hours before finally falling asleep.

Damn it—it's real.

"Remind me again why we're moving here," I said, leaning down to shove my feet back into my Chucks. We drove seven hours in a moving truck full of our stuff (that'd been incorrectly shipped to our old address in Minot—*thanks, Air Force*) so we could now live in a place where there appeared to be multiple feet of snow on the ground and the windchill was subzero—like, make it make sense. "I mean, why not California?"

"We've been over this. Too expensive, too hot in the summer, and you're going to love living here," my mom said, shutting off the truck and pulling the keys out of the ignition. "You loved it when you were younger, remember?"

The main reason I loved it was because of Alec.

My stomach instantly knotted at the thought of him and the reality that I was going to have to face him after he'd ghosted our long-distance friendship. I was dreading that awkward reunion with every fiber of my being, and still slightly pissed, but I was also hopeful that once the embarrassing moment passed, he'd be the best thing about the move.

Or at least he'd help it be . . . marginally less nightmarish.

Because Alec Barczewski had always been a hilarious ray of sunshine with the uncanny ability to make everything better. It'd been a long time and we were obviously different people now, but in my heart I knew that my dorky friend would somehow make this okay.

"Loving a place you visit once a year—in the summer—is totally different from living there year-round," I muttered, opening the door and jumping down from the truck, the icy wind slapping at my cheeks as I jerked up the hood on my jacket. "Especially when the winter climate is abysmal."

Dear Lord, it feels like there are shards of glass in that wind. Whyyyyyy do people choose to live in a place so cold? I'd lived in the cold before, so it wasn't new to me, but I'd somehow managed to forget just how harsh it felt.

"Quit complaining. I just drove through White Castle, so you've got a slider and fries in your bag," she said, coming around to grab my arm and loop it through hers after I shut the door.

"Seriously?" My stomach growled and I caught a whiff of onion as I looked down at my tote. "Perfect last meal before I freeze to death, thank you."

"And we are now officially residents of Southview," she proclaimed with a terrifying amount of finality in her voice. "Like it or not."

I sighed and thought *a thousand times NOT* as I pulled out a tiny burger and lifted it to my mouth. I took a bite and stared at the big white house in front of us, my stomach heavy with dread as I chewed.

Which kind of made sense, since the last time we'd been there, my dad and I had been loading the car in silence while my mom argued with my grandpa in the driveway.

You traded in your family and your entire life to follow that asshole from base to base—was it worth it? Do you like your rootless existence, where Dani doesn't even know what family looks like?

"He doesn't appear to be home," I said, taking in the closed curtains and empty driveway. "He knows we're coming, right?"

"Of course he's home," she said. "He's probably just parked in the garage."

"He never parks in the garage," I corrected, taking two more huge bites and saying through a mouthful of food, "That's where he keeps his tools."

Or it was where he *used* to keep his tools before he decided to cut us out of his life.

"It's been a few years—he could have cleaned it out," she said. "And don't talk with food in your mouth."

"Then don't engage me in conversation while I'm eating."

But when we went up to the door, he wasn't home.

My mom gave me a smile and acted like it was fine, but there was the telltale wrinkle between her eyebrows that let me know she was nervous. She dialed his number and raised the phone to her ear, nibbling on her bottom lip as she waited for him to answer.

"Oh. Dad. Hey," she said, her words making puffs in the frigid air in front of her face. "We're here with the moving truck—are you on your way?"

I crossed my arms, trying not to freeze to death as I watched her listen to his response.

This wasn't good.

The wrinkles stayed on her brow, and she started pacing.

"Well, I know. Yes, that's fine," she said, "but we thought you'd be here to help."

Fabulous. Grandpa Mick was AWOL on the moving. I'd be pissed, only I was too cold to feel human emotion anymore.

My rage was an icicle.

"Sure. I get that," she said. "But you knew we were coming, right?"

Of course *he knew we were coming,* I thought. It was probably his way of giving us the finger.

God, I still couldn't believe we were moving in with him.

To be fair, I had a childhood full of good Grandpa Mick memories. As quiet and surly as he was, the man had taught me to fish and skate and used to call me his "Danigirl" while giving me rides on his shoulders.

But those memories had all been written over the day he literally kicked me and my parents out of my grandma's funeral when I was in middle school.

In front of a crowd of mourners.

So it was still baffling to me that somehow, some-freaking-how, we were about to move our things into his house as if that nightmare never happened.

Technically, he'd built an apartment for us in the upstairs of his house—my mom loved to say this as if that made a huge difference— but I still couldn't understand why this was a good idea.

Yes, please, let's move in with the grumpy old guy who doesn't like anyone but especially not us.

It was going to be so much fun.

"Oh, okay," my mom said into the phone. "It's fine. There's nothing heavy, so we'll just get started."

She nodded and disconnected the call, but before I could open my mouth, her finger came up and she pointed at my face. "I don't want to hear a word, okay?"

"Oh geez," I said, shaking my head. "What's up? What'd he do?"

"Nothing," she said, shrugging like this was fine. "He just had to help a friend up in Minnetonka with his boat."

I waited for more, but that was apparently it.

"And . . . ? How far away is that? How long is he going to be helping a friend with a boat?" As soon as the words came out of my mouth, I was irritated by how ridiculous it was. "Also, it's the freaking tundra out here—what could someone possibly be doing with a boat in this weather? Every drop of water in the place is frozen solid."

"Dammit, Dani, this is Minnesota," my mom snapped, her voice rising in frustration. "Boats are always in play!"

I opened my mouth but had no idea how to respond to that statement.

"I think I might've just come up with a kick-ass tourism slogan." Her forehead smoothed and her mouth turned up into a little grin. "Let's start moving our stuff, and he'll be here when he's done."

"We're seriously moving all our stuff in by ourselves—is that what you're telling me?" I burrowed my chin into the top of my coat, trying to block the icy wind.

"I will buy you a large cheese pizza and a freaking pony if you cut the sarcasm and just help me carry boxes into the house," she said, pulling a key ring out of her pocket.

"Can I eat the pizza while riding the pony?"

"As long as you're safe."

"Fine, I'm in," I said, watching her open the screen door. "But I really feel like I was just hitting my stride on the negativity."

My mom used her key—*yes, the key from when she was a child still worked in the door*—and we went inside. The main level was like a throwback, everything seemingly unchanged from the last time I'd been there. The only difference was that it didn't smell like cookies anymore; my grandma always made chocolate chip cookies when we visited.

But when we got to the staircase, instead of looking up and seeing the upstairs hallway like it used to be, we saw a pair of French doors. The glass was frosted, so you couldn't see anything through it, but natural light shone from behind the doors and made them look like they were glowing.

"Wow," my mom said, running up the stairs.

"Yeah," I agreed, following. "Wow."

The upstairs had been completely transformed. Warm wood floors and white trim made it feel sleek and contemporary, the polar opposite of the old-person vibes of the main level. Two of the bedrooms had now been made into a living room, the walls removed so it felt like it'd always been that way. Big windows made it bright—too bright with all that freaking snow—and a white brick fireplace was centered on a wall of white bookshelves.

"This is amazing," my mom said breathlessly.

It was hard to even remember how it'd looked before.

The two remaining bedrooms were equally gorgeous, with new furniture and a huge shared bathroom, and the small kitchenette had everything the two of us non-cooking people could need.

And when my mom opened the second set of French doors next to the fireplace, we found a deck with stairs leading down to the garage behind the house, where we'd be parking.

It was actually an apartment with its own entrance.

"Are you sure he did all of this himself?" I asked, truly in awe of the transformation. I knew Grandpa Mick had a woodshop and liked to build things, but this was next-level.

"Positive," my mom said, and for a split second it almost looked like she had tears in her eyes.

But then she gave her head a little shake and said, "Okay, let's get moving."

We went out to the truck and started bringing stuff in, but with just the two of us it felt like it was going to take forever. There were so many boxes of random things—books and clothes and pictures and shoes, and taking them in one at a time was just depressingly slow.

"Dani?"

I turned around when I heard the voice, and it took me a minute to recognize the tall dude in the blazer when I saw him smiling at me, breath puffing out in clouds in front of his face. He was bigger and had a facial-hair thing going on now, but, holy crap—it was him.

"Benji?"

Benji had always lived next door to my grandparents. Well, actually, his *dad* lived next door to my grandparents, and Benji just spent random weekends there. His mother, who he lived with the majority of the time, was loaded and lived in a lakeshore mansion.

In an exclusive gated community.

Alec had always called him King Douche—long before we were old enough to even use the word "douche"—because he went to a fancy all-boys private school and acted like he was better than everyone else.

You got a bike for your birthday? That's hilarious. I got a racehorse named Titus.

"I go by Ben now," he said with a funny smile. "And can I help you with that? Please?"

He gestured toward the saggy box I was holding, the box that appeared to be moments away from losing its bottom.

"Thank you," I said as he reached for it, remembering the last time I saw him.

God, I'd completely forgotten about that day.

It was a couple of years ago, and we'd flown in so my mom could see Alec's dad in the hospital after his car accident. We'd been days away from the move to Germany, so we literally only had a few hours to spend in the Twin Cities, and Benji had been on our flight from Minot.

I'd been horrified when he switched seats with a middle-aged guy so he could sit beside me, but after a few minutes we connected like the old friends we weren't. Which was a total shock because Benji had always been such a tool to me and Alec when we were little.

But I was so lonely at the time that the mere fact he was kind to me was . . . well, *nice*, even if he was still a douchey rich kid (the guy showed me no less than fifty pictures of himself on his phone, doing things like riding a horse on the beach while shirtless in Bali). And

Alec had disappeared from my life by then, which was why I opted not to join my mom at the hospital when we visited, because I was worried Alec didn't want me there—for reasons I still wasn't sure about. Benji was kind and warm and comforting. It was surprisingly wonderful.

I glanced over Benji's shoulder and noticed the car that appeared to be idling at the end of my grandpa's driveway.

"Wow, is that your car?"

I wasn't into cars, but my dad was, so I definitely knew that was a Maserati Grecale.

Of course Benji had a hundred-thousand-dollar SUV.

"It is," he said with a smile so proud, you'd think he *built* the vehicle. "Want to go for a spin around the block? Warm yourself up on my heated seats?"

Gross. "Sorry, but I have *this* whole thing going on."

And I pointed to the box he was holding.

"Oh yeah," he said with a disappointed smile. "This goes inside?"

"Yep."

"Excellent." He nodded and started walking toward the house. "What *is* the story with the boxes, by the way?"

"Oh, you know," I said, grabbing a floor lamp as I followed him. "We're kind of moving here."

"What? Are you serious?" He said it like he couldn't believe it, but in a good way. Like he was happy to hear the news. "You're moving to Southview?"

"We are," I said, reaching for the front-door handle and pushing it open for him. "My mom and I are moving in with my grandpa."

"No way," he said, walking into the house.

"Oh yes," I said, my stomach sinking because I just hated moving so much. I knew from experience that I was about to hate the next couple of months of my life, and after that it was TBD. Might get better, might get way worse. "Apparently, this is home now."

"Well, that is fantastic news," Benji said, smiling with his whole face. "Staying with Dad just got a lot more interesting."

I didn't really know what he meant by that, and to be honest, I didn't really care. When moving to a new place, I welcomed anyone who could be moved into the "ally" category, whether they were a harmless rich douchebag or not.

Too bad he went to a fancy academy, or I might've actually known someone at my school already.

"Thanks, and we'll stay off your lawn, I promise," I teased.

"Trust me, the last thing I'm worried about is my dad's little yard," he replied, his tone rich with condescension.

He'd always seemed to be embarrassed that his dad was a regular middle-class guy, which kind of made me wonder how his parents ever ended up together—even for the short term—in the first place.

"It was great seeing you," he said, setting down the box. I'd been kind of hoping Benji might help a girl out with the moving in, but that went up in flames as I watched him unironically pop the collar on his jacket. "Welcome home."

Ughhh, how is this home?

I just smiled and nodded too, because I didn't really know what to say to this version of Benji—ahem, I mean Ben.

Please don't linger.

How can your teeth be so white?

17

Is Titus still alive?

"Do you want my number?" he asked me, and I must've made a confused face because he quickly added, "In case you guys need anything, being new in town and all that."

"Oh," I said awkwardly. "Um—"

"That would be great." My mom suddenly appeared from nowhere, shooting me a *be nice* look. "Wouldn't it be great, Dani?"

"Yes," I agreed, forcing a perky grin while pulling out my phone. "That would be great."

He put his number in my contacts—*Ben Worthington*—and then he was out of there, saying he had to get to practice. I could almost hear Alec making a joke about what kind of loser activity little Benji would be practicing—*crumpet dipping? speed neckerchief tying?*—because the guy seemed way too fancy for any sport where one might be required to sweat.

"Benji boy got cute," my mom said with a smirk. "And still looks just as smitten around you as he always did."

"It's *Ben* now, Mother, and I thought we agreed 'smitten' was a terrible word," I corrected, not sure why *Ben* was funny, but it was.

It kind of made me want to call him Benji forever.

"We did—my apologies," she said with a smirk, her gaze on the front window. "Dear God, is that a Maserati?"

"Yup."

Just as she said that, someone laid on their horn outside. I turned around in time to see a big black truck pull up behind the fancy car, and whoever was inside impatiently hit their horn—over and over—until *Ben* finally pulled away.

It made me laugh, imagining Benji's distaste for the slush-covered F-250, until I saw the truck whip into our driveway behind the moving truck.

Then I saw him get out.

The man somehow looked taller—and tougher—than I remembered, and I swear to God he was cursing as he slammed his truck door and gestured toward Benji's house.

Grandpa Mick.

"Looks like Daddy's home," my mom said, but she was smiling like his behavior was amusing.

I knew my mom had had a *lot* of phone calls with him since my parents separated and we ditched Germany, so it was possible that my grandpa had earned my mom's tolerance for his grumpiness.

But he hadn't earned mine.

Because what kind of grandfather just stopped talking to his grandchild?

I braced myself for his entrance, dreading the reunion because there was no way it wasn't going to be weird. He was probably going to make some big apology, and I was probably going to have to lie and say *oh, it's fine* and hug him and pretend that it was all water under the bridge.

I hope he doesn't cry.

The door flew open, almost as if he kicked it in, and suddenly there he was, looking more like a character from an action movie than somebody's granddad.

"I can't believe that little shit was blocking my driveway—why was Worthington here?"

He pulled off his Ray-Bans, and in spite of the rant about his neighbor, I felt something warm in my chest when I saw his eyes. Probably because his eyes looked exactly the same as they had when he'd been my favorite human.

Even though he was a colossal jerk, some part of me wanted to hug him. Desperately.

"He helped Dani carry a box," my mom said as she crossed the room to hug him. "Benji was being nice."

"Sure he was," he muttered, sounding like a grump but wrapping her up in a big hug and kissing the top of her head. "How was the drive?"

"Good. Cold," she said, and when she pulled back, I couldn't ignore the expression on my mother's face. She looked relaxed for the first time in . . . wow, maybe *ever* as she grinned at her father and added, "Dani's officially an ice cube now."

"Eh. It's not too bad out there today," he said with a shrug, looking over at me.

I didn't know what to say, so I just made a weird noise, like a harrumph, because Grandpa Mick's gaze was locked in on me and it was . . . *unnerving*.

He stared at me like he was searching for something, like he was trying to find an object that'd been hidden on my person or something. I bit down on my lip and fidgeted under his hawklike watch, but then I realized he was probably just searching for the right words to apologize with.

I mean, how *does* one intro an apology for years of absence? *Listen, kid, I'm a dick* could work, or perhaps *let's talk about the jackass elephant in the room.*

20

I crossed my arms, and my breath felt a little bit stuck in my chest as the silence hovered, but then he finally opened his mouth.

And said, "You got tall."

You got tall.

What?

"You got tall"?

That is all you have to say to me?

I cleared my throat and tucked my hair behind my ears. "I'm five-seven."

"Yeah," he said, nodding like I'd confirmed something. "Pretty tall for a girl."

What is happening?

He kept looking at me, and nodding, and I wanted to die from the embarrassment of this reunion. The man who'd let me steer his boat when I was four because I was his "Danigirl" could only muster up enough politeness to hit me with the small-talk gold of *tall for a girl*.

Such a poignant moment.

Such a glowing apology.

"I'm going to go get more boxes," I said, pointing toward the door, and then I quickly left the room before he had a chance to offer a follow-up inquiry about my shoe size or perhaps question whether I liked pickles on my hamburgers.

"We're right behind you," my mom sort of yelled, but I didn't care.

I was suddenly all in on the box moving, because it gave me a reason to avoid my life for a couple more hours.

And it worked.

When the U-Haul was finally empty, I was about to go inside and close myself into the bedroom that was now officially mine when my mom said, "You guys ready to go get some dinner?"

I wanted to remain distant and unapproachable, really, I did, but the truth was that I was famished. And frozen. And exhausted.

A hot meal sounded heavenly.

"I'll drive." Grandpa Mick pulled out his key ring and hit the start button on his truck. "They still live on Fairacre, right?"

Wait.

"Yep," my mom said. "I'll go grab my purse and lock the door if you guys want to get in the truck."

Wait, wait, wait. *Fairacre Road.*

What??

"Where are we going?" I asked calmly, even though I already knew the answer and my stomach had suddenly dropped to my feet.

"We're going to the Barczewskis'," my mom said as if it was a given. "Sarah cooked us dinner."

"*What?* You didn't tell me that," I said, my voice a little louder than I'd intended.

"I'm pretty sure I did, but do you have a problem with that?" She gave me a weird look, and I could feel Grandpa Mick's eyes on me. "I thought you'd be thrilled."

"I mean, I *am*," I lied, trying to be cool because I didn't want my mom to question why I wouldn't want to see Alec. As far as she knew, we'd happily said goodbye five years ago and that was it.

Which was true, but she didn't know about the postcards we'd secretly exchanged since elementary school, postcards that had just stopped coming one day.

That was what filled me with dread.

The sheer awkwardness of the ghosting.

"But we just drove in a moving truck all day and unloaded our stuff," I said, hoping for the thousandth time that Alec wouldn't even remember the silly postcard thing.

The silly postcard thing that hadn't been silly to me at all.

But whatever.

"I don't exactly feel fresh and ready to see people—I'm kind of a mess after all the moving." I knew it was stupid to care, but I really didn't want the first time I saw Alec after all this time to be when I looked like *this*—in sweats and a messy bun.

"I mean, if you wanna hang back," Grandpa Mick said slowly, "I can stay too, and we can grab a pizza or something."

At the exact same time, my mom and I both whipped our heads around to look at my grandpa because . . . well, that was absolutely unexpected. Was he trying to spend time with me? I didn't know how I felt about that.

"No," my mom snapped, pointing at him. "You are antisocial and eat microwave food for every meal. Sarah invited you over and has cooked food for us, so we are going, end of story."

"God, I forgot how bossy you can be," my grandpa said, but something in the way he looked at my mom made me think he appreciated it.

"I wonder who I get that from," she replied, rolling her eyes. "I'm going to get my purse and we're leaving. Get your butts in the truck."

She turned and ran for the house, leaving me standing there with Grandpa Mick in the driveway. He didn't even look at me as he opened his door and said, "It's probably warm already."

"Oh. Cool," I said, opening the back door and climbing inside, trying to remain calm when I was about to see Alec.

In mere moments, dear God.

How can this be happening?

CHAPTER TWO
Alec

"Hey, sweetie. How was work?"

"Good," I said, shutting the kitchen door behind me and kicking off my shoes. "Quiet, thank God."

I worked at my uncle's hardware store every weekend (and any other time I could squeeze in extra hours, to be honest). Usually it was only on Sundays during hockey season, but since we'd had a game the night before and just an early practice that day, I'd been able to get in a bonus Saturday shift.

Which was perfect, because I needed new skates.

Like, yesterday.

"After you shower, will you make sure the twins look presentable?" My mom was rolling out dough on the center island—fucking beer bread, *yes*—and had three pots going full steam on the stove.

Which made me want to cry little happy baby tears, because I was fucking famished.

"They're watching TV in the basement," she said. "Dad was supposed to get them ready, but Andy swung by, so odds are good he forgot."

"Yeah, but why?" I pulled off my jacket, being extra fucking careful with my left arm, and put it on a hook. "Andy doesn't care what they look like."

Andy was my dad's best friend and basically like another member of the family.

"The Boches are coming over for dinner," she said casually as she focused on the bread.

The *Boches*?

"What exactly does *that* mean?"

I was impressed by how chill I sounded when I felt like I'd been kicked.

She couldn't mean Dani was coming over tonight.

She hadn't brought up Dani and Hannah since last month's announcement that they were moving back, and I'd been delusionally hopeful that something had changed.

I definitely wasn't expecting her to come to my house for a meal.

"Mick, Dani, and Hannah," she said. "Duh."

"They're 'the Boches' now?" I asked, because Dani and Hannah had never gone by Hannah's maiden name before.

Or at least not that I'd known of.

"Well, Dani still goes by Collins," my mom said, "but Hannah's back to Boche."

She said it with a triumphant smile, probably because she'd always hated the colonel, but I was starting to feel like something was sitting on my chest.

This couldn't be happening.

I knew I was going to have to run into her eventually, but why tonight, when my shoulder was fucking killing me and all I wanted to do was eat and fall into my bed? Doing *anything* sounded like too much, but seeing Dani?

Nope.

"And they're all coming over for dinner *tonight*?" I opened the fridge and looked inside, trying to wrap my head around the knowledge that *she* was going to be *here*, in my kitchen, within the hour.

No fucking way.

Seeing her was going to suck, but seeing her at a meal with my family, who'd always loved her and would kiss her ass and treat her like a long-lost beloved niece, was going to suck nails.

"Hey, Sarah," I heard as the door opened behind me and cold air whooshed in.

I turned around as Doug (my dad's other best friend) slammed the door behind him and said to my mom, "Is Mick Boche really coming over for dinner?"

"God, I told John to keep his mouth shut," she said, but she was grinning.

Mick Boche—Dani's grandpa—was a hockey legend. He'd been the best player to ever come out of Southview for sure, a superstar enforcer in the NHL until an injury forced him to retire in his prime.

And even though he lived in town, the guy was notoriously anti-social, which made him even more of an elusive icon. When spotted around town, people ID'd him with a Sasquatch level of excitement.

"So it's true, then," he said as he took off his boots and went around me to grab a Busch Light from the top shelf. "We're breaking bread with Mick Fucking Boche tonight, holy shit."

"*You* are doing no such thing," she said with a laugh, pointing a finger at him. "This isn't a fan meet and greet; it's a nice family dinner for my best friend, and he happens to be her dad."

"Am I not part of this family? Nice game last night, by the way, Al."

"No, you literally are not," she replied.

"Thanks," I said at the same time.

"Sarah. Come on." Doug shot me a smile before he said to my mom, "You *have* to let me stay. You're having dinner with my hero, for God's sake, and all I'm asking is to quietly sit at the table and witness the greatness. I won't say a word, and I'll—"

"You *always* say a word—too many of them, in fact—and the answer is no."

"He can have my spot," I said, shutting the fridge. "Because I just want to sleep."

"And you can," she said in her authoritative voice, "*after* dinner. Besides, I thought you'd be dying to see them."

"I mean, I am," I lied, "but if they live here now, I'll see them all the time, right?"

"I'm going downstairs," Doug said, disappearing down the steps while yelling, "but I'll be back up for supper, Sar."

"No, you will not, Doug—"

"What's this I hear about Mick Boche coming for dinner?" The back door opened and Ed, one of my dad's other buddies, came inside and went straight for the fridge. "Hey, Al—great game last night."

"Thanks," I said.

"He is, but you're not," my mom answered, not even looking up.

"She doesn't mean it," Doug yelled from below.

"But Big John said I could," Ed lied, because everyone knew my dad would never have the balls to go against my mom. "He said I could sit directly across from Mick, actually."

"Bullshit," I muttered.

"Worth a shot, though, right?" he murmured to me with a smirk.

28

"Go downstairs before I hurt you, Ed," my mom said, which was basically her caving on the whole no-fanboys-at-dinner thing.

Which would make it slightly less terrible.

More people to focus on while trying to pretend Dani Collins wasn't in my house.

But, like, *shit*—it wasn't fair.

I had enough to worry about right now.

Seeing her again—in my house—was just too damn much.

I cannot believe she's going to be here.

That we're going to have to speak.

Fuck.

I followed Ed down to the basement and was pleasantly surprised to see that the twins were fully dressed and not in need of my assistance. *Thank God.* I was good with helping my mom, but five-year-olds were a *lot* sometimes. Cole and Ashton were staring at the small TV in the toy corner of the room, fully immersed in a show about crime-fighting dogs, while my dad and his buddies watched ESPN on the big screen.

"How was work, kid?" my dad asked, grabbing the handle of his cane and slowly getting out of his chair. His eyes narrowed and he winced as he reached his full height, and I realized that I could barely remember what it looked like to see him moving without pain.

"Slow," I said. "Thank God."

"Killer game last night, Al," Andy said from his spot on the couch. "How bruised is the shoulder?"

Dude, if you only knew.

"Fine," I lied. "Deep purple but not black."

"Nice."

"Mom told me to check on the twins before I get in the shower," I said to my dad. "Are they good?"

"Yeah—they're under the spell of Disney, so go shower. The Boches are gonna be here in an hour."

"Is that what we're calling them now?" I wasn't sure why I found that so annoying. "The Boches?"

We'd *never* called them that.

"I just repeat what your mother says, you know that."

But it bugged the shit out of me as I went back upstairs and turned on the shower, especially when the Bluetooth speaker cued up "Little League," the song that always made me think of her.

Of us, back then.

> *When we were younger*
> *We didn't know how it would be*

"Next song," I shouted at my phone.

Everything about this sudden social event was bugging the shit out of me. So they'd moved to Southview—why the fuck was this a big deal?

People moved all the time, for God's sake.

My breath hissed out between my teeth when I lifted my shirt over my head because *shiiiit*.

It was getting so much worse.

I could handle my shoulder's fuckery when I was playing, but for some reason, stupid things like lifting my arm over my head while getting dressed were nearly dropping me lately.

Even with the steady rotation of ibuprofen, Tylenol, and ice.

I was setting my phone next to the sink and about to step into the shower when I got a text.

Vinny: Zack's bonfire is tonight and it sounds like everyone's going

The word "everyone," when paired with "bonfire," was no longer part of my vocabulary.

I was supposed to be keeping my nose clean.

I *needed* to keep my nose clean and steer clear of any parties that could get out of control.

But as I stepped under the hot water, turning to soak the throbbing shoulder that scared the shit out of me because I couldn't afford—literally or figuratively—to be taken out by an injury, I was tempted.

Getting a little bit numb suddenly didn't sound like such a bad idea.

CHAPTER THREE
Dani

It looks exactly the same.

Grandpa Mick put the truck into park and I felt transported back in time as I stared at the house.

My favorite place in the world.

Or, well . . . the place formerly known as.

The Barczewskis lived in a small Cape Cod–style house, gray with white shutters and a curvy sidewalk leading to the door that was always lined with flowers—daylilies and roses—in the summertime.

Today it was lined with knee-high snowbanks, yet it still managed to somehow look ridiculously charming.

But also terrifying.

Intimidating.

I was so unbelievably nervous to ring that doorbell.

I was never at ease in social situations. *Ever.* I overthought each word that was spoken and worried too much about the tiniest of details. I stressed over what everyone was thinking about me, how I looked, what I was doing; on a normal day, social gatherings gave me anxiety.

But tonight—this felt ten times worse.

The idea of reuniting with these people whom I'd loved but who were now strangers was even scarier.

Mostly because I didn't know what things would be like with Alec.

I stared out the window and just wished I knew if it was a distant memory for him now, where he barely remembered our couple-few years of correspondence and his departure from it, or if it would be all he thought of when he looked at me.

There's the postcard-sending dork.

God, I couldn't believe I was about to see him.

And how was I supposed to look at his always-readable face and decipher his thoughts when I hadn't seen that face in five years? And this was going to be happening in real time while the rest of the family watched us?

It was too much, and I was starting to breathe too fast.

Calm down, I told myself. I inhaled through my nose and counted slowly, trying to remember all the ways to stop myself from spiraling.

"You okay?"

I looked away from the window to see Grandpa Mick watching me in the rearview mirror. His face was as serious as it'd been all afternoon, but there also wasn't any judgment in his expression.

"Yes," I said, clearing my throat. "I'm fine." Though I was really embarrassed that he seemed to know something was up with me.

"I'm so excited," my mom said, jumping out of the car and slamming the door.

She deserved this excitement. After so many years of living far away from her friends and family, she was like a kid at Christmas about this move.

And I got it.

My mom was a social person who'd settled into a solitary, unsocial life for a very long time. It'd pretty much been the three of us—Dad, Mom, and me—as we moved from base to base, and even though that might've been normal for me and the only life I'd ever known, it'd weighed on her.

She'd had a *lot* of arguments with my dad about it.

Just as I was climbing out of the truck, the front door flew open and there was Sarah. She yelled my mom's name and ran down the walkway, not stopping until she'd wrapped my mom in a massive hug. The two of them squealed and said unintelligible words that made my mom look so damn happy.

Once again I glanced at my grandpa and he was looking back at me. It felt like we shared . . . *something* in our silent exchange, watching my mom squeal in joy.

Sarah hugged me next, smelling—as always—like dryer sheets. She said into my hair, "Look at you; you're so gorgeous, Dani!"

I *loved* Sarah and hugged her back *so* hard.

"And how are you, Mick?" she said to my grandpa.

I think he might've said *fine*, but it was more of a grunt, to which she replied, "Oh good."

I wanted to laugh for the first time since we'd pulled into town.

"Dani, it's about damn time!" Big John was standing inside the doorway, and it was impossible not to grin as he pulled me into a big bear hug. He'd always been my favorite uncle, even though we weren't technically related, and just hearing the long northern vowels made me feel warm inside.

It was a little shocking to see him with a cane—I hadn't seen him since the accident—but from the way it sounded, it was a miracle he was standing at all.

He asked, "How was the drive, kiddo?"

"It sucked," I said as he let go of me. "Too long, too cold, too boring."

"It's only the beginning of February, hon," he said with a grin. "This is like a crisp fall day. Better toughen up."

"You sound insane when you say things like that."

"You sound exactly like my favorite little smart-ass," he replied. "It's been too long. How's it goin', Mick?"

My grandpa gave another grunt, to which Big John replied, "Right?"

Sarah and my mom exploded into conversation after that, the way they always had, wandering toward the kitchen in a cloud of giggly exclamations. I followed, nervously wondering where Alec was.

In the kitchen?

Upstairs in his room?

Was he going to pop out of a closet?

God, I just needed to get this over with.

"Who are you?" I heard, and when I turned around, there were two little kids—one boy and one girl—standing beside the staircase that led to the second level. They looked like they were probably four or five years old, dressed alike in Vikings hoodies, and they were obviously waiting for me to answer the question.

"I'm Dani," I said.

"No, that's a boy's name," the girl said, her little eyebrows wrinkling together as a half-dressed Barbie dangled from her fist.

"It's also *my* name," I countered, wondering why I was justifying my name to a preschooler.

"I like your hair," the boy said with a chin nod. "Your bun is real big."

"Um, thank you," I said, raising a hand to my messy hair, and I swear to God when I looked over at my grandpa, he almost looked like he wanted to smile.

But only almost.

"Can you believe we had more kids?" John said, shaking his head like he couldn't believe it himself.

"Wait—these are *yours*?" I said, shocked to the core. "These two are *your* children?"

"Whoa—don't seem so shocked," he said with a grin. "We're not *that* old."

"No, it's not that," I explained with a laugh, my mind totally blown. "I just had no idea. My mom didn't tell me."

She'd been very careful to not discuss anything Minnesotan around my dad because he blamed this place for everything, so it wasn't especially weird that she'd forgotten to mention something so huge.

I looked at the twins again, and now I could totally see it. They looked a lot like Alec. Dark hair, dark eyes, mischievous faces; they were like his little clones.

Or clones of who he *used* to be.

I wanted to ask John what Alec thought of being a big brother, but for some reason I was scared to bring up his name.

But it was like he read my mind.

"By the way, Al had to run his friends somewhere, but he should be back in a bit."

"Oh," I said, not sure how to respond. I didn't want to seem too interested, but I didn't want to seem too disinterested, either.

"I don't think he'll be back in time to eat with us, but he'll be here before you leave."

"Okay, cool," I replied, relieved he wouldn't be there for dinner. I felt myself relax a little, knowing I'd have at least another hour to get used to the situation before he showed up.

"Grab a seat at the table—the food is ready," Sarah said, and my stomach growled, because she'd always been the most amazing cook, and it smelled like that hadn't changed.

"You don't have to ask us twice," my mom said, and motioned for Grandpa Mick and me to come sit beside her. I sat on her left and my grandpa on the right, and as I scooted my chair in toward their big dining room table, I was a little surprised to see plates at every spot.

A lot of other plates.

"Go get your friends," Sarah said to John with an eye roll, and he headed for the basement stairs.

"Friends?" my mom asked, taking the glass of white wine Sarah was holding out to her.

"As soon as I told John you guys were coming over for dinner, he opened his big mouth and told Dougie, Andy, and Ed. And even though I informed them multiple times that they weren't welcome, the knowledge that you guys—and Mick Boche—were going to be here was too much for their hockey-addled brains and they refused to listen."

Just as she finished saying that, three guys followed John upstairs. One was wearing a Vikings sweatshirt, and the other two were in flannel.

"No way," my mom squealed, jumping to her feet and running over to hug the guy in the Vikings hoodie. As soon as she let go of that dude, she hugged the other two.

Which, to be honest, shocked the hell out of me.

The four of them obviously knew each other, and it was a little bit of a mind blow to me, seeing her this way. My mom had been an officer's wife my entire life, not really having any friends of her own who weren't just spouses of my dad's coworkers who she occasionally attended base events with.

But here she was, beaming at this man trio as they gave her shit like they were the oldest of friends. I guess I'd always known she'd had a life before us, but I'd never thought about what it might've looked like.

"This is my daughter, Dani," my mom said, "and my dad, Mick."

These grown men smiled politely and said hi to me, but then they turned to beam at my grandpa like he was a god. They immediately launched into NHL game recollections and statistics without even pausing for small talk, stumbling all over themselves to kiss his ass and tell him how good he used to be at hockey.

It was so bizarre.

Like, I knew my grandpa played when he was younger, but these guys were acting like he was Wayne Gretzky.

Grandpa Mick still only gave them one-word answers and grunted replies, but he also didn't look uncomfortable with their attention. Obviously people treated him this way a lot.

"Will you shut up so we can eat?" Sarah said to Ed, gesturing toward the line of Crock-Pots on the counter. "You said you'd be good."

"I *am* being good," he said with a huge smile. "You think I'm being good, right, Dani?"

I was a little surprised as he gave me a conspiratorial smirk and a wink.

"I mean, sure," I replied.

"See?" he said to Sarah, pointing at me. "Dani thinks I'm being great."

"I don't think that's what I—"

"Dani thinks you should lighten up and let us talk freely," Doug said, also giving me a grin. "Right, kid?"

I coughed out a laugh as these grown-ass men—strangers—pulled me into their jokes.

"Don't let them speak for you," Sarah said, pointing a big spoon at me. "They're overgrown children who need discipline."

"Don't talk to our Dani like that," Andy said with a big smile, and I couldn't help but smile back at him.

Who were these guys?

As someone who usually hated chaotic gatherings where I didn't know anyone, I was surprised to find myself having a decent time. I sat there, shoveling food into my face, having trouble not smiling as these guys all talked over each other about hockey, hockey, and more hockey.

What is the deal with the hockey insanity?

Fifteen minutes later they were still recapping someone's game from the night before, and I wondered if they realized that hockey was literally the only thing they'd talked about.

Even Sarah—and my *mom*—were in on the conversation.

Since I didn't know a puck from a Popsicle, I was able to listen to everyone else without having to contribute. I was relaxed and enjoying the show, so much so that I kind of forgot to be nervous about seeing Alec.

He'd completely slipped my mind until I visited the restroom and saw his bedroom across the hall.

And—*no way*—it'd barely changed.

I couldn't stop myself from stepping through that doorway, because seeing his room was like stepping into a time machine.

There was still a twin bed in the center of the room, though it was now covered with a gray comforter instead of the Vikings bedspread that'd been there the last time I visited. Hockey posters still hung on his walls, though they made a lot more sense now.

I used to think it was funny that unathletic Alec had a sports-themed bedroom, but now I understood that hockey was obviously part of life up here, whether you played or not.

I looked at the little desk in the corner, the same oak desk he'd always had, and my fingers itched to open the drawer. To see if there were still postcards and stamps.

Does he still have them somewhere the way I still have mine?

A shiver of nervousness slithered through me, but what came with it was a bright side.

At least the unknown, with Alec, was almost over.

By the time I went to bed that night, I'd be back to having him in my life again.

CHAPTER FOUR
Alec

"Why are you being an antisocial dick?"

Richie dropped into the chair beside me, giving me a look like I was ruining his fun.

Which was ironic when he seemed to be having the time of his life.

I swear to God he'd already gone down that hill fifteen different times.

Every year for as long as I could remember, the Novotnys had a massive February bonfire out at their place, where all their friends brought their discarded Christmas trees and they basically burned random shit all day and drank beer while the little kids took sleds down their massive hill.

We used to be the little kids sledding during the day, but for the past few years Zack had taken over bonfire duties after dark, when the adults went inside, and had *his* friends over for sledding and burning.

"I'm not," I said, reluctantly taking out my AirPods and shutting down the "hell of a good time" I'd been listening to on repeat while staring into the fire. I considered myself to be a social guy on most days, but tonight I wasn't feeling it.

I pulled my beanie down to my eyebrows because even though the bonfire was roaring, it was fucking cold.

And Richie wasn't wrong.

Not the dick part, but I *was* being antisocial because—dammit—I couldn't stop thinking about Dani.

And it wasn't helping that my mom kept texting to see where I was.

Mom: Are you on your way?

Mom: Dani looks bored—you need to hurry.

The joke was on her, because I wasn't planning on going home until Dani was gone. I knew I was going to have to face her eventually, but I'd prefer to do it at school.

From afar.

I didn't need to participate in a freaking welcome dinner for the prodigal blonde.

No, thank you.

"The only person you've talked to since you got here is Tawnee, and she said—and I quote—that you're 'too drunk to be fun.'"

I looked over in Tawnee's direction, and, as if hearing her name, she glanced back at me and smiled. She and her best friend, Kylie, were wrapped up in blankets, standing on the other side of the fire, and I knew I probably should ask her out before someone else beat me to it.

"Bullshit," I said, raising my cup and smiling back at her. "The drunk is my attempt at *being* fun."

But I wasn't drunk.

I was attempting drunk, I was working my ass off to get myself drunk, but I was way too sober and in my own head at the moment.

Vinny, who I hadn't even noticed behind us, asked, "Didn't you say you were done drinking until after the season?"

"Can you please get off my ass, Ma?"

"Oh, but you're not being a dick, right?" Richie said with a smart-ass grin.

"Touché," I muttered with a shrug, because they were right about everything.

I *had* committed to dry December and January (and February) because there was too much at stake for me to enjoy partying. Everything was lined up for me, and I couldn't risk a mistake, not when everyone— every fucking one, I swear to God—was counting on me.

But tonight the risk had taken a back seat to the burning annoyance with my inability to stop thinking about *her*.

"Shut off the music and join us. It's like you kind of set the tone at a party, as much as I fucking hate to admit that," Vinny said, shaking his head like it was a ridiculous concept. "When you're having a good time, everyone's having a good time. Remember the massive sled train last year?"

"The one that broke Dex's thumb?"

"I don't give a shit—it was fucking epic, and that was all you," he said with a laugh. "But when you're quiet and dickish, everything is chill and no one gets crazy."

"(A) That's not true," I said, "and (B) if it *were* true, that wouldn't be my fault. Maybe you should be more interesting, and then *you* can set the tone."

"I'm so fucking interesting it's ridiculous, assbag," he said with a grin. "If hockey didn't exist, you would *so* be in my shadow."

That was probably true. Between his stupid-long mullet (hence the nickname Vincent the Flow) and the way he looked more like a linebacker than a hockey player, he was probably the most interesting man in the room at all times.

My phone buzzed, and I sighed before pulling it out of my pocket and taking a look.

Mom: They're leaving soon—when are you coming back? I think Dani thought you'd be here.

"Yeah, well, I don't give a shit what Dani thought," I muttered under my breath.

"What?" Richie asked, his ratty mullet looking like straight-up flames in the glow of the bonfire. Calling him a redhead was like calling the pope slightly spiritual: a wicked fucking understatement. "Who is Danny?"

I sighed and gave my head a shake. "She's Mick Boche's granddaughter."

And my former best friend.

"Wait—Boche's got a granddaughter? How old is she?"

"Our age."

"No shit?" Vinny finished his drink and tossed the paper cup into the fire.

"Yeah. I kind of knew her when I was little, and she just moved here." It wasn't a lie. "She's going to be going to Southview now."

"The hell you say—what does she look like?"

"I'm picturing Mick with long hair, and it's fucking terrifying," Richie said with a laugh.

"I have no clue," I said, not wanting to think about it. Her hair, her freckles, her height . . . *has she gotten even taller?*

"So why are you pissed about her?"

"I'm not," I said defensively, knowing I sounded like a pouty little shit. "My mom is just all on my ass to go over there and see her when I don't want to leave this party."

"And you shouldn't," Zack said, stepping into our conversation and lowering his voice. "Because Reid brought megabong."

"Of course he did," Vinny laughed, shaking his head.

Reid was the only guy I knew who legitimately behaved like he was something out of an eighties stoner movie. He didn't really drink, but he was all about it when it came to smoking.

I was the opposite.

I didn't mind having a few beers when I wasn't driving, but contrary to popular belief (because of a few shenanigans that got blown way the fuck out of proportion), I really wasn't into partying.

Especially not Reid's version of partying.

But an hour later, when the beer had yet to slow the steady stream of Dani-focused thoughts (and my mom texted Dani is GORGEOUS now, btw), it suddenly felt like a good night to make a few mistakes.

"Has anyone ever gotten lit *while* going down this hill?" Richie asked, falling into the high-pitched giggle that only came out when he was buzzed. "Reid would look like a fucking steam locomotive if he megabonged on a sled in motion."

"He'd never have the balls to try something that legendary," Vinny said, shaking his head. "Are you kidding with that?"

"No lies detected, Vincent the Flow," Reid agreed, nodding while wearing a half-baked smirk. "But I bet I know who would."

"Who's that crazy?" Zack said, throwing a handful of sticks into the fire.

"Our boy Zeus."

CHAPTER FIVE
Dani

I'm not nervous; I'm focused.

I looked in the bathroom mirror and repeated the reminder, even though it was total bullshit. Nothing was worse than the first days at a new school, and nervous didn't begin to cover it.

But over the years I'd discovered that if I focused on what *I* needed to get out of a new school, it made me feel more in control and marginally less . . . well, *powerless*. Instead of worrying about things like people judging me or where I was going to sit at lunch, I zeroed in on what mattered.

For example, I wanted to go to Harvard next year.

I wanted to go to Harvard *so badly*. I wanted to go to Harvard like Lorelai wanted Rory to go to Harvard.

When I was in grade school, my dad was stationed at Hanscom Air Force Base, just outside Boston. My mom used to take me to Harvard for fun, and we'd spend entire autumn days exploring the campus while the leaves were in full color. She fed me Lunchables in Harvard Square, and I fell madly in love.

I'd never been able to put my finger on exactly *what* I loved about it, but Cambridge was my happy place.

So, yes, my only goal in life at the moment was Harvard.

I'd discovered over the past few years that when everything in your life sucked, making an absurd college goal your primary focus became an extraordinary diversion.

Lacking in the friends department at your new school?

Who cares? You need to focus on getting into Harvard.

Is that volleyball player mocking you behind your back again?

Who cares? You need to focus on getting into Harvard (and that bitch could never get in, by the way).

So what I needed from Southview was Harvard insurance, since I'd been freaking *deferred* and was still waiting on acceptance. I needed to maintain my perfect GPA, meet with a counselor to keep my goals on track, and make sure that the only thing admissions saw when they finally reviewed my application again was that I'd landed in Minnesota with my Harvard-destined nose to the grindstone.

The focus of my first day was to solidify those important things and not worry about anything else.

I put my hair in a clip and turned off the bathroom light.

But when I walked out to our little apartment kitchen, there was a note on the microwave from my mom.

The electrical in the new kitchen still isn't working, so come downstairs for breakfast.

Wonderful.

Last night, as soon as I'd climbed into bed, I'd realized that I still hadn't had a single one-on-one conversation with my grandpa. Aside from "you got tall," we hadn't really exchanged any words.

Which left me with this annoying nervousness about how things were going to be with him.

Mick Fucking Boche.

I rolled my eyes as I thought of everyone's attitude toward him Saturday night, the way a table full of grown men had behaved as if he'd been Taylor Swift popping in for dinner, instead of an old man with a bad attitude.

Obviously, hockey made people nuts.

I grabbed my coat and backpack and went downstairs, wondering if I should even bother with breakfast.

Seemed like a bad idea when my stomach was so knotted.

Grandpa Mick was sitting at the table when I entered the kitchen, reading the newspaper while my mom appeared to be making scrambled eggs at the stove. He had reading glasses on the end of his nose, glasses that should've made him look old but instead just accentuated how intimidating he was.

"Good morning," my mom said in a singsong voice, glancing over her shoulder and giving me a smile. "How'd you sleep?"

"Great," I said, not knowing what to do, so I sat down across from *him* at the table.

"The beds are so comfy, right?" she said, sounding like a Disney princess with her happy breathlessness.

"The comfiest," I muttered, pulling my phone out of my pocket.

"You don't like the bed."

I looked across the table, taken aback by the quiet rasp of his voice and the way it hadn't sounded like a question at all, and Grandpa Mick was watching me with his eyes narrowed.

"N-no, um, I do," I stammered, shrugging and adding, "It's great."

"Because I can get a different bed." He pulled off the readers and said, "You need softer or what."

What is a bed again? I felt like I was under the harsh lights of an interrogation room as my grandfather looked at me like I'd murdered someone and he wanted to know where the body was buried.

"No, really, I love the bed."

"Oh." He crossed his arms over his big chest, giving me hardcore direct eye contact, then said, "Today's a blackout."

"What?"

He gave my bulky sweater a chin nod. "At school. The kids are wearing all black because it's rivalry week, starting with Simley."

"Oh." I crossed *my* arms and said, "I'm just going to wear this, but thanks." The thick, warm wool of my fisherman sweater seemed more important than school spirit.

"You sure that's wise." I *thought* he meant it as a question, but there was a period at the end of his statement.

What was happening?

"It's warm and I don't even know what a Simley is, so yes—it's perfect."

"Dani," my mom said, "it's rivalry week. Maybe it wouldn't hurt to wear black today."

Oh well, if it's rivalry week.

I knew my mom meant it in the best way. She knew how much I loathed first days of school, so she was more concerned about me fitting in than anything else.

But the truth of the matter was that I knew all the rules of fitting in at a new school; I could write the damn rule book.

Rule #1—It's not about fitting in; it's about blending. Be invisible.

That wasn't me being melodramatic; it was me knowing how to survive.

As a new student, you need to be relatively in style so the assholes won't see a clueless dork and move in for the kill, but you can't be too in style or it might look like you think you're cool.

And you don't want to be ugly because the jerks love that, but prettiness can be perceived as a threat too, so it's best to be vanilla.

To look like everyone else.

To be utterly forgettable and absolutely uninteresting.

"Yes, I'm sure," I said. "I'm too new to care about rivalries."

Wearing spirit-week clothing on your first day might be perceived as try-hard.

"Southview should win," Grandpa Mick said, his eyes on the newspaper. "Simley's got no answer for Zeus."

"I'm assuming you're not talking about the Greek god . . . ?" I regretted it the minute the words left my mouth, because I couldn't care less about sports.

"Helluva defenseman," he said to me with his eyebrows up like he genuinely thought I wanted to talk to him about sports. "The kid back-pedal hits like Kronwall, I swear to God."

"What's a Kronwall?" I asked.

"Niklas Kronwall," he said, his eyebrows scrunching together in disgust. "Played for the Red Wings? Legendary checker?"

Now, I knew what he meant by "checker," because even *I* knew the Red Wings were a hockey team.

But I couldn't stop myself from saying, "Wait, 'hits'—is this baseball? What's this Kronwall's batting average?"

"Hockey. It's hockey." He managed to scowl at me while also looking confused by my stupidity, like he couldn't fathom that someone might actually respond that way. "I'm talkin' about hockey."

Minnesota men and their propensity for dropping g's, I swear to God.

"Are you ready to go?" my mom asked, giving me a look that told me she knew I was being a pain in the ass on purpose.

"As ready as I'll ever be," I said, wishing I could just be homeschooled. I tried very hard to convince my parents to let me do online high school when they decided to divorce, but good ol' Mom and Dad were adamant that the things you learn socially are just as important as what you learn in your textbooks.

Sure, I thought. *It's super important for me, as a senior, to continually relearn that I hate high school.*

My mom chattered the entire drive to school. I knew she was trying to distract me, but all I could do was stare out the window at the snow and houses while trying my hardest not to throw up on my own lap.

My heart started beating faster when my mom turned into the parking lot, as I stared up at the ridiculously large brick high school that loomed in front of me.

Everything about it looked ominous.

Foreboding.

So freaking cold.

"It looks so different from when I went there," my mom said, leaning forward to look up through the windshield. "But it's a great school. And I gave you Alec's number if you want to text him, right?"

Alec never showed up the other night, which was a relief at the time but left me still dreading the reunion. My mom gave me his phone number so I could text him if I needed anything, and I was contemplating sending *something* in hopes of getting the awkwardness out of the way before we had to meet face-to-face.

"Yeah," I said, reaching down to grab my backpack as she drove closer to the doors.

"Text me as soon as you can, just to let me know how it's going so I can stop worrying, okay?"

"Okay," I said. "But don't worry—it'll be great."

I didn't believe that, but what was the point of letting her into my stress? It wouldn't make anything better for her, and she was already struggling to bounce back from the whole failed-marriage thing.

"I'll text you later," I said, reaching for the door and climbing out. Only the air punched me in the face as soon as I straightened.

God, how can it be so freaking cold?

"Bye, sweetie," she said, giving me a wave before pulling away.

I swallowed and headed for the doors, careful to take deep breaths in through my nose to try to keep the panic at bay. An anxiety attack on day one would be a nightmare, so I was going to make sure that didn't happen.

Please, God, no panic attack.

As soon as I entered the school, I saw the office.

Which was nice in that I didn't have to wander around looking more lost than I felt.

But as I walked over, I couldn't help but notice the massive amount of hockey . . . *enthusiasm* decorating every surface of the school's interior.

It was ridiculous.

An enormous poster of the school's hockey team hung from the rafters of the high ceiling, and posters of individual players were slapped up all over the walls. I understood school spirit, but it was laughable that a bunch of high school boys were taped up all over the place like they were actual celebrities.

I opened the office door, only to see even more hockey signage inside the bustling administrative area.

IT'S PACKER GAME DAY!!

Calm down, people.

"Can I help you?" asked the woman behind the desk, who was holding a phone up to her ear.

"Hi, um, my name is Dani Collins, and I'm new. It's my, um, my first day," I stammered.

"Well, good morning, Dani," she said with a big smile, her tone laced with familiarity, like she'd been expecting me. "You're a little early, so if you want to take a seat in one of the chairs, I imagine Cassie will be here in the next ten or fifteen minutes."

"Cassie?" I asked, wondering if I was supposed to know who that was.

"The student who'll be showing you around," she explained. "You'll love her—Cassie's a doll."

"Oh," I said, nodding. "Good."

"She knows everyone and everybody loves her, so she'll be a great point of contact for you."

"Awesome," I said, nodding again.

I sat on one of the chairs and looked out the office window, where it was getting busy in the hallway.

Students yelling to each other, groups walking together . . . God, I hated it so much.

Because on day one, there was no way to know who the threats were.

The group of four girls who were laughing, with their pretty hair and perfect teeth? At this moment, they looked harmless.

Nice, even.

But they could actually be the girls capable of making someone's life hell.

My life.

And the same went for guys. The four dudes standing by the trophy case, smiling and looking cute—they could either be nice guys, or the ones with the potential to ruin everything.

There was no way to know, no warning signal to give you a hint of danger.

A group of dudes in hockey jerseys walked by, strolling down the hall like they were icons. They walked past the multiple banners with their own images on them, moving like they ruled the world.

Which wasn't shocking after the hockey-themed dinner Saturday night.

It was clearly the culture.

Still . . . *spare me*.

To be fair, I knew that I was prejudiced when it came to jocks. It was wrong to judge an entire group of humans by the actions of a few, but over the years, it'd been my experience that the overconfidence that accompanied athletic successes created narcissistic social monsters.

If mean girls were a thing (and they were), then cocky jocks were even worse.

Because they wielded ridiculous amounts of power.

A jock could offhandedly say "the new girl is hot," and even if he meant it in a complimentary way, it just led to all his friends feeling the need to contribute their opinions as well.

No she's not.

She looks like a bitch.

Her nose is weird.

Those nerdy glasses, though, come on.

"Just breathe," I told myself, trying to keep the anxiety at bay.

Watching the hockey players strut down the hall, I noticed another huge banner hanging from above. This one was strung all the way across the common area, and it had an image of the back of a hockey player on it, the name ZEUS stretched across the broad shoulders.

Ridiculous.

I took another deep breath, slowly inhaling through my nose.

Everything is going to be fine.

As if on cue, a girl with long brown hair walked into the office. She was wearing black leggings and a black SOUTHVIEW HOCKEY crewneck, and she went straight for the secretary.

"There you are, Cassie," the woman said. "This is Dani." She gestured toward me and added, "Dani, this is Cassie."

Cassie looked over and smiled like she was happy to see me, which was better than her looking irritated, I supposed.

Of course, it was also my experience that the student who volunteered to show new kids around was usually either (A) a genuinely nice person who liked their extracurriculars, or (B) a control freak who was insane about their extracurriculars.

Hopefully she was the former.

"Hi," she said with a grin. "Do you have your schedule yet?"

"Yes, they emailed it to me," I said, gesturing toward my pocket like she would somehow know my phone was there.

"Same, and I'm in awe of the way you're taking AP and honors everything," she said. "By the way, I love your sweater—it's very Harry Burns rolling out the rug with Sally while discussing dating."

"Thank you," I said, wanting to smile at the reference but knowing it was better to keep my mouth shut.

Because another important rule?

Don't share personal information with the volunteer who shows you around on your first day. No matter how nice they might seem, you don't know where they fit into the school's social hierarchy.

One minute you could be sharing with someone you think is friendly how *When Harry Met Sally* is still your comfort-watch, only to discover two days later that she mockingly told all her friends that you are a loser who still watches old rom-coms with your mother on DVD.

The less you share, the better.

Cassie led me out into the hallway and immediately turned on her tour-guide persona. She pointed out everything we passed, and I did my best to focus on her while being very aware of people looking at us.

Just as she was showing me where in the cafeteria you could get breakfast, we walked by a few more hockey players, and one of them yelled her name.

"What?" she said with a smile. "Can't you see I'm busy?"

"Yeah, but we have a question," the red-haired guy said.

"And it would be . . . ?"

"Where did you go Saturday night after you left the bonfire?" he asked. "One minute you guys were there, the next second you were gone. And we couldn't help but notice Kyle was gone too. So we were wondering . . ."

"So don't do that," she said, rolling her eyes and kind of pushing him a little bit, but in a teasing way. "I have no idea what Kyle did after the party—don't be an ass."

"I'm not an ass," he said around a little laugh. "I just wanted to make sure you both got home safely."

"Sure you did. By the way, this is Dani—she's new."

"Hi," I said.

"This is Richie," she told me, pointing to the redhead. "And this is Vinny."

Vinny had a blond mullet that was so long it went halfway down his back. As if that weren't jarring enough—what was *with* that hair—he was ginormous.

"Wait—your name is Dani?" Vinny asked, raising his eyebrows.

"Yeah . . . ?" I replied, my cheeks warm as they looked at me.

Richie said, "Oh shit—are you Mick Boche's granddaughter?"

Okay, this is weird.

"Yes . . . ?"

How would he know that already?

"Do you guys know each other?" Cassie asked, looking back and forth between me and these strangers.

"No, but Zeus mentioned her the other night at the party," Richie said.

What?

"You know *Zeus*?" she asked, her eyes wide like this was a very big deal.

"*No,*" I said, unsure why this dude thought I did. "No, I think he must have me confused with someone else. I have no idea who this Zeus person is."

Richie said, "Yes, you do! He's—"

But then the bell rang and all I could hear from Richie was . . . absolutely nothing.

Because it was like we were standing *inside* the bell, it was so loud.

"Later, Cassie! Dani"—Mullet Boy smirked before bowing—"it was a pleasure."

What the hell . . .

And with that, the hockey guys immediately dispersed, leaving me with unanswered questions.

How would some puckboy named Zeus have ever heard of me?

"Okay, let's get you to class so you're not late on your first day; no one likes being the center of attention that way, right?"

Oh, thank God she gets it, I thought. "Right."

"Okay, so I'll walk you to your first class, and then I'll be waiting when it ends to get you to second period. Cool?"

"Perfect," I said. "Thank you."

But as we walked and she pointed out classrooms and hallways, I couldn't shake the annoyance that some hockey jock had mentioned me. Like, *howwww*? I mean, it didn't make sense, because I'd literally met no one since I'd been here, but I supposed the tie-in to my grandpa made it possible.

Maybe Richie's dad was one of Big John's friends.

It irked me because I just wanted to be invisible. I needed whoever the hell Zeus was to forget he'd ever heard my name, if he had actually heard my name at all.

"Here we are: AP Lit," Cassie said, interrupting my thoughts by pointing to a classroom. "That's Mr. Hunter and he's really cool, so I'm sure you'll have no problem with him. Actually, let me help you."

She grabbed my arm and pulled me into the classroom.

"Hey, Mr. Hunter—this is Dani, and she's a new student."

He looked down at the piece of paper Cassie was holding out, which pretty much just had my name and schedule on it, and he narrowed his eyes.

I tried my best to pretend the people in the classroom weren't looking at us, even though I knew they were.

"Well, it's nice to meet you, Dani Collins," he said.

I nodded and smiled, wishing he would lower his voice and let me go sit down.

"There's an open desk in the back of the room—have a seat. I'll get you a textbook as soon as the final bell rings."

"Awesome," I said, my face on fire.

"I'll be back when it's over," Cassie said with a smile.

I was torn between being relieved she was leaving, because she was outrageously perky in a way that made me feel like a noncommunicative boob, and wanting to grab her arm and beg her to stay and protect me.

"Cool—thanks," I said, then headed toward the empty desk in the back of the room.

Where I would do my very best to become invisible.

CHAPTER SIX

Alec

Is that her?

I walked down the hallway, listening to Vinny's conspiracy theory about Kyle and Cassie while my eyes stayed glued to the back of an unfamiliar blonde's head. From what I could see, she was shortish, with wavy blond hair, and she was walking toward the history hall.

"Are you listening to me?" Vinny asked.

"Nope," I admitted, my eyes laser-focused on those curls. "Not at all."

It wasn't because I was interested in anything about her—*hell, no*—but because I wanted confirmation of whether or not it *was* her. For some reason, I needed to know.

Was she here?

Was Dani actually walking the halls of Southview this very minute?

That just seemed impossible.

God, seventh-grade me would've fucking *flipped* at the idea.

"Zeus!"

I turned around and Tawnee was smiling, walking toward me, holding the scarf I gave her just before I left the bonfire.

"I told you I'd return it," she said, and I had to force myself to smile. And not look over my shoulder to track the blonde's progress.

Tawnee was hot, Tawnee was cool, so why did I just want to crane my neck and see where the curls had gone? Dani was nothing to me, so

I definitely didn't need the mere idea of her to screw up any chance I had with Tawnee.

Although, to be fair, it was a long shot that Tawnee wanted something with me in the first place, because everyone knew she was still hung up on her ex.

"Thanks," I said, and shoved it in my pocket.

"How'd you feel yesterday?" she asked, her expression telling me she thought I'd been *wasted* at the bonfire.

I hadn't been, but I'd gone harder than I should have.

"Fabulous," I said, smiling like I meant it. "Like a ray of sunshine, thank you for asking."

She gave a little laugh as the bell rang, and I was glad when she went in the other direction.

Dammit.

I shouldn't be glad.

I needed a reset, because two days ago Tawnee Flanigan was all over my radar, but this morning I just wanted her out of my sight so I could play *Where's Waldo?* with some blonde's head.

Dani was messing with my mind and I hadn't even seen her yet, which was stupid. She was nothing to me anymore, literally nothing, and the sooner I stopped even remembering she existed, the better.

I put in my AirPods and cued up Hippo Campus. "Brand New" was the perfect song to make me stop wasting time and brain cells on someone who'd proved to me a long time ago that she wasn't worth it.

"Dude, I met Mick Boche's granddaughter."

"*What?*" I nearly shouted the word at Richie as we walked into the lunchroom, but the confirmation that she was within these walls fucking rocked me.

"Yeah, Cassie's showing her around, and Vin and I ran into them on the way to first period. She's fucking cute."

Vinny arched his eyebrow at me as if to say, *Typical Richard, our hopeless romantic.*

Richie grabbed a stack of like ten napkins because he was a neat freak and said, "She's got that whole librarian thing working for her, where you just want to see what's going on behind those glasses."

"This isn't Hallmark or Pornhub. Glasses are just glasses," Vinny said. "She's got bad eyes and probably a little stamp she uses in her home library that says 'This book belongs to Miss Boche.'"

"No less interested," Richie said with a laugh.

"How do you know she's Boche's granddaughter?" I asked, unsure why I felt like I'd been zapped by a stun gun.

"Cass said her name is Dani; isn't that what you said her name is?"

"Yeah," I said, grabbing a tray and sliding it past the salad bar, though I suddenly had zero appetite. "That's her."

"I didn't really get to talk to her because the bell rang," he said, "but trust that I'm going to find her by the end of the day."

That pissed me off for no good reason.

"I'd keep my distance if I were you," I cautioned, the idea of Richie going after her making me insane even though I didn't give a shit about her. "Because she was kind of a sketchball the last time I saw her."

"What do you mean, 'sketchball'?" he asked.

"I don't know," I said, trying to sound casual as I reached out to grab a chicken sandwich. "Just one of those people where you can't really trust them because they're all over the place. Sketchy."

"Ooh, did the librarian dump you?" Vinny asked with a smirk as he set three pieces of pizza on his tray.

"No," I said, because that was the absolute truth. You have to be *with* someone in order to dump them, and Dani was never *with* me at all. "We never went out; we were friends when we were kids, that's all, and she was—"

"Sketchy, yeah, we get it," Vinny interrupted.

"Tell me they have fiestadas today," Kyle said as he ran up to us. "I need my lucky lunch."

Kyle was our starting goalie and superstitious as fuck.

Like, worse than all of us put together.

"They have fiestadas," Richie confirmed. "I saw three on Bauer's tray when I came in."

"If that skinny fuck made them run out, I'll have to destroy him."

"Are you even capable of destruction," Vinny asked, "if you don't have your lucky lunch first?"

"Oh shit," Kyle said, shaking his head. "I don't even know."

I pretty much didn't hear anything anyone said at lunch because I was irrationally annoyed that Richie had called her cute and my mom had called her gorgeous.

For starters, I didn't give a shit.

But also, like, she shouldn't be cute.

She wasn't *allowed* to be gorgeous, dammit.

The last thing I needed was for Dani Collins to be beautiful *and* a student at Southview.

I had no room for distractions like that in my life. I put on my headphones and tried drowning out the chaos with "Come Apart," but it was useless. The idea of her drove me nuts for the rest of the day, my head turning every time there was blond hair in my peripheral vision.

But by the time we got out early for the pep rally, at least I convinced myself it was normal behavior.

I was curious—that was all.

It was absolutely normal to wonder what a childhood friend looked like as an adult.

This wasn't pathetic little Alec, searching for the girl he'd had a crush on since birth.

No; this was totally different.

I was different.

This was just me—Zeus—being curious if my shitty ex-friend had grown into a cute chick or not.

No big deal.

CHAPTER SEVEN
Dani

Thank God pep rallies aren't mandatory.

I made my way toward the doors, excited for this unexpected reprieve. I'd gone into the gym with everyone else when we were dismissed for the event, and I didn't realize until we were three cheers and a fight song deep that I had the option to leave.

Talk about a bonus.

It was weird, though. Even though it wasn't required, it looked like the entire school was sticking around for the pep rally. Not only that, but Grandpa Mick had been right: Nearly every person in that gym was dressed in black. I actually stood out in my off-white sweater, though I still stood by my tiny little act of rebellion, because it made me feel like I had a shred of life control.

Just as I reached the exit doors, the hockey team was announced, and I swear to God the entire student body jumped to their feet, screaming like they were at a concert and not a school-spirit event.

I turned back when it sounded like the crowd was booing, but as it turned out, they were just chanting "Zeus!" like a bunch of zealots.

I mean, even if "Zeus" was great at hockey, this adoration was absolutely unhinged.

And there was no way the boy wasn't a total egomaniac.

I narrowed my eyes and went down the row of players, curious to see if by some chance I might recognize the guy who'd apparently mentioned me. But the tall dude wearing aviators and raising a fist in the air like Bender from *The Breakfast Club* was no one I'd ever seen before.

Thank God.

I left and headed for the counselor's office, grateful for the empty halls and the extra time to get something accomplished. And when I got there, not only did I discover that my assigned counselor (Joan Hrznski, according to her name plate) had also chosen to skip the pep rally (obviously she was smart), but she had time to talk.

"Come in, Dani—have a seat. What can I do for you?"

I sat down, took a deep breath, and launched into the whole nightmarish story of how I was still in limbo.

I'd applied under Restrictive Early Action because I was all over my Harvard shit, but the divorce nightmare had had me so upset that my application hadn't been as strong as it might've been.

As it *should* have been.

Which led to me not being accepted, but being deferred.

God, I still couldn't believe it.

When I freaked out over the news, the counselor at my school in Germany had recommended not only that I keep my grades up—*Harvard is always watching*—but that I beef up my résumé with extracurriculars at my new school.

"Well, I'm inclined to agree with her." Ms. Hrznski nodded and said, "Keep writing to them, keep calling and pursuing the admissions office, and I'll do the same on my end. Nail down the extracurriculars here at Southview, keep your GPA up, and I'm confident we can still make it happen."

I had my doubts about her confidence, but I was going to delusionally believe her because what was my other option?

I wasn't about to face reality, for the love of God.

I would rather call admissions every other day until the breath left my body. I'd pictured my first year at Harvard for longer than I knew what the word "freshman" meant; failure was *not* an option.

"Do you know of some clubs that might be easy for me to get connected with?" I asked.

I'd always been good at finding activities that looked great on admissions applications—environmental club, math club, Amnesty International—yet didn't require a lot of social interaction.

Hopefully Southview would have the same.

"Well, it's February, dear," she said, her usage of the word "dear" irritating me because I wasn't some annoying spouse or child who was asking for the moon, for God's sake.

I just wanted to join a damn math club.

Then she added, "It's a little late to join a club."

So . . . why did you tell me to find an extracurricular if it's too late?

I swallowed down my frustration and calmly said, "What would you suggest for extracurriculars, then?"

"Maybe a spring sport—that'd be great," she said, nodding like she'd come up with the perfect solution.

Yes, Joan, that would indeed be great if I were magically athletic all of a sudden.

"Yeah, um, I don't play any sports," I said, trying to sound positive and not like I wanted to bang my head against a wall. "Isn't there like an environmental club or yearbook—"

"No, those are all closed by now," she said, cutting me off with a smile and a head shake. "If I were you, I would go home and rack my brain for potential activities that you might not be thinking of. Maybe track and field . . . ?"

Do you seriously think if I were a runner I wouldn't have thought of running, Joan Hrznski??

"Okay, thank you," I blurted out, climbing to my feet. I needed to get out of there before I lost my mind and did something stupid, like cry.

I walked out of the office, fuming because how ridiculous was it that my Harvard aspirations could be dead in the water unless I joined a team?

It was absurd.

It was just as absurd as the fact that legacy students were able to get in simply by being related to a former smart person, and jocks could get in on scholarship because they were able to dribble a ball while wearing a Harvard jersey.

How were those people seen as fantastic candidates, yet someone like me, who'd studied my ass off my entire life, could maybe only get in if I added to my permanent record that I'd *bowled* at a high school somewhere in Minnesota?

Insane.

I stepped out into the hallway and gritted my teeth as crowds poured out of the gym.

Fabulous timing.

I just wanted to be left alone to pout and be unhappy—was that so much to ask? The last thing I needed was to be surrounded by students losing their minds over whether or not the hockey team was going to be able to outpuck Simley's hockey team that night.

And how stupid a name is Simley anyway?!

Just as I was mentally raging, a group of hockey players walked by and I was suddenly surrounded. They didn't even notice me as I was absorbed into the center of their saunter pod, stuck because they were each hauling a huge hockey bag that served as some sort of duffel perimeter.

Please kill me.

I clutched the straps of my backpack, keeping my head down while trapped in the middle of the swagger sandwich as everybody in the hallway cheered them on as if their mere presence was the greatest thing to ever happen to the world.

The exit doors were just ahead, so I needed to keep my head down and make it a few more steps and then I'd be free.

"Zeus!"

One of the guys in front of me—the tallest guy—turned, which made his ginormous hockey bag come around and knock me to the floor.

Literally.

His body-bag-sized duffel laid me out.

"Oof" was the moronic noise I heard myself make as I fell to my ass, and something about that duffel slamming into me—and a random laugh I heard from somewhere behind me in the hallway—was the final straw.

"Can you maybe watch where you're going?" I snapped, too frustrated to hold back. "Just because you know how to hit a puck with a stick doesn't mean you're allowed to just mow people down in the hallway with your stupidly huge bag."

I wouldn't have thought he'd hear me, because it was so noisy in the hallway, but the guy stopped. The huge dude in the hockey jersey turned his head and looked down at me, and I gasped when those brown eyes met mine.

Brown eyes that were sort of amber and absolutely familiar.

Brown eyes that'd looked into mine countless times during those summer months. Brown eyes that I'd never forgotten, even when I tried my hardest.

His mouth kicked up into a cocky smirk, and he held out a hand.

"Nice to see you too, Collins."

Alec.

Alec was Zeus. Zeus was Alec.

I was too shocked to move, to speak. Words escaped me because the everything of us hit me harder than his hockey bag. Alec, *my* Alec, was standing right in front of me, close enough to touch. After everything and all the years, it was finally happening.

We were back.

"Zeus! You comin'?" yelled one of the guys ahead, breaking me from my trance. "The bus is here."

Alec's eyes narrowed as he took in my face. Silence lingered for too long until he lowered his hand away from me. The crowds in the hallway moved in slow motion, their cheers and yells a blur of noise. But I heard Alec's voice clearly.

"Yeah," he yelled back, his lips lifting teasingly. "I knocked some chick over with my bag."

Some chick?

His Adam's apple moved around a swallow. The smirk stayed on his mouth, but his eyes went hard.

Um.

I might not know him anymore, but I recognized that look.

He . . . definitely *wasn't* happy to see me.

CHAPTER EIGHT
Alec

How dare she?

How dare she look up at me like that? It was almost game time, but my mind was still on her face as I took a few laps, taking shots at the open net while picking up speed.

God, her face.

Richie was wrong.

She wasn't cute—she was fucking gorgeous.

Dani had always been pretty because of her laugh and the way she was so carefree. Her *Dani-ness* made her impossible to look away from.

The girl I'd knocked down in the hallway, though—she was a drop-dead stunner. All that wavy blond hair, those big brown eyes and black glasses . . . it fucking *worked*.

Not that I cared.

I wasn't a dick, but I'd be lying if I said it hadn't felt good to turn around and walk away like I'd never seen her before.

Because she didn't matter anymore.

"Fuck," I muttered under my breath when I heard the whistle, because warm-ups were over and I'd barely registered any of it. I was on fucking autopilot, which was the last thing I needed to be when I had a game.

I needed to be *on*. I needed to be intentional.

I needed to be proactively on top of every move being made by every player in a fucking blue jersey. Shutting down Simley was the only thing that mattered, especially when I knew there were scouts in the seats.

Fucking focus, *dipshit*.

A few years back, I used to get myself pumped up by imagining Dani watching me play in the NHL someday—while she was married to some loser and regretting her decisions. Regretting what she did.

It'd worked at the time, but I didn't need that motivational shit anymore.

She was nothing, and hockey was everything.

I jumped the boards and took down some water, redirecting my thoughts from her to the game as Coach started drawing out plays on his clipboard.

And by the time the puck dropped, she was long gone from my mind.

We struck first as Bauer snapped a shot past Simley's goalie on an odd-man rush, and then Richie made it 2–0 as he finished off a pretty passing play with Kirchner and Hardina. We had a shitty second period overall, and Vinny had to make some saves when we were leaking oil a little bit, but in the end we pulled it off and got the win.

A gutty effort, an ugly fucking dub.

But a win was a win.

CHAPTER NINE

Dani

"You came back," Cassie said with a smile, standing just inside the front doors as if she'd been waiting for me.

"Wait—did I have a choice?" I replied as I lowered my hood, welcoming the warm air on my face.

But the truth was that I was no less nervous today than I'd been yesterday.

Southview had A-days and B-days, with a different rotating schedule for each day, which meant that since yesterday had been an A-day, today was a B-day and yet another day of new classes.

Like a second first day of school.

And the fact that Alec hadn't looked happy to see me yesterday was messing with my head. I didn't understand his reaction—if anyone had a reason to look unhappy, it was me—but it made me nervous to run into him again.

And, as if all that wasn't bad enough, one of my B-day classes was public speaking, a requirement for all seniors at Southview.

So, yes—I was actually *more* nervous for my second first day than I'd been for my first.

Because I was the type of person who would've been queasy over public speaking even if I'd attended this school my entire life; speaking in front of other people just wasn't my thing.

But having this class at a new school—total nightmare.

I just prayed I didn't have one of those speech teachers who thought it would be great to force you to tell people a little bit about yourself on the very first day.

"I suppose you didn't, but I'm happy to see you, regardless," Cassie said. "Showing you around is way more interesting than just going to my boring classes."

"Yeah," I said, still a little unsure how to talk to someone so outgoing. Human nature made me want to open up because she seemed so nice, but experience had taught me that was a terrible idea.

"Let's head toward your first class," she said. "Because it's over on the northwest side of the building, which is a little farther."

We started walking, and I felt slightly less conspicuous than I had the day before, thank God. Cassie was so incredibly nice that even though I knew better, I found myself telling her about my visit to the counselor's office.

And dammit—it felt nice, having someone sympathize with my difficulties.

"So did you do anything last night, after that letdown?" she asked as we passed by the library. "I feel like everyone was at the hockey game, but I suspect you were not."

"No, I just stayed home and unpacked some boxes," I said.

I actually managed to get my entire room unpacked *and* talk to my dad on the phone, although that ended with me feeling emotionally drained.

I had such a weird, complicated relationship with him.

Ninety percent of the time, I thought of him as "the colonel" in my head. He was strict, by the book, a pretty distant father but a very good man.

Upstanding citizen and born leader, absolutely impossible to relate to.

But the other ten percent of the time, when he let his guard down . . . that was when I missed him so much it hurt.

Because during those rare moments, he'd do things like send a funny meme that I suspected he didn't understand but somehow knew I'd love, or have flowers delivered that let me know he was actually thinking of me. My entire life had been me watching him with wide eyes, breathlessly waiting for those few and far between occasions when he was "Dad" instead of "the colonel."

Yesterday had been one of those times.

He'd FaceTimed after I got home from school to see what my room looked like, and instead of saying my mom's name or the word "Minnesota" in the tone he always used that told me he didn't approve of the move and everything that went along with it, he told me that Germany wasn't the same without me.

And as nice as it'd been, it'd made me miss him so much that hours later, I still hadn't been able to sleep.

Because the thing I found so hard about the divorce was the lack of forced proximity. In a normal, intact family, both parents being nearby was the default, whether you liked it or not.

But in a divorce, that was never the case and never would be again.

I *felt* my dad's absence every day, just as strongly as I felt my mom's presence.

And it sucked.

"Well, the game was crazy," Cassie said, assuming I would be interested.

"Yeah?" I asked, trying to be a good conversationalist. Hockey was apparently interesting to everyone in Southview except for me. "Did we win?"

"We won, but we were down the entire third period until Zeus scored with five minutes left in the game."

"He *did*?" How could Alec be Zeus, the player my grandpa was going on about and the one who'd inspired a thousand posters? He'd been absolutely unathletic as a child, adorably clumsy in an *I'd rather play Roblox* kind of way.

So how could he be not just an athlete, but a varsity *hockey* player?

It didn't make sense.

I'd replayed our reunion scene in my head over and over again since it happened, getting angrier every time I thought about it. Not only had he *not* apologized for knocking me down with his bag, but he'd walked away like he didn't know me and laughed about it with his friends.

He'd called me "some chick."

I shouldn't care, but the knowledge that my childhood bestie had turned into an oversized, arrogant jock was just straight-up depressing.

So much for the one good thing about the move.

"Oh yeah—he single-handedly won the game for us, but that's not new. That's kind of his thing."

"So Alec is actually really *good* at hockey." It just seemed impossible, even though the new version of Alec certainly *looked* like a hockey player.

"Are you kidding me?" She gawked like I'd just asked if the earth was round. "Saying Alec is good at hockey is like saying LeBron James is an okay basketball player. He's broken a zillion high school records and he's a potential NHL prospect. He's like the *best*."

"Alec *Barczewski*." It was just too out-there to believe, even after witnessing the school's reaction to him at the pep rally. "Shut *up*!"

He'd been as unathletic as me.

"So *do* you know him?" Cassie asked, her eyes narrowing. "Yesterday you said you didn't."

"That's because I didn't know him by the nickname," I clarified, in total shock. "I knew him when I was a little kid, before he was Zeus. He's like an . . . honorary cousin of mine, if you know what I mean."

I didn't want her to think there was any tie between us, because the last thing I needed was for people to link me with the popular jock; that could mess me up before I made a single friend.

I added, "I haven't seen him in years, so he's basically a stranger." Right as I said that, we walked by yet another poster of the hockey team, and this time my eyes found him immediately.

Zeus.

Ugh.

Something about his expression in that image made me think of his black eye, the one he got playing baseball the summer after fifth grade. A fly ball came right to him, but instead of catching it with his glove, he caught it with his face.

And he'd been *happy* about it because he got to sit out the rest of the game, and his dad bought us Dairy Queen afterward.

That had been my buddy.

I couldn't believe Alec (sorry, *Zeus*) had become the exact kind of guy I'd learned to avoid at every single school I went to.

I guess it's time to avoid my former best friend.

Although, that was apparently going to be easier said than done. *Oh, universe, what did I ever do to you?* I thought when I walked into my speech class later that day and saw *him*.

I already wanted to vomit because of my aforementioned terror of public speaking and first days, but there he was, sitting in the back with two other guys, each smirking with legs stretched out under their desks like they owned the room.

"This is Dan Collins," Ms. Sykes said to the class, "and she is a new student. Everyone make sure to say hi to Dan and help her out. There's a desk over there for you."

I knew I should correct her—*it's Dani*—but I couldn't bring myself to speak.

So now I'd probably be known as "Dan" for the rest of the year.

I looked in the direction of where she was pointing and it was on the other side of the room from Alec, which was good, but the chairs were arranged in a big U shape, so I could still see him and his friends at all times.

Wonderful.

I couldn't stop myself from glancing at him when I walked by his desk, just as he tilted his head and met my eyes.

While smirking, like he was the king who found himself amused by the presence of a lowly peasant.

I clenched my teeth and was about to look away when he winked.

Winked at me.

He might've even made a clicking noise with his mouth, but I couldn't be sure my brain hadn't added that douchebag sound effect.

My face was on fire as I sat down and unzipped my backpack, torn between nervousness, embarrassment, and kind of wanting to rip his face off for winking at me.

Who did that? What kind of eighteen-year-old senior in high school *winked* at someone?

The arrogance it took to throw out a wink in response to someone looking in your direction was truly astounding.

Thankfully, the teacher started in on a lesson, and since we were required to take notes, I was able to forget about the freaking winker on the other side of the room. I threw myself into notes, writing every single word because it was a far better option than looking up from my paper.

Halfway through the class I glanced his way, only to see that his head was down on his desk, and he was asleep.

Alec was sleeping in class like he didn't give a shit.

And it kind of made me want to cry, honestly. It felt like I'd lost something (even though I'd technically lost him a long time ago), because over the past five years, through all the bad days, I'd imagined that my best friend still existed somewhere, even if he wasn't in my life.

I was able to think that *someday* we might be friends again.

But now I was forced to face the reality that the possibility no longer existed.

CHAPTER TEN
Alec

"I can't believe you fell asleep again," Kyle said.

"I can't believe Sykes let me," I replied, relieved as we left the classroom.

Because I'd needed that nap so badly.

Last night, after the game, my throbbing shoulder kept me up until my alarm went off, I swear to God. I was fucking exhausted, and that nap during speech had done wonders.

The only shock was that I'd been able to fall asleep at all after getting punched in the gut with Dani's presence. Somehow, even though I knew she went to my school now, I hadn't considered the reality that she might actually end up in one of my classes.

When she walked into public speaking, I could barely breathe.

How the hell was this happening? I didn't want her to be in Southview at all, but definitely not in my life, in my fucking speech class.

It was unbelievable.

Her cheeks had been bright red, and her eyes were down when she walked to her desk, and if I didn't know her, I would've thought she was super shy.

But Dani Collins wasn't shy. At all.

I wasn't sure if it was an act or if she was unhappy to see me, but it didn't matter.

She was just another girl at my school, and I would ignore her like I did any other girl I wasn't friends with. I loaded a little Connor

LYNN PAINTER

Kauffman into my playlist and moved the hell on.

Only for some reason, when I saw her through the library window at lunch, I couldn't do it. She was sitting all by herself at a table, and dammit—I couldn't ignore her.

"Hey, I'm going to go in the library for a sec," I said to Kyle, my eyes on blond hair and glasses. "I'll meet you in the cafeteria."

"I'll go with you," he said with a smirk. "I see what you're doing."

"It's not what you think," I said as he gestured with his head toward Dani. "I just need to grab a book."

"Sure, me too," he said, walking beside me as I pulled open the library door and went inside.

For a half second, I was able to look at her without her seeing me. Her eyes were on the book in her hands, so I took a moment to really take in my old friend.

Holy shit.

I might not give a damn about her now, but the kid who'd spent his entire childhood following her around like a puppy needed a minute to catalog this updated version of her.

The curly hair that used to stick out all over now fell in long waves around her face, like she'd figured out how to relax the wildness. Which could maybe be said for her personality, I supposed, since I'd yet to see the wild-ass grin that used to be her default expression.

She looked *good* in the black turtleneck sweater she was wearing. It was plain, nothing remarkable about it at all, but it was like it fucking showcased her soft skin and the—

"Dude," Kyle said, grinning at me like he just caught me staring at the new girl.

Because he had.

"Kiss my ass," I said, walking over to her table.

"Hey, Collins," I said, dropping down into the chair across from her even though I had no idea what I was doing there or what my plan was. She was like a magnet pulling me toward her.

I hated it.

She raised her eyes from her book, and for the splittest of seconds it looked like she might smile.

The moment held like a pause, long-lashed brown eyes I'd known *so* well watching me from behind black glasses, and I felt almost homesick for the person I used to know.

But then her eyes went to Kyle, and back to me, and then she blinked fast before quietly saying, "Hey, Alec."

"So how come you're hiding in the library at lunch?" I asked, telling myself to get it together and knock off the *homesick* bullshit.

"I'm not very hungry and I wanted to read," she said with a shrug.

Then she lowered her eyes back to her book, brushing me off.

Like she was finished with me.

Like she'd been finished with me back in the day.

And just like that, I wanted to get under her skin.

To mess with this unfamiliar quiet composure that I found to be irrationally irritating.

"Have you met Kyle yet?" I asked. "This is Kyle. Kyle, this is my old buddy Dani. Say *hi*, Dani."

She raised her eyes again, and annoyance was all over her face. "Hi," she said to Kyle.

"Hey," Kyle replied, smiling but looking confused.

Which made sense because the vibe between Dani and me was awkward as shit.

"So how do you like Southview so far?" I asked, setting my chin on my fist like I was dying to hear her answer.

"It's fine," she said, a crinkle forming in between her eyebrows as her eyes dropped down to my mouth, cataloging what I was sure appeared to be an asshole grin.

Good.

"What's this about?" I asked for no good reason, reaching out to flick the front cover of her book. "*The Blind Assassin* isn't actually about a visually impaired killer, is it?"

"No." She cleared her throat and closed the book, her eyes narrowing a little. "Is there something I can help you with? I'm trying to get some reading done before my next class, but I can totally move to a different table if you guys want to chat."

"But we want to chat with *you*, Dan," I said, unable to stop myself from being a tool.

"I don't think you do, though, *Al*," she snapped, but quickly covered it with a fake smile, seeming like the old Dani for a second. "It feels a little bit like you just want to interrupt me."

"You look fun to interrupt," I said, wondering as I looked at her frosted pink fingernails if she still insisted that her toes always match. "What can I say?"

"You could say *nothing*," she replied, so quiet I *almost* couldn't hear it.

"Jesus, you guys *are* old friends," Kyle said with a laugh. "You sound like siblings."

"There you are!"

All three of us turned as Cassie breezed through the library doors and ran over to the table. "I was looking for you everywhere, Dani, because I thought maybe you'd want to sit with me and my friends at lunch."

She was friends with Cassie already? *Shit.* The last thing I needed was Dani showing up everywhere I went with my friends.

"Actually, I think I'm just going to read through lunch, because this is a really good book," she said, her cheeks getting red as we all looked at her. "But thank you."

"Sure," Cassie said, looking at me and adding, "I see you ran into your old buddy."

Dani looked embarrassed, glancing my way as she said, "Oh, um—"

"You already told her about us, eh?" I couldn't help myself. "Your Zeus connection?"

That made her nose wrinkle like she smelled something bad. "It definitely wasn't like that."

"Yeah, she didn't even know you at first," Cassie said, then grabbed a chair and pulled it so she was sitting beside Dani. "By the way, I was thinking about your Harvard problem."

"Ooh, what's your Harvard problem?" I asked, grabbing Dani's book and picking it up.

Dani shot me a *butt out* look. "It's nothing—"

"Dani's been deferred by Harvard, the only school she's ever wanted to go to," Cassie explained. "So she needs to get in a couple of extracurriculars here at Southview so she can lock it down, but it's too late to join most of the clubs."

The only school she's ever wanted to go to.

I cleared my throat, forcing away the memory of how for the entire summer after fifth grade, Dani wore a bright red Harvard T-shirt almost every day.

I started to open the book I'd snagged, but Dani snatched it out of my hand.

"Hrznski didn't even help, she just told her to play a spring sport, which is ridiculous, right?" Cassie made a face and said, "Like someone can just start a new sport their senior year."

It pissed me off as I listened to Cassie talk about poor Dani, because I had zero choices regarding my education. It didn't matter where I wanted to go to college, because unless something changed, it wasn't the plan for next year. It was just assumed I'd play juniors or train over in Michigan.

And *yes*, it was a dream come true that I had these insane hockey opportunities, but no one had ever even asked what *I* wanted. If I was being honest, I wanted to go to college next year like everyone else, so fucking badly. I wanted to study history, to get lost in old libraries and sleep in university dorms, but I felt like shit even thinking that, because how many guys would kill to be in my shoes?

Still, Dani complaining because she might not get to attend the Ivy League school of her dreams didn't exactly have me bleeding sympathy.

"Regretting the unathleticism, Collins?" I asked. "Maybe you should've practiced skating instead of reading all the time."

"And risk ending up an egomaniac with a stupid nickname? I'd rather go to community college, but thank you."

Holy shitballs, there she is—the girl who used to play with me every summer.

"Whoa," Kyle said, laughing. "Did the new girl just destroy you?"

"I think she tried," I said, torn between irritation and wanting to smile.

"I think she succeeded," Cassie said around a laugh.

"I'm telling your mom," I said, dropping her book on the table in front of her.

"Snitch," she said with a tiny smirk, and then I watched as she realized what she'd just said.

Oh, the fast blink of regret.

We'd used "snitches get stitches" for an entire summer because it'd been hilarious in the way that middle school jokes were hilarious when on repeat.

It was interesting that the words had naturally fallen out of her mouth.

She might've left me behind, but she hadn't forgotten.

CHAPTER ELEVEN
Dani

"Come eat, kiddo!"

I set down my pen and stretched, because I'd been working on homework since I got home at three thirty and it was almost seven. Southview's AP classes were no joke, and I needed to stay on top of the curriculum because I had no room for anything less than an A+.

But I was starving and something smelled really good, so I ran down the stairs.

When I got downstairs, Grandpa Mick was twirling spaghetti around his fork, my mom doing the same beside him.

"Oh, praise God, spaghetti," I said under my breath, starving. I was famished because I hadn't eaten lunch at school.

It'd been *years* since I'd consumed lunch in a cafeteria.

It was another one of those important lessons of starting a new school. Far better to lose yourself in a library book over lunch than navigate a crowded cafeteria. It was peaceful and unthreatening, and a little bit of hunger beat a heaping helping of mortification every time.

Although today the mortification had nearly happened *in* the library.

Even after discovering he'd become some arrogant jockish version of his former self, I was still surprised that he'd seemed to find it entertaining to mess with me.

I would've assumed our family connection would at least make him ignore me, since he'd clearly decided I wasn't worth his jock-star time, so his plopping down and inserting himself in my life just for funsies had been a total surprise.

I hated that a tiny part of me just wanted to know why. And why he so clearly didn't want to be my friend anymore. Maybe *Zeus* was just too cool for me now.

It was also driving me crazy, wondering if he'd laughed to all his friends about the postcards.

"How was school today?" Grandpa Mick asked, pulling me out of my spin.

"Good," I said, glancing over at him because the way he'd asked didn't feel like small talk.

Did he know something?

"How do you like Southview?" he asked, picking up his garlic bread and taking a bite.

"As much as I like any school," I said, grabbing a plate and scooping a pile of pasta from the colander still in the sink. I didn't recognize the pot or the colander or the smell of the sauce—had *he* made dinner?

My mom was all jar sauce, all the time.

"It's Grandma's recipe," my mom said, reading my mind as she lifted a forkful of noodles to her mouth. "He nailed it, and the meatballs are to die for."

"You made this?" I asked my grandpa.

"What, you think I can't cook?"

I couldn't tell if I'd offended him or if he was messing with me.

"I think I have no idea," I said, which was the truth, but as soon as the words left my mouth, I realized they sounded like a jab about his absence from our lives.

Which was deserved, I supposed, but unintended.

"Did you make friends today?" my grandpa asked as I sat down across from him and my mom, but he was looking at his phone.

Why was he asking me questions about school?

"Sure," I said, even though the only person who'd been friendly to me was Cassie and it was because it was her job.

"Are there any concerns you have that you would like to, um, to talk about?"

Was he serious? Maybe my interaction with Alec—*ugh, Zeus*—made me suspicious about everything, but why all the questions?

"What do you mean?" I asked.

"I think he's just checking in to see if you want to talk about anything," my mom said, reaching out to grab a piece of bread while giving me a *be nice* look.

But he was *still* looking down at his phone and not at me.

"Is . . . that what you meant?"

He sighed and finally looked up. "Hell if I know."

So I shrugged and said, "I'm fine," just as the words "how to talk to your teenager about school" caught my eye before his phone buzzed with a notification and he snatched it up.

Wait. Was he googling how to talk to me?

I watched him looking at his phone, and I was dying to know if that was the case. *Can that be it?* Something warmed in my chest at the thought of it, because the idea of him actively trying to know me better was . . . well, *nice*.

But my body immediately sent a dose of anxiousness to my stomach, because it was foolish to toss hopefulness into this wildly confusing relationship, right?

"Oh shit," he said as he read whatever message had just come through.

"What is it?" my mom asked, leaning over to see his phone.

"Oh shit, this is not good," he said, holding it out for my mom to see.

"What's going on?" I asked.

"Is that *Alec*?" My mom grabbed his phone and squinted as she looked at the screen.

"What has the hockey god Zeus done now?" I asked, stabbing a meatball with my fork. "Walked on water?"

But when I raised my eyes, they were both looking at me like I was a jerk.

"What?"

"I'm going to go call Sarah," my mom said, and then she jumped out of her chair and ran upstairs.

"What happened?" I asked Grandpa Mick, suddenly worried. "Is everything okay?"

He gave his head a shake. "Someone posted this on social media."

He held up his phone, and there was a picture of Alec.

A picture of Alec holding what appeared to be the world's biggest bong, and his eyes were only half open; he looked hammered. And happy.

With a raging fire in the background.

"What was he thinking?" I said under my breath, relieved he wasn't hurt but also disappointed, because how was it possible that Alec had become *that* guy?

"He wasn't," my grandpa said. "And now he totally fucked over his future."

"But isn't weed legal in Minnesota?" I didn't know anything about it, to be honest, but my grandpa's response seemed like a bit of an overreaction. "I mean, I know he's a minor, but I doubt something like this will ruin his future. Like, he's not going to go to jail for drugs, right?"

"No, I'm talking about his hockey future."

"Oh. That," I said, and I must've sounded too casual, because he looked at me like I was an uncaring ass.

But I wasn't.

Even though I didn't know this stranger Alec had become, I didn't want bad things to happen to him.

My grandpa said, "He might've just screwed up his shot at making the US training team."

"I don't know what that is. Like, the Olympics?"

"Mm-hmm," he said. "There is literally a board of old hockey dudes who decide the roster, and if they think he's going to crash and burn once he gets to the next level or be a locker-room cancer, they'll choose someone else."

No way. *The* Olympics. He was *that* good? Like *Olympic training* good?

Alec may have grown into a complete tool, but this could not be good for him or for Big John and Sarah. I hated this for them. Not for *Zeus*, but for the old Alec who used to be my best friend.

"Is there anything he can do?" I asked. "He's a teenager. Can't he just apologize?"

"I don't know," he said as he scooped up a meatball. "If this was the first issue, they might let it go, but my buddies said he got an MIP last year, and he's been in a few fights, so he might seem like too much of a risk."

Fights. Like plural? As in multiple fights. "I cannot believe Alec has become someone who fights and parties all the time," I said, shaking my head. How much had he changed from the last time I saw him?

"He's *not*," my mom said as she walked into the room, looking absolutely offended by my words. "He got in a couple of fights back when John was in the hospital and things were super tough for their family. And the MIP was just teenagers being dumb. It looks bad when you put it all together, but he's still a good kid."

Her words punched me right in the gut. I reached for my water and wondered if she was right. Maybe I was being too judgmental.

"Sarah said all of Alec's coaches are on their way over right now to talk to him and come up with a plan."

"*All* of them? Like, an entire coaching staff is en route to yell at him over a random photo?"

"I'm sure," Grandpa Mick said. "Because it's not just *his* future that's at stake."

What is that supposed to mean?

"But we're talking about hockey here," I clarified. "Not his entire future."

"They go hand in hand. It's hockey with the potential to change the trajectory of his entire life," my mom said in a scolding tone, her eyes narrowing at me. "Now eat your spaghetti."

CHAPTER TWELVE
Alec

"Are you okay?" my mom asked, pushing open my door, letting the light from the hallway flood into the dark bedroom where I was lying on my bed.

Was I okay?

Fuck if I know.

She stood in the doorway with her arms crossed, watching me with the same overworried, overprotective look she'd worn for most of my life.

Especially since the accident.

Everyone had finally left, thank God, so she was checking in after witnessing me getting yelled at for two hours straight.

God, it was so stupid.

I hadn't even put my mouth on megabong. As much as I'd wanted to get hammered at the bonfire, I'd been a good boy and steered clear of Reid's party favors. I'd laughed my ass off when I saw his ridiculous apparatus, of which Tawnee had snapped a photo, but I'd hardcore passed on that nonsense. In the end I'd known better, but now no one believed that I'd just been holding it.

Not even my dad.

I mean, my biggest lapse in judgment had been letting Tawnee take a photo at all. I didn't have any social media accounts (that were public or searchable) because of potential situations like this. I knew better than to post anything about my personal life for the world to see.

But *she* didn't know better. Tawnee's harmless "photo dump" had ensured that half the hockey players in the Twin Cities—a large number of them my rivals—laid eyes upon that picture of me holding a fucking bong.

And now the guys up north, the ones with all the power, had already seen the photo.

Gee, I wonder how that happened? Fucking Maserati-driving douchebag.

I was so screwed.

I paused my playlist—"undressed" by sombr didn't feel right while talking to my mom—and took out my AirPods.

"Yeah," I said, staring up at my ceiling. "I mean, I deserved that."

"You did," she said with a smile in her voice, "but you're just a kid. Screwing up is part of growing up."

Her understanding made my throat tight, because she of all people needed me to be *on*. Out of everyone in my life, she and Dad were the ones who should've been yelling the loudest, because I was potentially fucking things up for them.

But here she was, asking if I was okay.

"Do you think they can fix it?" I asked, hating how weak I sounded. How unsure.

"I do," she said. "I know it'll be fine."

After my coaches hollered at me for an hour, they came up with a tentative plan. I was going to behave like an angel and be fucking perfect—perfect grades, perfect behavior—and they were going to see if they could get the newspaper to do a story on me and my family and the whole ride we'd been on. They thought maybe if they showed who I was—and the shitstorm we'd (sort of) weathered—the decision makers would be more prone to forgive the stupid things I'd done.

"Just do everything they said, kiddo. You've got this."

Her faith in me almost made it worse, because it just added to the pressure that'd been crushing my skull for the past year. A tiny part of me wished this mistake would ruin everything. Then I wouldn't have any more pressure to get the wins and make the training team and eventually get the NHL deal that was going to change my family's life forever.

I could go to community college next year while working at the hardware store, and no one would even notice my presence. Finally, I'd be able to breathe.

But my hockey future had become the most important thing to my family's long-term security. It was the thing with the potential to make the grind less grinding. I didn't think my parents had even realized that we'd stopped talking about other options for me a long time ago.

Which was fair, because life had been hard since the accident.

My dad still couldn't work, aside from part-time, because his back seized up if he sat too long (or stood too long). And the medical bills we still owed from all those surgeries and hospital stays weren't going away, especially since my mom was a teacher and not a millionaire.

I'd been doing my part to cover hockey expenses by working a lot, but the Barczewskis as a whole were way the fuck away from being in the black, so the life-changing lotto win of a future contract would mean everything.

God, I wanted to deliver that so fucking badly.

But what if I failed?

What if things never got easier for my parents?

"I promise not to screw up again," I said, my voice cracking.

"I know you won't, honey," she said. "By the way, you didn't even tell me how things went with Dani. I'm assuming you two have run into each other by now?"

Like I need this right now.

"Yeah, I saw her," I said, rolling with her attempt to change the subject without going too deep into a Dani discussion. "It was fine."

"Just fine?" She sounded shocked.

"What'd you expect?" I asked. "I haven't seen her since middle school."

"I don't know—you kids were always like two peas in a pod, so I think I imagined you immediately going back to business as usual, the way you did every summer."

"Yeah, well, it's been a long time, and I only saw her for a few minutes."

"Oh."

"Don't sound so disappointed," I said, smiling in spite of everything because sometimes my mom was so ridiculously delusional that it was kind of adorable. She always had an attitude like she knew everything was going to work out.

Even in the worst of times.

"Well, now that you've seen her, I'm sure you'll get to know each other again."

"Maybe," I said, just wanting to end the subject.

For some reason, talking—hell, even *thinking* about Dani hurt my chest.

"Well, if you have the chance, make sure you go out of your way to be nice to her. Make sure she's hanging out with good kids and making friends."

"She's a senior in high school—I'm sure she can handle this," I said.

"Yeah, but Hannah said she's changed. Apparently she's not the same outgoing kid she used to be."

Ugh. There was that pain in my chest again.

"What do you mean?"

"I don't know, she didn't really go into it, but I get the impression that all the moves kind of messed with her. She sort of closes herself up, and has some social anxiety."

"I can't imagine Dani being an introvert," I said, and the idea of it made something in my heart pinch as I pictured her red cheeks and lowered eyes in the library over lunch.

Nope—not my problem, I quickly reminded myself.

"Yeah, me either, but I've never had to switch schools every two years. That'd really have to screw with your head, y'know?"

"I'm sure she's fine," I said, unable to sympathize with Dani when I had enough shit to worry about.

"Yeah, I'm sure she is too," my mom said. "I'm going to go check on the twins, but get some sleep, kid."

"I will," I said, even though I wouldn't.

Between the ache in my shoulder and the stress in my brain, I could tell it was going to be a long night.

CHAPTER THIRTEEN
Dani

"Grandpa's going to drive you to school today," my mom said as I walked into the kitchen. "Because I have an interview, remember?"

"Oh yeah," I replied, though I hadn't realized it meant having to ride with *him*.

"You look nice," I said. "That dress screams 'I would be an exemplary employee.'"

"Sure it does," she said, walking over to pull me into a hug. "I think it screams 'I don't know what's cool anymore,' but thank you just the same."

"Anytime. You're going to totally wow them."

My phone buzzed.

Ben Worthington: I'll be at my dad's tonight if you need anything.

What? I could not imagine any scenario where I'd be needing Mr. Maserati, but also, like, why would he just send *me* a random text out of the blue? I supposed it was nice that he was checking in, but his message felt a little too familiar when we were basically strangers.

"She's the best bullshitter I've ever met," my grandpa said, smiling at my mom.

God, he should smile more. He almost looks . . . nice.

"Ready to go, kid?"

His smile disappeared when he looked at me.

Of course.

"Yes," I said, sliding my arms into my winter coat.

Yesterday had been pretty uneventful at school (thank God), without any Alec sightings. His name was impossible to avoid because *everyone* was talking about the bong picture—I wondered how he was handling it—but I hadn't *seen* him at all.

Unfortunately, I wouldn't be so lucky today because it was a B-day: public speaking day.

Not only would I be seeing him, but there was a chance I'd be called upon to give a speech to the entire class.

Please, God, no.

My grandpa turned on a hockey podcast when we got in his truck, which was good because I still hadn't figured out how to talk to him. It seemed like we talked around each other a lot, but never directly *to* each other. We rode in silence, which was helpful because I started going through my speech in my head, over and over again.

Ms. Sykes had told me I still needed to give the intro speech that everyone else had given at the beginning of the semester, so I was practicing what I'd written out, trying to make myself sound somehow interesting but boring, unremarkable but not mockable.

But the closer we got to the school while I practiced, the more nervous I got.

By the time we pulled into the parking lot, I felt almost dizzy with stress.

"You okay?"

I looked over at my grandpa, who I'd kind of forgotten was there, and he was once again watching like he knew what was going on with me.

I just nodded, unable to speak; that was how close I was to a full-on panic attack.

No. No. No. Not in front of him.

"Just take deep breaths through your nose," he said, his hawklike gaze on mine. "They always save me."

Wait. Is he saying . . . ?

I cleared my throat, and all the questions I had must've been in my eyes, because he simply said, "I guess you get it from me. Sorry about that."

He didn't say anything else, just met my gaze.

And I could tell he wasn't going to expand on that, which was okay, because it was enough. For the first time since arriving in Minnesota, and in the midst of my panic, I smiled at my grandpa.

"You should be," I said. "Because this sucks."

"Like I don't know that." He winked and said, "Now get out of the truck and go to school. Just keep breathing and you'll be fine."

"Okay," I said, unbuckling my seat belt with unsteady hands. "Thanks."

His reminder helped, but only short-term.

Because the minute I walked into speech and saw Alec and his friends, draped across their desks like nothing fazed them, my fingertips felt numb. I breathed in through my nose and took my seat, desperately hoping I wouldn't get chosen to give my speech that day.

But the universe was clearly out to get me, because Ms. Sykes sat down behind her desk and as soon as the bell rang, she called on me.

"All right, it's a day full of speeches, so let's not waste any time. Since one more student needs to give their intro speech, let's knock that out before moving on. Miss Collins, why don't you start us out for the day?"

I swallowed and stood, grabbing my notes, praying I wouldn't do something like pass out or throw up.

I walked to the podium at the front of the class, and my chest felt tight as I looked out at all the faces. Unfamiliar faces that didn't look especially friendly.

And then I made eye contact with Alec, who just swallowed and stared at me but didn't even smile.

I took a deep breath, but my heart was beating so fast. I could feel it. It was too fast.

Too fast.

"My name is Dani Collins," I said, my voice thin and shaky. "I—"

"Louder, please," the teacher interrupted, smiling but holding her chin up like she was trying to show me how to project my voice.

But I couldn't catch my breath.

I knew what this was—I always knew what this was—but it still felt terrifying.

It's just a panic attack, I told myself, but at the same time I wondered if I needed to go to the nurse or dial 911 because I just couldn't get a good breath.

Help!

I tried taking another deep breath, but it wasn't working. A wave of dizziness came over me, and I clutched the sides of the podium and tried it again. "My name is—"

"Ms. Sykes!" Alec yelled, and when my eyes shot to him, he was waving his hand in the air like he desperately needed the teacher's attention.

"*What?*" She looked at him like he'd lost his mind and snapped, "Mr. Barczewski, can this wait?"

"I am so sorry," he said, kind of in my direction but also to her, "but I just got a message that I have to leave early for an appointment, and I really, really want to get my speech done today. Since she's new and obviously not too excited to do this, is there any way I can go in front of her?"

A few people laughed, and I didn't know what to think as he stared at me. His brown eyes were serious and direct, like he was trying to tell me something.

"I'm not going to make her stop just because you want to get your speech done today, Alec," she said. "I appreciate your—"

"I—I don't mind," I interrupted, a little shocked I was able to find my voice at all. "He can totally go now." I let my eyes move over Alec's bizarrely familiar yet unfamiliar face, not sure if he was aware that he was saving my ass.

The teacher gave a heavy sigh before saying, "Well, if you truly don't mind," her tone both beleaguered by his request but also amused. "Then, Alec—get up here and get your speech finished."

A few people laughed as my shaking hands grabbed my notes and I went back to my desk, passing by Alec, who wandered up there with empty hands (not a *single* note card) and a confident smile like this was no big deal.

"Thank you, Ms. Sykes, for letting me do this," he said, to which she gave a closed-mouth smile and tilted her head.

"Have you ever wondered what it's like to work in a hardware store?" he said, causing snickers around the classroom. "It sounds wildly fascinating, I know, but you'd be surprised that a lot of the things that occur inside the walls of your local Ace Hardware are actually not that exciting."

Even though I knew I was still next, I felt my heart rate slowing down as I took in a deep breath *that felt so good* through my nose while he casually delivered his speech.

Which almost didn't feel like a speech at all.

I was a little frozen while I listened, because hearing him speak that way, relaxed and self-deprecatingly funny, reminded me so much of my friend Alec.

And the little half smile he wore was exactly the same.

I missed him as he spoke, missed being someone he spoke to. I knew he was either a full-time jerk now or at the very least uninterested in rekindling our friendship—which was fine—but as someone who'd never had a lot of friends, I was homesick for the ease I used to feel around him.

As soon as he finished the speech, he left, briefly arguing with the teacher because he couldn't seem to produce the pass that proved he was allowed to leave.

But he was so good at insisting that she ultimately let him go (while smiling).

As soon as he was gone, she called on me to give my speech.

I still had all the butterflies, and my hands were still shaking, but this time I managed to do it. I wasn't sure if it was because I didn't have to look at Alec because he was gone, or if his distraction had been enough to convince my body I'd be fine.

Whatever it was, I made it through the speech without passing out or throwing up.

Which felt like a victory.

Until lunch, when I looked up from *Invisible Man* and saw him entering the library.

Dammit.

Not only was it Alec, but he had three hockey guys with him. And Cassie.

I quickly looked down at the book that I was rereading in preparation for AP Lit, pretending I hadn't seen them while I delusionally hoped that they were either in the library for some other reason or were going to ask me a quick question and leave.

"Can we sit here?" Alec asked, pointing to the chairs at my table.

"Sure," I said, my eyes moving to his friends, who were all looking at me as they pulled out chairs and sat down. "I can move to a smaller table if you guys need the big one."

"No," Cassie said. "Alec said it was too noisy in the cafeteria and he wanted to go to the library, so we came too because, well . . . why did we come again?"

She grinned at the other three guys, and I realized she was impossible to dislike.

"Well, *I* came because I wanted to ask Dani here about her grandfather," said the enormous wall of a human with the ridiculous hair.

I thought I remembered that his name was Vinny.

"Yeah, okay, that was why I came too," the redhead (Richie?) agreed, grinning in a way that made me think maybe he was okay.

"I was just following Cassie," Kyle said with a shrug. He was the one who'd been with Alec in the library the other day, and he *also* had a mullet, though his was *normal* compared to Vinny's. Just a dark-haired version of the whole business-in-the-front-party-in-the-back ugly hairstyle.

"Silly me," Cassie said, smiling at Kyle. "I came because I actually agreed that it was noisy in the cafeteria and thought it would be fun to eat my lunch quietly in the library."

"The only one without an ulterior motive," Alec said. "I need to grab a book."

Without another word he walked over to the history section—was he seriously getting a book?—while his friends gave me shy smiles like they were little boys.

"So what was it like growing up with Mick?" Richie asked.

"Is he always intimidating," Vinny asked, "or is he super real when you know him?"

"Um, he has always been a little intimidating, to be honest," I said, surprised that they just wanted to talk about my grandpa. "And I didn't really grow up with him. We moved a lot, so I kind of only saw him once a year when I was a kid."

I wasn't sure if I should lean into this interest or downplay everything. Having a sort-of-famous grandfather had never come into play before, so I had no rule book to check for this.

"So you don't really know him any better than anyone else—is that what you're saying?"

Kyle was looking at Cassie when he said that, but she was listening to me and had no idea that her admirer was staring at her with the real-life equivalent of heart eyes.

"I mean, I did when I was little," I said. "He used to take me fishing and let me drive his boat and stuff. We were pretty close until I hit middle school."

"Does he talk about hockey all the time?" Vinny asked. "*Tell* me he'd sit at Thanksgiving dinner and talk about bashing Guy Gustafson's face in."

"Can you even fucking imagine?" Richie said with a laugh. "'I busted the shit outta his nose—hey, pass the stuffing.'"

I glanced at Cassie and she was grinning at me, rolling her eyes at her friends.

"Actually, he never really talked about it—Guy's face bashing or anything else. It wasn't until recently that I even realized he was more than just, like, someone who played hockey when he was a kid."

"Are you kidding?" Vinny asked. "No way. You can't be serious."

"Totally serious," I said, kind of realizing for the first time how strange that was.

"Wow," Kyle said, shaking his head.

"So, Dani," Cassie asked, playfully nudging him out of the way. "Did you come up with anything on the extracurriculars?"

"No, because I honestly can't think of anything that will work," I said.

I'd spent *a lot* of time trying to figure something out, clicking through all the teams on the Southview High website, hoping to find some random activity that might be an option, but so far there was nothing.

Cassie filled the guys in on my situation, which made Richie say, "Can't she just be another manager?"

"Oh my gosh," Cassie said, her eyes going huge. "Why didn't I think of that?"

"Think of what?" I asked slowly. Very curious what they could be talking about.

LYNN PAINTER

"I mean, you've been doing it by yourself since Lillie quit," Vinny said. "Couldn't Dani just take her place?"

What? I heard from behind me. Alec came over with a couple of books in his hand and a scowl on his face. He sat down, his eyebrows furrowed like he'd just overheard us saying something obscene.

"Dani's still trying to find an extracurricular, and these guys thought maybe she could be a co-manager," Cassie said excitedly. "And that seems like a really good idea."

"A co-manager?" I asked, suddenly slightly panicked by Alec's reaction. "Of what?"

"Hockey," Cassie said. "I'm the team manager."

What? I couldn't be a hockey manager—was she kidding?

No, no, thank you.

Nope.

"Well, I'm sure it's too late," Alec said as if it was out of the question. "I don't think Coach would be into bringing on someone new that he doesn't even know."

"It couldn't hurt to ask, though, right?" Cassie said with a shrug, looking at him like he had a say in the decision or something. "You should totally ask."

NO! I wanted to shout.

You definitely shouldn't ask.

Because not only did I know nothing about the sport, but I had zero interest in frequenting a world where Alec was the king. Especially not when he was looking at me as if that was the last thing in the world he wanted.

CHAPTER FOURTEEN

Alec

"I don't know," I said, trying to sound casual and open to the idea when I absolutely was not. "Maybe."

Yeah, I'm not fucking asking.

It was too bad that Dani was having issues making her Harvard dream come true, but that wasn't my problem. The last thing I needed was to have her in my world, messing with my concentration when I'd already jeopardized every fucking thing with megabong and needed to focus now more than ever.

Hell, just seeing her for three seconds had *almost* messed with my focus against Simley; I definitely didn't need to see her during every practice and game.

It wasn't my problem that she was having problems.

I was actually pissed at myself for letting her get under my skin during Sykes's class. I hadn't *planned* on giving my speech early, and I was probably going to get a C now because I hadn't even had my note cards, but after what my mom said the other night, I couldn't stop myself from helping her.

Because, I swear to God, she'd looked like she was five seconds away from fainting, vomiting, or having a massive heart attack as she stood in front of the class. Before I'd known what was happening, my hand was up and my mouth was moving.

It was probably because the girl I used to know had a stubborn grin and attitude for days, and that girl was *not* in my speech class. And she wasn't hiding out in the library at lunch like she was scared of the cafeteria, either.

Aside from a fleeting moment the other day when she'd thrown me some snark, that girl was missing.

And the girl in her place seemed to need me.

Correction: She seemed to need *someone.*

Or something.

Which explained why I was in the library—fucking *again*—at lunch. As soon as we turned down the hallway and I could see her through the window, sitting at a table all by herself with her eyes on her book, all I could hear were my mom's words.

Social anxiety.

And I couldn't help but wonder what'd made her go from the Dani I'd known to this quiet version. Had she been bullied? I didn't *want* to talk to her, but I hadn't been able to suppress the need to make sure she wasn't hiding out all alone every day during lunch.

God, I was as big of a chump as I'd ever been.

Only—no.

No, dammit.

I wasn't chumpy little Alec; I just wasn't an asshole.

It was entirely possible not to give a shit about someone, yet still behave like a decent human being.

But I sat there for the rest of lunch, regretting my decision to be nice, because while my friends exchanged small talk with Dani, I looked at her face and couldn't stop the memories.

The barely there freckles that were sprinkled across her cheeks reminded me of the Eighteenth Avenue pool and the way she'd always lied about wearing sunscreen because she hated the smell.

And her dark eyelashes reminded me of the way they'd bunched together in wet triangles when we ran around in the pouring rain.

But when my eyes dipped down to the cursive scrawlings on her notebook, memories of the idiotic postcards clawed at me and I had to look away.

Because, God, those postcards.

I was a grown-ass man with a car and a job, for God's sake, but every time I accidentally came across that bundle in the back of my closet, I was reduced to a little boy with a thousand fucking feelings.

I blamed the Como Zoo.

After she'd bought a postcard at the zoo one summer morning (we'd been nine-ish at the time), I—of course—had to make fun of her. *Hey, Grandma, are you going to send that to your pen pal?*

"I love postcards," she'd said, shrugging while leading me toward the polar bear exhibit. "You get to send a cheesy picture and get credit for being thoughtful, but the tiny square keeps it short and sweet."

"But everyone can read what you write," I said, eating (and dropping) handfuls of popcorn while trying to keep up with her.

"True," she agreed, then pointed at me and said, "Unless you come up with a code."

We never made it to the polar bears, because we stopped to sit on a rock and brainstorm the code idea instead. We went back to our shed that day and proceeded to spend hours—and the entire next week—creating our own alternate alphabet of symbols, which Dani made into two decoders that she had laminated at the library.

We were out of our minds over the idea of sending each other coded messages.

By the end of our month, the postcard pact was enacted.

Once a week, we would send each other a postcard—in code.

Fucking little dorks, I thought as I remembered how committed we'd been to our plan.

One postcard a week, and they had to adhere to our strict guidelines.

The guidelines: one sentence of greeting, two sentences describing random things that'd happened to us that week, and one sentence of goodbye.

That was all that was allowed.

It was asinine, but we'd sent those weekly postcards to each other for years.

Years.

We're talking hundreds of motherfucking postcards.

I sent cards I picked up at truck stops; she sent back vintage cards she had to have found in thrift stores. I bought meme postcards online, and she sent me cards that gave tiny hints about what life was like where she was living.

They started in messy elementary-school chicken scratch and ended in artistic freshman symbols where she dotted her *i*'s with tiny hearts.

So, so idiotic.

Alec—

Hey, loser!

1. Yesterday I found a cat in our back-

yard and gave him tuna, which he wolfed

down and then proceeded to immediately
barf up on my shoe, leaving me no choice
but to name him Sir Pukesalot. :D
2. This morning, my dad told my mom
that he was disappointed that she'd never
cared about him enough to learn to cook,
leaving me no choice but to name him
Lieutenant Colonel Pukesalot.
Counting down the days until summer,
Dani

And then they just stopped.

I kept sending them like the chump I was, convinced it was a post office issue because I was a delusional little shit, but apparently she was just done.

And a couple of weeks later, when she came to town and fucked me over, I realized that was just who she'd become.

The girl who'd laminated our decoders had left the chat, and now Dani Collins was just somebody that I used to know.

CHAPTER FIFTEEN

Dani

"Okay," Cassie said, "but you really need to listen to me."

I walked down the hall with Cassie and two of her friends—Liz and Lillie—after school, pleasantly surprised that not only had Cassie yelled my name when she saw me so I could walk with them, but her friends seemed nice.

Like *genuinely* nice.

And they'd invited me to go with them to Applebee's for half-price apps later.

It wasn't in my nature to trust this, but I couldn't seem to stop myself.

"I know you know nothing about hockey, but being a manager is *so* easy. Sometimes I film practice, sometimes I keep stats, sometimes I go on a hot dog run if someone's hungry; anyone can do it."

"For sure," Lillie agreed, nodding. "You don't have to know hockey at all."

"I'm sure Alec is right, though," I said, remembering how unhappy he'd looked when she'd suggested it. "It's probably too late."

"Yeah, but that's the thing," she said as we went past the office. "First of all, I don't think that's true; Coach Osman is super chill. But second of all, you're friends with Alec."

I felt like I should correct her—all of them—because that definitely wasn't true, but I kept my mouth shut.

"Zeus *is* hockey around here," Cassie said. "And he's the captain. So if *he* brings it up, they will totally let it happen."

"I get that he's good, but he's still just a student, right? He can't have that much power."

"Are you serious?" Lillie said, making a face like I was absolutely clueless. "I know you're new here, but trust me—if Alec Barczewski wants something related to hockey, he's going to get it."

"But I don't think he—"

"You need to ask him," Cassie said, cutting me off. "Even if you guys don't know each other anymore, your parents are still friends, right? I'm sure he'll happily do you this tiny little favor, because he's a good guy. I'm positive that if you ask him, he'll make it happen."

But is *he a good guy?*

"I don't know," I said, dreading the idea of swallowing my pride and going to him for a favor, because if he'd wanted to even be a simple acquaintance, he would have at least smiled at me by now.

But so far he was all cold sarcasm and avoidance.

"Do this for me because I'm sick of doing it by myself and I think we'll have a blast," she said. "*Pleeeeeeease.* Come on."

"And I won't have to feel guilty anymore for quitting," Lillie said. "Do it for me, too."

"And for me so I don't have to listen to *this* ever again," Liz added.

"Hmmm." My stomach was heavy with dread as they tried convincing me, because it sounded like a terrible idea. Not only did I know nothing about the sport, but the last thing I wanted was to be around Alec on a daily basis.

In a cold arena.

I was stressed at the mere *idea* of it.

But I wanted Harvard—so badly.

"How about this: Go with me to practice today," Cassie said. "They have a game tomorrow, so it's shorter than usual, just a run-through. Ride over with me, see what I do, and then you can make the call. If you want to do it, you can wait for Zeus and beg him after practice to talk to the coaches."

"Maybe I should wait—"

"Think about it," she interrupted, emphasizing her words with hand gestures. "If Harvard said you needed to lick the floor to get in, would you?"

"Eww," Liz said with a look of disgust.

"Eww, but you would, wouldn't you?" Lillie said, pointing her finger in my direction. "Wouldn't you? You might go behind a locker so no one could see you, but you'd definitely touch your tongue to the tile, right? Don't lie, you know you would."

"Gross," I said around a laugh. "But yeah—I guess I would."

"So be willing to ask a simple favor, then," Cassie said. "It's way less disgusting."

It was a stupid analogy, but she was right.

Of course I could beg Alec for help if it meant getting into Harvard. *Who cares if he's a dick now?* Swallowing my pride and begging him to help me was *nothing* if it gave me the extracurricular I needed to get in.

Honestly, I probably wouldn't even have to see him at practice because I'd be too busy doing manager-y things and he'd be . . . like, hitting pucks with sticks and stuff.

"Okay," I said, nodding and suddenly kind of excited. "I'll do it."

• • •

"See? This job is *so* not hard," Cassie said as we walked around the hockey arena. "If you can fill water bottles, take skates to get sharpened, and press play on a video recorder, you'll be fine."

"I can do all those things," I said, relaxing a little.

"Of course you can," she said with a smile. "Let me show you around."

She showed me the girls' locker room, the maintenance closet, the equipment room, the snack bar—basically every nook and cranny of the Doug (what everyone called the Douglas Gowo Arena, apparently). She walked me past the huge mural that stretched all the way down the back wall, a photographic history of Southview hockey.

"I think that's your grandpa, isn't it?" she asked, pointing at a team from the seventies. I narrowed my eyes and, *holy shit*, the big guy in the back row was, in fact, Grandpa Mick.

He was grinning—something he rarely did now—but his eyes were exactly the same. He was young and handsome, sweaty, holding up a finger just like everyone else in the picture.

It was shocking, in a way, to see him looking so unabashedly happy, like he'd burst into laughter the second the photo was snapped.

What happened to change him so much? I wondered.

"Yeah," I said, running my hand over his image, curious if he'd been here when they'd unveiled the mural.

Surely he had, and I wondered how he'd felt.

I knew so little about his life, aside from being my grandpa, and suddenly I wanted to know more.

"Come on."

After that, Cassie did a quick tutorial of the skate-sharpening machine—the Sparx—which she talked about like it was the easiest thing in the world to use (but it terrified me).

"What if I screw up someone's skates?" I asked.

"You won't," she said with the wave of a hand. "Most of the guys have a specific preference on how they want them sharpened, and the ones who don't usually go with the average. It's not a big deal at all."

It was *so* a big deal, I suspected.

"Okay, let's go closer to the ice and I'll show you how to film."

Yes. Filming. That I could handle.

And as I followed her, I knew this was manageable, that this extracurricular was something I could do without screwing up. Every muscle in my body felt more relaxed, less tense, because I could finally check the "find an activity" box on my whole "make Harvard love me" list.

That was if *Alec would help make it happen.*

As if my brain conjured him just by thinking his name, suddenly the guys started coming out of the locker room and onto the ice. I felt . . . breathless as I watched them warming up, and I wasn't sure why.

Surely it had everything to do with the impressive speed as they took a few laps and nothing to do with my eyes locating the tallest player as he appeared to sprint down the ice in skates.

Cassie showed me the camera and let me do the filming while she sat down beside me and started her homework, which was apparently what she did at practice a lot of the time.

But my eyes kept wandering to Alec, even as I told myself I didn't care. I knew nothing about hockey, but it was easy to see he was the leader and insanely good. In every drill, he seemed to go faster and harder than everyone else.

It was like the rest of the guys were playing a high school game while he put on an exhibition of the sport.

And how did he skate that fast? *Backward??*

A tiny part of me was proud of him—my little Alec—but it was hard to remember that version of him while watching him be so big and physical.

Those were two characteristics I never would've linked to my former best friend.

"So he actually *is* good, holy shit," I said to myself, watching as he shouted something to the guys who were doing the drill he'd just finished doing. I couldn't make out his words, but he was definitely cheering them on or yelling something . . . *athletic*.

The job really *was* pretty easy. And the time went by pretty quickly.

"I think we're done," Cassie said after she locked up the camera. "I have to leave to pick up my little brother, but you're waiting around to talk to Alec, right?"

"Right," I said with a smile and a nod, even though the word "dread" didn't begin to cover how I felt about the idea.

"Make sure you're *very* convincing, okay?" she said, pulling her car keys out of her coat pocket. "I don't want to do this alone anymore."

"Okay," I agreed.

"By the way, he's always the last one out, just FYI," she said. "He reads scouting reports and does . . . hockey shit after practice, I don't know, but he's usually the last one in there. So don't feel like you missed him."

"Got it."

It was loud for a few minutes while players filed out of the locker room, but then it got quiet, as in I was literally the only one left at the rink. For what felt like hours.

Where is he?

I nearly had a heart attack when my phone started ringing with a FaceTime call, sounding crazy loud in the big empty rink. I was shocked to see it was my dad, because this was the second time he'd FaceTimed me since we'd arrived in Minnesota.

We didn't usually do that at all, much less twice.

We'd always been way more into tense telephone calls filled with guilty silences.

"Well, hey," I said in a perky voice as I answered, smiling when his face appeared on my screen.

"Hi, honey," he said back, wearing the beige T-shirt that was like a second uniform for him after-hours. He squinted and said, "Where the heck are you?"

It was dumb, but I didn't want to say it. I didn't want to tell him I was at a hockey rink. My dad had always acted like Minnesota, and everything tied into it, was a problem. My grandparents, Sarah, my mom's childhood . . . it was all bad in his eyes.

When I was a kid, Southview was something he rolled his eyes about but begrudgingly let my mom run away to for a month every summer. He'd always had zero interest in joining us, but he accepted it for what it was.

His wife wanting to go home.

But the more they argued and didn't get along, the more he behaved as if it was part of the problem. It was like he was jealous of the things that'd mattered to her before him.

"I'm actually at a hockey rink," I said, smiling as if I'd never wanted to be anywhere more. "I might be helping out the hockey team just to keep my extracurriculars where they need to be for college."

"Dear God, there's not anything better than hockey for you to do?" he said disapprovingly, his dark eyebrows down. "I would think something like math club would be far better, wouldn't it?"

"Yeah, it's a whole thing here where it's too late for me to join most clubs," I said.

"So your mother picked a fantastically backward school—got it."

I didn't want to have a conversation about his opinions on Southview or my mom, so I said, "How are you doing?"

I wanted to say *I miss you*, but we didn't talk to each other like that.

"Everything is going well, Daniella, but something came up that I need to discuss with you. Do you have a minute or should I call when you are *not* at an ice rink?"

He said it with the same tone he would use if I'd said I was at a circus.

"Actually, I'm waiting around for things to finish, so your timing is perfect. What's going on?"

"Well," he said, "I was in a meeting earlier, discussing my potential next assignment, and as it turns out, there is a very good chance that I might end up at Offutt."

"Really?" Offutt Air Force Base was in Omaha, which was only like a five-hour drive from where we were.

That would be *amazing*.

Because I hated the reality that I *couldn't* see him if I needed to.

I knew he was hard-edged half the time, but he was my dad and I wanted him around. I wanted him to be able to come to my graduation and I wanted to be able to smell the mix of aftershave and soap that'd always made him seem like the cleanest man on the planet.

So him moving closer was the best news I'd heard in ages. "When will you know?"

"Really it's less a question of when I'll know and more a question of when I'll decide what I want to do."

"Wait—you get to decide?" I asked with a laugh. "That's very un–Air Force–like."

"It's a complicated situation, but basically there are parties who would really like me in both places, so I kind of have the upper hand. That being said, I want to discuss where *you* would like me to end up."

"At Offutt for sure," I said, looking around to make sure nobody heard what an excited little kid I sounded like. "This is the best news!"

"I'm glad to hear that," he said, sort of smiling but maintaining his composure like the officer that he was. "Because if it were simply about location, I'd probably stay here; I *like* Ramstein."

It was true—he did.

My mom and I, on the other hand, had *not* liked Ramstein. Germany had been incredible, but on a daily basis we'd felt a million miles away from everything familiar, stuck on a faraway military base.

"But the opportunity to be with *you* trumps location," he said, and warmth shot through me, because my stern father was admitting he missed me. That meant everything.

"Obviously your mother and I will have to carve out the details on how it would work, because it's too far to do the every-other-weekend type of thing, but I think it'd make sense for you to come live with me at Offutt until school ends. It's fine if she wants to run around up there, but you shouldn't have to be stuck in the tundra just because she's reliving her childhood, right?"

I looked at his face on my phone and was confused for a second.

"You can spend the summer with her before you go away to school, once the weather's nice up there."

"Wait. What?" I couldn't be hearing him right.

He wanted me to leave my mom?

"Well, I prefer Germany, but I prefer my daughter's company more, of course. So if you want to live with me, then I will take the offered assignment. If you want to stay up in Minnesota with your mother, then I will probably re-up my assignment at Ramstein."

"Those are the only options?" I asked, hating that my voice sounded thick and like I was going to cry. "You're only coming back to the States if I leave Mom and live with you full-time?"

"There's no need to get emotional, Daniella; I'm just trying to have a conversation."

"I'm not emotional," I said, fully aware of how defensive I sounded. "I'm just trying to understand."

"It's simple. I'm happy to leave Ramstein to spend time with you, but if that's not what you want, I'm probably going to stay here. Does that make sense?"

God, I hated the way my dad always said that. *Does that make sense?* He never failed to make me feel like a stupid little kid when he threw out those four words.

He was watching me with zero emotion on his face, sternly observing my pathetic attempt at holding mine in. Why couldn't he ever make things easy? All I wanted was an easy relationship with him, and it felt like all he wanted was the opposite.

Or that he wanted me to prove my devotion to him by hurting my mom.

"Yes, it does," I managed, lowering my voice to sound chill while I struggled to keep it together.

He couldn't really be serious about this, could he?

"I know your mother won't be thrilled with this plan," he said, "But I think if she knows it's what you want, she'll be okay with it. She's so determined to live with your grandfather that I don't think she's focusing on anything else."

"Um, when do you need to give an answer?" I asked, forcing my face not to fall, hating how high-strung I sounded.

"I'd prefer to knock this out as quickly as possible," he said, steepling his fingers under his chin like he was having a business conversation and not asking his daughter to tear out her mother's heart. "Since you just moved there, the pieces should still be simple to reconfigure."

"I don't think I can do this to Mom," I admitted in an almost whisper, trying to blink away the tears that were filling my eyes.

"But you found a way, with me," he said quietly, and I was shocked by his words and how hurt he looked. Colonel Collins didn't *get* hurt; he was a robot.

Wasn't he?

"That's not—"

"Sometimes choices aren't easy, Daniella."

"I know, but . . ." I turned the phone away from me, pointing it toward the roof so he couldn't see me wiping away the tears.

"Okay, so now we're crying," he said disappointedly, sighing loudly, and I was glad I couldn't see his face. "I'm sorry if you're upset, and I'm not going to force you to move. I thought this might be something you'd want."

My chest was so tight it hurt. "I *do* want to—"

"No, I don't think that you do," he interrupted.

I couldn't believe I was crying in the middle of a hockey rink, like full-on crying, but I couldn't seem to stop the emotions as I listened to his voice. He went back and forth between making me feel guilty and making me feel sad; it was an infinite loop that had me in a choke hold.

I kept wiping at my cheeks and trying to get it together, but I felt precariously close to sobbing when I heard him disconnect the call.

And then—*shit, shit, shit*—I heard voices.

I didn't have a visual on who was coming or where they were, but I also couldn't see through my tears. All I knew was that I couldn't have anyone at this school or on this hockey team see me bawling like a baby at the hockey rink.

I got off the bench and ran for the maintenance closet. I needed to lock myself in a dark room and get my shit together before I saw anyone.

Please be unlocked please be unlocked.

As someone who didn't cry a lot, I found it alarming how freely the tears were flowing. There was no hiding that I was crying, and there was no stopping my eyes from whatever they were doing.

I reached for the handle—*thank you for being unlocked*—and opened the door, then quickly slipped inside and shut it behind me.

But I immediately knew I'd screwed up when, even through the tears, I could see that the room was big and bright. Not a closet at all. And it smelled like dirty socks in a heater. I wiped at my eyes and realized I was in a locker room, holy *shit*.

Thank God no one is in here.

I leaned my forehead against the cold wall and took a big gasping breath, but it came out as a hiccuping sob. I covered my eyes with my hands, giving in to the despair for a second.

"Dani?"

Fuck! I quickly wiped at my eyes before turning around, hoping somehow I didn't look as bad as I knew I looked.

But when I turned around, my heart sank to my feet. It was Alec.

Oh God.

Not only was I mortified that he was seeing me bawling, but also—dear Lord—he was naked.

Not *completely* naked—he was wearing black boxer briefs—but his hair was wet and his muscles were everywhere and I could smell his soap or shampoo; he'd obviously just gotten out of the shower, *shit shit shit*.

"Oh my God," I said, hating that I was still crying. I could *hear* the crying in my voice as I muttered, "I'm so sorry, I did *not* mean to come in here."

"Dani?" He took quick steps toward me and grabbed my upper arms in his hands, his voice so serious when he asked, "What's wrong?"

His dark eyes swept over my face, and it felt like he was holding his breath, waiting to hear what had happened.

And I was mortified that it was *nothing*. No terrible thing had just happened to me, I was just a sad little girl who couldn't please her dad.

"Nothing. Really, my dad called and . . . I mean, I'm fine," I said, sounding like a frog because my throat was so damn tight.

"You're not, though," he said, and something about the concern in his voice did the opposite of helping me get myself together.

His concern made me shatter.

"Collins," he said, almost with a question mark, pulling me into his arms as the stupid tears wouldn't stop, wrapping himself around me. His hug felt like home, like something I could count on, and there was nothing I could do but snake my arms around his neck and take refuge.

Anyone else in the world, including my mom, would've told me all the ways that it was going to be okay, that it was fine and everything was going to be great.

But Alec knew me and the way I felt about my father.

Or at least he used to.

He just hugged me tighter as I attempted to get myself together.

"I'm s-sorry," I managed to hiccup out after a few more minutes.

The tears were finally stopping, thank God, so I pulled back, wiping my cheeks, and gave him what I knew was a pathetic smile.

"I don't know what's wrong with me," I said, sniffling, "but thank you for being cool about my little breakdown."

"There's nothing wrong with you," he said, his voice scratchy, his forehead creased.

And as he looked down at me with those dark eyes and that impossibly handsome face, I realized that I was still wrapped around his nearly nude body.

"Sorry—" I managed, but when I tried pulling away, I was jerked forward.

127

"Your necklace," he said, and I looked down and saw that his chain was tangled up with my necklace. I literally couldn't pull away from him because we were tied together by jewelry.

"Oh," I breathed, incapable of more than that, because it was so absurd that my face was literally right next to his neck, which smelled really freaking good—*holy shit*—and I could feel his breath on my collarbone.

"Hang on," he murmured into my neck, and then after a second I felt the necklaces separate as he said, "Got it."

"Thank you, Alec," I said, looking up at his face but not letting go of his shoulders. Not yet. I was thanking him for more than the necklace, and I could tell by the way he was looking at me that he understood. "I didn't mean—"

"Whoa!" I heard from behind me in a deep, growly voice. "What the—Barczewski . . . ?"

We both whipped around, and I wanted to die as I saw not only the hockey coach standing there, scowling at us, but three other grown men beside him who stared like they'd just caught us having sex in the locker room.

"What the hell is going on here?" the coach yelled, and we quickly jumped apart.

"This isn't what it looks like," Alec said, and I was amazed at how calm he sounded.

"Really?" the coach said in a near shout. "Because it looks like there's a girl in my locker room."

I said, "I—I accidentally—"

"Dani," Alec interrupted, his face absent of the kindness I'd seen moments ago. His jaw flexed and unflexed, like he was fighting to hold it together, before he said, "You should go."

"But—"

"*Go,*" he repeated, his dark eyes on mine.

"He's right," the coach agreed. "You shouldn't be in here, young lady."

"I'll explain what happened," Alec said to me, but he looked volatile, like he was about to lose his shit.

I nodded dumbly, because what else could I do? I was standing in front of four scowling men and my former friend, who I kind of suspected hated me. I nodded one more time and turned, walking so fast out of the locker room that it was almost a run.

I texted my mom and told her to pick me up as soon as she could, and she said she was on her way, but I felt sick as I realized what I'd done.

The hockey coach was a teacher.

A teacher who'd found me in the boys' locker room, where one of those boys was changing.

I was in so much trouble.

CHAPTER SIXTEEN
Alec

Fuck, fuck, fuck.

I swallowed and rubbed the back of my neck as the door shut behind her.

What the hell had just happened?

I'd been getting dressed when I remembered I left my chain in the shower. I went back, put it on, and when I returned to my locker, there she was, holy *shit*.

Facing the wall, but I'd have recognized those blond curls anywhere.

And when she turned around, her tears took me straight back to the night when I dried her tears and kissed her.

I almost couldn't breathe as she blinked up at me, and then I was hugging her while fucking "sweat" played on the Bluetooth speaker in my locker like some kind of joke.

Sweat, get into it
Let me show you how to use your legs

I still wasn't sure how it'd happened when I was committed to keeping my distance, but in an instant I was punched by the flowery smell of her hair, buzzed on the warmth of her body in my arms, fucking hypnotized by the slide of her hands on my skin, dear *God*.

What the fuck even *was* that? I'd gone from zero to under-her-influence in three seconds.

Although in my defense, it had to do with the colonel. Dani's dad was a controlling dickhead, a controlling dickhead she'd always been insanely devoted to even though he didn't deserve it, and I'd always had a soft spot for her daddy issues.

Because while she'd do anything to please him, that man wouldn't lift a finger to throw her the tiniest of crumbs.

So color me unsurprised that he was still making her cry.

But how the hell was I going to fix this? Coach looked like he wanted to kill me, and I couldn't blame him.

I mean, talk about your shit timing.

This would have been bad enough if Oz were alone, but he was with two coaches from Wisconsin and with Gordy Frye, a local sports reporter who was *super* connected.

Like, the dude knew *everyone* in hockey.

"I know that probably looked weird," I said, working hard for a casual smile like this wasn't a big deal, but the bottom line was that this was huge. I was supposed to be fixing my reputation, but now these dudes were thinking they'd just witnessed me fucking around with a girl in the locker room—the night before a game—like my head wasn't in it. And just after the picture of me with the bong.

Dammit, Dani.

Fuck, even *thinking* her name made me feel unsteady.

Coach said, "If you guys want to step into my office, the stat sheets we were talking about are on my desk. I just need to yell at my player really quickly and then I'll bring him in and we can all have a nice conversation."

They gave big laughs like this was all fun and games, but I could tell by the way they were looking at me that they thought I was screwing up again.

As soon as they went into his office, coach went off.

"What the *fuck* is wrong with you, Barczewski? All you had to do was keep your nose clean—that's it. What has it been, like, a *day*? These guys are here to watch you, and it was a perfect opportunity to prove you're not what you seem, but you screw it up by bringing a *girl* into the locker room," he said, his yelling kind of a spitting growl because he was trying to keep the volume down. He was totally in my face as he raged, "As if that isn't bad enough, you're not even dressed. Like, what the fuck? And who the hell even is she? I've never seen that girl in my life. Please tell me you didn't bring a Simley girl into our locker room or someone from another school."

"God, no," I said, a little pissed that he didn't know me better than this. Like why the fuck did everyone always assume the worst? "She's new here and wants to be a team manager. She was trying—"

"Was she or was she not in the locker room while you were changing?"

"It's not like that—she's Mick Boche's granddaughter!" I said—yelled, actually. "She just moved here, and I've known her since we were kids."

"She's Boche's granddaughter?" he said, his eyes narrowing like he couldn't believe what he was hearing.

"*Yes,*" I said, glad that little nugget had slowed him down. "She and her mom moved in with him last weekend."

"No shit?" he said, squinting like he couldn't keep up. "Does she play hockey?"

"No," I said, hoping he'd stay distracted by her pedigree. Maybe if I talked about *her* he'd forget what he thought he just walked into. "She's a brainiac goody-goody who's going to Harvard next year. Like the opposite of Mick."

He crossed his arms. "You said you grew up with her?"

"Our moms are friends," I explained, "so I've known her forever. We were childhood buddies until she moved away."

"Whoa, whoa, whoa." Gordy popped out of the office wearing a huge grin, the Wisconsin coaches behind him. "I couldn't help eaves-dropping, and did you just say that the girl you were with in the locker room—your childhood sweetheart—is Mick Boche's *granddaughter*?"

"Childhood sweetheart" wasn't exactly right, but it was interesting the way everyone's faces changed. Suddenly they didn't look like they were accusing me of being a screwup; they looked like they were interested in the story of me and Boche's granddaughter.

Whatever it takes.

I wasn't about to lie, but I wasn't about to skip away from a bailout, either. I gave my best version of a secretive smile when I said, "Yes, Dani is a direct descendant of Mr. Boche."

"No way," Gordy said with a grin. "If you'd told me he had a grand-daughter, I'd have thought she'd be a girl who fights, spits, and curses like a sailor. You're telling me that blonde with the glasses comes from Mick?"

"Yes, sir," I said, leaning into it. "Doesn't drink, doesn't smoke, and would rather read a book than watch a game. The apple fell *far* on this one."

"That's hilarious," he said, shaking his head. "Who would've guessed."

"Gentlemen . . ." Coach said.

Gordy pointed to the office. "I know, I know—back to the office so you can finish your lecture."

"I'll be right in, thanks," Coach said, but his smile disappeared as soon as the door closed.

"Coach, I swear to God—"

"Shut up and listen to me, Zeus," he said, lowering his voice. "I'm about to go in my office and make sure those guys understand that you're tight with Boche's granddaughter. That doesn't make this okay, for God's sake, but at least it's *her*."

Her.

"Maybe the fact that you're seeing a Boche will distract them from not only the picture that people are still whispering about, but also what we walked in on, since the two of you'll be like goddamn hockey royalty, I don't know," he said, glancing toward the office. "But I like what you said about her. You dating someone more into books than parties is exactly what you need right about now."

Dating?

Oh, shit, he thinks I'm *seeing* her . . . ?

I tried deflecting with, "I was telling the truth about what you walked in on, though."

"And I believe you," he said, and I hoped he meant it. "But Gordy talks to *everybody*, and if the committee is already wondering about you, we don't want the news he brings them to be that instead of watching game film, you were making out with a girl in the locker room. Isn't it better if he goes back with the news that you're dating a serious girl who just happens to be a direct descendant of Mick Fucking Boche?"

His eyes bored into me, willing me to understand the importance of what he was saying. But I didn't want to believe it. Refused to believe. And yet, deep down, I knew that as fast and wild as the gossip had spread about that stupid picture, this was going to be much, much worse.

Shit. He's right.

I didn't have a choice.

CHAPTER SEVENTEEN
Dani

I almost had a heart attack when I heard the tap on the front door.

It was after ten, and I was the only one in the house still awake, doing homework.

We had a massive test in calculus next week, but if I was honest with myself, I was studying to avoid thinking about my dad.

And the locker room.

And I was too emotionally exhausted to start crying again.

I half expected it to be Cassie, because she hadn't wanted to take no for an answer when I backed out on Applebee's, but when I looked through the window atop the door, I saw Alec peering through.

Shit shit shit, I did *not* want to face him. It was bad enough that he'd seen me bawling, but the whole . . . *thing* that followed was mortifying.

Mostly because, for a split second, I'd forgotten about everything in the world except his brown eyes and the way it felt to have him hug me again.

Idiot!

But what choice did I have? I'd been freaking out all evening, expecting a call from the superintendent telling me I'd been expelled.

I went over to the door and pulled it open, my stomach full of butterflies.

And God, there he was.

He was so tall now, so big as he looked down at me with a smirk on his mouth and amusement in those dark brown eyes.

"Wow," he said without even saying hi. "You look hot."

I rolled my eyes. I was wearing flannel pajama pants and a threadbare Philadelphia Eagles jersey, and my hair was still wet from the shower I'd taken twenty minutes before when I'd been too cold to concentrate.

Yes, I looked atrocious, but that wasn't important.

"What happened after I left?" I asked, lowering my eyes to the zipper on the front of his jacket because I couldn't bear to look directly at his face for another second.

"Can I come in?" he asked. "Because it's a long story and your hair is going to freeze if the door stays open."

"Oh. Sure," I said, stepping back to hold open the door. "But my mom and grandpa are asleep, so you have to be quiet."

"Yeah, I wasn't planning on yelling the house down," he said as he walked inside, and I wasn't sure if he was joking or being a sarcastic ass.

I quietly shut the door and went into the living room, hyperaware of him following me. I didn't know what to do with myself, so I sat down on the couch and crossed my arms over my chest.

"So what did he say? How much trouble am I in?" I asked, knowing my cheeks were bright red because it felt like my skin was on fire.

"You're not in any trouble, actually," he said, dropping down into the chair across from me.

"What? But he seemed really mad," I said, confused. "And I *shouldn't* have been in the locker room."

"Okay, so let's just say things got weird after you left. I've got a lot to tell you, so I need to ask—respectfully—for you to just be quiet until

I'm finished. I need you to hear everything I have to say before you respond."

This can't be good.

"All right," I said, grabbing one of my grandma's flowered throw pillows and hugging it to my chest. "I'm listening."

"So you were right—Oz was crazy pissed. He thought I brought some random girl into the locker room for . . . um, reasons that were not hockey-related. Like he saw—"

"I get it," I snapped, wondering how much more mortification I could take without spontaneously combusting in shame.

"Okay, good," he said, and it annoyed me that it looked like he wanted to laugh. "He was livid, so I had to explain that we knew each other when we were kids and that you aren't some random girl. I explained to him who your grandpa is—"

"Oh my God, is he going to tell my grandpa?"

Just when I'd thought the embarrassment couldn't get worse.

"No," he said, then added, "Well, I mean, I don't think so. He didn't really say."

"What *did* he say, then?"

"You were going to be quiet while I told you, remember? From five seconds ago . . . ?"

"Go already," I said with a sigh, just wanting this to be over.

"Thank you," he said, and when he offhandedly rubbed his shoulder, I noticed how exhausted he looked. "What I was saying is that Coach didn't respond the way I thought he would. When I said I knew you when we were kids, he and Gordy mistakenly thought that meant we were, like, childhood sweethearts or something."

"Weird," I said, looking down at my lap and trying not to remember the kiss.

We hadn't been childhood sweethearts except for that one night.

"For sure weird. But the guys who were with him are hockey dudes. Two of them are D1 scouts, and the one with the bad haircut is a sportswriter who has ties to everyone who matters in USA hockey, right?"

"Okay," I said, remembering what Grandpa Mick had said about those guys.

"They came to see me play, which was great, because I'm trying to convince them I'm not a fuckup, because a picture that, uh, might've made it look—"

"Like you were smoking the world's largest bong?"

His eyebrows went down. "You saw the picture?"

"Yeah, it was our dinner entertainment the other night," I said.

"Shit—did Mick see it?" he asked, looking panicked.

"Would it really matter if my grandpa saw a picture of you with a bong?"

"Mick Fucking Boche?" He looked at me like I'd just said something ridiculous. "Of *course* it would matter."

"He's just a man, you know."

"Oh, okay," he said, rolling his eyes.

"Back to the story," I said, gesturing with my hands for him to get going.

"They came to see me when I'm supposed to be proving I'm not a locker room distraction, so the fact that they walked into the locker room and saw what they thought was me hooking up with a girl is a fucking nightmare."

"I bet," I said, almost feeling bad for him.

Almost.

"But when they heard who you were from my coach and his incorrect assumption that you and I are maybe an item—"

"What?" This day was a nightmare. "They think we're an 'item'?"

"Shhhh and listen," he said, shaking his head. "It was inferred by my coach because he misunderstood what I said. Anyway, once they heard that you're a genius who's going to Harvard and Mick Boche's granddaughter, all of a sudden they started looking at me in a different light. Like maybe I wasn't a fuckup and maybe I'm dating somebody who's going to be a good influence on me."

How could four dudes have it all so wrong? I wondered.

"But we aren't dating," I said dumbly.

"No shit, Sherlock," he said.

"No shit, Sherlock," I mocked in a stupid voice under my breath, irritated by his attitude.

"Dani." He leaned forward, his elbows on his knees, and said very seriously, "Obviously this is a shit show, a misunderstanding that got way out of hand."

"Obviously," I said.

"But while I'm trying to get people to see who I really am—not a partying fuckboy—this could be a good thing."

"For *you*," I said, trying to keep up with his direction. "So, what—you want to just let them think the wrong thing because it makes you look better?"

"You promised to be quiet until I was done," he said with raised eyebrows and a tilted head, like he was reasoning with me.

"No, I didn't," I argued. "I believe I said, 'I'm listening.'"

"Dani," he said through gritted teeth. "Please?"

"Fine," I said with another eye roll.

"So," he said, clearing his throat. His face got super serious as he put his big hands together like he was praying and said, "I have a proposition for you. I will get you the hockey-manager job so you can have Harvard, if you agree to go along with this and maybe, like, let people think we're kind of dating a little bit."

"What?" Whatwhatwhat the *hell*?? "You want me to pretend we're *dating*?"

"I mean, it'd be low-key," he said, looking offended by my reaction. "It's not like we're going to make a formal announcement or anything. We'd just, y'know, kind of act like we're seeing each other."

"Absolutely not," I said, irrationally irritated by his nerve, his assumption that I'd just do him the tiny favor of ruining my own not-yet-formed reputation.

I could just imagine how it would go.

I'd be his little nerd beard, giving him the credibility he needed, yet all his friends would know the truth and laugh behind my back about the way Miss Four-Eyes was fake prostituting herself for an extracurricular.

Meanwhile, I would be on display for the rest of the school to notice me—*who even is she?*—and make judgments about me because I was suddenly dating their superstar.

Talk about landing on everyone's radar in the very worst way.

The new girl is dating Zeus? Ew.

And eventually, when he didn't need the alliance anymore and fake dumped me, I'd be left alone to deal with whatever my undeserved tattered reputation might look like.

"Don't shut it down without considering it first," he said with narrowed eyes, like he found my reaction to be ridiculous.

He was ridiculous.

And then he said, "Keep in mind that regardless of what we do, people are going to hear about what the coaches thought they saw earlier. So do you want the rumor to be about two people who barely know each other, or two people with history who might be reconnecting?"

I wanted to hit him. I wasn't a violent person, but I wanted to hit him for saying something I hadn't considered, for speaking out loud something that was a freaking nightmare.

People were going to be talking about me tomorrow, about me and Alec in the locker room together.

I knew he was right, but I was too mad to give in.

"Listen," I said, my throat tight because everything was going south at Southview so freaking fast. "It sucks that you're having to face the consequences of your actions, but I'm passing on this opportunity."

He squinted a little more, looking like he was trying to see in the dark as he glared at me. "You're not at all interested in helping when it might actually help you, too?"

"Nope," I bit out, glaring back at him.

"Harvard isn't worth a tiny little favor to you?" he asked.

"Not even a tiny little bit," I replied, overwhelmed by the stress of what tomorrow was going to look like at school.

"Wow," he said, his lips turning up in a mean smile as he gave his head a slow shake. "Some things never change."

"What is *that* supposed to mean?" I asked, because I'd *always* been Team Alec until I couldn't be anymore because he'd disappeared.

"Just that I thought maybe this one time you could think of someone other than yourself, maybe like a cool new thing for you to try out, but obviously I was wrong."

"You cannot be serious." Was the guy who'd ghosted me after a lifetime of friendship actually calling *me* an asshole? "You're saying *I* don't think of anyone but myself?"

"That's exactly what I'm saying," he said, his voice rising. "I guess I expected—"

"Yes, you expected me to drop to my knees and do whatever you asked because now you're Zeus the Hockey God," I said, standing up. "It's late and I need to study, so maybe you should go find someone else to pretend to be your girlfriend. I mean, it seems like the ladies line up to be on Zeus's radar, so it shouldn't be hard—"

"You don't have to be an asshole," he said, rising to his feet.

"I don't? Because it seems to me that you've been an asshole since the second I got to Southview for no good reason. If the big hockey star doesn't want to be friends with his old nerdy buddy, that's totally fine—I don't want to be friends with you, either—but don't act like I'm a jerk when you're the jerk."

Just then, there was yet another knock.

"Are you freaking kidding me?" I muttered under my breath, because who else could possibly be dropping by this late on a weeknight? I walked over to the door and was shocked when I pulled it open and there was Benji.

"Hey . . . ?" I said, surprised to see him because I hadn't seen him since the day we moved in and also why the heck would he stop by when we weren't even friends and Grandpa Mick hated him? *Also, it's ten o'clock at night!* "What's up, Benji?"

"I saw the lights on and I'm about to go on a food run, so I wondered—oh, hey, Zeus," he said, looking around me with a big smile. "I didn't know you were here."

"You didn't see my car?" Alec said, and his voice was so tense it made me turn around. "Really?"

And he was *glaring* at Benji. Not with the mild distaste he used to have for my grandpa's annoying little next-door neighbor, but glaring like he wanted to annihilate him.

"Now that you mention it," Benji said with a creepily huge grin, "I guess I *did* see a rust bucket in the drive."

"Listen, um, Benji," I said, having no idea what this tension was but not in the mood for it. "I really appreciate—"

"Bye, Ben," Alec said, suddenly standing beside me.

"Alec," I said, looking up at him in disbelief.

"Well . . . ? Are you hungry, Collins?" he asked abruptly, angrily.

"Um, no . . . ?" I answered, looking back and forth between the two of them.

"She's not hungry, you fuck, so get the hell out of here," Alec said to Benji, reaching for the door, looking like he was going to take it off its hinges with a slam.

"Alec," I said in disbelief. "What are you—"

"Is he bothering you, Dani?" Benji asked me with a face full of fake concern. "Because if he is, I can—"

"You're *both* bothering me," I interrupted, having no idea what was

144

going on with this angry machismo. "Thanks but no thank you on the food, Benji, and I think we're done here, Alec."

I took a step back so Alec could join Benji on the porch.

"Oh, hey—did you get my text the other day?" Benji asked, smiling at me as if we texted all the time.

"Um, yeah," I said, crossing my arms as the cold air poured in. "I—"

"Fucking *go*, Worthington," Alec said, stepping out onto the porch and into Benji's face, giving his chest a push. "She already said you're bothering her."

"I think that was for you," Benji replied, smiling like he was absolutely unfazed by angry Alec in his personal space. "By the way, *love* the oversized bong, Zeus. *Very* classy."

He turned and went down the steps, and I shook my head, because nothing made sense to me anymore. I looked at Alec and slammed the door, just needing to be done with the day.

But then he knocked.

I sighed and pulled it open. "Did you forget someth—"

"You already reconnected with fucking Benji, are you kidding me?" His voice was low and gravelly, his eyes narrowed as he said it like . . . like it mattered, like I'd done something terrible to him by talking to the neighbor.

"He . . . lives next door," I said slowly, unsure what he could possibly mean by "reconnected."

Alec's face was hard, and even though he looked nothing like my old friend anymore, something about the moment was straight from our past, grabbing at my chest with a hard squeeze.

"But we *hate* that guy, Dani," he said with a scowl, giving his head a shake of disbelief.

"I don't even know him anymore," I said, so confused by his reaction and the way he said my name like we were still friends. "Do you?"

"Oh yeah," he said. "I sure as hell do."

"Then I guess I'll have to take your word for it, because I don't know either of you now," I said. "Good night, Alec."

"Good night," he said, sounding like he definitely didn't wish me good night as I slammed the front door again.

But I couldn't sleep when I climbed into bed, not when his words kept playing in my head, over and over again.

I thought maybe this one time you could think of someone other than yourself, maybe like a cool new thing for you to try out, but obviously I was wrong.

We'd exchanged weekly postcards for *years*, our own little coded system of keeping in touch, and then one day he'd just stopped responding.

I never heard from him again.

NEVER.

So if anybody was guilty of not helping somebody else out, it was him.

CHAPTER EIGHTEEN
Alec

What the fuck *was* that?

I was still sitting up in bed at twelve thirty, "ricochet" in my ears and a pounding in my skull, because how the hell was Benji already sniffing around when she'd *just* moved back? He'd always been like a puppy at her heels, so I shouldn't be surprised.

For all I knew, they were best friends.

Did you get my text?

Why would that fucking asshole even have her number?

It doesn't matter anymore.

But yes—it kind of fucking mattered because I hated him.

Benji Worthington had been an annoyance as a kid, a douchey little irritant who lived next door to Dani's grandpa and liked doing things like tattling behind my back and being passive-aggressive when he was too little to even know what passive-aggressive meant.

But once we hit middle school and I had to deal with him on the ice, he became a fucking menace. He was always on the best teams, the teams that recruited even though that wasn't supposed to be a thing, and it bugged the shit out of me. He had a hockey IQ of zero, yet somehow always managed to make the cut.

Surely it had nothing to do with all that expensive equipment and those unlimited resources.

But as much as I didn't like him, he fucking *haaated* me. It seemed to piss him off that no matter how much money he had, I was always the better player. Since he couldn't do anything about that, he used to talk shit on my family all the time.

And I could handle assholes chirping at *me*—that was part of the game, right?

But Ben always managed to come up with "jokes" about my life that were too personal, that had just enough truth to sting. My mom's crappy minivan, the time my dad got laid off when I was in eighth grade . . . he always had something to insinuate, then loved playing innocent when I lost my cool and lit into him later.

Then *I* was considered the "aggressor," the one who was out of line.

I finally beat the shit out of him at a party after my dad's car accident, which was probably what started the whole "Barczewski's a loose cannon" storyline (even though it wasn't true).

I'd been at the hospital that day, waiting for my dad to wake up after yet another surgery (he'd had seven), when my mom told me Dani and Hannah were on their way. Apparently they'd heard about the crash and decided to fly in for the day to see my dad and be with my mom.

And I'd been so fucking happy to hear that, not only because I hadn't seen Dani in a couple of years, but because we were all drowning from the fallout of the accident, and I needed my friend—who'd stopped responding to my postcards—so fucking badly.

But when Hannah showed up, she was alone.

I asked about Dani, and she looked embarrassed when she said, "She's not good at hospitals and wasn't sure if she'd be intruding, so she had Benji just take her to the hotel."

I knew I couldn't have heard her right. "Benji?"

To a hotel?

"Yeah, remember Benji Worthington, the kid who lived next door to us?" Hannah said it like it was hilarious, grinning as she told me that he'd been on the same flight and had offered them a ride.

Small world, right?

"That kid is so sweet," she'd said, and I wanted to put my fist through a wall.

What a small fucking world.

I'd been so bummed that Dani hadn't wanted to see me; it was like her refusal to come to the hospital made everything that was already horrible feel even worse.

And the idea of that jackass getting to see her brought it even lower.

But when I let Vinny drag me away from the hospital and to a party in White Bear later that night, and Benji was (of course) there, everything hit rock bottom.

"Zeus! I saw our old friend Dani today," he said in that sniveling rich-boy accent that had nothing to do with geography and everything to do with the silver spoon that was jammed all the way up his ass. He'd grinned and pulled out his phone. "Check it out."

I'd been so drained that fighting wasn't on my mind.

At all.

I'd been interested to see what Dani looked like, honestly, even as I felt so damn disappointed in her.

But instead of showing me an awkward selfie of them at the airport where I could convince myself she looked like she hated him, it was a photo of just her.

Sitting in a chair, grinning up at the camera.

149

A chair I recognized as one we'd stolen from my dad's shop.

Holy balls, she'd taken him to our spot.

She hadn't come to the hospital to see me or my critically injured father, but she'd taken King Douche to our secret spot and was laughing with him.

It made me want to puke.

I'd kept my cool for another hour, but as soon as Benji started in on his shit—*is it true your dad was drinking when he got in that crash?*—I hit him.

Multiple times.

Knock it off, I told myself, leaning the back of my head against the wall and skipping to the next song as I tried to figure out my next move. Because no matter how much I racked my brain, I couldn't come up with anything better than Dani. More specifically, (fake) dating Dani.

I didn't want to let her in, but I needed her, dammit.

"Screw it," I said, pulling off my headphones and dialing the number my mom had given me in case I wanted to be nice and reach out.

While it rang, my mind went back to the locker room yet again.

How could someone's neck smell so good?

"Hello?"

Something about her voice when she answered (I couldn't believe she answered), the way she sounded tired, brought back memories that I didn't want to remember.

"Hey, it's Alec," I said, realizing we'd never spoken on the phone before.

How is that even possible?

"Hey," she said, and I was surprised she didn't hang up or say something about the Benji incident earlier.

"Listen, I know you already said no," I said, jumping right into it as I switched on the Bluetooth speaker next to my bed to its lowest volume, "but I'm wondering if you'd consider letting me try to change your mind."

She sighed, but since it wasn't a no, I kept going. "You can still reject me, but I've come up with more reasons why this might benefit you."

"Have you?" she asked.

"I have," I said. "Can I share them with you?"

"Okay," she said.

Okay? "Wait—are you awake?"

"What?"

I said, "I'm worried maybe you're sleeptalking or something, because you sound very agreeable."

"I'm always agreeable. Now talk before I hang up."

"Okay." I took a deep breath and said, "So, for starters, I think you need to look at this in a pros-and-cons sort of way because I'm having a hard time coming up with any reasons why this would be a bad thing for you."

"Of course you can't," she said. "Because why would any girl not want to be linked with Zeus the Hockey God?"

"I feel like you're prejudiced against me for being athletic now," I said, wondering offhandedly where she was in Mick's house. Was she in bed, wherever that might be, or back down in the living room, where she'd been lost in studies when I showed up earlier?

I'd seen her through the window of the door, deep in thought with her eyes on her textbook and her bottom lip between her teeth.

I hated how pretty she was; I didn't need that shit.

151

"Are you jealous—is that it?" I teased, hoping to soften her. Regardless of anything else, I needed her to be receptive to this. "We both used to be klutzes together, and now you're left all alone . . . ?"

I heard her cough something that sounded like a laugh, and it felt a little bit like a win.

"Believe me, I'm not jealous," she said.

"Okay, so back to my outline. I'm going to give you reasons why this is a good thing for you. Number one—obviously—you get the extra-curricular. You can be a hockey manager, which will get you the activity you need for Harvard. Since going to Harvard is very important to you, pretending to like someone to make it happen seems like a small sacrifice, don't you think?"

"That was a pretty good argument," she said, "but it's the no-brainer. What's next?"

"You're not going to make this easy, are you?"

"Not at all," she said.

"Okay, so number two . . . well, actually, who am I kidding, I only have two."

"Wow," she said. "Did you spend all of five seconds on this outline?"

"I spent a solid twenty minutes, if you must know," I said, wondering if number two was going to piss her off or embarrass her. It was a gamble, but it was the only other reason I had.

"Give me number two, then," she said.

"All right. So, I've never had to go to a new school, but I don't imagine it's fun. Being the new kid probably sucks, and you seem to be a little on the introverted side now. And I don't mean that in a bad way; I just—"

"Get on with it," she said, but she didn't sound mad.

"Okay, so wouldn't it be nice to be linked to someone who knows everyone? I could introduce you to everybody, and then you would have, like, a social cushion, right? You wouldn't have to stress or be nervous, because you'd be *with* me."

"All I hear is arrogance," she said, but I could tell she was teasing.

The old Dani is still in there.

I explained, "It's not arrogance; it's just a fact. I've lived here my whole life, so of course I know everybody. Which means if you date me—"

"*Fake* date you," she corrected.

"*Fake* date me," I said with a sigh, "you're in. You can be confident and comfortable because you'll be instantly part of the group. *Surrounded* by friends."

"Okay, your number two is stupid, because the fake friends would be yours, not mine," she said.

"Potato, potahtoe. And don't you want to have a little bit of a social life?" I asked.

"Like you, the Bong King of the Twin Cities?"

"Not that you'd believe me," I said, torn between wanting to laugh at her smart-assery and wanting to scream because I was never going to live down that photo, "but I was just holding that—"

"For a friend, right?" she said. "Also, I like the way you assume I will never have a social life without your help. It *is* possible that I will once I'm here for more than a minute."

"That's not what I meant."

"And what exactly would this look like?" She sounded irritated again, like the idea of it was too much, and I knew I was losing her. "Not that

153

I'm considering it at all, but in this scenario, would *everyone* think we were an item, including our families?"

"Hmm—I haven't thought about that—this idea is new for me, too," I said, picturing my mom; shit, she'd lose it if she thought I was seeing Dani. "My gut says yes, though, because letting people in on the secret seems like a bad idea, like a quick way for it to fail. If we were to do it, I think it'd be best for everyone except us to think it's real. Do you disagree?"

"Um, no," she said, "I think you're right. Not that we're doing this."

"Of course not," I said, smiling in spite of myself because she was flipping back and forth so fast it was hard to keep up.

"And how exactly does this work? How do two people *pretend* to date?"

"Come on, Collins, quit being all Harvard and overthinking things. How hard can it be?" I reached over and pulled open my nightstand drawer, rifling through junk papers with my hand as I felt around for that old Polaroid. "We just need to be seen together a couple times a week, looking like we like each other, and maybe go to, like . . . things together sometimes. I can get on Instagram and post pics of us being a couple. As long as the guys on the team see us—and the guys I play against—it'll get back to the right people."

"So you really don't know," she said.

"Well, I've never pretended to date anyone before."

"Fair."

Found it. I grabbed the picture and pulled it out. "All I know is that I need to do whatever it takes to convince the fucking world that I'm gaga for a good girl and have my shit together."

"But, like," she said quietly, suddenly sounding nervous, "won't it be hard to pretend when we don't even know each other?"

"Isn't that what dating is, though—getting to know someone?"

I looked down at the faded snapshot between my fingers, the photo I'd looked at hundreds of times over the years, just as "Want Me" by Stephen Dawes came on.

And you're too cool for me to be yours

It was Dani and me, soaking wet after a water-balloon fight in my backyard. I was pretty sure we'd been ten or eleven at the time. Our clothes were drenched—she was wearing a Spider-Man T-shirt and I'd been in my bro-tank phase where I cut the sleeves off of every shirt I owned to show off my (soft) biceps—and we were sporting matching rainbow sunglasses that we'd gotten for free at the Southview Days parade.

We looked like little idiots.

"So your plan would be for us to get to know each other *while* we're pretending?"

Where the fuck had those kids gone? I wondered. How was it possible that they needed to get to know each other? I said, "I mean, why not?"

I put the photo back—*fucking sentimental dipshit*—because I kept forgetting the important piece of this puzzle.

I wasn't the same guy anymore.

Since the minute I heard she was moving back, I'd been all twisted up trying to convince myself I didn't give a shit about her. Because when we were kids, I'd always been half-obsessed with her, pudgy little Alec chasing Dani around while she laughed and chased me back.

But Dani Collins didn't have any power over me anymore, because I was no longer that kid. Faking nice with her wasn't going to kill me or make me fucking sprout feelings, for God's sake, because it was just a means to an end.

"And if I don't want to do this," she said, "is the hockey-manager position off the table?"

Yes, it's off the table, I wanted to snap, but I didn't. "I wouldn't say it's off the table, but if you do this, it's on the table with ribbons and bows and I'll make it so easy that you will thank me and name all your sons after me."

"That's hard to imagine," she said, "because isn't your middle name Herbert?"

"RIP Grandpa Herb, do not disrespect his glorious name," I said, surprised she remembered.

"I would never—Herb was an icon," she said, and I heard a smile again.

"So . . . ?" I prodded.

Please, please, please.

"Hmmm," she said slowly, like she was really weighing her options.

"Please?" I added, just in case it helped. "I promise you won't regret it."

"Don't make promises you can't keep," she said. "And I'll let you know in the morning."

"How about I pick you up?" I heard myself blurt, throwing out words and ride offers in a desperate attempt to convince her.

"Are you sure you're not just going to drive your car through Benji's house like a jackass when you get here?" she asked.

"I can't promise anything," I said.

She sighed. "So mature."

And then I couldn't stop myself. I asked, "You aren't seriously texting buddies with that piece of shit, are you?"

She was quiet for a minute, but then she just said, "I'll see you in the morning. Don't be late."

CHAPTER NINETEEN
Dani

I groaned when my alarm went off, because I was *not* a fan of mornings.

At all.

That being said, I turned it off and jumped out of bed because I wanted time to "casually" chat with my mom before Alec showed up. I couldn't guarantee he wasn't going to run into the kitchen and hijack the narrative, so I had to get to her first.

"Good morning," I said to my mom as I went into the kitchen and straight for the cupboard. "Are we ever going to use our kitchen in the apartment upstairs?"

"I'm sure we will," she said. "But this one is bigger and brighter, and the cabinets are always stocked. Since I haven't really grocery shopped since we moved here, I gravitate toward the one with food."

"Okay, fair," I said, pulling out a little bag of Hostess Powdered Donettes. "Can I have some of these?"

"Sure," she said.

"I just want to make sure they aren't Grandpa's," I said, because my mom *never* bought teensy trash donuts (that were delicious).

"He's your grandpa, so I'm sure he wants you to help yourself to anything in the pantry," she said.

"Hmm." I took the white bag over to the table and sat down, still a little unsure if I should be eating the sugary donuts.

"By the way . . ." My mom cleared her throat and looked weird.

"Have you talked to Dad lately? Is something going on with him?"

"Why?" I asked, feeling like my stomach suddenly weighed more than usual.

"I don't know . . . he sent me this voice memo where he was being really nice, saying that we are adults and that, because of you, he wants to make sure we have a good relationship."

"That sounds nice," I said, instantly stressed, because what was he up to? Was he trying to butter her up so he could talk to her about me possibly moving? That couldn't be it, because he'd hung up on me for not loving the idea, right?

"It does, but it sounds a little *too* nice," she said.

"Dad can be nice," I said, even though I wholeheartedly agreed with her suspicion.

"Bullshit," my grandpa said with a fake cough as he walked into the kitchen.

That irritated me, though Mom beat me to any response. "Dad, don't."

"I was just coughing," he said, going over to the cupboard and pulling out his mug, the same old North Stars mug he'd used for my entire life.

I don't know what got into me when I asked, "When was the last time you saw him? Like five years ago? And before that you maybe talked to him once, twice a year? Do you really know him?"

Though I was annoyed with my grandpa, the ask was sincere.

He crossed his arms and looked surprised by my questions. "I know enough, trust me."

Okay . . .

159

"Are you eating my Donettes?" he asked with his eyebrows down.

"Mom said they were for everyone."

"She was right if everyone means me," he growled.

"You're not going to share your donuts with your granddaughter?" my mom asked, looking irritated by the entire conversation.

"Not if she's gonna defend that jackass you used to be married to."

"Language, Dad," my mom said before turning to me, and then, anticipating my sarcastic response, quickly blurted out, "But back to my initial question—you didn't have any unusual conversations with Dad or anything? I've known him long enough to know that when he gets all nice like this, it's usually because he's setting me up for something."

"No," I lied, injecting my voice with all sorts of casual. My stomach knotted with guilt as I looked at her, because I loved my mom more than anyone in the world. *I shouldn't be lying to her.*

But I also wasn't going to bring up the conversation we'd had, because how would that even go?

Hey, Dad was trying to see if I would move to Omaha and leave you behind and I didn't exactly tell him no because I want him to move back to the States.

Yeah, no.

I was beyond happy when I heard the sound of Alec's noisy car pulling into the driveway, saving me from having to lie anymore. I hopped up from the table, grabbing my backpack.

"I don't need a ride today because Alec is picking me up," I blurted out, opening the fridge to grab a Red Bull.

"What?" my mom asked, looking surprised.

"Who the hell is Alec," Grandpa Mick asked in that not-a-question tone of his.

"Alec Barczewski, Sarah and John's boy," my mom said, still looking at me like she was trying to figure things out.

He took off his readers. "Who?"

I wanted to roll my eyes but I didn't. "Zeus? The one you said reminds you of, like, Conners or Krampus or—"

"Kronwall," he said, closing the newspaper with a sigh. "Niklas Kronwall. They both backpedal hit—"

A knock sounded at the kitchen door, interrupting my grandpa's hockey briefing.

I'd hoped to run outside and avoid this, but here we were. I opened the door, and once again, I was unprepared for Alec's appearance.

He was wearing black joggers and a Southview jersey—nothing unusual—but his size kept surprising me. I was five-seven, yet he seemed to be like a *foot* taller than me.

And a *filled-out* tall boy, not some gangly stick guy.

"Good morning, Collins," he said, grinning down at me.

He smelled good, like he'd just stepped out of the shower, and I put my hand on my stomach to quell whatever riot was happening when he smiled at me that way.

"Good morning, Barczewski," I said. "We were just talking about you."

"Obsessed already," he teased, his eyes moving all over my face.

It's only an act, I reminded myself, because one second of his flirting was already showing me just how powerful it could be.

Dear *God.*

161

"It was him, actually," I said, pointing to the table. "My grandpa thinks you backpedal hit like a cornball."

It was comical, the way Alec's face immediately changed when he looked at my grandpa. The teasing went away and he looked like a nervous little boy, like a kid who had no idea what to say.

His throat moved around a swallow, and my eyes got a little stuck on his neck.

Grandpa Mick shook his head like I was pathetic. "For God's sake, I said you hit like *Kronwall*," he corrected.

"Oh." Alec looked like he *definitely* didn't know what to say when he was being complimented by my grandpa. "Thank you."

"Hey, kid," my mom said to Alec with a big smile. "Thanks for being her chauffeur today."

"I figured you needed a break from this one," he said, again with the cute teasing.

"We should go," I said, looking back and forth between him and my mom, who was freaking *beaming*.

"You've got everything you need?" she asked. "You have lunch money?"

"Yep," I said, noticing the way Alec looked at me like he knew I was pocketing her money and avoiding the cafeteria entirely.

"Text me later so I know how things are going," my mom said, pulling me in for a big hug.

"I will." I took a deep breath, feeling like a little kid as I inhaled the Eternity she'd worn my entire life, and wished I could just stay home with her all day long.

"You guys ready for tonight?" my grandpa asked, zero warmth in his tone.

I pulled back from my mom as Alec gave Grandpa Mick a nod. "Eagan's playing good hockey right now, but as long as we stick to our game, they shouldn't be a problem."

"Right, *another* game tonight." I groaned. "Please tell me there won't be another pep rally."

"No, that one covered the rest of the season, so you're safe."

"Thank God."

Alec held open the door for me as we left, and as soon as the cold air blasted me in the face, I was filled with nervousness, because what was I doing?

Like, was I seriously going to do this?

Also—what the hell was Alec driving?

It was a silver car, but the bumper and one of the side panels were black, like they'd been taken from another vehicle.

And he was missing the passenger mirror.

I didn't care about cars, but I would've thought someone as slick and smooth as "Zeus" would drive something monster-sized that he called a chickmobile or something.

"Don't judge Burrito," he said as I opened the passenger door. "She isn't pretty, but she's reliable."

"It's more than I've got, so no judgment," I said. There hadn't been a reason for me to get my license at Ramstein, so I was still like a middle schooler with no wheels and no prospects.

"Good morning, Dani," I heard, and when I turned, I saw Benji standing beside his running Maserati in his driveway, smiling.

"Oh, hey, Ben," I said, uncomfortable after what had happened the night before.

"Hey, there, *Benji*," Alec said, giving my neighbor a total dickish smirk. "Do all the Cadets have douchebag cars, or is it just you?"

"We can't all drive pieces of shit held together by duct tape, bro."

"I'm not your bro, asshole," Alec said before climbing into the car and slamming the door.

Neither of us spoke as he backed out of the driveway, and I was stunned for a second to hear "Dopamine" playing in his car because I *loved* that song. As far as I knew, it wasn't a radio hit, so did that mean, like . . . Did *he* like it too?

Focus, Dani!

I scrambled to get my words together to ease whatever tension was rolling off Alec thanks to Benji, but also because I'd come up with my own demands for this "fake dating" situation.

I opened my mouth to start when he said, "By the way—are you okay?"

I looked over at his profile while he kept his eyes on the road, having zero idea what he was talking about. "What?"

He shot me a look for a brief second, his dark eyes moving over my face before he went back to the road. "Whatever the colonel did to make you upset yesterday—are you good now?"

Oh.

"Um, yeah, I suppose," I said with a shrug, because I was shocked that he was asking. "He's just being . . . y'know, *Dad*, I guess."

Alec looked at me like he understood, but before he could derail me further with unexpected concern, I jumped in. "So listen. I've been thinking about your proposition, and I have a counteroffer."

"Oh?" He glanced over again, and my face must've been intimidating or something, because he said, "Oh God."

"Yes, you probably *should* call out to him."

I'd barely slept at all last night because I couldn't stop thinking about the way Alec said people would for sure find out about what the coaches had walked in on in the locker room.

If that was true, I was screwed.

Because, since Alec was this big popular guy that half the girls in the school wanted to date, a rumor about me being *with* him in the locker room was going to get me a lot of hate.

So the game of pretend was absolutely necessary if I was going to stand a chance at not becoming a pariah.

But I was only going to feel safe if he did it my way.

"Here's the thing. As much as I don't want to do this, I feel like there's no way for me to *not* do it."

He looked surprised. "Really? You're seriously going to help me?"

"This isn't for you," I said, making sure he knew I wasn't at his fake-girlfriend beck and call. "The sad reality is that I'm going to be part of a rumor now. People are probably already gossiping about what they think was going on in the locker room."

"Yeah, probably," he agreed, which made my stomach drop.

I didn't want it to be true.

"So, to your point last night, I'd much prefer them to think that we are childhood sweethearts who reconnected, as opposed to me being cast as the new girl who's canoodling with hockey players in the locker room in her very first week."

"Did you seriously just say 'canoodling'?" he said with a smirk.

"Whatever—you get my point. Can you please focus here?"

"Fine," he said. "So you're saying the game of pretend works for you, too, then?"

"Yeah, but I'm going to need something more," I said, nervous because there was a good chance he was going to refuse.

"What is it?" he asked, turning onto the street where the school was. Which meant I needed to speak quickly.

"Well, we can still be super casual, but I'm going to need this fake relationship to last until I say it's over," I said, then quickly added, "Not as a power trip thing, but I just need—"

"You really *are* obsessed with me," he said with another smart-ass half smile, and I was glad he was joking.

It was good he was feeling funny.

"No, no, but I need you to agree to this," I said. "I want to have the final say in the breakup timeline. I want you to agree to stay with me until I say so, even if that keeps us together for a long time. Like, even . . . until graduation."

He made a noise like he thought I was kidding before he slowed at the stoplight and turned his full attention to me. "You want to be my fake girlfriend for three *months*?"

"I don't *want* that, ew," I said defensively, "but it might be necessary."

"How would it b—"

"Because the girl in a breakup always gets the bad rap, okay?" I snapped, hating the truth of it. "You're offering me this social protection as a new person, where I get to go everywhere and be part of your magical friend group, blah blah blah, but what happens if you decide to fake dump me in a few weeks and I haven't had a chance to make my own friends yet? Then *your* friends can start trashing me, and it might end up being worse on my end than if we'd never done it."

"My friends aren't assholes—they wouldn't do that," he said, brushing it off like I was ridiculous.

"Oh, they definitely would," I insisted, knowing from experience just how quickly people could turn. "But the bottom line is I'm not going to do this unless I have your guarantee that it's not over until I say it's over."

Could I sound like a bigger psycho?

"But." His eyebrows were scrunched together. "What if one of us wants to go out with someone else?"

I knew this would be the problem. Zeus the party boy wasn't going to accept the idea of potentially not being able to chase girls for the next few months.

"I know it's not ideal, but it's the only way."

"We can't just start and see how it goes?" he asked.

"This is the only option."

"Not to play the devil's advocate *for* you," he said, sounding like he thought I was being ridiculous, "but how do you know I'm not going to agree to this and then dump your ass anyway in a month if you start annoying me?"

Nice.

"Because if you do that," I said, digging deep for my badass bravery, "I'll tell everyone—including my grandpa and every hockey dude he knows—that it was all a lie in order to help your image."

"Whoa." His head came around for a quick second, and I could tell I'd shocked him. "You'd seriously do that?"

"I mean, I wouldn't want to," I said with a shrug, feeling like the world's biggest demanding jerk but knowing it was the only way.

"Mm-hmm," he said, looking back at the road, and I wished I knew what he was thinking.

Are we doing this or not?

When we finally got to school and started walking toward the door, he still hadn't said anything. And it was killing me. Did he agree to my demands?

But when he grabbed the handle to the front door, I got my answer.

"Let me ask you this," he said quietly, looking over his shoulder to make sure no one was close. "Do you want to soft launch this thing or go hard?"

"So we're doing it?" I asked, the cold wind sending a shiver up my spine.

"Yeah," he said, those dark eyes on mine. "So how do you want to play it?"

I had no idea exactly what he was asking, because we were walking into a public school building—it wasn't like "hard launch" could mean much, right?

"I guess that's your call."

"All right." His jaw did a little flex thing as he looked at me, and then he pulled open the door and gestured for me to walk in front of him.

"So . . . ?" I said quietly, glancing over at him as I walked through the door he was holding. "What do you want to do?"

"What I always want to do," he said. "Go hard."

I looked down when his hand grabbed mine, when he linked all five of his fingers in all five of mine. My eyes moved up to his face, and he was watching me like he was waiting for my next move. Somehow I sensed that if I didn't like this, he would totally back off, and I didn't know what to do.

Because something about him holding my hand scared me.

The school was already noisy, with everybody arriving and hanging out in the halls, and my heart started beating a little bit faster. What were people going to think? What was going to happen? Did I really want to do this?

The panic started rising again.

But then his fingers flexed, squeezing mine, and it felt like a reassurance.

I gave him a tiny nod, my wordless attempt at letting him know I was all in on going hard.

"Let's do this, Collins," he murmured, and then he started walking, pulling me alongside him. I nervously let him tug me along, hyperaware of people looking in our direction.

Because he was holding my hand like my boyfriend.

This was a statement.

And then—then he went harder.

"By the way," he said, yanking me a little closer as we walked. It was playful—flirtatious, even—as he gave me a teasing look and said, "I like this coat. It's cute."

"You like this coat?" I asked, looking down at it.

"I do. It reminds me of the one you were wearing in your Utah Christmas photo."

"The *sheep* jacket from third grade, are you kidding?" I asked around a laugh. "I forgot all about that. I *loved* that coat."

"It's got the same kind of fluffiness," he said, releasing my hand long enough to grab my sleeve and sort of yank me in his direction. "But what's really ridiculous is that scarf." He nodded his head toward the huge knit scarf around my neck. "You dress like you're in Antarctica."

"Because it *feels* like Antarctica here," I said. "I think I've been frozen since the second we rolled into town."

"So soft," he said, shaking his head like I was ridiculous.

"What's so soft?" I heard as Vinny and Richie came out of nowhere.

Alec slowed and turned in their direction, which meant I slowed too.

"She is," he said, bumping his shoulder against mine and smiling. "Dani dresses like it's fifty below all the time and runs for the doors whenever she's outside. Soft as hell." He whispered the last words, slowly, teasingly, his breath tickling my ear.

Jesus.

"You'll get used to it," Vinny said to me, his eyebrow lifting as Richie bit his lip to keep from smirking at this obvious display of flirtation.

Alec gave me a look that was so laced with . . . *something* that I felt my cheeks get hot. Even as I knew this was all for show, butterflies went wild in my stomach because of the way he was watching me.

Holy God, Alec at full power is a lot to handle.

"Listen," I said abruptly (and a little too loudly), "I need to go to my locker because I don't want to be late, so I'll see you later." I wasn't sure if I was talking to Alec or all three of them.

"Lunch in the library?" he asked, his eyes on mine as he reached out a big hand and grabbed the end of my scarf. Our gazes stayed locked as he slowly unlooped the yarn, his knuckles grazing my skin as he casually unwrapped my neck.

What is he doing?

A shiver slid down my spine, a shiver that was either from the cool air suddenly touching my throat or from the way he was audaciously peeling away one of my layers while looking at me *that* way; I couldn't be sure which.

But he was daring me with his eyes, wordlessly challenging me to respond; I'd have recognized that expression anywhere. He might be *Zeus* now, but my little friend Alec had given me that look a hundred times.

Usually in the context of *you won't* while waiting to see if I would.

So I raised my chin, snatched the scarf from his fingers, and said, "It's a date, *Zeus*."

CHAPTER TWENTY
Alec

Me: I heard that cool chicks hang out in the library. True or false?

I watched Dani grab the phone out of her pocket and look down at the message, and then—*dear Jesus*—her shiny mouth curved up into a smile as she texted me back.

Dani: I heard the same thing so I'm going to say TRUE

I shouldn't like her grin as much as I did—after all, she *was* my shitty ex-friend—but today I was all in on convincing her to help me, so that was my only focus.

Until graduation.

I still couldn't believe she'd suggested that, although her reasoning was sound.

And fucking sad.

If I were in her situation, it'd never have occurred to me that people might turn on me post-fake-breakup. I wouldn't have thought that far ahead, because in my experience—for the most part—people didn't act like assholes.

But she'd obviously had a different experience.

I replied: Rumor has it hot guys like to swing by sometimes . . .

She was still smiling when she texted: Only douches call themselves hot guys

There she is, the old Dani.

I sent: WHOA. COLLINS. I'm simply telling you the rumors that travel within these halls. I would never think to call myself that. Also . . . totally unrelated . . . I just walked into the library.

Her head came up and she was grinning when she looked at me.

And whoa—her full-throttle smile was still exactly the same.

It made me feel kind of . . . *off-kilter* as I walked over to her table.

"Did you already eat?" she asked, pushing up her glasses as I sat down in the seat across from her.

I don't know, what is eat? "I'm good."

Her eyebrows scrunched together, probably because that wasn't an answer. "And you *want* to hang out in the library instead of the cafeteria?"

I think I do. "Yes. I'm in need of a good book."

"A good book." That made her set down *Invisible Man.* "You didn't like the history ones you got the other day?"

The ones I blindly grabbed so I didn't look like I cared you were in the library?

"They were for school. I need a book for fun."

Her eyes narrowed and she watched me for a second before asking, "Do you want me to help you?"

A laugh came out of me as I remembered all the summer mornings we'd walked to the library together. She'd always been annoyingly excited about getting a new book, whereas I'd always been annoyingly excited to log into a library computer and play *Fortnite.*

But, to appease my mom, Dani always found a book for me to check out.

"Do your best, Collins."

"Come on." She left her stuff at the table and gestured for me to

LYNN PAINTER

follow her. The smell of her perfume was like my guide rope, leading me by the nose, and I cleared my throat and pushed that thought away because I couldn't afford to lose focus.

"*Billy Summers*," she said, moving through the book stacks with purpose.

"It's actually Alec Barczewski," I quipped, following her.

"The dad jokes, come *on*," she muttered, not slowing until we were standing in front of what was obviously the Stephen King section. She paused for a second, searching, before she pulled out a thick one. "*Billy Summers* is one of the best books I've ever read. Read it. I know you'll love it."

"Okay," I said. "I'll start it tonight."

"Aren't you going to read the back of the book?" she asked, looking at me like I was nuts. "To see if you'll like it?"

It was ridiculous how much I loved being taller than her now. It was like physical proof of the shift in our dynamic, a reminder that everything had changed.

"No, I trust you," I said. "You're the only person I've ever trusted to pick out library books for me."

That made her forehead get a tiny crease. "Let's go read."

We went back to the table, and it took a lot of mental toughness to start reading the book when her smell was messing with me and her blond curls were in my peripheral vision. Her perfume reminded me of apple juice and flowers, and something about that combination wreaked havoc on my senses.

It was annoying as hell.

I tried popping in one AirPod to take the edge off, but every random

174

song that came on made me think of the girl next door—"Famous," "Gateway Drug," "Picasso"—so I had to yank it out.

But once I focused on the words in front of me, I was immediately hooked.

Dani was right.

"Psst," she whispered a few minutes later, and when I looked up, she was holding out a granola bar. "Eat this."

"Why?" I asked, unsure why she was giving me a library snack.

"Because I heard your stomach growl and you have a game later and I'm fairly certain you're blowing off lunch for this," she said.

"Don't flatter yourself, Collins," I said, giving her an exaggerated smile. "I would never give up for lunch for you or for anybody. But I will take your proffered granola bar and devour it because I am fucking starving for no reason whatsoever."

That made her laugh, a quiet little tinkle that did nothing to help the grip I was losing on my focus.

"You know," she said, lowering her voice and leaning her face in a little closer, "there's basically no one in here, so you don't have to waste your lunch when we've got zero visibility."

She wants me to leave.

"Yeah, but if we're doing this whole thing, there needs to be a little bit of authenticity to it, right?" I asked. "We actually might need to spend time together if it's going to work."

"Probably . . . ?" She shrugged. "I have no idea."

"Same," I said, and we both smiled because *of course* we didn't know how to pretend date. It wasn't a thing. "But trust me—we're getting invisible visibility from this."

"What do you mean?"

"Well," I said, taking a bite of the bar, "Richie and Vinny couldn't believe I was skipping lunch to go to the library, so I guarantee they sat their wiseasses down at the table and started yapping about the fact that I'd rather hang out with you in a foodless library than join them in the caf."

"Oh." She bit down on her bottom lip, and I could tell her mind was going a mile a minute.

"I know the stereotype is that girls gossip," I said. "But no woman has anything on those dudes. They want to be in the know on everything and everyone."

"So," she said, leaning in even closer and lowering her voice to a true whisper. "Have you heard anything about the locker room? Is anybody talking about it?"

Her eyes were big as she waited for my answer, and I didn't know what to say.

Because, for starters, her whispering to me while apple juice and flowers floated around my face made it difficult to think. But I actually hadn't heard anything about it yet, if I was being honest, so maybe it *wouldn't* become a rumor.

But if she knew that, would she back out on the plan?

"Some of the guys definitely know, but it hasn't become a thing yet," I said.

Which wasn't *really* a lie, because Gordy and the coaches were, in fact, guys, right?

"Thank God," she said, then picked her book back up and started reading.

The rest of lunch flew by, the library a nice break from the chaotic lunches I was used to, and I'd be lying if I said I wasn't disappointed when the bell rang.

I waited while she put her books in her backpack so we could walk out together.

"Are you going to your locker?" I asked when we stepped out into the noisy hallway, because I needed to stop at mine.

"No, I'm going that way," she said, pointing toward the south corridor.

I leaned my head closer to hers because she was so short that it was hard to hear her in the crowded hall and said, "Shit, am I going to have to memorize your schedule?"

She looked up at me like she wanted to smile—her eyes crinkled at the corners—but she kept it together. "Don't burden that brain of yours when you have hockey to think about, Zeus. Trust me, I'll let you know where you need to be."

We agreed to meet at her locker after school and went our separate ways, but as I looked down at the scrap of paper in my hand where she'd written her locker number, I got an idea.

The best way to make sure she didn't flake on our deal was to show her that it was going to be fun, right? That she'd not only get Harvard, but she'd also get the social interactions she'd been denied with all the moving.

I needed to go harder on making her see it'd be fun.

She used to be all about a good time, and it might be entertaining as hell to see just how much I could make her like Zeus.

I shot off a text to my mom's cousin, who also happened to be the school's maintenance technician.

Me: I need a favor. Are you in your office?

CHAPTER TWENTY-ONE

Dani

"So I'm not sure if I should go or not."

Cassie stood next to my locker as I put in my combination, trying to get me to help her decide if she should go out with someone I hadn't met. I didn't have an answer, but she'd finally stopped questioning me about why I wasn't *quite* sure if I had the manager job locked down yet, so I was willing to discuss people I didn't know all day long.

Also—I didn't hate that she seemed to genuinely want my opinion. Like we were friends.

"He sounds nice," I said, pulling up on the release latch. "But what's the chemistry like? Is there awkward silence when you're together, or is he someone you can—"

Gummy bears.

I stopped talking because when I opened my locker door, a bag of gummy bears dropped down from the top shelf, swinging out at me from where it was connected by what appeared to be a strand of twine.

"What the heck is that?" Cassie reached out and grabbed the bag, holding it so she could read the note that was attached to the front of the candy.

COLLINS—

I DON'T KNOW IF YOU STILL INHALE

THESE LIKE YOU USED TO, BUT I SAW

THEM IN THE MACHINE AND THOUGHT
OF YOU.
—A

P.S. MY BOOK SMELLS LIKE YOUR
PERFUME AND IT'S DISTRACTING AS
HELL

Oh wow.

I stared at the scrawled-out note and couldn't believe what I was see-ing. Thoughts were bouncing around in my brain, chaotic little com-ments that were all over the place.

He remembers my gummy bear addiction.

There are obvious security concerns at Southview if he was able to get into my locker.

His handwriting is surprisingly nice.

Does his book actually smell like my perfume?

This is so thoughtful.

This is an act.

"Okay, Dani," Cassie said, letting go of the swinging bag to look at me with huge eyes and a gaping mouth. "What the hell is going on? Who put this in your locker?"

"I, um, I think—"

"I mean, you don't even really know anyone yet, right, except for Zeu—oh my God, *Zeus*?" She screeched his name when she realized, grabbing my upper arms. "I thought you guys were just old friends! You said you were like strangers, didn't you?"

I was torn between being excited that this fake thing might be easy to pull off, and terrified because I still really didn't want to do it.

"Shhhh," I said, ripping down the bag of bears, trying not to smile but failing. I lowered my voice and said, "It's no big deal. We *were* like strangers, but we've started talking a little, kind of . . . reconnecting. We're just, um, old friends catching up."

"Sure you are."

"Seriously."

"Holy *shit*, though," she said, giving my arms a shake. "You gave him your locker combination already?"

"No," I said with a shrug, shaking my head because my dismay at this was absolutely genuine. "I have no idea how he got in."

"That's so sweet," she said, smiling.

"Or felonious. He broke-and-entered."

"Because he wanted you to have candy," she added in a singsong voice. "The boy is out here committing crimes for you."

That made me laugh and kind of wish I weren't lying to her.

But there was no way I could trust her enough not to.

Why was I feeling giggly when this wasn't even real?

The warning bell rang, which meant we had two more minutes.

"I'll see you later," Cassie said, taking off in the other direction as I pulled out my phone.

I texted: Thank you for the gummy bears.

He was quick with the response.

Alec: I cannot see a bag of gummy anything without thinking of you.

That made me smile, the fact that he remembered.

It wasn't easy to concentrate after that, because I was a little keyed up.

Playing this game with Alec was kind of fun, which I hadn't expected. He seemed a lot like the old Alec, in this world of pretend, and every tiny piece of me wanted that to be true so badly, because I missed my best friend so much.

But I needed to remember that that wasn't him anymore.

He might be capable of fun, but he was now Zeus the Hockey God, a guy I couldn't trust.

Keeping that in mind proved difficult, however, because he was a very entertaining fake flirtation. He showed up at my locker with Vinny and Richie after sixth period just to say hey and see if I'd eaten all the bears yet (I had, which made him grin like I was adorable), and when he met me there after school, he grabbed the scarf from my hands and wrapped it around my neck like he was a parent bundling up a child about to play in the snow.

I laughed in spite of myself, and then I laughed even more when he took his Southview beanie out of his coat pocket and put it on my head with both hands, saying, "You lose a lot of body heat through the head, Collins, so a wimp like you needs to get a hat."

I rolled my eyes, and then my stomach flipped all the way over when he bent at the knees so our faces were level, gave me a half smile, and said, "You look good in mine—you should keep it."

My breath was stuck in my throat as he flirted so well that I had trouble remembering how to speak. I met his gaze and said, "Thanks."

"You got it," he said, tugging on a strand of my hair. His eyes were all over my face before he added in a murmur, "Danigirl."

Sweet holy God.

It was confusing to stare up into the face of this incredibly attractive guy, an oversized specimen of a world-class athlete with a hard jaw, while getting a glimpse of the old Alec Barczewski when his mouth slid into a smile.

"What the hell is this?" Vinny said with a questioning smirk, and—God—I hadn't even noticed he was there.

"Yeah, get a room," Richie added, and it was wild the way I hadn't noticed either of them because all I'd been able to see was Alec.

"So good luck tonight, you know, at your game," I said like a dope, blinking fast in hopes that I wasn't looking at him through pathetic heart eyes or something.

I was positive he got that from most human females because, well, *damn*.

Like, bravo, Mother Nature.

"Thanks," he replied in a low voice, his eyes getting a playful squint as he raised my scarf to cover my chin, like he was helping me stay warm (again).

I felt a little hypnotized as his . . . *bigness* surrounded me. Tall body, wide shoulders, big hands—he was obviously a very physical guy, always nudging with a shoulder or yanking on a curl, and it was going to take some getting used to.

Especially when he wielded direct eye contact like some kind of weapon.

I needed to start reminding myself to breathe or there was going to be a lot of passing out during the course of this fake relationship. I said, "Call me later?"

I could tell by the quick blink of his eyes that I'd surprised him, but he quickly recovered.

"Try and stop me, Collins."

CHAPTER TWENTY-TWO
Alec

I thought about her all the way to the arena.

Even with headphones on and my Pregame Calm playlist sending me chill shit like "The Black Dog" and "In the Kitchen," I couldn't shake the image of her big brown eyes blinking up at me from point-blank range.

This was going to be tougher than I thought.

I mean, I could handle it, but *fuck*. As much as I didn't want to accept it, the truth was that there was still a part of me that saw her the way I'd always seen her.

The guys gave me shit the second she left us alone, because apparently I looked like a "lovesick little bitch" when I was around her, which made me defensive for a half second before I remembered that was how I wanted to look.

The clouds parted because, *oh yeah*—it was all an act.

She was playing her part, and I was playing mine.

Boom—no worries.

I swallowed down a few ibuprofen when I got to the locker room, then rubbed a shit ton of Icy Hot into my shoulder before suiting up.

And then everything else disappeared.

It didn't make sense, really, that when I wasn't playing hockey, I spent every waking minute stressing about it. The banners, the articles, the recognition—it all just reminded me that I was going to let down a lot of people if I wasn't the best.

If I wasn't better than the best.

I mean, I'd gotten a text from my agent already that afternoon, just checking in to see how things were going and to wish me luck for the game.

And to remind me that a couple of scouts were going to be there.

Forgetting was impossible.

Especially when there wasn't just *my* post–high school career and everything that came with it to worry about, but also Southview—like, the town itself. The Packers had gone to the tournament more times than any other school in Minnesota, yet we'd never brought home the title.

There was no championship banner hanging from the Doug's rafters, no championship trophy sitting on a glass shelf in one of the Doug's trophy cases.

We'd made it to the finals last year but lost to St. John's Academy (and fucking Ben Worthington), so even though I scored a goal at the Xcel Energy Center, it was the worst game of my life.

Because we'd come so damn close.

I'd cried like a fucking baby afterward, swear to God.

And now it was my senior year and I was playing the best hockey of my life. It was cool that the entire town was insanely supportive, but it also felt like everyone was counting on *me* to finally make it happen.

To lead the team to the historic thing that'd never been done before.

It kept me awake (when my shoulder wasn't already keeping me awake) more nights than it didn't.

But the second my skates connected with the ice—praise Jesus—all of that disappeared.

I forgot about pressure, pain, and curly blondes with brown eyes. My brain pressed pause on everything that wasn't connected to my skates, my stick, the puck, and the ice in front of me.

"What the fuck is this I hear about you and Boche's granddaughter?" Kyle said as I skated past him during warm-ups.

Fuck.

He was always lazy until game time, yapping about random shit, but I needed to get in some good laps before we stretched and didn't need him messing with my focus.

"If you can catch me, I'll tell you," I said, knowing I was safe from having to discuss Dani, because he wasn't even going to try. I cleared my head of everything, and from the second the puck dropped that night, we were fucking on fire.

I got lucky from the jump with a rim around the boards that led to a turnover behind the goal line. Kyle got the puck with space behind the net and wrapped it around the right post into the low slot to Richie, who got enough on his shot to get the puck past their goalie.

It felt slick and easy, one minute in, and we never let up.

Everything worked that night, and we fucking destroyed them.

After the bus brought us back, I stopped by the team offices to see Kuhn—one of the assistant coaches—and get his okay on Dani being a team manager. I dropped it casually, like *Are you cool with a new kid helping Cassie?* and he—of course—agreed.

I mean, I wasn't an idiot.

Going to Coach Oz, after what he thought he'd walked in on the day before, would've been a terrible idea.

"He was cool with it?" Richie asked as we walked to my car.

"Yeah," I said, a little surprised myself.

"I mean, she's Boche's granddaughter," Vinny said, "Of course he's gonna be cool with it. You really think he wants Mick kicking his ass for turning her down?"

"Boche's not going to kick anyone's ass," Richie said. "Probably."

"Of course he isn't," I said, although the old enforcer was crazy intimidating.

After dropping off the guys and wolfing down some leftover meat loaf that was in the fridge, I went up to my room to get started on my homework since I needed to stay on top of my shit now more than ever. My parents weren't home yet, which I didn't hate because I could use a little quiet.

But first I needed to text Dani and make sure we were all good. I flopped onto my mattress and stretched out, then decided to hit the FaceTime button instead.

She answered on the second ring.

"What are you doing?" she asked as the call connected, her eyebrows down behind those big glasses. "Don't you know it's considered a breach of etiquette to assume the FaceTime call without asking first?"

It looked like she was also sitting on her bed, because there was a white headboard behind her.

"My bad," I said, rolling over onto my good side. "I just thought talking would be easier than texting to let you know that you're in as manager. So tomorrow just check with Cass on where you should go and what you should do at practice."

"What did he say?" she asked, her eyes wide. "The coach was fine with it after . . . y'know . . ."

186

That made me want to laugh, the way she looked too innocent to finish the sentence, even though nothing had been going on. "He's fine with it."

"Oh, thank God," she said, putting a hand on her chest and looking so relieved that I almost felt guilty. "So I'm officially one of the team managers."

"You are." I cleared my throat and said, "Hockey manager and my, uh, not sure what to call you . . . *person of interest* . . . ?"

"Sounds like I'm being investigated by the feds," she said.

"Lover?"

"Gross."

I heard the slam of the door downstairs, so either my parents were home or my grandma was back with the twins.

"My boo?" I suggested.

She sighed but I could tell she wanted to smile. "How about the brilliant girl you're suddenly obsessed with?"

"That doesn't sound right," I said, and then she *did* smile. "You can't be brilliant and mistake Kronwall for cornball."

"Can I tell you a secret?" she said with a shitty little smirk.

"You knew it was Kronwall and just wanted to annoy Mick," I said.

She coughed out a laugh. "Little bit."

"What's it like so far, living with him?"

She shrugged. "He doesn't really talk to me. He barks out random questions and statements when we happen to cross paths, but that's pretty much it."

"What a game—ooh, sorry," my dad said from the doorway, putting up a hand when he saw the phone.

I didn't know if she was ready for a public outing with our parents, but what the hell? Might as well start ruffling our family's feathers with the shock of this. I watched her face as I sat up and said to my dad, "No worries—it's Dani."

She looked back at me and I saw her register who I was talking to, and then she tilted her head and gave me a little squint, like she knew exactly what I was doing.

"Danigirl!" my dad said, gesturing for me to hold up the phone. He fucking *loved* her, so this was going to be interesting. "How's it goin', kiddo? You like it so far? Is Al showing you everything you need to know about being a Packer?"

"Well," she said, smiling in that way that told me she was up for the challenge, "I actually thought he was avoiding me when I first got here, but suddenly he has become incredibly helpful."

"Has he now?" my dad said.

"Also, John—what happened to your squishy little son? I mean, not that I'm complaining," she said, "but he has definitely changed."

That made my dad throw his head back and laugh, which was still my favorite sound.

It was weird how tragedy could do that to you.

My dad had been fine(ish) for a long time now, but after everything, I still cherished his loud-as-hell laugh, because we'd almost lost it forever.

"Yeah, he grew and then suddenly he became less klutzy—go figure," my dad said.

"Did he tell you that I'm going to be a hockey team manager?" she asked.

"Oh yeah? I thought you didn't know anything about hockey," he said, giving me a confused look.

"Oh, I don't, but it seems to me like when your boy wants something, he somehow manages to make it happen."

Good Lord, she is good.

She was dripping little bits of flirtation without blatantly saying that things might be progressing past friendship.

"So I guess I'm going to have to learn all about it now," she said.

"I'll teach you," my dad said, which I knew he'd love. "Come over anytime and I'll teach you everything you need to know."

"Yeah," I said. "You should come over right now, Collins."

Something about the way she looked embarrassed when I said that, the way her cheeks got a little bit pink, made me smile in spite of my exhaustion.

"I'm pretty sure you have studying to do, Barczewski," she said in a perfect tease. "By the way—my mom said she was going somewhere called the Crow to celebrate her new job and it's been hours and she still isn't back—should I be worried?"

"Nah, she was with us," my dad said. "We stopped by after the game."

"I'm assuming the Crow is a bar?" she asked.

"The Croatian Social Hall," I said. "The Cro."

"Oh," she said, looking no less confused and distracting me with the way she was blinking fast.

She had the coolest fucking eyes.

"It's basically a bar," I added, clearing my throat and my mind. "That everyone goes to."

"Got it. Listen, I should probably go study," she said, smiling at my dad. "But am I going to see you and Sarah soon? Will you guys be at the next game?"

"They're my parents, Collins," I said. "Of *course* they'll be there."

"I was talking to your father, not you," she said adorably.

"Yeah, we'll be there. And you missed a helluva game earlier; Al really had his legs moving tonight, holy moly."

That made her eyes land on me as she smirked. "He brought both of them, did he?"

My dad laughed again and went off, describing the game, completely oblivious to the fact that she had no idea what he was saying.

She tilted her head and that smirk slid into a grin. "So . . . you scored?"

My dad lost it, howling as he told Dani she needed to get her ass over to the house soon so he could teach her about hockey.

"I will, I promise," she said. "Al, are you picking me up for school on Monday?"

I hadn't been planning on it, we hadn't discussed it at all, and something about the way she was looking at me told me she knew that.

"Of course I am," I said, slowly shaking my head because she was a little shit.

"I'll have him bring some deer sticks," my dad said. "And some of El's cinnamon rolls."

"That would be great. See you then, Zeussy," she said with a big grin, and I laughed because she'd obviously tricked me. I'd made a deal with a harmless shy girl, not this mouthy version of classic Dani.

"I love that kid," my dad said after the call was disconnected. "So she's gonna be a manager, huh? Where the hell did this come from?"

I told him about the Harvard thing, and he said, "Well, I'm glad you were able to help her. She's a good kid and it sounds like she went through some shit, so hopefully Southview's a great place for her to land."

"What sort of shit?" I asked. "Besides the divorce."

"I think it was just typical mean-girl stuff in junior high," he said. "But it sounds like it left her a little on the skittish side. God, I'd love to slap whoever messed with Danigirl. She seems fine now, though."

"Yeah," I agreed, thinking that that tracked with how suspicious she seemed of me and my friends.

The doorbell rang at that moment and my dad gave me a look. "Sounds like Grandma's here with the twins, so close your door if you expect to get any studying done."

"Good call," I said, and watched my dad wince as he turned to walk out of my room.

He was so good at living through the pain that sometimes I actually forgot about the accident, which was insane, because it'd blown our world apart.

But then little facial expressions like that reminded me.

Of the call: *They said the semi T-boned your dad's truck.*

He'd had a ruptured spleen, internal bleeding, swelling on the brain— and those were just the things the doctors told us could kill him. He'd also had a broken back, broken femur, broken wrist, and four broken ribs, but those were almost cosmetic compared to the critical injuries.

He'd been more smashed up than not.

So the man who winced today was a walking miracle.

He was also a walking reminder that Dani had disappeared during the time I'd needed her the most. When my world fell apart.

It was a sobering thought when I was still so fucking drunk on her damn smile.

CHAPTER TWENTY-THREE
Dani

Fake dating Alec quickly became the easiest thing in the world.

My favorite part? The way he kept showing up for my library lunches.

Because the truth was that I didn't necessarily *like* being alone for that hour, yet I was too scared of the cafeteria to do anything about it.

So seeing him walk in made me feel . . . like, some kind of way.

Safe.

Happier . . . ?

Not alone.

"Is that a new book?" he asked one day when he showed up at my table looking ten feet tall, towering above me.

"It is," I said, taking my foot and pushing out the chair across from me. "Where's *your* book?"

He gave me a little half smile as he looked down at the chair; then he sat down and unzipped his backpack. "In here, but my book is much fatter than yours, so I'm still working on it."

"You don't have to make excuses for being a slow reader," I teased. "It's fine."

"Please, I could totally kick your ass in a speed-reading competition," he said, pulling out *Billy Summers*. "Not that something that nerdy has ever been an actual competitive event."

"Here." I pulled the sandwich out of my bag and set it on the table in front of him.

"What the hell is this?" he asked, his eyebrows all squished together as he looked down at it.

"What does it look like? It's a sandwich," I said, rolling my eyes.

"First of all, what kind of sandwich, because it looks weird," he said with a smirk. "Second of all, why did you bring me a sandwich?"

"Because an oversized man-child like you is going to starve to death and probably pass out if he doesn't eat lunch."

"Are you concerned about me, Collins?" he asked, his voice dropping into a lower octave that made my stomach flip.

"Not at all, but if you pass out like a little old lady and bash your face on the ground, it'll make Sarah sad, and I would hate that," I said with an eye roll. "And it's ham and cheese."

"It doesn't look like ham and cheese," he said with a scowl, holding up the baggie.

"That's probably because I couldn't find sandwich fixings in Grandpa Mick's kitchen, so it's queso with Spam. And pickles."

"Are you serious?" He stared harder at the baggie. "You brought me a Spamwich?"

"It was a last-minute idea, and that was all I could find in his fridge," I said, laughing at his ridiculous word.

I went back to my book, but I could see in my peripheral vision when he took out the sandwich and cautiously raised it to his mouth.

"This is . . . interesting," he said in a weird voice as he chewed.

"I'm so happy you think it's delicious," I replied, my eyes on the pages of my book.

"I don't think that's the word I used," he said.

He opened his book and started reading, and I couldn't help but notice he finished the entire sandwich as he read. The fact that he'd wolfed it down made me think he was either more polite than I'd given him credit for, or absolutely starving.

We read in silence for the rest of lunch, but when the bell rang and I looked up from my book, he was watching me with his arms crossed over his chest, a smirk on his mouth.

"What?" I said, closing the book and pushing up my glasses. It was impossible not to smile when he looked at me that way.

"The rest of the world just disappears for you when you're reading, doesn't it?"

"Yes, thank God," I said, nodding and unzipping my bag. "It's like magic."

"I bet it is," he said, and I noticed his book was already put away, his backpack on his back.

"Oh, so you're already packed up," I said, a little embarrassed that I'd been *that* out of it. I quickly shoved my paperback and my water bottle into my bag, zipped it, and stood. "Sorry."

"Don't be," he said, and then he came around the table to slide those fingers between mine yet again.

The familiarity of the move, the way it was beginning to feel natural even though our game was still new, made me look up at his face.

I wanted to see what he was thinking.

"It's weird, right?" he said quietly, his eyes all I could see as he read my mind the way he always had when we were kids.

I just nodded, too sucked into his gaze to think of words.

The moment held, and the rest of the world just disappeared like magic for a split second.

I watched his Adam's apple bob around a swallow, and then he said, "We should go."

"What?" I blinked and realized there was movement everywhere around us. The librarian was carrying a stack of books, students were filing through the hallways, and my heart was pounding in my chest.

"Yes," I said a little too loudly, clearing my throat and nodding. "We should go."

We walked out of the library, and just as he let go of my hand because we had to go in two different directions, he leaned down and said, "Hey, thanks for bringing me a sandwich."

His eyes were a little squinty as he grinned at me.

"Hey, thanks for eating it," I said, smiling back at him.

"I'll never look at Spam the same way again."

I didn't see him for the rest of the day or after school, since Cassie whisked me away to ride with her to practice.

Being a team manager, so far, had been easy, and I was actually having a good time.

There were still a million things about hockey I didn't know, but she was making it fun to learn.

Weird, right?

"Do you want to film today, or do you have homework you need to do?"

"I'll film," I said, mostly because I knew I wouldn't be able to focus on homework while Alec was hockeying.

It was becoming a problem. Every day, as soon as I set up the camera and started recording, I couldn't do anything but watch him play.

I was obsessed.

On each play and on every drill, he played like his life was at stake and the only way he was going to see tomorrow was if he beat the other guy to the puck.

He was beyond impressive.

When the guys finished drills and I was able to hit pause, Cassie walked over and said, "I'll see you at Vinny's . . . ?"

"Vinny's?" I repeated, having zero idea what she was talking about.

"The team dinner is at his house tonight."

"What? Do hockey managers *have* to go?" I asked, having no interest whatsoever in going to a team dinner. Me and a table full of obnoxious hockey players I didn't know?

No, thank you.

"Yeah, it's mandatory," she said, and I felt like she was giving me a little side-eye for sounding so disinterested. "For all players, coaches, managers, and trainers."

"Oh—I didn't know," I said dumbly, as if that weren't obvious.

But I felt stressfully unprepared for this kind of social interaction.

I needed time to mentally prep for outings.

"It's tradition," she said as she put on her coat, "and super chill. It's usually something like pasta or soup, and you just eat a plate and leave. I don't think I've ever stayed for more than an hour."

"Oh," I said, my stomach filling with dread.

"Zeus said you're riding with him."

"Oh yeah," I played along, even though I knew we'd discussed this. My stomach sank deeper inside my body at the thought of unwelcome social interaction *while* playing pretend with Alec—ugh. "I forgot about the whole thing."

As if on cue, my mom texted at that very minute:

Mom: Sarah says there's a team dinner after practice tonight—are you going?

I texted: I literally just found out about it. It's mandatory, apparently.

Mom: Just stick with Alec and you'll have a great time!

She'd seemed fine with my aversion to social situations before we moved here, but now it was like someone had lit a match under her. It was all the little things she said, her perky suggestions.

You should go!

Maybe you should see if Cassie wants to study with you at Starbucks.

Do you want to have anyone over for the game?

It kind of made me feel like she thought I was a broken weirdo who needed an intervention before my entire life was ruined. I could *feel* her stress that I wasn't running around with a group of friends already, but the truth was that all the school bullshit wasn't worth it.

It wasn't.

I *used* to do it. I *used* to move to a new school and work my ass off for friends and sleepovers, feeling like everything was right and settled when I found people I connected with.

And I'd be the first to admit—that shit felt *good*.

But eighth grade was a nightmare of mean girls and embarrassment so terrible that I'd been excited to move, and then ninth grade was better but ended up being the worst.

After I left.

Because the awfulness that came with being forgotten felt ten times worse than the discomfort of assimilation.

It was never intentional, the forgetting, but it was always a given.

At some point, you would just literally never hear from your "best friends" again.

I probably would've played that soul-crushing game forever if it hadn't been for Jackson Ford.

I dated him for six months my freshman year—*six* months. I'd been head over heels in love with him and it felt like a movie when we were together. I slept in his COIN sweatshirt every night (before his mom made him get it back because it'd cost a hundred bucks at the concert) and he held my hand in the hallways.

We were inseparable.

I'd seen literal tears in his eyes when we said goodbye and I moved away.

We talked on the phone and texted continuously. FaceTimed whenever we could.

But after about a month, he sounded different when I called. I convinced myself I was paranoid, but something was off.

And suddenly I was the only one calling.

That should've had me prepared for the end, but I'd been stunned when I'd seen the Instagram post making him and Olivia Lowell official.

It was a picture of them grinning at the movie theater, holding hands, and he was wearing the COIN sweatshirt that had once been my uniform for dreaming.

They were a couple.

It absolutely destroyed me, but the realization that he hadn't even felt the need to break up with me was what shattered every little piece of my heart. I'd been so forgotten that it hadn't even occurred to him that he needed to end our relationship before starting another one.

I was just somebody that he used to know.

I cleared my throat and forced myself back to the present, because revisiting all the crap never helped anything.

It *was* a good reminder, though, that all these people I was suddenly spending time with were wrapped up in our fake arrangement and not real at all.

And right on cue, I heard Alec's voice. "You ready to go, Collins?"

Right. Relationships hurt, and I wasn't about to let Alec—and the toe-curling smile that dared me to answer—make me forget that.

"Sure."

Alec pulled up in front of a cute yellow house and put the car in park. There were a lot of cars lined up on the street, so we definitely weren't the first ones to arrive.

I took a deep breath through my nose, wishing I'd just said no to this. I was new enough that no one would've missed me.

"So what do I need to know about this dinner?" I asked, my stomach filled with butterflies at the thought of walking into a house full of people I didn't know.

"You eat," he said, shrugging. "That's it."

"Wow, you've really illuminated what I can expect from this experience, thank you." I pushed open the car door and stepped out, wondering if I'd ever stop gasping at the wicked snap of the cold on my skin.

And it was snowing *hard* now, big, fat flakes that slapped you in the face.

"It's just something the parents do to make sure we have a good meal the night before a game," he said as we both walked toward the driveway. "Nothing to overthink."

He didn't know that was all I did.

Overthink.

"I feel like my sandwich might've ruined other meals for you, though," I said, filling the quiet of the night with rambling to cover my nerves.

"For the record, today's sandwich was actually not bad," he lied. I was sure of it.

When we got to the front door, Alec didn't knock or ring the doorbell—he just walked in.

I followed, having zero idea what to expect as we stepped inside.

Ahhhh, warmth.

"Alec!" A woman, presumably Vinny's mom, looked over from where she was standing in front of the sink and smiled before she set down the towel she was holding and came over. She was wearing jeans and a Packers crewneck, her brown hair pulled back in a ponytail, and she smiled like she loved us. "The guys—and Cassie—are out in the garage already. You must be Dani."

"Hi," I said, nodding, a little surprised she knew of me when I'd only just found out I was coming.

"Are you adjusting to the weather yet?" she asked. "Big John said you're not a fan."

She knows Big John and they've discussed me?

I was so confused by this place. Why in God's name would *I* ever come up in conversation?

"I mean, it's brutal, right?" I said. "It's snowed every day since we moved here."

201

"Believe it or not, you'll adjust," she said warmly, like she really wished the best for me. "So what do you think of hockey so far?"

"She thinks I look hot in my breezers," Alec said with a grin, and then he wrapped his arm around my shoulder and pulled me closer. "Right?"

I rolled my eyes while every nerve ending in my body shorted out. I was impressed by how chill I sounded when I said, "No one has ever looked hotter in tiny padded pants."

That made Vinny's mom laugh, and before I had a second to say anything else, Alec's hand slid down to mine and he was pulling me away from her and toward what looked to be the patio door.

Now he's holding my hand in front of adults.

He'd held it at school, but this felt like more somehow.

Tighter. More physical.

I said, "Don't you think this is a bit much—"

"Hard launch for the over-eighteen crowd, baby," he said in my ear, his voice deep and quiet and for some reason making my heart beat just a little faster.

Probably just because he'd startled me.

But . . . *baby.*

"Oh," I managed, looking at his face while my brain just kept repeating, *He's holding your hand like that he's holding your hand like that Alec Barczewski is holding your hand.*

Like that.

"Come on." He opened the sliding glass door, then let go of my hand the minute we stepped outside in the cold, dark, snowy evening. The snow seemed to insulate the world, making it strangely quiet as he closed the door behind us.

It was freezing, so I cleared my throat and said, "Are we seriously going to eat in the garage? Won't we freeze to death?"

"Oh, Dani," he said, shaking his head like I was a ridiculous child. "It's like you've never seen the inside of a Minnesotan garage before."

I followed him through the backyard and out to the detached yellow garage that matched the house. When he pulled open the door that was right beside the two-car overhead door, I was shocked to feel warmth.

To see bright lights.

To hear noise.

We walked in, and the garage barely resembled a garage at all.

It had shiny floors and finished walls, so the space felt more like a basement rec room than a place to park cars. There were three TVs mounted on a wall covered with sports posters, and two refrigerators sat underneath them.

Neon beer signs hung on the other wall, above a line of tables that were set up as a slow cooker–rich buffet, and I half expected to see servers and bartenders milling about the place.

In the center, a bunch of rectangular multipurpose tables had been shoved together to form a supertable (with PACKERS HOCKEY tablecloths, of course), which was where the team appeared to be sitting.

Coach Osman was standing next to the refrigerators, talking to the other coaches and some guys who I assumed were team dads, and I felt like they were all looking at us as the door closed behind us.

Probably just paranoia.

"Danigirl!"

Big John stood on the other side of the garage with a couple of the guys I'd met at his house during dinner my first night in town.

Just seeing him made me feel a little more comfortable as I waved back.

I heard multiple people shout "Zeus!" but Alec was looking at *me* when he said, "Should we get some food?"

I nodded, eyeing the three different kinds of casseroles, four different types of pasta, three different sauces, and the two lasagnas displayed on the table.

Oh—and three kinds of bread.

These moms were *not* playing.

We filled our plates and sat down at a table beside Cassie just as Kyle said, "No, they're my dad's venison meatballs."

Venison meatballs?

I didn't say anything, but I must've made a face because Alec said, "I promise they're good."

I shrugged like I had no issues with Bambi meatballs because I knew it was technically the same, right? Cow or deer, either one had me eating an animal. "I'm sure they are."

But something about the cuteness of deer messed with me for no good reason whatsoever.

"If they're *your* dad's," Cassie said to Kyle, "then my dad helped."

"True," Richie agreed.

"They cook together?" I asked. "That's really nice."

"That's not *exactly* it; it's not that sweet," Alec said, smirking.

"Yeah, no," Cassie interrupted, shaking her head. "Our dads all have this little . . . shit, I don't know what you'd even label it. Call chain, maybe . . . ?"

"On-call group," Kyle corrected, nodding.

"Yeah," Alec agreed.

"During hunting season, if one of them bags a deer, they put it out on the group text so by the time they get home, each person in the group is already there and waiting to help break down the deer," Cassie explained.

"Big John still tells the story," Richie said, "of the time Cassie came out to where they were breaking down a deer, and peed her pants."

"Shut *up*," she said, but she was laughing. "First of all, I was three. Second, no one warned me I'd be walking into a scene from a horror movie or I would've hit the bathroom first."

"Mm-hmm," Kyle said with a grin.

"Third," she said, flipping him off, "Big John gave me twenty bucks to stop crying, so I think I was actually the winner."

"Are you saying twenty bucks can erase childhood trauma?" Alec said.

"I'm saying twenty bucks bought two kick-ass Barbies."

The four of them started laughing—I mean, I did too—but I felt a pang of envy in my stomach for what they had, what I would never have. There was this long-game history between all of them, a braided-together past that made them more like cousins than friends.

I wondered what that felt like.

Everyone smiling and reminiscing about the collections of stories they didn't run out of telling—it was warmth and sunshine, and I was jealous.

Just as I was thinking that, the basket holding the plastic forks toppled over as Big John stumbled into the table, grasping his knee and grimacing in pain.

"Dad!" Alec jumped out of his chair and was at his dad's side in an instant, joining another guy in helping Big John right himself. He hadn't gone all the way down, but it'd been close. They each grabbed an arm, and my heart sank as Big John plastered a smile onto his face, dismissing their help.

"Damn leg keeps locking on me whenever I stand up. I'm fine," he said, as if it happened all the time."

Wait. *Did* this happen all the time?

"Give us the word and we'll get one of the boys here to give you a piggyback ride," Vinny's mom said.

And she laughed.

And Big John laughed.

Everyone laughed.

Everyone except Alec.

CHAPTER TWENTY-FOUR
Alec

"So I feel like this is going well, don't you?" she asked. Her voice was soft, and I knew she was trying to break the tension.

I nodded as I drove because I wasn't really sure what to say.

Yeah, it went really well at the team dinner—*except when my dad damn near collapsed in pain!*—and Coach seemed happy to see us together. Our fake relationship was going great at school, too, except for the fact that I kept getting distracted by her.

Logically, I knew it wasn't a thing, that *we* weren't a thing, but when it was just the two of us, I kept fucking forgetting.

None of this is real.

Which was why I appreciated the wake-up call tonight. The gut-wrenching dose of reality that hit me when my dad's knee buckled was exactly what I needed. Seeing him like that was an instant reminder of one of the worst times of my life, when my friend chose not to be with me but to instead take my fucking nemesis—that twat—to our spot.

His presence helped ground me.

"Yeah, it was good," I said.

"Are you okay?" she asked, holding her hands in front of the heating vents. "With your dad, I mean. I didn't know . . ."

"Just tired," I said, which absolutely wasn't a lie, but I also didn't want to talk about my dad. Not with *her*. Whenever he sat for too long, pain shot up his leg. It happened often, but that didn't make it any better.

"So do you have trouble sleeping the night before a game?" she asked, clearly avoiding the subject of my dad. "I've never played any sport, but it seems like since you're decent at hockey, it might be a little stressful."

"No more than any other night," I said.

"What does that mean—you *don't* sleep well?" she asked.

"You're not my real girlfriend, Collins—you don't need to worry about how many hours of sleep I'm getting, okay?"

It came out a little harsher than I'd intended, but I needed to create a little distance.

Her eyebrows went together and I knew she felt that one.

"I was just asking," she said.

I pulled into her driveway, and when I opened my door to get out, she said, "You don't have to walk me to the door. No one is around."

"It's dark, so I'm walking you to the door," I said, feeling like an ass. But when I got to her side of the car, I saw that fucking Benji Worthington was out on his porch with a vape pen in his mouth.

Forever a douche.

"Fucking Worthington," I muttered under my breath.

"Why do you guys hate each other?" she asked quietly as she climbed out of the car, looking in Benji's direction. "I mean, we never liked him because he was a tool, but obviously things got worse."

"Yeah, he's an asshole."

"Oh, well, that explains everything," she said sarcastically.

I sighed. "He's just my enemy and I fucking hate him, okay?"

"Your *enemy*?" she repeated in a tone that told me she thought I was being dramatic.

"Okay, so maybe not my enemy, but he's a dick weasel who gossips

208

like an old church lady," I said, wanting to punch him just for sitting there. "I guarantee you he's the one who spread the bong picture."

"Seriously?" She glanced toward Worthington's house.

"Oh yeah. He plays for St. John's Academy—"

"The ones who beat you in state last year?" she interrupted with a gasp.

"I can't believe you know that," I said.

"I can't believe you scored twice in that game," she said, closing the car door. "Apparently that's impressive for a defender."

"Look at you, doing all your research," I said, looking down at her mouth.

She smiled up at me, and it was insane how badly I wanted to kiss her.

Wait.

What? Where is this feeling coming from?

It was insane and plain fucking stupid.

Get it together.

"He's watching us now," she said quietly, "so I'm going to laugh like you're hilarious and charming."

She let out a little giggle and, yeah—he noticed us.

His attention was all ours, but he had no idea we'd spotted him.

"Holy shit, that's it," I said, my mind spinning. "With the way he gossips—we should totally kiss."

"*What?*" she said loudly, with a laugh, like she thought I was kidding.

But I glanced over her head and could tell Benji was staring, completely psychotically watching us, and I wasn't above begging.

Because if I could use him to broadcast this *and* make him jealous, that was a huge fucking win.

"Please let me kiss you please let me kiss you please let me kiss you please let me kiss you, Dani," I muttered, looking into her eyes and groveling. "I just hate that fucker so much and this is going to kill him please fucking let me kiss y—"

"Okay," she quietly interrupted.

I hadn't realized how sure I was that she was going to say no until she said okay.

"*What?*" I couldn't believe I'd heard her right. I looked down at her upturned face and said, "Really?"

"If you think it's going to get back to the right people," she said, her voice a near whisper as she leaned a little closer so Benji couldn't hear us, "then why not? We did it before just for fun, so why not do it now for public-relations purposes?"

Just for fun, my ass.

"Are you sure?" No matter how I felt about her now, I'd never want to pressure her into doing something she didn't want to do.

Even though it was suddenly the only thing I'd *ever* wanted to do.

So much for keeping it together.

"I'm sure," she whispered, nodding. "Lay it on me, *Zeus*."

It was the shitty little twinkle in her eye that made my knees weak. And the way she lifted her chin and tilted her head the tiniest bit, like she was getting ready, dear *God*. Suddenly my heart was pounding and my breath was frozen in my lungs and the smell of her perfume—*apple juice and flowers*—was jamming up my senses, making it impossible to breathe normally.

Because there she stood, in the dark beside my car, looking up at me *exactly* the way I'd always wanted her to.

Lay it on me, Zeus.

I forgot all about Benji when I watched my fingers slide into her hair as if they worked independently from my brain. I held her in place, the curls soft against my hands, and as I lowered my mouth, one word was transmitted through to every corner of my mind like a chant.

Dani's Dani's Dani's Dani's

The blond hair wrapped around my knuckles, the unsteady breath that hovered in a cloud between us, the long eyelashes fluttering closed—the reality that they all belonged to *her* hit me like a blow, like a punch that knocked me all the way down.

This was Dani, holy shit.

I felt her lips underneath mine—*sweet cherry lip gloss, oh God*—and it was like being struck by lightning. I felt a jolt in every nerve ending in my body when she opened for me, and I was electrified when her fingers fisted in the front of my coat and her tongue—

"What the *fuck* is going on out here?"

Dani jumped away from me, and I felt like I was going to die when I opened my eyes and saw Mick Fucking Boche standing on the porch, glaring at me.

Oh shit.

He was wearing all black, like an angel of death, and his big arm was extended, his finger pointed directly at me. "Get your ass inside. Now."

Shit, shit, shit.

Dani turned and started for the porch, but Mick said, "I mean you, Barczewski!"

Fuck, fuck, fuck.

"Yes, sir," I said, my heart beating so fast that it was possible I was going to faint from the fear like a little old lady. I followed Dani up the path to the porch and into her grandpa's house, where I was surely about to be destroyed.

But as I went inside, I realized that the bright side of my death was that Benji was being eaten alive by jealousy at that very moment. He'd always been into Dani, so it was just *chef's kiss* that he'd had a front-row seat to me winning.

Take that, jackass.

He may have been too jealous to give me props, but having witnessed Mick Boche catching me with his granddaughter and hollering at me to come into his house?

Ben was probably already running inside to share the info.

Dani said, "It's not Alec's—"

"I don't wanna hear it," Mick bellowed, cutting her off. "You need to go upstairs so I can talk to him."

"What?" she gasped in disbelief.

He pointed toward the staircase that led upstairs. "You heard what I said—go."

"You can't—"

"I can and I will—and I know what you're thinking, Danigirl. You're thinking I'm not your dad and I can't do this. But you're wrong—I *can* do this. I'm the one who's here, I'm the one who's around, and I'm the one who gives a shit. Go upstairs and I'll talk to you later."

She blinked fast, like she couldn't believe what he was saying, and then she mouthed the word *sorry* to me before she turned and went up the staircase.

Traitor.

"Sit down," he barked, gesturing toward the kitchen table.

I obediently dropped into a chair, grateful for the opportunity to sit because my legs felt like they might give out and the odds were good he wasn't going to punch me in the face if I was sitting at his kitchen table, right?

"From what I know, you're not a bad kid." Mick crossed his arms over his chest and glared down at me. "But did you seriously think you could date Dani for a minute and then be all over her in my own fucking driveway? Are you kidding me right now?"

"I—"

"Were you trying to prove some kind of point, like you're a tough guy who's not afraid to disrespect Boche's granddaughter right in his own goddamn yard?"

"Oh my God, no," I said. "And we'd barely even—"

"Really." He didn't believe me. "You weren't remotely aware of the fact that I might look out a window?"

"*No,*" I insisted, shaking my head.

"Really."

"*No,*" I said, even louder. "Respectfully, I wasn't thinking of you at all. I kissed Dani because I really like her and then I forgot about everything, especially where I was. This had *nothing* to do with you."

"So Dani was the only one you were thinking of when you decided to kiss her."

Is it hot in here? I tugged at the scarf around my neck and said, "*Yes.* I mean, I was kind of hoping Worthington saw because I hate that guy, but yeah—it was all about Dani."

"I hate that little shit too. Did you know he has a Maserati?"

What is happening right now?

"Yeah," I said, shaking my head. "He had a Cayenne last year but drove it into a light pole."

"Figures," Mick said in disgust. "Fuckin' idiot."

"Right?" I agreed.

"Listen—I'm going to be honest with you," he said, tilting his head and looking at me like I was a bug. "I don't like you dating her."

"You don't." I didn't know why, but that mattered to me. Even though it was a fake relationship, there was something about knowing someone you respected thought you were a piece of shit that felt . . . well, really shitty.

"No, I don't. Not at all. Dani and her mom have spent the past seventeen years with a manipulative little pecker. I look at her and I don't even see a spark of the kid I used to know."

I don't know what I'd expected, but it wasn't *this*. Mick was looking out the window, sounding more like he was talking to himself than me as he said, "Every once in a while she gives me sass and I wanna fucking cheer because it's so good to see, but I know she doesn't want that. And she shouldn't want that, because—well, it doesn't matter, but she's right to be mad at me, but my point is that I want her to figure out who she is and find her voice without some guy in her way."

"I—I don't want to be in her way," I said, rolling my eyes at myself when my voice cracked like I was a nervous middle schooler. "I want the same thing you do, I promise. And I hate the colonel too."

"You do?" Mick said, looking surprised.

"God, yes, but it doesn't matter because Dani still worships him," I

said, realizing the second the words left my mouth that that was probably an overshare.

Dani would probably be super pissed if she overheard me saying that.

"I know," he said with a sigh. "She won't hear a single critical word
about him, but he's her dad, so I have to respect that."

"Even after he called her the other night and made her so upset that I
found her crying in the locker room, she still defended him."

"Did she say what he did? To make her cry?"

I shook my head. "No, but I didn't really have a chance to talk to
her."

He grunted and went back to looking at me like he was trying to figure out where he was going to bury my body after he killed me.

So I said, "Mr. Boche, I don't want to be on your bad side. I just
really like your granddaughter, that's all."

"Well, you're allowed to like her," he said, crossing his arms. "Just
knock off the handsy shit and let her breathe."

"Okay," I said, nodding, because odds were good there wasn't going
to be any more handsy shit regardless. I still wasn't sure why she'd agreed
to let me kiss her in the first place, but I was positive that after this, I
wasn't going to get the chance to finish what we'd barely started.

"By the way, what are you doing about that shoulder?" he asked.

"*What?*" I said it a little too loudly, but he was looking at me like he
knew everything, and there was no way that he could.

"I see the way you drop it when you're tired, the way you rub it sometimes when you're talking. Your shoulder's fucked up, isn't it?"

His words made my blood run cold, because what the fuck was that?
I drop my shoulder when I'm tired?

215

Was this something people other than Mick might've noticed? Shit, had scouts noticed?

Shit, shit, shit. I couldn't let anyone think I was injured.

"No," I said, shaking my head and making a face like he was nuts. "Bruised as hell from when I got checked last week, but I'm—"

"Okay, okay," he interrupted, shaking his head. "Spare me the bullshit—it's your body, not mine. How are you feeling about the game tomorrow?"

I shrugged because this was all over the place and also, I never knew how to answer that question. I always felt like we were going to win, even when we lost.

"We're going to win," I said.

"Yeah, probably," he agreed, then pointed his thumb at the door. "Go home now."

I nearly leapt out of the chair because I was so damn happy to be leaving without being skinned first. If I could've sprinted to the door and out to my car, I would've.

But when I got to the door, I stopped and looked back, because I felt like I had to say something. "Mr. Boche?"

"Mick," he corrected.

Mick?

I said, "Thanks, uh, thanks for not killing me."

"No problem," he said, and I swear to God he sort of smiled. "If you accidentally tap the Maserati next door with that piece of shit you drive, by the way, I didn't see a damn thing."

"Noted," I said, and then I left, getting the hell out of Dodge.

When I finally looked at my phone after getting home, I had multiple texts from Dani.

Dani: Are you okay?

Dani: I'm so sorry.

Dani: What did he say?

Dani: Please send me proof of life.

I took a selfie, then sent: I'm fine and he was actually pretty cool. He just wanted to make sure I wasn't being a dick to you.

I thought about what he'd said about her. It was interesting, the way she always assumed he was an old jerk when in all actuality, it seemed like he'd missed her and was worried about her.

Like he was trying to help her.

I texted: This might sound crazy, but I think he's trying to fix things with you.

Dani: How is he doing that exactly? By grunting a lot in my presence?

I could see how she could miss it. The old guy was shit at communicating. But as much as I wanted to help Mick out a bit, I needed to cover the kiss *immediately*.

I texted: So . . . subject change.

Dani: Yes . . . ?

Me: About that other thing that happened in your driveway.

Dani: What other thing?

Okay, so she clearly didn't want to discuss it. And yet all I could do was think about it.

Me: Fair enough. See you tomorrow.

She didn't respond, but just as I plugged my phone into the charger and switched off the lamp, my phone buzzed.

Dani: My grandpa just came into my room and told me to tell

LYNN PAINTER

you to ice the shoulder before you go to bed, even if you're too tired.

I stared at the message in disbelief. I wasn't sure why it made my throat feel a little tight, and I had no fucking idea why it made me feel a thousand times more exhausted.

I texted: Tell him thanks.

And then I went downstairs and got some ice.

CHAPTER TWENTY-FIVE
Dani

Game day was a series of shocking events.

For starters, Alec looked ridiculous when he picked me up for school. I opened the kitchen door and almost dropped dead from a heart attack. I opened my mouth but the only words that came out were "Where are your contacts?"

"Too tired to put them in," he said, looking confused. "Why?"

What does "why" mean again?

I knew that the team dressed up for *some* game days, but they hadn't for the last one. He'd worn joggers and a hoodie, for God's sake, so I wasn't prepared for *this*.

I hadn't pictured him dressing up so . . . *well*.

Alec was wearing perfectly tailored black pants that somehow showed off how muscular his thighs were (or maybe that was just my foggy brain still shocked by the change in him). He had on a nice belt that matched his *very* stylish dress shoes, and the gray cashmere sweater he wore clung to his pectorals and amplified just how hard and wide his chest was.

And he was wearing glasses—dear *Lord* he looked good in those tortoiseshell frames. I remembered him getting contacts in sixth grade, but apparently he still wore glasses from time to time.

It wasn't an exaggeration—it really wasn't—to say he looked like he could be in a photo shoot for hot young businessmen, and it kind of freaked me out.

I wasn't *comfortable* with how attractive he was, and I could tell he'd noticed me looking.

Dammit.

So I said, "Your mom has the *best* taste."

"What?"

"I like your outfit," I said with a heavy dose of teasing condescension. "It looks like Mommy got you really nice church clothes."

His mouth slid into an arrogant smirk and he shook his head. "I know I look good; don't be a little shit."

"So humble," I muttered, going around his big body because I couldn't look at him for another second. My cheeks were hot and I felt unaccountably nervous, and the feeling didn't get any better when I nearly broke off the car door handle.

I yanked, but it was still locked.

"Can you please unlock the door?" I asked with a sigh, glancing at him over my shoulder.

Only he was *right there*, much closer than I'd thought. My eyes met his, and a thousand images of him kissing me in that very driveway slammed into me.

It might've only lasted for mere seconds, but God, I could still *feel* his big hands tangled in my hair and see the intensity in his dark eyes as he'd lowered his face.

As his mouth had landed on mine.

He cleared his throat.

Gah!

I jumped a little and said, "God, it's freezing out here."

"Yeah, let's go," he said, unlocking the door and quickly walking over to the driver's side.

I could *feel* the awkwardness between us.

Like every moment together was edged with tension.

Inflated.

And I had no idea what to do with it.

Looking to talk about anything not filled with weirdness, I asked, "Are you excited about the game tonight?"

"Are you mocking me?" he asked as he started the car.

"No, I mean it," I said, watching out the window as he backed out of the driveway and started driving. He was so serious about hockey that it *had* to stress him out. "How do you feel on game day? Are you excited or nervous? Listening to pump-up music in your headphones while playing air guitar in the locker room—that sort of thing?"

He was rarely serious with me; he was either the obnoxious jock boy or a flicker of silly little Alec, so I was surprised when he swallowed hard and his jaw clenched. There was *something* in his dark eyes when he said, "I think I'm more stressed out when it's *not* game day."

"What? Really?"

"I can control my game, so I can't wait for that," he said. "Everything else is out of my hands, but when I get out there, it's all up to me, so I'm just counting down the hours."

He looked uncomfortable, like he was thinking unhappy thoughts, and I realized it was probably because I was sounding too interested.

I couldn't have him thinking I was a hockey groupie or something, so I said, "This morning my mom told me she's going to the game tonight, and when I asked her why, thinking she felt like she had to go just because I'm sitting on the bench filming, do you know what she said?"

"I'm sure it was brilliant," he murmured, which made me roll my eyes because he'd always adored my mom.

"She said that she's going to the hockey game to support the team. That she plans on going to *every* hockey game for the rest of this season," I said, shaking my head. "That she plans on going to the Cro before the game tonight because apparently the parents all go there beforehand."

That made his mouth turn up into a grin. "Why do you seem annoyed by this? This is what all the hockey parents do every game day."

"But she's not a hockey parent," I said. "Her daughter is a manager just to get the extra-credit points."

"Have you ever considered that maybe it doesn't actually have to do with you?" he asked.

I flipped him off.

"No, seriously," he said, giving me a little head shake. "It's a Southview thing. Like, everybody here goes to the hockey games—they just do. And since your mom grew up here, I'm sure she probably spent her whole life going to them."

"I suppose," I said, wondering why I hadn't thought of that.

All of *this* was what she'd grown up around; I just couldn't imagine.

The Doug felt very different on game night.

The place was electric, packed to the rafters, with music playing, a rowdy student section, and adults everywhere dressed in maroon and white.

Alec was right—it was a community thing.

I set up the camera, and as I waited for everything to start, I was a little shocked by the number of familiar faces I already knew. We'd *just* moved there, so it was wild that I recognized anyone at all.

But I could see all the guys who'd been at Alec's house the night we got to Southview, sitting with people I assumed were their wives and children. And all the adults who'd been at Vinny's the night before were sitting together—the hockey parents—and that group looked just as rowdy as the student section.

I could see my mom, sitting beside Sarah, Big John, and the twins (who were wearing adorable little number-seven hockey jerseys), and she looked like she was one of them, like she'd always been a part of this.

I forced my eyes in the other direction, not sure how I felt about that.

Because it looked right for her, if I was being honest, like this was where she was *supposed* to be, but that felt disloyal to my dad, the one who'd taken her away from all this.

My dad, who'd texted me twice since our call, and I'd yet to respond.

Dad: We still need to have that conversation—please text me your availability, kiddo.

Dad: I'd appreciate a response. I AM the one paying for your phone, Daniella.

I knew I needed to respond, but every time I tried, I ended up writing multiple paragraphs that I ultimately deleted because I knew he'd find them too emotional.

And I was too scared to call him.

Man, I'm losing it.

Thankfully, when the puck dropped, I had no choice but to snap out of my own head.

Because the game was unreal. It was a lightning-fast back-and-forth that had me on the edge of my seat, my eyes struggling to keep up with the speed of that little black puck.

And Alec was a sight to behold.

If he was intense at practice, he was *sublime* in a game. He was insanely physical with the other team, slamming into players as he got his stick in there and fought for the puck like his life depended on it. He got sent to the penalty box *twice*, although the crowd definitely thought the second time was unwarranted.

My heart was in my throat, and I felt a little emotional—in a good way—while watching him kick ass on the ice.

I was proud of my little friend Alec, who was a certified hockey god.

Southview won by two, and Alec had two assists—in addition to a goal that made me scream so loud my throat hurt.

I'd never had so much fun watching a sporting event in my entire life.

Who was I turning into?

After the game, I found my mom near the locker room with Sarah, Big John, the twins, and a couple of John's friends.

"What'd you think of your first game, kid?" Big John asked, and I found it adorable how huge his smile was. My entire life he'd always reminded me of a happy Santa, and this was no exception. "That was one hell of a match."

"I kind of loved it," I admitted. "And Alec was amazing. It's tough to reconcile the kid who used to take three naps a day with this badass hockey player."

"One day he was wasting hours of his life playing video games," Sarah said, her arms full of the big blanket she was holding, "and the next he wanted to spend every waking moment on the ice."

"So are you his lucky charm?"

A tiny woman with cute brown eyes and curly black hair—and the most adorable northern accent—asked the question, and she was giving me a sweet smile.

I looked at the guy next to her and remembered them—*Ellen and Gary*. Big John's parents, Alec's grandparents.

"We've been talking about how this season he's playing better than he ever has," she said. "So we're wondering if maybe that's because of you."

Wow—news traveled fast. I was pretty sure Grandma Ellen's time-line was off, but it tipped in our favor, so I'd take it.

I looked at Sarah and John and my mom and they were *all* watching me with cheesy smiles.

"I think he's just really good at hockey," I said, shrugging, because I didn't know what else to do.

"Yeah, there is that," my mom said, throwing me a wink.

Players started coming out of the locker room, and I couldn't help but think how sweet it was the way everyone's parents were waiting around to say "good job."

There were also a couple of news reporters, standing on the edges of the crowd, and they definitely started filming when Alec walked out.

But dear *God*, my heart flipped all the way over when he exited the locker room, looking somehow better in his dress clothes postgame—with shower-dampened hair—than he had before. His gaze landed on me, and his mouth slid into a smile that was dangerously swoony.

Oh no.

What is happening to me?

He didn't glance at anyone else as he headed straight in my direction, dark brown eyes all over my face.

Pull it together, Collins!

"Want me to take your stuff?" John asked, his voice bringing me back from the Alec-only universe I'd drifted away to.

"Nah, I'm going to go home and change before heading out," Alec said.

Everyone started talking hockey then, gushing about how great Alec had played while also trash-talking the referees, and I just watched the show.

I'd always rolled my judgmental eyes about the jocks at every school I attended, walking around with their chests all puffed up because they knew how to throw a ball really far.

But I'd never thought about their parents.

Or their uncles.

Or their neighbors.

I looked around, and little groupings were all over the place, people bunched around *their* respective hockey player. Moms dressed from head to toe in Southview gear, dads laughing with their buddies—it was . . . not at all how I thought it would be.

Was this a hockey thing or a Southview thing?

"You goin' to Richie's?" Big John asked.

"Yeah," Alec said before those deep brown eyes found mine. "You should come to Richie's, Collins. I'm sure Cassie'll be there."

Everyone had been so welcoming and Cassie was great, but why did I suddenly feel like maybe I didn't belong? *Why do I feel nauseous?*

"I think I'm just going to head back with you," I said to my mom. "Maybe next time."

"Well we're stopping at the PNA on the way home," she said, obviously trying to nudge me to find another ride, "so it might be a while."

"What's a PNA?"

"The Polish Lodge," Mom said.

The Polish Lodge. First the Croatian Hall, now the Polish Lodge.

I'm pretty sure we're of Irish and German descent, Mom.

But I didn't ask any more questions as I piled into a truck with a bunch of adults, watching Alec leave, part of me wanting to go with him to wherever he was going but scared I'd regret it if I did.

Instead I was left regretting my current choice minutes later as I followed Big John toward a stucco-looking house.

What the . . . ?

I had doubts, but then my mom grabbed my arm and said, "Prepare to be wowed."

We followed Big John through a side door and went down the stairs, and . . . well, it was like a dive bar.

In a basement.

There was a bar with beer taps and TVs on the wall, a pool table, and darts, but also—it was a basement.

A basement *packed* full of people.

At least it's warm, I thought, walking with my mom as Sarah and Big John led us to a table and started taking off their coats.

"Am I allowed to be here?" I asked. "As a minor?"

"As long as you're not drinking or serving," John said. "Now tell Sarah what you want to drink so I can tell you all about this place."

"Must you?" I teased.

"You're a Southview girl now, so yes—I must," he teased back.

I am not a Southview girl, I thought. *I am a nowhere girl.*

But a tiny part of me *wished* I were a Southview girl.

John leaned a little closer so I could hear him over the noise, and launched into a history lesson as if we weren't in *just* a bar. He told me all about how in the early 1900s, a large Polish immigrant population arrived in town, drawn to jobs in big meatpacking plants. They built the social hall as a place to get together for drinks after a hard week, and to have things like weddings and funerals.

"The Cro's got a similar history," he said, sounding like all this was personally important to him, and I wondered if Alec felt the same way.

I mean, he *did* seem to read history books for fun.

"But for the Croatian immigrants, yes?"

He grinned. "You got it, kid."

The funny thing was that Big John's little story made me look at the dive bar a little differently. It'd been a long time since 1911, and I was pretty sure there were no more meatpacking plants in Southview.

Which meant that all these people at the PNA had kept the place alive by choice.

In a metropolis full of trendy bars and restaurants, this community chose to celebrate their win at the tiny historic bar in the middle of their neighborhood.

Why do I find that charming as hell?

"Well, hi, Dani," I heard, and when I turned around, it was Jessie Osman, the coach's wife, whom I'd met at the team dinner but hadn't really talked to.

And standing beside her, but talking to someone at the moment, was Coach Oz himself.

I immediately felt panicked, because I'd actively avoided eye contact with the man after he'd seen me groping his half-naked defenseman.

"Hi," I said, clearing my throat.

"How's it going?" she asked. "Getting all settled at Southview?"

"Yes," I said, though it was kind of a yell because the place was so crowded and noisy.

"Alec played great," she said, crossing her arms over her chest and leaning closer. "Where is he?"

Shit. Had he said he was going to Richie's, or to Kyle's? I seriously couldn't remember, but his actual girlfriend would know, right? "Um, he's hanging out with some of his teammates."

"Where's Zeus?" the coach yelled to me.

He obviously hadn't heard my answer to his wife's question, and I was even more scared to answer *him* than I was to answer her. I didn't know who knew what about anything, but since our act was *for* the audience of hockey people, I didn't want to mess up.

"Richie's," his wife said to him, apparently more in the know than me about which teammates were having people over postgame.

"Ah," he said, nodding.

"So I'm curious," she said, narrowing her eyes and smiling. "I heard that you two are old family friends, but how did that turn into dating?"

"Um." I cleared my throat again, wishing I had any idea what details Alec had given his coach about our fake relationship.

"Yeah, I'd actually really love to hear this," Big John said with a huge grin, his mischievous eyes looking a lot like Alec's as he crossed his arms and waited for my response. "Because one day you hadn't even seen each other yet, and the next you're FaceTiming at all hours of the night."

"Collins!"

I looked toward the door as Alec and his friends walked in.

Thank God.

He was grinning as he cut through the people, laughing at something some old guy in an I'M MORE SOUTHVIEW THAN YOU T-shirt said as he passed, and as I watched him work his way in our direction, it occurred to me that he looked like he *belonged* in that basement bar.

Like he was part of it, like he was somehow related to every one of those people who chose to spend their Friday night together in a basement where a mural of Poland was painted on the cement-block wall.

And I was jealous.

I was always jealous, at a base level, of people who'd lived in the same place their entire lives and didn't have to move every few years, but this was different.

Because I'd lived most of *my* life in an isolated family of three.

I *liked* my little trio (and was struggling at the moment to deal with its dissolution), but seeing Alec move about in this community, where it felt like every adult was his fun uncle, teasing him like they'd always been in his life and genuinely cared about his well-being, made me wish I knew what that felt like.

"Hey," he said when he reached my side, giving me a questioning grin, like he was wondering what I could possibly be saying to his coach.

"Hey, yourself," I replied, snaking my arms around his right bicep and giving him what I hoped looked like a girlfriendy grin. "Your timing is perfect, because Mrs. Oz was just asking me how we went from old childhood friends to dating."

"Yeah?" He grinned down at me like he liked this, though I wasn't sure which *this* he might like, to be honest.

"Yeah," I said. "And I want to hear your version."

"I bet you do," he said, and then he winked. "But the best things in life should be kept secret."

I wanted to roll my eyes *so* badly as all the adults laughed at him, but I didn't.

And then he kissed the top of my head.

I gasped because *what the hell*, but thankfully the room was so loud that no one heard it.

Alec's eyes shot to mine and were unreadable as he watched me, and I cleared my throat and tried to look calm.

But I was shaken up by the fact that his stupid little kiss, all part of the act, had felt natural.

Like it was something he'd done before.

Which he hadn't, right?

God, I'm losing it!

"I wonder if you still suck at darts," I said abruptly, desperately needing to untangle myself from him and get a little breathing space.

"You little shits used to fill my wall with holes when you played with my metal-tipped darts," Big John said with a laugh.

"I wonder if you're still a sore loser," Alec replied, the cautiousness in his gaze disappearing. "Come on."

He grabbed my hand and led me over to the dartboards, and when we stopped, he turned and asked, "Do you actually want to play darts, or were you looking for a rescue?"

"Oh my God, Alec, I was freaking out," I said, letting out my breath. "When his wife started asking me to tell the story of us and I had no idea what you'd actually already said, I was convinced I was going to blow the whole thing."

"Well then, I'm glad I showed up just in time," he said.

"Yeah, why are you here?"

"Richie's brother kicked us out."

"Oh," I said.

"Do you want to play?" He gestured toward the dartboards.

"I'm in," Richie said, suddenly beside us.

"Me too," said Cassie, popping up next to him.

"Yeah, same," Kyle said, and then it was set.

Apparently we were all going to play darts.

I took off my jacket and put it on the back of a chair, feeling slightly unsettled by how social this suddenly felt. I'd purposely left with my mom to avoid this very scenario, for God's sake.

But once we started playing, it was surprisingly fun.

Ridiculously fun.

Alec's friends seemed to be addicted to gambling, because they couldn't play a single game without wagering something. At first it was a couple of bucks, plus they kept buying tickets for a meat raffle (a bizarre fundraiser that's apparently common in Minnesota in which people try to win a package of meat) when the board came around, but then they all agreed that they didn't have any more money to throw away.

So they started betting absurd things.

Loser of the next game has to take a sip out of someone's drink without them noticing.

Loser of the next game has to do a cartwheel.

Loser of the next game has to freestyle dance for two minutes without stopping.

Alec lost that one just as my grandpa walked in.

And yes—he stared at Alec like he was a moron.

I couldn't stop cackling as Alec continued dancing, his cheeks red, and my grandpa continued scowling at him.

"I officially request that someone kill me," he said when he walked back over to the table where I was sitting with his friends, "because my soul has already left my body."

"I cannot believe you just danced for Mick Fucking Boche," Richie said.

"Yeah, I definitely want him to forget he ever saw that," Alec said, shaking his head.

My phone lit up from where it was sitting in the center of the table, and every single person in our group looked at it as the words BEN WORTHINGTON showed up on the screen.

"You're getting a text from Worthington?" Vinny said, looking at me like I'd just gotten a text from Ted Bundy.

"What the hell is that about?" Kyle said, looking at Alec.

"No—he's my next-door neighbor," I said defensively. "Sometimes. I mean, he lives with his mom most of the time—"

"That doesn't explain why he's *texting* you," Vinny said.

"It really doesn't," Alec said, looking . . . so serious all of a sudden.

"Wait—how do *you guys* even know him?" I asked Vinny. "He goes to school at—"

"St. John's. Yeah, he's a fucking Cadet, we know," Richie said.

"Everyone hates Ben," Cassie said, as if that explained everything.

"Feel free to read the message," Alec said to me, his face very unreadable (but definitely not happy). "Go ahead."

The entire group was watching me like they suspected me of . . . *something*. "You guys, my mom made me put his number in my contacts, but I don't ever text with Benji—"

"You should read it," Cassie said, "so it doesn't drive these guys nuts. They *really* hate Ben. We all do, after what he did."

"What'd he do?" I asked.

"Nothing," Alec said. "It doesn't matter."

I could tell it absolutely *did* matter, but I could also tell no one was going to share because Alec had told them not to. I grabbed my phone and held it out to Cassie. "You can read it. I honestly barely know the guy."

She gave me a look that said *good move* before taking my phone and reading his text aloud. "'FYI big party in Mendota Heights tonight. I'll drop the address if you and your friends are looking for something to do.'"

"Gross," Kyle said.

"Can I respond?" Richie asked with a grin. "Pretty please?"

"I'm on it," Cassie said, reading out loud as she texted: "'No thanks, too busy celebrating with our hockey boys.' And . . . send."

And that was it. The group went back to their silly games instead of looking at me like I was colluding with Satan.

"Okay, all or nothing," Cassie said. "Loser of this last one is at the mercy of the winner of this game."

Everyone let out a collective "oooh," as if this was a *very* big deal.

All I knew was that I did *not* want to be the loser.

And I wasn't.

But my fake boyfriend was not so lucky.

He was the loser, and Richie the Obnoxious was the winner.

"Zeus, Zeus, Zeus," Richie said, grinning as he looked at Alec.

I giggled.

Which made Richie look at *me*.

His mischievous grin kicked up a little higher as he looked back and forth between the two of us, and a niggling of unease settled into the pit of my stomach.

"I dare you to kiss her for thirty seconds," he said to Alec, pointing at me. "Right here, right now."

"What?" I said, or kind of squealed, actually.

No. No. No. No. No. NO.

"How is that a punishment?" Alec said casually, as if he really *were* my boyfriend and didn't understand the stupid request. "I actually *like* kissing her, and though I appreciate you thinking of me, I don't understand why you'd choose this as my punishment."

He was so cool that I almost believed his act.

But gahhhhhhh what the hell what the hell??

I'd barely recovered from the driveway kiss, and that had only lasted for a heartbeat.

I wasn't sure my heart could *take* a real kiss.

Also, I was *not* about PDA.

No, thank you.

Richie said, "I dare you to kiss her right here—"

"Yes, I got that part," Alec interrupted.

"—where you are directly in a certain someone's line of sight."

The entire group turned their heads in unison and saw my grandpa sitting at the table just behind ours, his chair directly facing us.

"Where Mick Boche can see you," Richie said, smiling like he was supremely proud of himself.

"No way," Alec said definitively, looking offended by the suggestion. "I don't have a death wish."

"But you lost," Richie said. "Rules are rules."

"I don't care, I'm not doing it," Alec insisted, which I understood, but it also made me feel a little rejected for no intelligent reason whatsoever.

"Come on, you wimp," Kyle said quietly. "What do you think is going to happen—he's going to punch you in the face? You played your ass off tonight, and we need you for the postseason. He won't do dick."

"So why do you want me to do it, then, Kyle?" Alec asked. "Why do *you* care?"

I expected Kyle to say *to show you have big balls* or something stupidly macho, but he said with the utmost sincerity, "Because you've never reneged on a game challenge before. Can't start now. Not sure why you're even questioning it, to be honest."

Kyle's eyebrow rose, and Alec's mouth closed as if what Kyle said was worthy of consideration.

"Zeus doesn't back out on anything. Hasn't *ever*. Period. Aren't you worried about messing up the team's mojo?" Richie pressed on.

As if that reaction weren't weird enough, the rest of the group all nodded as if this was something important that needed to be factored in.

And they collectively said, "Ooh."

"Wait. What does that mean?" I asked.

"Zeus here, our *captain*, hasn't reneged on a game challenge the entire time we've been undefeated," Kyle explained. "He can't start now when we're looking at the tournament. When we have a legitimate shot at finally going all the way."

"It's true," Cassie added. "We've made the state tournament more than any other team in the state. For *years*. And now the odds are in our favor."

Why is it suddenly getting so heavy in here? I looked at the group around me—their faces were as serious as ever.

"You aren't kidding, are you?" I said, glancing back and forth between Alec, who wouldn't meet my eyes, and his friends, who were staring me down as if my decision was of the utmost importance.

"She doesn't have to do it," Alec said to his friends, but he wasn't smiling. He looked . . . *uncomfortable* as he threw me a lifeline. "Seriously."

I wanted to laugh, because it was ridiculous the way they were all behaving as if this were a logical concern. But I couldn't, because Alec's face was all tension as he watched me, and also my stomach was filling with raucous butterflies at the thought of what the punishment entailed.

Kissing Alec.

For thirty seconds.

Here and now.

I must've waited too long to answer, because he glanced at me, swallowed, then said, "We're not doing it."

My mind was racing, my heart beating fast. Alec's eyes were pleading, and my whole face felt like it was on fire. And before my brain could stop my lips from moving, I heard the words "I think we have to" escape from my mouth.

Ohhhhh, holy shit, we were doing it.

CHAPTER TWENTY-SIX
Alec

Holy *shit*.

If there was one thing I knew, it was Dani Collins's facial expressions.

Or at least I used to.

And as she looked up at me with her eyebrows raised, I recognized the challenge. She was daring me, wondering what I was waiting for.

Shit, shit, shit.

It felt like my head was spinning, because how was this happening? I still hadn't been able to brain-scrub away last night's driveway situation, the way her mouth felt underneath mine and the way she'd grabbed my jacket, yet now—here we were again?

I swallowed and tried to be cool.

"Fine," I said, glancing at Richie, "but not here."

"What? That's part of the challenge," he said, sounding outraged. "The challenge is for you to be within Mick's line of sight."

"I get that," I said. "But I want her to have a little cover. You might be a weirdo voyeur who wants her grandpa to see that we're kissing, but we don't need everyone in the PNA to watch, do we? This way you're getting what you want and I'm terrified that Mick is going to murder me, but Dani doesn't pay the price."

"Okay, I'll allow it," Kyle said, as if he were on the governing body of stupid dares.

I grabbed Dani's hand again, this time pulling her away from my friends and over to the back wall. Technically we were probably more in Mick's direct line of sight than before, but I was able to angle us so my body was kind of a shield.

"Are you cornering me, Zeus?" she asked in a low voice that made my body go hot.

Her eyes were narrowed in a dare, her pretty mouth kicked up at the edges, but her voice was a little breathy, like she felt unsteady about this.

Which made me feel better, because I was ready to pass the fuck out. I could see the freckles on her cheekbones as she looked up at me, and it was all too close yet not close enough.

"Just trying to block you," I said a little too harshly, not sure why my voice was coming out all scratchy or why the lyrics to "No One's Ever Kissed You" were suddenly pinging around on full blast in my mind.

"Listen, um." I cleared my throat, trying to give her one last chance to tap out. All I wanted was to kiss her—suddenly it felt like I *needed* to kiss her more than I needed to do anything else—but some part of my brain needed her to know it was her choice.

"It's okay if you don't want to—"

"I swear to God, I'm going to hurt you," she said through a fake smile, raising her hands to my shoulders as she darted a glance behind me. "Let's just get this over with, okay?"

"Get this over with"?

Why did that make me want to kiss her more?

My heart was pounding hard in my chest, and I wanted to shout for the entire place to shut the hell up so I could think.

"Just forget it's me and *go* already," she said through gritted teeth.

As if I could ever forget that, I thought.

240

Dani hissing to "*go* already" was so on-brand for the girl I used to know.

And her "get this over with"?

Yeah, fuck that. Her words fired me up, filling me with the urge to make sure what was about to happen was something she'd never want to get over.

Like she'd done to me the first time it happened.

In our spot, before everything went to hell.

I took her face in my hands and very nearly growled, "Let's do this, then."

I lowered my mouth, and I don't know what I expected, but it wasn't for her to *immediately* pull me closer. The noise, the people—it disappeared into a blur of white noise as I leaned into her, grateful for the solid wall against her back that pressed us together.

God, Dani, I thought as her body cushioned mine, as my fingers slid over her soft neck so my thumbs could stroke along that delicate jawline.

God. Dani.

What is it about her? I wondered as the sweetness of her cherry-flavored mouth became my whole world. Kissing her felt like razor-sharp relief, like we'd been denied a thousand fucking perfect kisses in our lifetime and were finally allowed to feast. I dove in, starved, and it was like I had some kind of sensory-deprivation experience the minute our lips touched, where everything else ceased to exist and the tiniest of her details were so vivid I felt them excruciatingly.

The way her fingertips flexed against my shoulders, the way her teeth nipped at my bottom lip, the way her curls rested on my hands, dear *Jesus.*

Never getting over this, I thought as I took it deeper, obsessed with the way she kissed me back like she was trying to outkiss me. *You won't win this one, Collins* was the thought that whispered through me as I dragged my teeth over slick cherries before angling my head and—

"Enough," I heard as I felt myself being jerked backward by my shirt.

I came around, ready to level whoever was interrupting, but Mick stood there, glowering at me as he let go of my shirt so hard I stumbled.

He kind of threw me.

Oh shit.

Like being awakened by a bucket of cold water to the face.

A bucket of cold water that was going to *murder* me.

"God, Mick, I—"

"Don't," he said, raising his hand—a signal for me to stop talking, which I may or may not have thought was him about to hit me.

"I need a beer," he growled, and walked away, the crowd parting in front of him as he headed for the bar.

Oh God, oh God.

I turned back to Dani as my heart rate started to slow, and I wished I knew what she was thinking. She looked disoriented as her brown eyes moved over my face, like she was having a *lot* of thoughts.

Shit, shit, shit. Something about the way she was watching me made me nervous.

"Come on," I said, grabbing her hand. "Do you want to get some air?"

She bit down on her lower lip—*oh honey, I was only getting started*—and nodded.

"Let's go." I linked my fingers between hers and headed for the

242

stairs, ignoring my laughing friends (who'd already moved on to the next dare), her grandpa's glare from the bar, and the entire side of the room where I knew our parents were surely watching us.

We went up the steps without speaking, and when I let go of her hand and pushed open the door, it felt like we were stepping out into another world.

The moon was high and full, the snow a thick blanket that insulated us from the sounds of the world. It was cold and quiet, and even though it was almost midnight, the moon's brightness allowed me to see the wrinkle of confusion between her eyebrows.

"What's up?" she said quietly, and somehow I just knew. It felt like she was forcing calmness in her eyes as she looked up at me like it was no big deal, but I watched her swallow, and I knew she was as freaked out as I was.

Because even though we kept getting interrupted, those seconds where our lips connected felt fucking insane.

Huge.

"I just want to make sure we're good," I said. "I got a little carried away with the whole . . . everything, and—"

"No, I got carried away too," she said, raising a finger and mindlessly touching her bottom lip—*mine*—like she was thinking about the kiss. She looked distracted when she said, "We're okay."

Thank God, I thought. *Thank God we're okay and thank God she looks as unsettled as I feel.*

"I mean, neither one of us has ever been able to turn down a dare," she said, shrugging. "So why would a kiss dare be any exception?"

Wait.

Dani looked up at me with a smirk that made me think maybe it *was* just me who was freaking out. She looked . . . not unsettled, actually.

She looked completely settled.

"Well, I'm glad we're on the same page," I said, unable to look at her face without wanting to lean in and try again.

Dammit.

"Same," she said, nodding and tucking her hair behind her ears. "We didn't mess with the mojo and all is well."

Apple juice and flowers. "Yeah, thanks for that."

"We should go back inside before we freeze, don't you think?" she said with a breezy smile. "I mean, I'm sure *you* would never, because you're Minnesotan . . ."

"Yeah, of course, never—feels like summer to me," I said, following as she started walking back toward the building, irrationally disappointed that she was unfazed by the kiss.

I mean, it was good. It meant things were fine with us.

But . . . *fuck.*

My hands were literally shaking and I didn't know what to even do with that. I'd kissed a fair number of people since Dani's and my first time in the shed, right? I knew what I was doing now and I was *good* at it.

So the shaking hands didn't make a damn bit of sense.

Right? Wrong.

No. Everything was fine.

Except . . . wait.

Why the fuck is Benji texting you??

CHAPTER TWENTY-SEVEN

Dani

What the hell what the hell?

I paced around my bedroom, all keyed up and unable to relax because there were multiple problems with this pretend-dating situation already.

Like the fact that we'd already kissed twice.

Both kisses fit into the scheme, because they were both for the optics of gossipy hockey people, but if I was being honest, I liked them too much.

Way *way* too much.

I mean, maybe it was just because I hadn't kissed anybody in a really long time, but my brain wouldn't stop constantly replaying the way Alec's brown eyes got all intense just before he lowered his head and put his mouth on mine.

God.

"Kid," I heard from the other side of the door.

I assumed he was talking to me, because *of course* Grandpa Mick didn't knock like a normal person.

No, he just barked out a word and waited for doors to open.

I pulled open my door and he was standing in the hallway.

"Hey, Grandpa," I said, dreading what was coming.

Because the idea of Grandpa Mick lecturing me for kissing Alec?

Nightmare.

"You okay?" he asked. "I heard you walking around in circles, and it's one in the morning."

So far, so good.

"Sorry, did I wake you up?" I looked down at his flannel Snoopy pajama pants and said, "I forgot that your room is underneath mine."

"No, I was up reading," he said. "I just thought maybe you were awake and might need to talk about something."

What was he doing? Had he read more articles about how to talk to teens?

I kind of wanted to just say *no, I'm good* because it was easy, but after what Alec had said about my grandpa, maybe I needed to give him a chance.

But in *my* way.

Here goes nothing. . . .

"I need to play twenty questions with you," I said.

He made a growling sound. "What the hell does that mean?"

"It means I have a lot of random things I'd like to ask you."

I hadn't planned on this little game, but I *did* have a lot of things I wanted to ask him.

He squinted, like he was waiting for the universe to translate my words, and then he said, "Fine. Go."

"Oh. Okay," I said, surprised. I cleared my throat and asked, "Question one. Do you miss playing hockey?"

"Yes," he said.

Oh-kay. So much for learning something new about my grandpa.

I tried again. "Question two. What's your favorite memory of Grandma?"

He sighed and looked uncomfortable, which made me think he was going to walk away and quit the game. But then he said, "The way she used to sit by the penalty box during every one of my games."

"What?" It was hard for me to even imagine her watching hockey, to be honest. She'd just always been the woman who smelled like Jergens cherry-almond lotion, owned a closet full of floral dresses, and giggled like a scandalized child every time my grandpa cursed in her presence. "She didn't sit with everyone else?"

"Nope."

"Why not?"

He looked like he wanted to smile (but of course he didn't). "She said she knew I'd end up in the box at some point, and she thought if I saw her sitting there, I'd have to settle my ass down and focus."

"Grandma said the word 'ass'?" I said with a laugh, feeling shocked by the thought.

"Maybe I'm paraphrasing."

"Or not," I said, for some reason intrigued by this new-to-me version of her. "Did it work?"

"Like a fucking charm," he said, and then he *did* smile.

"Smart lady," I said.

"The smartest," he agreed, and then I felt guilty for even bringing her up.

"I'm sorry," I said.

"For . . . ?"

I shrugged. "For bringing her up, I guess."

"Don't be," he said quietly. "My favorite thing to talk about."

His face was softer for a second, and a small part of me felt like hugging him.

247

"Okay, then—question three," I said, because I didn't think he'd appreciate the hug. "How many times did she turn you down when you asked her out the first time?"

I used to love this story.

"Twelve," he said with a smart-ass grin. "I asked her out for twelve days in a row, showing up at her mom's house every morning with a cruller from Kriz's and an invitation to the movies for that night. And for twelve days in a row, she took the donut, said, 'Thank you but I must decline,' then walked her sweet ass back inside."

I laughed even though I knew this one, because it was so romantic.

"And on the thirteenth day . . . ?" I prodded, loving this part.

"And on the thirteenth day, I opened my front door to see her standing in my yard with a donut in *her* hand. She told me she'd broken up with her long-distance boyfriend—who I hadn't even known existed—and she was wondering if I'd want to go to the lake with her."

"And the rest was history?" I leaned against the doorframe and wondered what it'd be like to have the power to make a man so tough fall so hard.

"The rest was fucking legendary," he said with a grin. "Any more questions?"

"Actually," I said, not wanting to let him walk away when he was sharing like this. "Question four: Was there ever a time that you got along with my dad?"

Since he was opening up (as much as he opened up), I wanted to know more about why he hated my dad so much. Grandpa Mick was a grumpy jerk in general, but now that I'd been around him a little more, I knew he wasn't like that to everybody.

So why was he like that with my dad so very much?

"What kind of question is that?" he asked, lowering his voice like he didn't want my mom to hear.

"I don't know. I was just wondering, because my parents got married in college, but it wasn't until years later that you . . ." I hesitated for a second, my voice going soft before I said, "That you . . . flipped out on him."

I'd always been scared to bring up this black mark. This scar of a memory between us was still tender, but I felt like it was now or never.

"Yeah?"

"So I guess I want to know if you got along when they first got married, or if you've always . . . hated him."

He sighed. "Maybe you should ask your mother about this."

"No," I said, grabbing his sleeve and pulling him into my room. I closed the door behind him and said, "I don't want her version of this. To be honest, I think you're unfair to my dad, but I want to know why. There are two sides to every story, right? I think it's maybe fair to hear it from your point of view."

He sighed. "I'm not going to bash your dad, kid. I think he's a prick and I can't stand him, but he's your father."

"You do know that calling him a prick is bashing him, right?"

"Eh," he said, like he disagreed.

This made me smile a little. "Okay, so tell me about the first time you met him."

I knew I wasn't going to agree with what he said, but I was curious what things had been like in the beginning. Or if it had always been capital B-A-D bad.

"I'm only gonna state the facts," he said like he was dropping a legal disclaimer.

He walked over to my bed and sat down. "The first time I met your dad, I acted like a jackass."

"Wow, the self-awareness," I said, the smile I had tugging harder at my lips.

"Do you want to hear this or not?"

"Sorry."

He cleared his throat. "So your ma told us she met a guy in one of her classes and they were dating. He was stationed at the base an hour away but was working on his master's. Sounded like a decent guy, but right away I didn't like that, because she was only a freshman."

I wanted to explain to him that this wasn't reason enough to hate my dad. But I kind of understood. The fact that he was five years older than my mom wasn't a big deal now, but when she was eighteen?

That would've felt huge. Especially to her parents.

As if he'd read my mind, he continued, "Not a reason to hate him so much, sure. But when she called a few months later to tell us she was quitting school to marry him?"

"Wait, *what*?" It felt like someone had doused me with a bucket of ice water. I knew they got married in college because she was pregnant, but I hadn't realized it'd been like *that*, so sudden. *So* soon after they met.

"Out of nowhere, she calls to say she wants to give up a full-ride academic scholarship to be an Air Force wife. She worked her ass off to get the Fricklinhauger Fellowship, but suddenly she says she wants to leave." My grandpa shook his head and said, "I still can't believe it."

If I had felt that I was slapped by ice water, now I was drowning in it. Breathing became harder.

"*S*he had a Fricklinhauger Fellowship?" This was literally the first I'd heard of this—in my *life*. "This can't be true. Like, I knew she was smart and that she met my dad at school, but she was a Fricklinhauger *fellow*?"

What the hell? This was *unbelievable*!

They awarded like *five* Fricklinhauger Fellowships a year to high school graduates, fellowships that covered all expenses because the recipients were literally geniuses.

It felt like my world was imploding. How much more didn't I know about my parents? *Why* didn't I know this?

You'd think, as I rambled incessantly about Harvard for most of my life, she might've mentioned it.

"She's brilliant, your ma," Grandpa Mick said, his mouth curving into something close to a smile. "She used to work on math equations at my games—when she was like six—because she said it was more fun than watching hockey."

I couldn't quite form any words—my brain was still processing everything. My mom, a genius. We had never talked about that. *Ever.*

What else didn't I know about my mom . . . ? And why did it make my heart hurt?

"But she bailed on the fellowship after less than a semester."

Instantly, I thought of Harvard, of how badly I wanted it, of how hard I'd worked to hopefully get it.

Had it been like that for my mom . . . before she had to give it up?

I looked at his face and realized she'd quit because of *me*.

Me.

The silence felt heavy.

I'd taken her Harvard away from her.

The panic and anxiety I'd been fighting the past few years started rising and rising, stealing my breath the way they always did, until a rough hand found mine.

"And don't you for one minute think it was because of you," he said firmly. Protectively.

My heavy eyes met his and he said, "She could've stayed; your grandma was ready to move there and help. We had a plan all figured out."

"You did?" I pictured my grandma's face, and, yeah—that tracked. She'd been the sweetest, so *of course* she would've moved to another state to take care of her daughter and a baby.

"But your mother was adamant that the only option was to marry your dad and move with him—he'd just gotten a new assignment when she got pregnant."

"Why wouldn't she—"

"It doesn't matter now," he said, cutting me off.

"Oh." I thought of my dad's persuasiveness when he thought he was right, the way he couldn't even fathom that his way wasn't the only way. "So *he* said it was the only option."

My grandpa shrugged, confirmation without him actually confirming. My stomach dropped.

"It gets worse," he said, a soft but guarded smile cracking his weathered face. "I showed up at your mom's dorm and told her she was coming home with me."

"You did?"

"I did. I was in the middle of telling her to start putting her shit in boxes when her boyfriend showed up and asked me to leave."

"My dad asked you to *leave*?"

"That was when I put him in a headlock just to shut him up so he'd listen, and your mother started crying, and the little dorm RA announced that if we didn't knock it off, she was going to have to issue a residential citation."

I watched as Grandpa looked down at his hands—he was clutching them so tightly they started to turn red.

Wait—was he *nervous* to tell me all of this?

"In hindsight, I should've slowed down, because I probably drove your mom to be more stubborn about what she wanted to do, but it was clear to me what was going to happen. He was career military. And that meant moving from base to base and taking my daughter—and grandkid—with him."

I could tell he was reliving it, that Grandpa Mick had just been transported back to the night he learned he was losing his daughter.

"That's probably enough of twenty questions," I said, suddenly feeling tired.

"It was only four," he said, his eyes searching my face.

"Yeah, but it was enough." I didn't want him to see me try to absorb everything. Didn't want him to see the panic stirring in my chest.

Just breathe.

He watched me for another minute, then nodded and stood. "You should get to bed now."

"Yeah," I agreed, nodding. "I'm pretty tired."

"Good," he said, walking to the door. "That means I can finally sleep because you're done walking in circles."

"I thought you said it wasn't keeping you up."

"Sometimes I lie," he said, and then he was gone.

And I was left sitting in my room, completely in the dark as I tried to digest the enormity of what he'd just told me.

CHAPTER TWENTY-EIGHT
Alec

Where the hell is she?

I waited for her in the Rainforest Cafe, dreading our "date."

It'd been her idea to schedule a fake date at the mall, where anyone and everyone could see us, and on paper it was a solid idea. We could get food and do something *datey*, all in one place, snapping a few pictures for social media before calling it good.

But that kiss was destroying my ability to think straight.

How could a fucking split-second kiss be making me so damn crazy?

Yes, it had been the result of a dare and we'd said it was all part of the act and blah blah blah, but if I was being honest, the minute her lips touched mine, I forgot who I was, where I was, and who was fake dating who.

I only knew I wanted more.

And I swear to God it seemed like she felt the same way.

Things between us almost felt too good to be an act.

Which made one thought about Dani keep creeping into my mind, dangerous but undeniable.

She'd let me down during the worst time of my life. That one motherfucking day that started with disappointment and ended with me at the police station.

"Hey, you," I heard, and when I looked up, it felt like something was squeezing my chest.

No, it felt like someone had punched me in the chest.

She was so pretty, holy *shit*.

I swallowed and tried to be cool, but that little skirt showed off amazing legs, and the dark blue of her sweater seemed to amp the pink of her cheeks, and had her hair always sort of glittered when she stood underneath recessed lighting?

She gave me a nervous smile, like she wanted me to like the way she looked, and it made me feel weak.

Get it together, dumbass.

"Collins," I said as she sat down on the chair across from me. "Can I tell you that you look hot without you punching me or getting pissed?"

"I'll allow it," she said with a little smirk. "And you look really, really nice, Alec. Like a grown-up version of Zeus."

"Gee, thanks."

"Oh, someone doesn't like changing out of his sweats," she teased in a quiet voice, picking up the menu that was sitting on the table in front of her.

"If we were really dating," I said, "would you actually want me to wear this when I took you out?"

What the hell is that?

I wasn't sure why I wanted to know, but I did.

"I mean, you look good like this," she said with a breathy giggle, like she was embarrassed. "But if we were *really* dating, I wouldn't care what you wore."

"Can I get you two some drinks?"

Dani looked at the server with an appreciative smile, like she felt rescued from . . . *something*.

Yeah, same.

We both ordered Cokes and then I asked the waitress, "Would you mind taking a picture of us?"

"Of course not," she said, taking my phone and stepping back. I moved my chair over and put my arm around Dani, the smell of her perfume and the way I could feel her hair on the side of my neck making me a little nuts.

"Say cheese," the server said, but I was too hypnotized by apple juice and flowers to say anything at all. Before I could grab my phone, Dani took it and got busy making a post.

She'd been the one posting photos of us to my newly-created-by-her public social media accounts.

"Okay, what do you think?" Dani asked, holding out the phone.

The picture was great. I looked like I was trying with the Ralph Lauren shirt—and my hair was on point—but Dani was stunning. We were absolutely pulling off two good kids on a date, which was what we were going for.

But the caption was what nailed it.

Dinner at the Rainforest Cafe because she likes the sound of thunderstorms, then book shopping at B&N. #perfect-date

She was fucking *good* at this game of pretend.

"Wait," I said, looking at my profile. "How do I have hundreds of followers already?"

"I followed Cassie and a couple guys from the team, so since you're you," she said with an eye roll that for once didn't feel like judgment, "everyone wants to be your friend."

257

"You really think I'm a douche now, don't you?"

"No," she said, shaking her head. "I did at first, especially when I was 'some chick' you knocked over with your bag, but now I think the Zeus hype happens because you're pretty decent at hockey and there's not a lot you can do about it."

"Wow, that feels like a raging compliment coming from you," I said.

"I'm not a jerk," she said defensively. "You've just changed a lot since we were kids, and it caught me off guard."

"Trust me, so have you," I said, wondering if she was still ticklish. I used to be able to drop her to the floor with just a touch on the back of her neck. "You came back as this quiet, shy, uptight girl, but every once in a while I see the Dani I used to know, so I literally can't figure you out."

"Well, that's good, because I don't like to be figured out," she said teasingly, and I wished I didn't know that her lip gloss tasted like cherries.

Suddenly I've got a killer sweet tooth.

The server came back and took our food orders, and after she left, I heard myself say, "So tell me everything that's happened since the last time I saw you."

She was picking up her drink, and her hand froze halfway to her mouth when she heard my question. "That's, uh, a lot of time."

"Yep," I said, suddenly wanting to know everything.

"Well," she said, shrugging. "Not long after we were here for my grandma's funeral we moved to Texas, which I hated."

"Why did you hate it?" I asked.

As much as I didn't want to bring up trauma, I wanted to hear about the years that sucked. For some reason, I wanted her to *want* to tell me about them.

"I don't really feel like getting into the mess of it," she said. "But let's just say when you're an Air Force kid, sometimes you move to schools that are fine and sometimes you move to schools that are *not* fine. Like, not necessarily the school itself is bad, but, like, maybe just a group of people suck, right?"

"Right," I agreed, glad I didn't actually have any personal experience with this.

Her voice was quiet, and she looked down at her hands for a minute before her eyes came back to mine. "So my middle school in Texas wasn't fine. I'd like to say they were all terrible people because it makes me feel better, but the truth is that I didn't really make friends at that school. I just know there were a few girls who decided they didn't like me, which made my experience there kind of not great."

"Bitches," I said, really feeling that. Really fucking hating whoever made her face look the way it looked right now.

"Whatever, it's all part of growing up; at least that's what my dad always told me," she said with a fake smile and a shrug.

"What'd your mom say?" I asked.

"Oh, my mom called the principal and the mean girls' mothers and she raged," Dani said, smiling. "So eventually I stopped telling her, because *of course* that made it worse."

"Oh shit," I said.

"Oh shit, indeed."

"Where'd you go after that? I feel like my mom said it was, like, North Dakota . . . ?"

"Yeah, we moved to Minot, and after that we moved to Germany, and now we're here."

"Did you like Germany?" I asked.

"I mean, I loved the country," she said. "If I'd been an adult who could just freely explore Germany whenever I wanted, it would've been great, but as a high school kid living on an American Air Force base that just happened to be in Germany, I didn't love it. My mom was really unhappy there, because it was when things got bad with my dad, and it just felt like we were sort of isolated."

"I'm sorry about your parents, by the way," I said.

"Are you?" she asked with a funny grin. "You never liked my dad."

"But I love your mom and hate the thought of her being sad," I said. "Did you know it was coming?"

"Yes and no," she said. "I knew my parents were fighting more than they ever had—well, fighting with them was just passive aggression and snapping—but I knew my mom was unhappier than I'd ever seen her. Still, though, I just assumed that was who they were together. I didn't actually envision them coming to an end."

"I'm sorry for bringing this up—are you okay about it?"

"Yeah," she said, shrugging. "Mom's happier now, but I also still feel bad for Dad and miss him. Even if he can be a jerk sometimes. It doesn't make any sense, right?"

"It does, though," I said, surprised I'd never considered that that was what it'd feel like in a divorce. "I can't imagine not seeing my parents every day, even if they were being assholes. At the end of the day, he's still your dad."

She just nodded in response, before saying, "By the way, your date conversation is a real downer."

"Yeah," I agreed, and as she looked at me with sad brown eyes, the thought that it might be time to confront the past between us suddenly hit me in the gut. Knowing just a fraction of what she'd been going through made me want to understand what *really* happened back then.

But just as I was about to form the words, something stopped me.

Why did it still feel so raw? After all these years?

"So tell me about *your* life in the time we've been apart," she said. "Unless you don't want to talk about it. The accident sounds like it was a nightmare. I'm so sorry—I don't think I ever said that."

Here was my chance. Get it all out in the air. She'd opened the door; all I had to do was step through it. But . . . "Yeah, actually, I don't really want to talk about that," I said. "The bottom line is that Big John is a fucking force of nature and overcame it all."

"Thank God," she said, shaking her head. "So let's talk about hockey, then. The last time I saw you, either you weren't playing hockey yet or you never talked about it during the summer months when I was here. So how did you go from that to this?"

My chest loosened, and I was thankful for the change in topic. "I've played hockey since I was four," I said, "but I sucked until eighth grade. Then I grew like a foot and a half, and I don't know if my body was always waiting for me to get bigger or something, but all of a sudden I was coordinated. And faster than everybody else."

"And the rest is history?" she asked.

"Pretty much," I said, because it'd almost felt that simple.

She had a million questions about hockey, which I fucking loved, and I was laughing my ass off when she pulled out her phone and proceeded to take notes—*crease is half circle in front of goal*—so she could "keep it all straight."

"Have I told you that you have nice legs, Collins?" I asked as we walked out of the restaurant, because, according to Dani, we still had some book shopping to do.

"I don't think you have," she said, biting down on that gorgeous fucking lower lip like she was trying not to smile.

"Am I allowed?" I asked as I reached for her hand.

She had a little crinkle in her forehead when I asked that, which served as the perfect reminder.

"You know," I said with a shrug. "Public space and all. A lot of people from school hang out here."

"Okay, yeah," she said, her smile relaxed as she looked at me out of the corner of her eye.

And suddenly, I felt daring. Hungry.

"Then let me just say you have amazing legs."

Her eyebrow lifted. Had I crossed a line?

Could I help it anymore?

But I was saved by a group of girls from my calc class who stepped off the escalator that very second. *Yes.* I nodded in their direction so Dani could see them.

"Showtime," I said, lowering my voice and yanking her a little closer. "Am I also allowed to say you have a great ass?"

"No," she said, but a shy smile curved her lips and her cheeks went pink.

God, what is happening to me? I needed to take a step back.

"Fine, fine," I said, holding up my free hand in a gesture of innocence. "I won't tell you that you have an amazing ass that I steal peeks at all the fucking time."

"Stop," she said, still smiling, and suddenly it didn't matter.

It didn't matter that we were pretending, because the honest-to-God truth was that I was on the best date I'd ever had in my entire life.

I was so screwed.

CHAPTER TWENTY-NINE

Dani

"*I'm* picking out a book for *you* this time, Collins."

"Okay," I agreed, because I was curious to see what he'd choose.

"But don't even look toward romance," he said, pulling me further into the store. "We're going to history."

"You're not going to make me read nonfiction, are you?" I asked, thinking for the hundredth time since I'd shown up at the Rainforest Cafe that he looked insanely handsome.

Those glasses, that shirt—he was almost too pretty to look at.

"You're going to Harvard next year—you can handle it."

I kind of wished he hadn't brought that up. I was still working my ass off because I refused to give up, but the not knowing weighed on me. I'd wanted to go there for so long that it felt like if I didn't get in, I wouldn't even know who I was anymore.

Which was weird, especially when I didn't even know *specifically* what I wanted to study, but I'd made it my entire identity, so failure wasn't an option.

"I didn't say I can't handle it," I said. "I just like escapism."

"But books about history are interesting enough that they often feel like fiction," he said. "Come on."

"Says you."

"That's right *says me*," he said, tugging on my arm a little.

God.

When he used that teasing voice and literally pulled me around, it messed with my head.

Because most of the time, Alec was Zeus, the cocky smart-ass who spoke in sarcasm and kept me at a distance. He was the guy who'd ghosted me, the guy I tolerated for the sake of our mutually beneficial ruse.

But sometimes his hockey-god mask slipped a little, and I got a glimpse of someone who reminded me a lot of the boy I used to know.

And it gave me whiplash.

Who had I kissed? Was it Zeus the Untrustable, or Alec?

He led me over to the history section and proceeded to behave like a professor, familiar with nearly every topic on the shelves. He walked around, pulling out hardcovers and paperbacks like he spent every weekend shopping at Barnes & Noble, and it was a little *too* attractive.

A hockey player with glasses and a big fat brain?

A girl could faint from that shit.

"I'm impressed, Barczewski," I said, because I *so* was.

"And you thought I was a stupid jock who can't read," he said.

"Yeah, now I just think you're a stupid jock," I teased.

"You do not, don't lie, Collins," he said with a wink.

A wink that did things to my stomach.

Knock it off!

"Do you know how badly I wanted to punch you in the face when you winked at me during my first speech class?"

"What?" He coughed out a surprised laugh. "Seriously?"

"Yes," I said, still a little outraged as I remembered. "After pretending you didn't know me the day before and then walking around school like an obnoxious jerk, you had the gall to look down at me and wink. You're lucky you didn't get your face scratched off."

"I was being charming," he said, grinning unrepentantly.

"You were being a douche," I corrected.

"Come on, let's not fight, baby," he teased, his voice deep and quiet as he grinned down at me.

"Baby?" I said with a laugh, my stomach flittery as he looked at me like I was someone he was allowed to call *baby*.

"Do you prefer *honey*?" he asked, lowering his voice even more. "What's your favorite pet name, Goldilocks?"

What is happening? I thought as I scrambled to remember my *actual* name.

"How about we go with Collins," I said, embarrassed by how out of breath I sounded.

His flirty grin slipped away and he cleared his throat.

Gave a nod.

"Yeah, that's perfect," he said, his jaw flexing before he gave another nod. "Let's take a bookstore picture, *Collins*, so we can get on with it."

"Good idea," I said, working hard to pull off a smile as I took out my phone to grab a selfie. In an instant, things between us felt tense and awkward again, which was probably why I failed to notice the three steps behind us that led to the store's coffee shop.

I missed the step and stumbled, but Alec had quick reflexes. His long arm shot out and he pulled me back, but when he did, he let out a loud noise like a groan, and then he stopped, holding his arm.

"What happened?"

He gave his head a little shake and said through clenched teeth,

"Nothing. Hang on. I'm fine."

"You don't look fine," I said slowly. "Are you okay?"

"Yes," he bit off, obviously in a lot of pain. His left hand was clamped over his right shoulder like he was holding it in place.

"Is it your arm or your shoulder?" I asked, stepping closer as he stood there, clutching his arm with a grimace on his face.

"Fuck," he said under his breath, then managed, "It's my shoulder, and I'll be fine in a second."

His face was bright red, like the pain was killing him, and I noticed a couple of people in the coffee shop looking at him.

I touched his good arm and gently moved him toward the hallway that led to a back area.

"What happened?" I asked as soon as we were out of foot traffic.

"It's nothing," he said, but his jaw was clenched and it seemed like he was struggling to even form words. "I hurt my shoulder a few games ago, and sometimes if I raise my arm too high or in a bad direction, it messes with me."

"What can I do?" I asked, because he was still growling out words instead of speaking. "Do you need some Motrin, or do you want me to go get some ice?"

"It'll be better in a sec," he said. "But thanks."

"Is it, like, a muscle pull or a strain or something?" I remembered Grandpa Mick telling him to ice his shoulder—was this the same injury? "What'd the doctor say?"

"It just needs to heal—fuck *me*," he ground out. "It's going to be a little touchy for a few days."

He could barely speak, so it seemed like more than "a little touchy" to me, which was saying something, because he'd always had a high tolerance for pain.

He'd giggled about his black eye, for God's sake.

But right now he looked like he was suffering, and I hated it.

"Is there something maybe we can get to help?" I asked, wanting to do something—anything—to make him look less . . . terrible. My stomach hurt as I watched him swallow hard. "My grandma used to use, like, Aspercreme on her arthritic knee."

"Sometimes I use Icy Hot," he said, and I could tell that it was starting to feel marginally better. He was speaking more and grunting less. "I don't know if it actually helps or if it just convinces my brain it's helping."

"Okay, well, you stay here and I'm going to run down to the Walgreens by the food court."

"The pain is in my shoulder," he said, and he almost looked like he might smile. "I can manage walking."

"Are you sure?"

"*Yes,*" he said, and then he *did* smile. "This isn't new, so you don't need to look so freaked out. I deal with this every day."

"Oh my God, you do?" How awful. "How long has this been bugging you?"

"A few weeks," he said. "It's fine."

"It's *not* fine," I said, carefully grabbing his good arm, gently pulling him alongside me. I didn't know what kind of an injury this was, but he shouldn't be in this much pain. Something wasn't right, and I was going to lose it if his face didn't go back to looking . . . *not like this*. "Let's go get you some Icy Hot, but a few weeks isn't okay, Alec."

What if it was serious? Could something be broken?

We didn't say anything as we walked to the Walgreens, which thank God was close. We went right to the Icy Hot—he obviously knew where it was located within the store—and I pointed to another product. "Have you tried these?"

I read the back of the lidocaine patch and said, "Not only does it mess with the temperature to trick your brain like Icy Hot does, but it works on the nerve, so it might be better, actually."

"Yeah, no," he said, not even considering it.

"What do you mean, 'no'? Why wouldn't you try it? Do you like being in pain?"

"For fuck's sake, Dani, just trust me on this."

"But it doesn't make sense," I said, not wanting to be a nag but wanting him to feel better. "Why not do both? Put the patch on the worst part, then use Icy Hot around—"

"I can't put on the patch, okay?" he snapped.

"Wait, what?"

"When it gets like this," he explained quietly, "it's all about the motion of my shoulder. I could go play hockey right now and it'd be tolerable, but lifting my arm to take off my shirt is going to destroy me. I can go at it from the other side when I put on Icy Hot, but I can't put on a patch without taking off my shirt."

Ohhhhh. I cleared my throat and said, "I'll help you."

He just raised an eyebrow, which made me roll my eyes and say, "I've already seen you in the locker room and managed to control myself, so I'll be fine—let's buy the patch."

I was impressed by how casually I said it, because I was freaking out.

Seriously spiraling.

On the one hand, my stomach was in knots, because seeing him like this was just, like, too much. The way his jaw was hard and his Adam's apple kept bobbing and his forehead was creased: He was in so much pain, and I needed to find a way to fix it. To help him.

But at the same time, at the very same freaking time, I was out here saying things like *I'll help you* and offering to apply first aid to his naked, muscular (and injured) shoulder when I was still losing my shit over the way he'd kissed me at the PNA.

Because he hadn't given me a normal kiss.

I'd *had* normal kisses before, and whatever that'd been was the opposite of normal.

It'd been competitive and athletic and sexy and bossy and domineering, and it kind of pissed me off, in a way, because I'd loved every terrible, magical, *holy shit* thing about it.

What the hell is wrong with me?

My eyes were on the floor as we went over to the checkout, but when I raised them, I could see that he was still in a lot of pain. His jaw was like stone and there was a red flush on his cheekbones.

Although compared to his reaction when he'd stopped me from falling on my ass, it was a big improvement.

As soon as we walked out of Walgreens, my heart started beating a little too fast.

It's just first aid—chill out.

I saw the vacant family room/lactation lounge across the hall, so even though we hadn't discussed the *where* of this scenario, I pushed him in that direction, then locked the door behind us when we got inside.

"Whoa, whoa, whoa, Collins," he teased, but his eyes were serious. "I don't know what you have in mind, but I am not interested in any—"

"You're hilarious, shut up," I said, pulling the box of patches and the tube of Icy Hot out of the Walgreens bag. The quiet of the tiny room seemed deafening as I said, "So, um, I think you should unbutton your shirt but don't even try to take it off, okay? You don't need to make your shoulder worse, so tell me when you're done and I will just, like, lower the shirt enough to put on the patch. Okay?"

His eyes moved over my face like he was having a lot of thoughts, and my breath was a little frozen in my chest as those dark brown eyes held me in place. "Okay."

He looked down at his shirt as he unbuttoned it, and I gnawed on my bottom lip and opened the patches, keeping my eyes on my hands as if completely unaware of the unbuttoning going on in front of me.

"Okay, I'm unbuttoned," he said, making *me* swallow hard and clear my throat.

What a thing to say.

"Good," I said, my voice sounding a little . . . *airy* as I raised my eyes to the shirt hanging open in front of me, a long vertical strip of bare skin exposed.

"So, um, I'm going to lower your shirt," I said, painfully aware of how close our faces were as I looked up at him. The air was charged, and it felt like the room was too small.

And my face was too hot.

I said, "Tell me if I'm hurting you."

His Adam's apple was all I could see as it moved around a swallow. "You won't."

271

I reached up with both hands and grabbed the two sides of his shirt carefully, gingerly, lowering it around his shoulders. I tried hard not to touch him, but my breath got stuck in my chest when my fingertips grazed his skin.

He didn't say a word, only took a deep and sharp inhale.

Is he cold? Or . . . ?

My throat was so dry all of a sudden.

My carefulness was a failure because the shirt slid off his arms and immediately fell onto the floor.

Which meant he was completely shirtless and so close that our bodies were almost touching.

"Dammit," I whispered, feeling so flustered that I was a little lightheaded.

"Just. Leave it." His entire face looked hard, like he was so flexed that his tight jaw might just shatter at any moment.

I nodded, swallowed, then nodded again, trying not to look at the ridiculously muscular chest in front of me, dear *God*.

"I want to make sure I get it in the right spot," I said. "Tell me when I'm in the right area, okay?"

He swallowed again and his jawbone tightened. "Okay."

He turned around, and for some reason I felt no less . . . *unnerved* looking at his back. It was ridged and hard, like his skin was stretched tight over those lean muscles. I held the patch in my left hand and raised the fingers of my right hand to his shoulder. I gently set my fingertips on his skin, my heart beating in my ears as my fingers slid over his shoulder blade.

"Right here?" I asked in what came out as a whisper.

"A little higher," he said, and everything between us was somehow in slow motion all of a sudden. My fingers brushed his skin, slowly, and I swear I felt him shiver under my touch as I traced higher.

"Here?" I managed to croak.

"Yeah," he said.

I peeled the backing off the patch and stuck it to his shoulder, using my palm in slow circles to gently press it to his skin.

"You're fine," he said in a gravelly voice. "You're not going to hurt me."

"Good," I said, my voice more a breath than a sound as my palm smoothed over the patch. "Turn around so I can get the front with Icy Hot."

He obeyed, his dark eyes full of questions as he looked down at me, but he didn't say a word.

I placed the cream onto the right side of his collarbone, set down the tube, then lifted my fingers to his shoulder.

"Is this all right?" I asked, noticing my hands were shaking just the tiniest bit as I put them on his body. I had no idea what I was doing anymore, I only knew that I was under the influence of *something* as I started rubbing the slippery lotion over his skin.

"Yeah, but you don't have to do this," he said, his jaw flexing and unflexing. It felt like something huge was hovering between us, something thick and heavy that stole the air from the room.

I didn't know what it was, but breathing was suddenly difficult.

"I—I want to," I managed, feeling like I couldn't think when he looked at me like that. I wasn't even sure my lips were moving when I said, "I don't like when you're in pain."

He raised his left hand and cupped my cheek, his eyes impossible to read as those big fingers grazed my skin. I wasn't sure how, but the moment felt more intimate than the kiss that hadn't left my mind since last night.

His gaze locked with mine, both of us breathing harder as he leaned in, inching closer—

"Is someone in here?" The door handle jiggled as someone said through the crack, "Is this open?"

"Y-yes," I yelled, looking up at Alec while jumping away from him, quickly wiping my fingers on my skirt, my heart about to explode in my chest. "I'll be out in one minute!" I yelled.

Oh God, oh God, oh God.

He was watching me, his expression unreadable, and I wished I knew what he'd been about to do. I bent down and quickly picked up his shirt, then helped him slide his arms into it before gathering my bags off the floor while he buttoned.

"Okay, we're good," he said, and when I turned around, he was all put together again.

But he was still looking at me in that way, the way that I couldn't figure out.

What the hell just happened?

CHAPTER THIRTY
Alec

Everything changed after that date. Not only between us, but *about* us.

And it was confusing as hell.

At school, everyone suddenly recognized us as a couple. Dani thought it was because of the Instagram account, but no one seemed surprised to see us together anymore and everybody accepted it at face value.

Which was great.

In addition to that, the team was on fire at every practice. All of a sudden, *everyone* was playing at another level, and the general superstitious consensus was that it had something to do with Dani being my good-luck charm. It was asinine, the way we were all so superstitious, but even I bought into it a little bit.

Because our game had been elevated to the nth degree ever since Dani and I started "dating."

As if that weren't all fucking great enough, things were moving in the right direction on the reputation front too.

The *Tribune* ran an article on me and my family, and as much as I hated that it was necessary, my parents were an open book about everything and it made for a fantastic feel-good story. And I knew Dani's and my PR work was paying off when the interviewer actually asked me about my dating life.

"I know you're only in high school, but rumor has it that Zeus, the guy who's been a little bit of a loose cannon, has been straightening his ways and focusing on other things. Do you want to comment on that?"

"I know what you're getting at," I joked. "All I'll say is that I reconnected with a childhood friend who is ten times better than me in every way. She inspires me to be more."

And that wasn't a joke, to be honest. It felt . . . *true*.

And I liked seeing Dani coming out of her shell. I noticed her dressing less . . . monochrome and oversized, and she gave an informative speech in Sykes's class and didn't even look like she was going to faint.

The only thing that *wasn't* great (aside from my shoulder, which was definitely not fucking great and probably getting worse by the day) was that it felt like my head was constantly spinning when it came to her.

Because it was all pretend, right? Everything between us was supposed to be pretend, but more and more it felt, well . . . *not* pretend.

Starting with the damn lidocaine-patch incident that would not leave my memory. I teeter-tottered every hour, I swear to God, between thinking she'd been doing a good deed that night, rendering first aid, to thinking we'd been *this close* to something hot happening in that tiny room.

My brain replayed it on a loop, over and over again, torturing me.

But ever since we'd left that room, I felt like she was pulling away. It was probably my imagination, because she was still doing all the fake-girlfriend things she'd done before, but there was something in her eyes that made me feel like she was putting up a wall.

And I didn't know how I felt about that.

Because wasn't I supposed to *want* there to be a wall?

I couldn't remember what I was supposed to want and how I was supposed to feel anymore.

And then, to make matters more confusing, she kept bringing me bizarro lunches in the library, which was somehow charming as shit because like the patches, it felt like she cared.

See?

Total mind fuck.

This time it was a peanut butter wrap with pickled jalapeños, a slice of bacon, and crunched-up potato chips.

"So you smoke a *lot* is what you're telling me," I said as I looked down at the lunch I had zero interest in eating. "This is something you discovered when you were high as fuck, right?"

She rolled her eyes but giggled, a sweet little sound that made me want to do whatever it took to make her giggle again. "Just trust me, okay? Something about the flavor combo *works*."

"I don't believe you."

"Grandpa Mick used to eat one before every game," she lied, her eyes dancing like she thought she was hilarious as she dared me to eat her shitty wrap. "He calls them his secret weapon."

"I think it's cute as hell, the way you suck so badly at lying."

That made the giggle turn into a laugh. *God, she should laugh like that all the time.* The Dani I used to know was *always* laughing, and I hadn't realized until now that I'd been missing it.

"By the way, what exactly is boot hockey?" she asked, taking a bite of her wrap.

"Basically just a version of hockey that people play in street shoes on ice, usually at the park," I said, taking out my questionable tortilla. "Why?"

"Because Cass and Lillie were talking about it. Tell me everything

277

you know," she said, taking another bite.

Did I always find the way she ate adorable?

I took a bite—*what the fuck*—and said, "The bar down the street has a league, but around here most people just play it for fun, like pickup basketball games. The guys in leagues usually wear broomball shoes for better traction, but when my friends play, they don't."

"Good God, what is broomball?" she asked with a snort, like this was the funniest thing she'd ever heard. "Wait—are *literal* brooms involved? Like Quidditch from Harry Potter? I could get into that!"

Is she being this cute on purpose?

I started describing it, trying to focus on anything but whatever the hell was in my mouth, but she interrupted after she swallowed her food, shaking her head.

"Ah, so not Quidditch. Hmm. But broom, though? I guess that makes as much sense as hitting a little ball around with a hockey stick."

"You didn't just call a puck a ball, did you?"

"No," she said, her eyes big but her mouth smiling as she pushed her napkin forward. "I would *never*. I mean, I'm Mick Fucking Boche's granddaughter, thank you very much."

"Uh-huh." *She* has *to be doing it on purpose. Good God.*

Now I was focusing too much on her mouth. *Get it together!*

I cleared my throat. "Actually, a bunch of people are playing tomorrow," I said, taking another bite because I couldn't *not* finish the atrocity she'd made just for me.

"I know," she said with a funny look. "I'm asking these questions because I'm probably going to go."

"You actually want to *play*?" I asked, fucking shocked because it was the last thing I would've imagined her wanting to do.

She hated the cold.

"I mean, how hard can it be, running around on the ice, hitting a puck with a stick?"

"Oh, sweet little baby girl."

"Screw you, now I'm for sure playing," she said with a laugh. "I mean, if Cassie can do it, I can do it. Probably without any help."

"Cassie played hockey until her junior year," I corrected. "Not an equal situation."

"Says you," she said, waving a hand as if it was no big deal before she finished her wrap and went back to her book.

But going back to *my* book wasn't so easy.

Because the sight of her destroyed my concentration.

She gnawed on that full bottom lip, lost in her book, while my brain shorted out, getting lost in the idea of her.

Of what she'd do if I leaned across the table and kissed her.

Long lashes, cherry lips, apple juice.

Of what *we* could do behind the tall book stacks on the other side of the computers.

Soft curls, pink fingernails, flowers.

Of how—

"You're not going to read?"

"Huh?" My eyes snapped into focus and Dani was looking at me strangely, which made sense because I'd literally been staring into space like a total dipshit.

"Not in the mood to read?" she asked, those glossy lips turning up into a smirk. "Or is little Alec getting sleepy?"

I dragged a hand over my hair—*you fucking moron*—and just said, "Both."

CHAPTER THIRTY-ONE

Dani

"It's all about anticipation, kid."

"Okay," I said, nodding, even though I truly had no idea what that meant.

"You don't know what that means, do you?" Grandpa Mick asked, squinting because the sun was setting behind me.

Not that it was doing its job.

So freaking cold.

"No idea," I admitted, clouds of frozen breath puffing in front of my face as I pulled Alec's hat down a little lower on my forehead.

I'd been foolish enough to casually mention boot hockey to my mom and grandpa via text, and before I knew what was happening, Grandpa Mick was picking me up from school and I was on my way to some random guy's backyard pond to train.

Apparently, according to them, I needed to "not embarrass the family."

Which made me roll my eyes but also have some kind of feelings about the sentiment, because I'd never felt like I had "family" to embarrass before.

So now I'd been freezing my ass off in Bilch's backyard for an hour, but I was having a surprisingly good time running around in the near-dark with my grandpa.

"All right, think about it like this," he said, leaning on his stick. "In hockey you have speed, but in boot hockey you don't. It's small and slow and kind of clumsy."

"So the sexiest sport," I said, grinning.

"Sure," he said, rolling *his* eyes at *me*. "So you don't want to go too fast and overcommit. If you don't time your slide, you can actually hustle *too* much."

"I would never overhustle, Grandpa, I swear on my life."

"Yeah, I can see that about you," he said, giving me one of his begrudging half smiles. "You could take a lesson on hustling from the Barczewski kid. He's only got one speed."

The Barczewski kid.

Ugh.

I'd been working so hard at not thinking about him, at trying to constantly remind myself it was all pretend.

Because I'd fallen, *God help me.*

I felt a million real feelings for him and I needed to get them in check.

The kiss, the hand-holding, the tension-filled patch application—it was *all* part of the game, but it *all* swam around in my brain like the very best memories of my very real boyfriend.

Which they weren't, and he wasn't.

It might *feel* like we were both feeling things, but that wasn't factual.

So now I'd shifted to being mentally proactive. When we were together, I reminded myself over and over again—in my head—that it was fake. And when he held my hand, I reminded myself that he was just acting.

Because even if he wasn't always pretending—*which he was*—I was going away to college in a few months and he was going to be hockeying somewhere.

Only a fool would start something that wasn't going to last.

"Quit daydreaming," Grandpa Mick said, sending the ball in my direction.

"For the record, I'm very disappointed that we play with a ball. I was really looking forward to hitting a puck."

"I'm looking forward to seeing you hit *anything*," he quipped.

I swung my stick, hitting the ball as hard as I could.

Grandpa Mick didn't even move.

He just stuck out his stick and stopped it.

"You suck," I said, laughing.

"No, *you* suck," he said, laughing too.

He ran me through more exercises, trying to improve my stick handling, but I really *did* suck, and then his buddies—Kris and Mel—showed up to watch.

"Why don't you guys make yourselves useful," my grandpa said, "and get your asses out here."

"Two-on-two?" the one with the long white beard asked, smiling like he'd never wanted to do anything more.

It only took a minute, and suddenly we were in a game, my grandpa and me playing against the two old dudes.

"Control the puck," my grandpa yelled from the other end of the ice.

"I'm trying," I yelled back as Mel and Kris ran around on the ice as if they *weren't* senior citizens.

"If you manage to get it, just haul ass toward the goal and keep your

283

head up," Grandpa Mick instructed as I swung my stick and tried getting at the ball.

"But I can't see the ball if my head is up," I said.

"Don't say that shit out loud, for fuck's sake," he yelled, laughing.

"And don't call it a ball," Mel said in outrage.

I ran around chasing those guys, but I had nothing on them.

Which meant I was going to have nothing on Alec and his friends.

"You didn't do too bad, kid," my grandpa said when we came off the ice.

"That's a lie and you know it," I said, shaking my head. "I just got my ass kicked by some old guys."

"And your grandpa," he added, his mouth actually turning up into a legitimate smile.

God, I've missed that so much.

"Hey, you guys," I said to his buddies, "will you take a picture of us?"

"What for?" Grandpa Mick asked, looking surprised.

"I just want to send Alec a picture. He's going to lose his mind when he sees who's teaching me boot hockey."

That made him laugh, and something in my heart felt warm and full when I put my arm around Grandpa Mick's shoulders and we grinned, together, for the photo.

I texted it to Alec with the caption: Check out who's teaching me boot hockey.

His response was almost immediate.

Alec: Damn, Collins. BADASS.

Me: Right??

Alec: Also I like the braids.

I was positive he was saying that in character—*he's just pretending, he's just pretending*—but even so, the comment made me feel a little gooey.

Me: Prepare to see them whip past you tomorrow when I break free with a clapper.

I wasn't sure if I got the slang right, because he just responded:

Alec: That is the most adorable thing you've ever said to me.

CHAPTER THIRTY-TWO
Alec

"She doesn't suck as much as I thought she would," Kyle said from his spot beside me on the park bench.

"Must be Mick's genes," I said in agreement.

"I can hear you, y'know," Dani yelled from where she was scrambling on the ice, and I fucking loved the attitude. She was giving my friends shit and laughing, looking cute as hell in one of Mick's old jerseys as she tore around like the scrappy little shit that she was.

"If you can hear me, answer this, Collins," I yelled. "Why do you keep slamming into the boards?"

Since the game started, she'd be running just fine and then, boom— she'd go full speed into the boards before turning and getting back to it.

"Because I fall down every time I try to switch directions," she said, running and holding out her stick like it was a baton and she was in a relay race. "I think it must be my shoes. So it's easier to just slam into the wall."

"Did Mick teach you that?" Kyle asked, laughing.

"No, but I guarantee he'd appreciate it. He's a 'do whatever it takes' kind of guy, and I would rather body-slam the wall than keep falling down."

"I actually respect that," Richie said.

"So do I," agreed Kyle.

"Yeah, because I'm sure that's her goal," Cassie said as she smacked the puck. "To gain your respect."

"I think everyone who isn't playing should just shut up," Dani said, panting a little as she straightened and leveled a glare in our direction.

"Oooh," Richie said, giving me a grin.

Dani had, for some reason, thought that *we* were going to be playing.

But it was hockey season—no *way* would we fuck around on the ice when the tournament was in play. Even if we were stupid enough to *want* to, Coach would kill us.

Her team got their asses kicked, of course.

But I was impressed.

Dani went hard, even if she didn't go pretty.

When she came off the ice, she was whining to Cassie about how sore her thighs were, holding one of Mick's sticks (which we'd all freaked out about when she showed up).

"Do you want me to carry you?" I asked.

Her gaze shot to mine, the tiny furrow between her brows letting me know I'd surprised her. She covered it by saying, "I'm still mad at you."

"You can't still be mad," I said, distracted by the way her brown eyes looked when she teased me. "It was a misunderstanding. I never told you we'd be playing."

"It was implied."

"Was not," I said.

"Fine, you can carry me because my thighs are burning," she replied, smiling in the relaxed way that was becoming more frequent, like she was finally feeling comfortable here. "But I reserve the right to still be pissed at you."

"Good girl." I turned and pointed my ass in her direction. "Get on."

"Wait, no—your shoulder," she said quickly, stopping herself. "I don't want to hurt you."

Fuck, fuck, fuck. I straightened and turned around to see not only Dani looking at me with worry on her face, but the guys, too.

"What's wrong with your shoulder?" Kyle asked.

"Zeus?" Richie looked over at me with raised eyebrows, waiting.

"He hurt it in a game," Dani explained, "and it's—"

"Fine," I said, cutting her off and smiling. "It's fine."

"No, it's not," she said, looking at me like I'd lost my mind. "It's killing him—"

"Honey," I interrupted, very aware of the way the guys were looking at me, "I might've been a *little* dramatic about the shoulder."

Her eyes narrowed. "What?"

I could tell she wasn't buying it but couldn't figure out why I was being dishonest.

"You were being such a good nurse," I said, hoping she wouldn't be pissed at my lie. "I maybe leaned into it a bit."

Richie started laughing, and I just shot her a look and said, "Get on."

"Okay," she said, handing me her stick while eyeing me suspiciously. "But we're going to talk about this later."

And she jumped onto my back.

"Must we?" I asked, which made Richie laugh even harder.

"We must," she said into my ear, and I swear to God she touched my earlobe with her lips on purpose, sending a shiver down my spine.

"Devil woman," I said under my breath as I grabbed her legs, which made her giggle.

"Why are you keeping your shoulder injury a secret from your friends?" she asked as I carried her toward my car.

Don't focus on the feel of her breath on your neck.

I tried, but it was impossible.

"I'm not," I lied, trying to sound casual. "It's just not that big of a deal."

She lowered her voice. "You absolutely *were* keeping it a secret. You lied like it's not even an injury. Why can't you tell them?"

Her lips are too close to my neck.

"It's not that I can't tell them; it's—"

"So it's fine if I talk about the way you can't lift your arm over—"

"Please let this go," I begged, glancing at her over my shoulder, glad the group had spread out during the trek to the parking lot. "Please?"

"Alec." Her eyes moved over my face. "*Of course* I'll keep your secret. But, like, you really can't tell me?"

She said it like it hurt her feelings, and it reminded me so much of the old her that I lost my damn mind. I set her on the trunk of my car and told her the honest-to-God truth.

"I don't want anyone to know about it, okay?" I said quietly, reaching out a hand to adjust her (my) hat. "It's getting better—I can tell—but if scouts or recruiters think I'm busted up, it could affect fucking everything."

She blinked fast, kind of staring up at me like she was weighing my words.

"*Everything,*" I repeated, desperate for her to understand.

"Well, then," she said quietly, "we're going to have to get some more patches on the way home, aren't we?"

I wanted to hug her, but I restrained myself.

"Fuckin' A right we are."

"No way."

Richie looked down at my phone and started laughing as we walked around to the back of Bryce's house. His dad was ice fishing at Mille Lacs, so he was having a few people over. "I didn't know Mick knew how to smile."

The picture of Dani and Mick was so fucking funny that I couldn't stop looking at it and showing it to everyone I knew, even a day later. Dani looked cute as hell, laughing in her fuzzy hat and long braids, and it felt like the perfect shot of the Dani I used to know.

"Normally I'd agree," I said around a laugh, "but he's different around her."

We went in the back door and straight to the basement, because that was the only place we hung out when Bryce's parents were gone. And holy shit—the party was in full swing already, looking like a fucking casino with all the card games going on down there. King's Cup at the table by the laundry room, Fuck the Dealer (my favorite) at Bryce's dad's bar, and some variation of beer pong on the Ping-Pong table.

Everyone not engaged in a game was standing around, talking and watching the Minnesota Wild on TV. "Sleep When We're Dead" was booming out of a speaker somewhere.

Richie grabbed beers for everyone but me, and I'd just taken a sip of my water when Kyle said, "Oh, it looks like Dani's already here."

"*What?*"

"Over there, with Lillie and Cassie."

If we were in a movie, I would've done a spit take when I turned around. I followed his gaze over to the corner, and sure enough, there was my Dani, smiling at something Lillie was saying while holding a red cup.

And she looked fucking *hot* that night.

Her long hair was down, her lips were red, and she was wearing a crop top under her flannel shirt that exposed a few inches of bare skin between the bottom of her shirt and the top of her jeans, bare skin that my eyes didn't want to look away from.

There was nothing wild about her clothes and she was barely wearing makeup, but to me, she looked insanely gorgeous.

Because Dani seemed to be coming alive, more and more every day. She laughed as Lillie spoke, and the sound of her laughter made my fingers flex. This hybrid version of Dani Collins—part who she used to be and part something new—was someone I *wanted*, God help me, someone I suddenly felt panicked for, like I needed to get to her immediately before someone else beat me to it.

I didn't even realize I was walking in her direction until her eyes met mine, like I'd made it impossible for her not to see me because I was suddenly *there*, in front of her.

"Al!" she yelled, grinning at me and launching herself into my arms.

I wrapped my arms around her waist and said into her ear, "Are you drunk, Collins?"

She pulled back and gave me a flirty grin. "Just because I'm happy to see you doesn't mean I'm drunk."

"It usually does for me," Richie said.

Richie, who I'd forgotten even existed.

"But I'm assuming you've never kissed him," she said, smiling at my friend like she meant it as she pulled out of the hug. "That's what bumps him from *whatever* to *I am so happy to see you* status."

Wow, she was turning it *all the way* up.

My girl was definitely buzzed.

"Gross," Richie said, but I could tell by the way he was looking at her that he was surprised she was being so outgoing. "I'll just take your word for that."

"By the way, I meant to tell you after the last game, Richie," she said. "Great job. I saw you smacking that stick around lots of times, so . . . y'know . . . go, hockey."

He shook his head, but he was laughing when he said, "I swear to God there must've been a mix-up in the hospital. Mick Fucking Boche's offspring would never."

"But she does . . . and she just did," Dani said with a smirk. "And, oh yeah—nice apple."

"What?" he said, looking at her like she was nuts.

"You had an assist," she said. "Which in hockey is sometimes referred to as an apple."

"Oh, we've got a hockey expert right here," Richie said, fully laughing with her now.

"That's right, *Richard*," she teased, and something in my chest was warm as she messed with my best friends. I felt happy or proud or just *relieved* that she was finally being herself around them.

"Although you didn't exactly look like an expert at the park today," Vinny said as he joined the group. "How sore are you? Crashing into the boards so many times had to sting. You pretty bruised, Boche?"

I thought she might correct him on her last name, but instead she grinned like he'd complimented her and said, "Probably not as bruised as your ego after betting against me, *Vincent the Flow*."

I lost it at that, reaching out to grab the back of her shirt and pull her a little closer as I laughed my ass off.

"Funny girl," Vin muttered, shaking his head, but he was smiling.

"Did you tell Mick you scored?" I asked, lowering my head so she could hear me while trying not to breathe because her perfume always made me drunk. "Did he lose his shit?"

"As much as my grandpa can lose his shit," she said with a laugh. "I believe his response to 'I scored a goal' was 'congratulations, but how many did you stop?'"

"Fair point, though," I said. "Smart man."

"Hey, c'mere," Dani said, grabbing my sleeve. "Let's take a selfie."

She stepped closer to me and held out her phone to take a picture. She was grinning as the phone captured us, her tucked in front of me with the party in our background.

"You know you can't use this because of the beer," I said, trying not to focus on the smell of her hair.

"Then I guess this one's just for me," she said, holding out the phone to show me the photo.

I really fucking liked that picture.

I liked *us* in that picture.

And I liked her, right now. Whatever distance had been between us since the mall seemed to have disappeared, and she looked downright flirty at the moment. It was probably the result of whatever she had in her cup, but I wasn't hating it.

"Are you having fun, Collins?" I asked, also liking the way she was still leaning back against me with her head under my chin.

"I am," she said with a smile in her voice, and I swallowed hard when she turned around to look up at me.

I am in too fucking deep.

"So Alec." She tucked her hair behind her ears and nibbled on her bottom lip, like she didn't know what to do with herself, before she came up with, "Do you want to go watch Dumb Drink Dares?"

"Sure," I said, knowing it was fucking stupid the way I liked how nervous she looked. Because I felt the same way and had felt that way since she'd taken off my shirt in that bathroom at the mall. The memory of her soft fingers on my shoulders wouldn't go away no matter what I did, and the crackling electricity that'd been there in that tiny room had stayed with us ever since we'd left.

And for the next hour, everything was pretty fucking perfect.

I sat on a chair, soberly judging Dumb Drink Dares, and she sat on my lap because there weren't any other chairs. I'd be lying if I said I didn't take advantage of the opportunity, snaking an arm around her waist to pull her closer, anchoring her to me so her back was leaning against my chest.

She turned her head a little to look up at me. "You're kind of handsy, Zeus."

"Are you complaining?" I asked, wondering what she'd do if I kissed the side of her neck. I'd been obsessed with that particular spot since I'd been up close and personal with it in the locker room.

Her eyes roamed all over my face. "Nah, just stating a fact."

"Fact noted," I said with a wink, which made her laugh and pinch my thigh.

My heart might've stopped a couple times, but all was well.

But then her dad called.

She stared at the phone, biting her lip like she was nervous before she said, "I should probably just take this."

"Now?" I asked, selfishly not wanting her to get up.

"I mean, it's like five a.m. in Germany, and he's . . . y'know . . ." she said, shrugging.

"Your dad?"

She nodded. "Yeah. I'll be right back."

She took the call upstairs, but she was gone for a *long* time. So long that I started to worry something was wrong.

But when I went up to check on her, she was off the phone and talking to Cassie and Lil in the empty kitchen.

I swear to God I didn't mean to eavesdrop, but I was stunned into silence as soon as I stepped into the foyer.

"So I don't know," Dani said, sounding like she wanted to cry. "Like, I don't want to move again, but maybe I should go, y'know?"

"No way," Cassie said. "You can't leave; it's your senior year."

"I mean, I probably won't," she said, "but there only a few months left and I *just* got here. A school's a school at this point, right?"

I went back downstairs because I wasn't some asshole who was going to creep in a corner, listening to conversations that weren't meant for me. But I was confused as hell, wondering what her dad was up to now.

She might move again? *Already?*

I pretended to pay attention to the guys and the game, but every part of me was in a holding pattern as I waited for her. I needed to know what was going on.

How could he even consider doing this to her again?

She had to be freaking the fuck out.

But when she came back a few minutes later, she smiled like nothing had happened.

And she lied to me.

"Everything okay with your dad?" I asked, wanting to ditch the party so we could figure everything out.

She nodded and rolled her eyes. "He needed my Social Security number for Air Force stuff and couldn't remember it."

And . . . ?

I waited, but she didn't say anything else.

"That was it?" I asked. "At five a.m.?"

She nodded again. "Typical Dad, too impatient to wait. So what'd I miss?"

You're seriously not going to tell me?

"Vin did a back handspring and broke the card table," I said, but my mind was running, because what the fuck?

She wasn't going to tell me that she might be leaving?

I mean, she didn't owe me shit, right? This was just a fake relationship, so she didn't have to trust me with everything going on in her life. That was what people in *actual* relationships did, and I needed to get my head right.

She'd tell me if she wanted to tell me, and hopefully this was just the colonel being his normal asshole self.

It was fine that she was keeping it to herself.

But when I heard her talking to Cass and Lillie over by the keg a little later, I got a whole lot less understanding.

Because Lillie asked her about us, about the history of us.

"So you guys never dated or *anything* before now? It was strictly platonic?"

"Yes and no," I heard her say, but I refused to look. "We were always just friends, but he *was* my first kiss."

I was a big fan of the way her voice sounded when she said that, like it'd meant something warm-and-fucking-fuzzy to her, because, well, *hard same*. I focused on the hockey game playing on the TV as intently as I could—*quit eavesdropping, you pathetic fuck*—but then I felt gut-punched when I heard her giggle and say the most fucking ridiculous thing I'd ever heard.

"But we're together now, which is surreal because I thought I was still mad at him for what he did back in the day," she said with a laugh. "But how can I hold a grudge when he looks so good in a hockey jersey?"

What?

What the fucking *fuck*?

She was still mad at me for what *I* did?

Was she serious right now?

What the hell did *I* do, exactly?

I wanted to confront her, to finally have *that* conversation, because we probably *needed* to discuss our "back in the day."

But when I casually glanced her way a few minutes later, she gave me a conspiratorial grin and a motherfucking wink.

It was the smile of my partner in crime.

My fellow participant in the fake dating games.

She appeared to be having a blast, rewriting history while playing our game.

So fuck it, I thought.

Doesn't matter.

She could rewrite history and keep secrets all she wanted.

Hell, she wasn't my girlfriend, and I needed to remember that.

CHAPTER THIRTY-THREE
Dani

"Where'd you get that shirt, Goldilocks?" Alec asked, his eyes strolling over me as I leaned against his locker, waiting for him with Cassie.

"Your mom let me borrow it," I said, wishing I could read his mind as he stopped in front of me. I'd snagged his hockey hoodie because I thought he'd like that, but his face was impossible to read at the moment.

Which was disappointing when he'd been *so* adorably flirty at Bryce's party the other night. My stomach flipped over every time I thought about the way he'd pulled me against him during Dumb Drink Dares, the way he'd lowered his deep voice and teased me from the point-blank range of *in his arms*.

And on his freaking *lap*.

Talk about toe-curling.

I was pretty sure he'd assumed my behavior toward him at the party was drink-related, but as someone not fond of giving up control in social situations, I knew the Diet Pepsi I'd been chugging all night said otherwise.

"It looks good on you," he said, but something was missing in the *way* he said it.

What is with him?

"Why, thank you," I replied, batting my eyelashes in an attempt to be light while my stomach got heavy.

Because something *was* off with him.

"Why aren't you in the library?" he asked as he put in his combination, glancing at Cassie. "Isn't this prime reading time for you?"

"I'm kind of feeling like the cafeteria today," I said with a shrug, suddenly doubting myself.

He pulled open his locker. "You're Miss Social now, eh?"

"Finally, she is," Cassie said. "Now hurry up, Z, because they always run out of oyster crackers at the salad bar."

"Calm down," he teased, and I felt better when he gave her a smart-ass grin and looked a little more like himself.

Whew.

He dumped his books in his locker, and I was surprised that even with friends by my side and a surprising number of recognizable faces in the crowd, there was still something massively intimidating about a high school cafeteria during lunch. So much noise, so much obnoxious laughter; I always felt like the cafeteria was the high school equivalent of the yard at a prison.

Lots of energy after being locked up all day, the air full of volatility.

But I was ready for this. I'd played boot hockey with these people. Eating food with them would be nothing, right?

As if reading my anxious mind, Alec squeezed my hand.

And that, combined with the familiarity of the table he stopped in front of, completely calmed my racing heart.

Because Kyle, Richie, and Vinny were on one side of the table, eating their lunches, and a couple of other guys from the team, as well as Liz and Lillie, were on the other.

It was a safe table.

Weird in a good way.

Like we were all friends.

Of course, I had no idea if that would change once Alec and I ended our agreement. What would they think of me then?

It was getting tricky to remember the big picture of our situation when my feelings about everything had changed.

Like hockey practice, for example.

It felt a lot different all of a sudden.

Now, when I wasn't filming, I sat beside Cassie and we *both* did our homework (when she wasn't stealing snacks from the concession stand). I watched the guys practice and I cared about more than just Alec. I watched as the entire team worked their asses off, and almost as much as the school wanted it, I wanted them to make the tournament.

It was all they talked about, the only thing that seemed to matter.

You could almost feel it in the air when you entered the Doug.

The mural that hung on the wall, the one that showed the hockey history of Southview—it suddenly seemed larger and more visible, like it was waiting to have the BIG story added onto it.

And the team's intensity at practice was off the charts. Alec still seemed, to me, to be more locked in than everyone else, but there was a seriousness that couldn't be denied. This was the team that could potentially do the thing that'd never been done, and everyone appeared to be fixated on the importance of that.

But toward the end of the week, I started noticing the tension hanging over Alec.

He was the same funny guy, but it felt like he was distracted by his thoughts twenty-four seven.

He smiled, but it didn't quite reach his eyes. He joked, but his mouth wasn't as quick to slide into a grin. It was like he couldn't *not* think about the tournament and how badly he wanted it.

Only one more game and they were in.

And God only knew how much pain he was in. Every time I asked about his shoulder, he told me it was fine, and I could tell he didn't want to talk about it.

Part of me wanted to whisper to him that everything would be fine regardless of what happened, but I knew he wouldn't appreciate that.

I wished, for once, that I could be the one to reassure *him*.

That I knew how to make him relax.

Because all I wanted was for him to be happy.

CHAPTER THIRTY-FOUR
Alec

I think I might have an ulcer.

I probably didn't, but knowing how close we were to the game, my appetite was gone and my gut kind of burned all the time.

Section finals—one more fucking game—and we were going to the X.

No matter what I did, my brain couldn't let it go.

First and foremost, of course, I was obsessed with winning because we were *all* obsessed with winning. This was our year and Southview was destined to bring home the trophy.

It was ours for the taking, as Coach Oz reminded us every day.

But I also couldn't stop thinking about the rest.

Dani and I had been making strides with my reputation, but that wouldn't even matter if my game wasn't there. I knew scouts were going to be in the seats and writers were going to be in the box and my parents were going to be watching with their hearts in their throats, so I had to find a way to come through for all of them when my shoulder was getting so bad that I was on a steady rotation of acetaminophen and ibuprofen, mixed in with a near-constant dousing of Icy Hot.

But what if I didn't come through?

How would my parents ever get out of debt if I didn't get drafted?

I leaned into being Zeus and acting like I was unfazed (Dani called it my puckboy personality), but the truth was that I felt like a nervous kid, scared little Alec afraid to fuck up at sports.

My mom cooked my favorite dinner Thursday night—pepperoni casserole—and then my folks proceeded to be so fucking excited to talk about the game while I ate that I almost couldn't breathe from the weight of it on my chest.

Two days away, holy shitballs.

Every hockey team in the state that was facing their section finals was losing their shit right about now.

One more win until the X.

I was sick with want, I swear to God.

Elite play, elite hair, elite cellies—everything about the tournament was elite and everybody wanted to make it there. Add to that the lore of fucking Southview and I was *this close* to puking my guts out at any given moment.

"You okay, kid?" my dad asked, taking a break from his game talk to wolf down his dinner. "You've been quiet all week."

"*I* was quiet all week," Ashton said, mostly because she'd entered a phase where she just stole other people's conversations, all the time. If you said you took a walk, Ashton took a walk. If you said you were tired, Ashton was tired.

Yesterday my dad said Ed had been busting his balls about selling one of his duck blinds, and she looked directly at me and said, "Ed has been busting my balls."

"Yeah, I'm fine," I said. "Just tired."

"Is it possible you're taking this *too* seriously?" my mom asked. "I love how competitive you are, Al, but you need to relax. You don't want to psych yourself out."

"I know," I said, not wanting to take another bite of food.

"And the bottom line is it's just a game, right?" My mom gave me the smile she'd always given me when she was trying to make me feel better about something, the same one she'd given me when she used to put Band-Aids on the scrapes I'd gotten from being klutzy as fuck.

"Just a game"?

I had to stop myself from laughing.

We all knew it wasn't *just* a game.

Hockey was *the* game.

Especially in Minnesota, and especially in this household, where we were relying on hockey as a lifeline (though we'd never say it out loud).

Hell, I *wished* it were *just* a game.

But it wasn't. That was the truth.

She said, "Of course you want to make it to the tournament, and you guys are good enough this year so you probably will, but the thing is—if you don't, your road isn't ending, right?"

Right.

"Your high school career will end, sure, but this is only the beginning for you," she reassured me. "So go hard, but remember that this game isn't the end either way."

I needed a lightning bolt to just come down through the roof and strike me down.

"You'll be starting a whole new chapter," she said.

My dad grinned and said, "God, what if one day you were in an Original Six jersey . . . ?"

"What?"

What the fuck is that, Dad?

That was an insane thing to say, especially out loud.

Expecting me to one day wear the sweater of one of the most legendary hockey franchises in, well, like, the history of hockey??

"I mean," he said with a grin, grabbing the casserole and scooping out some more before setting the pan down, "I don't want to jinx anything, but a man can dream, right?"

Where the hell is that lightning bolt?

I didn't get a lightning bolt, but the doorbell rang.

"I'll get it," I said, nearly leaping out of my chair. "It's probably Kyle."

I had no reason whatsoever to think it was Kyle, but I needed to get out of there before I had a heart attack. *Please be Kyle please be Kyle.*

But when I opened the door, it was Dani, all bundled up in a scarf, hat and boots.

Every thought in my head immediately cleared.

"Hi," she said with a shy smile.

"Hi, yourself," I said, shocked as fuck to see her. "Can I help you?"

"Who is it—oh hey, Danigirl," my dad said from behind me. "Come in before you freeze."

"Actually," she said, grinning like she always did at my dad, like she was genuinely happy to see him, "I was wondering if your son would want to go on a walk with me."

Wait, what?

"You walked over?" my dad asked. "Is your blood finally thickening?"

"No, I've got three pairs of socks under these boots and pants under my pants."

My dad started laughing, and she gave me an eyebrow raise. "So? Do you want to take a walk or not?"

I was pretty sure I'd never wanted to do anything as much as I wanted to go for a walk with her at that moment. Not only was she rescuing me from that dinner conversation, but she looked cute as hell all bundled up.

And it'd been a long-ass time since I'd gone for a walk with Dani Collins.

Fuck, this is a terrible idea.

Because as much as I'd been denying it, things with Dani were starting to feel way too fucking real.

They had been for a while now.

Whether I liked it or not.

That didn't mean I had any clue what I wanted or what the hell to do with the realization, but it was suddenly my reality.

"Count me in," I said, slipping on my shoes and grabbing my coat.

As soon as I stepped out on the porch and shut the door behind me, I asked, "Where do you want to go?"

"Maybe the old route . . . ?"

When she used to stay with us in the summer, we walked the "old route" so many times, just wandering around away from our parents, talking about nothing and everything. We always walked to the end of the block, took a left into the loop by the elementary school, then went the long way by the big park before coming back.

"That works for me," I said. "But stick to the grass for traction."

It was a cold night, but not as bad as it'd been for the past couple weeks.

She might not freeze to death.

"So what is up?" I asked, pulling my gloves out of my pockets and

307

putting them on. "As much as I'd like to think you couldn't live without seeing me tonight, something tells me there's more to it than that."

"Wow, you're so intuitive," she said, bumping her shoulder against mine.

It was a buddy move, something that was so fucking nothing, yet the way she was always leaning into me just *did* something to my insides.

Because she didn't do it to anyone else.

I knew because I watched her way too fucking much.

"I know I am," I said.

"I actually wanted to swing by because you've seemed very stressed the past few days," she said, pulling her hat (my hat) down a little, "And I don't like it when you're stressed."

"You don't?" *She doesn't like when I'm stressed.* "What is this, like, you worrying about my soft little squishy former self or some bullshit like that?"

"Sort of," she said around a laugh. "I mean, you're kind of the same person."

"Asshole," I said, bumping *her* shoulder with mine. "Calling me soft and squishy."

"Missing the point, Barczewski."

"No, I'm not, Collins," I said. "And I'm fine. My mind is just on the game."

And on you and what you said at the party and that I'm starting to want to spend every second of the day with you but I can't because what the hell is going to happen in the future and I don't even know if you like me and what the fuck what the fuck?

"I get that," she said, shoving her hands into her coat pockets. "But, like . . . that's it? Every time I look at you this week, it's like the weight of the world is sitting on your shoulders. Am I wrong?"

I looked at the quiet street in front of me, flurries falling, and I wished I could tell her she was wrong, that I was handling it all.

I glanced over, and it must have been the way she was looking at me, that old familiar expression, because I heard myself say, "I'm just really feeling the pressure this week."

Instead of looking at me like that was shocking information, she kept her eyes on the path in front of her and asked, "The pressure to make sure the team wins?"

If it were anyone else, I don't know that I would've been able to say it out loud.

Explaining it to someone who wasn't me would be impossible.

But as I looked at Dani, I heard myself say, "The pressure to be Zeus."

Her eyebrows screwed together and she did look at me then. "Explain."

I couldn't do it. I couldn't look at her, especially when she looked at me like *that*, and tell her all my insecurities. I *couldn't*.

But then she slid her fingers between mine, linking our gloved hands as she patiently looked at me like she had all the time in the world to wait for me to muster the courage to say it.

So I did.

"I love the game, but there are so many people counting on me that I'm scared—all the fucking time—of letting them down," I said, and once I started talking, it was like I couldn't stop. "And, like, they've never said it directly, but my parents need me to go to the NHL so fucking badly. They still owe a fortune to the hospital for all the surgeries and

309

rehab, so if I don't make it big, there's no light at the end of the tunnel for them. It's going to be all foreclosures and bad shit."

The words came out of me as we walked down the block, they kept coming when we turned the corner, and I was still talking when we turned around by the elementary school. It was like the freedom to actually say out loud what'd been in my head for months now was fucking intoxicating.

"I hate that so many people are counting on me to fix everything, because what if I don't?"

She didn't say anything for a minute after I stopped ranting. She just walked beside me with the snow softly falling, and I wanted to file this image away because it felt important.

So very, very *us*.

It was the winter version of what we'd done so many summer evenings, walking around and talking.

"You have to know your parents will be fine, right? I mean, they love you and want you to be happy," she said. "I don't think you have to win a state hockey championship and go to the NHL in order for them to survive."

"Dani, they have spent half their lives—and their income— supporting me. Now they've been dealt this shitty hand where my dad can't really work even though he wants to, and the twins want to play hockey, which costs a fortune, and, like, I *need* to deliver this for them."

"I know," she said with a soft smile. "And you will—I can feel it. But if you don't, everything is going to be okay. It will."

"How do you know that, though?"

"I don't," she said with a shrug. "But I do."

"Genius," I said with a laugh, teasingly squeezing her fingers a little too hard. "That's really fucking genius, Collins. You don't but you do; that is a brilliant Harvard mind right there."

"Kiss my ass," she giggled, hard squeezing back.

"The perfect ass I'm not allowed to talk about?"

The giggles slid into laughter. "Kiss my ass, Vinny's ass, Oz's ass— just kiss an ass, Barczewski."

"Did you seriously come over here just to take me on a walk?" I asked as I noticed we were back on my street.

She shrugged. "It always worked when we were kids. It felt like we could talk about anything when we were doing this route."

"You're very wise," I said, swinging my left arm wide and hard to shoot her body a little forward, ahead of me, the way I always used to when we walked.

"A brilliant Harvard mind right here," she laughed, stumbling and squeezing my hand, jerking her right arm to bring me right back up with her.

Only she slipped on the dusting of snow, losing her feet entirely. She let out a squeal as she went down, landing on her ass in the snow, and I would've laughed at her but she pulled me down with her.

"Shit!" I managed as I landed right beside her (half on top of her), and I laughed while she cackled.

Thank God we had so much snow that it didn't hurt.

"You okay?" I said, pushing myself up on my arms, leaning over her. "Dani?"

She nodded, laughing as she propped herself up on her elbows. Her eyes were crinkled as she grinned and said, "That was very on-brand for the old Dani and Alec."

"It was, wasn't it?" I said, looking down at the face that was *just* underneath mine, upturned almost as if waiting for me.

The world went still, so quiet that all I could hear amid the dark and snowy night was my own heartbeat.

All I could see were brown eyes, staring up at me.

All I could want were those shiny lips, turned up in an amused pout, her soft breath so fucking close it gave me goose bumps.

I watched her eyes slide over my face, searching, questioning, and I no longer gave a shit about anything other than this moment. I didn't care about the past or the future, because nothing mattered but the present.

Her.

This.

Fucking *us*.

I lowered my head and took her mouth, needy. *Greedy.* I didn't give a shit about what was fake and what wasn't, because it was all real to me. This wasn't part of a game, and it wasn't for anyone watching.

No, this kiss was ours.

She sucked in a shaky breath, like she was about to dive in, and that sound was the flash point. It felt like something detonated, like the wick that'd been lit a long time ago had finally sizzled up and blown my fucking head off.

"*Fuck*, Collins," I said against her lips, but how could I not curse her when she was so fucking perfect?

She angled her head, *my genius*, drawing me in deeper, and I was instantly lost in her sweet mouth. My hands found her waist—*hate gloves, want skin*—while I attempted to consume her. Gluttony wasn't my goal, but once I had a taste of her kiss, I couldn't get enough.

More more more more.

Dear God, the way I want her.

Her lips, her tongue, and her apple juice smell were my world as I threw every molecule of my being into the kiss. Not because I was trying to prove something, but because I'd never wanted anything in my life the way I wanted her mouth at that moment.

Give me everything, honey, please, God.

I chased her tongue, nibbled on her lips, fucking *ate* at her mouth because I just needed more. I felt insatiable, ravenous, *feral* as she kissed me back, like I'd do anything not to have to stop kissing her.

Because Dani kissed me back like she felt the same.

Her gloved hands weren't just resting on my face; no, they were purposeful, holding me in place so she could kiss the ever-loving shit out of me, praise Jesus.

"Alec," she whispered, still kissing me.

"Hmmm."

"Porch light," she said, and I could hear the smile in her voice.

"Hmmm?"

"Alec," she said with a giggle, pulling back. "This house just turned on the porch light."

I opened my eyes, and the sight of her drowsy grin made me smile. "So?"

"So your neighbor is essentially turning the hose on us," she said, still giggling as she removed her hands from my face. "We have to go."

"But I don't want to," I admitted, because I was scared that if we moved, we'd never come back to this place again.

"Come on." Dani scooched away from me, climbed to her feet, then held out her hand. "Let's go, Barczewski."

I let her pull me up and lead me over to my door, but I realized when she left me on the porch that I still knew nothing. I watched her walk away under the streetlights, looking like everything I'd ever wanted, but I had no idea what the kiss meant—if anything—or where in God's name this left us.

CHAPTER THIRTY-FIVE

Dani

Friday started with annoyance in the form of a text.

Ben Worthington: If you ever need a ride to school, I go in that direction so just lmk

Yeah, no. The last thing I needed was for Alec or his friends to see Benji texting me, so I really wished he'd forget my number.

And then on the way to school, the day's theme switched from annoying to stressful.

Because my dad started texting.

Dad: Daniella Grace, I'd appreciate a call this evening. I'm out of time and patience.

Shit. I glanced guiltily at my mom, who was watching the road as she drove, blissfully unaware of my traitorous texting. I needed to respond, especially after he'd sounded so unusually . . . *nice* when I talked to him at Bryce's party. He'd been impatient for my answer, of course, but he'd also genuinely seemed like he maybe just missed me.

Which stressed me out because it made the decision harder.

I texted: Okay—sorry.

My heart started beating faster when my phone buzzed and he replied: It shouldn't be this hard.

I jammed the phone in my bag, feeling like a jerk reading his texts while sitting beside my mom. I couldn't stop thinking about it for the rest of the drive, my hands shaking and the panic clawing at my chest as

I ran through the scenarios over and over again in my head.

*Do what he wants and destroy my mom—and maybe myself—or tell
him no and lose the opportunity to ever get close to him.*

I had to go into the bathroom and splash cold water on my face when
I got to school, because my thoughts were getting too loud for my body
to ignore.

But every second I wasn't worrying about my parents, I was thinking
about Alec, which made my stomach *fill* with butterflies.

And not the fun ones that went crazy every time I thought about
the kiss.

No, these were the bad ones.

Because I had no idea what was going on with us.

Or how I felt about it—*gahhhhhh.*

Did I have real feelings for him? That was a big yes.

Had we had the world's most amazing kiss that definitely wasn't
fake?

Oh yeah.

Did that mean anything at all regarding my relationship with him?

No idea whatsoever.

Just because I liked him and *really* liked kissing him didn't mean that
(A) he felt the same, or (B) we should do anything about it. College on
the other side of the country was still waiting for me, and hockey was
still waiting for him.

So us = still not a great idea.

Especially when he was dealing with so much hockey pressure. The
best thing I could do as his friend would be to support him and *not* be
a distraction, right?

He didn't need our "relationship" messing with his focus.

But even as I had these internal heart-to-heart talks with myself, there was a part of me that didn't want to listen.

Because maybe . . . *God*, I was terrified to even think it. But maybe it was okay to feel more with him. Maybe it was okay to *be* more with him, because he was the exception.

Chill out, chill out.

I was overthinking everything, my nerves shredded, because in addition to my feels for Alec, I had tomorrow's section finals to worry about. Now that I knew how stressed he was and how much pressure he felt, the stakes felt out-of-this-world high.

He held my hand when I found him by his locker, and the look he gave me curled my toes, but nothing out of the ordinary (in our fake dating situation) transpired between us. We had speech and lunch together, but the entire day was exactly as it'd been before the kiss.

Which, of course, drove me to distraction wondering what that meant.

I was glad when the final bell rang because I needed a break from my own head.

I rode with Alec to the Doug, where the team had a quick run-through. They went over the game plan for the next day and did some skating, but it was low-key and relaxed.

Cassie wasn't there (she had a doctor's appointment), so I just sat on the bleachers and watched Alec like a stalker the entire time.

His big body, skating so effortlessly; the way he could casually maneuver the puck with his stick like it was an extension of his arm; the sound of his deep voice when he yelled . . . would I ever not be absolutely transfixed by it all?

I was already on a bit of an Alec high when he texted me while I was locking the storage room: I need your help.

Everyone else had already left, but I was used to Alec being last.

I texted: What's up?

Alec: You know how superstitious I am, right?

That made me smile, because he was a silly little boy when it came to that.

I texted: I do.

Alec: Well, after the practice before the best game of my life, this girl stumbled into the locker room and our chains got tangled together. It was a whole thing.

I giggled, then looked around to make sure no one had appeared out of nowhere to mock me for my idiocy.

Coast appears to be clear.

Me: Yeah?

Alec: Yeah. No one is in here, and I know for a fact the coaches have left, so . . . would you consider . . . ?

I gasped, and maybe giggled, as I looked down at the message.

Me: You're insane and NO WAY

My mind went back to his bare chest and the way his neck had smelled in the stuffy locker room. Like fresh soap.

Alec: PLEEEEEEEASE? You know how important this game is. I am desperate to re-create everything from that game.

I couldn't. I mean, I *couldn't*.

So why was I walking toward the locker room? I mean, he was in there, so it made sense to go talk to him about it in person instead of texting, right? That was all I was doing. I was going to where he was to discuss how ridiculous his request was.

I looked around when I got to the locker room, and I didn't see a single soul in the Doug. I knew there had to be people somewhere, the people who opened and closed the place, but they were nowhere to be found at that moment.

"Alec?" I said, pushing open the door, my stomach fluttery as my pulse pounded.

"Right here," he said, and if I'd instantly fainted, it wouldn't have been an overreaction.

There. He. Was.

I could see this time, my eyes absent of tears, and I suddenly wondered if this was a mistake. Because Alec looked *way* out of my league of knowledge at the moment.

He looked somehow dangerous.

He was bare-chested, and this time in perfect focus. He had pecs and abs and biceps—holy *shit* those biceps. I swallowed and was grateful that he had on sweatpants this time, because I felt like I would have turned and run out of the locker room like a schoolgirl if he'd been wearing boxer briefs again.

I would have spontaneously combusted or melted into a puddle on the floor.

The music that was playing somewhere in the locker room wasn't helping my calm, though.

Sweat, lose your breath
Any way you move, I'm into it

"I feel like this is a stupid dumb terrible idea," I said, walking toward him.

"Oh, honey," he said, his eyes wild with mischief, "most superstitions are."

I stopped in front of him, not too close but close enough. "Yeah?"

"Yeah," he agreed, and I could tell he wasn't paying attention to our words. His dark eyes were on mine, and it felt like we were both simmering, like water getting ready to boil.

"Okay." I cleared my throat. "So what exactly are we doing here *specifically*?"

"By 'specifically,' are you trying to differentiate what the goal is from the fact that we are inappropriately close in a locker room when I'm not fully dressed?"

"Yes, that is exactly what I'm looking for; thank you for the clarification," I said around a laugh.

"The way I recall it," he said, "I hugged you, you hugged me back, and then our chains got connected and I had to pull them apart."

"That is how I recall it too," I said, but my voice was almost a whisper.

"Then let's do this," he said.

Even though I knew it was coming, I somehow felt shocked when he wrapped his big arms around me. Butterflies went wild in my stomach and adrenaline pumped through my body as I slid my hands over his skin and hugged him back, like I'd touched a live wire or something.

I closed my eyes and let the smell of him into my senses, trying to be cool about the feel of his big arms wrapped around me.

But when I pulled back, our chains didn't get tangled.

"Come on," he said, grinning down at me in that way that made his eyes squint. "I guess we need to try again."

"This is ridiculous," I laughed. "Are you sure this isn't a ploy?"

"What are you saying, Collins?" he said, his deep voice making the flirt sound dirty. "That you think I like your hands all over my chest? Do you think I *like* canoodling with you in the locker room?"

"I actually think it's possible, yes," I said, wondering why it was so hard to speak.

"Yeah, I wouldn't hate if it took ten tries," he said. "Come here and let's get these chains to lock up."

He pulled me close again, this time wrapping his arms around my waist so tightly that I almost felt crushed against him in the very best way. He lifted me a little and I felt like I couldn't breathe, and when we pulled back, our necklaces were tangled together.

I felt his grin but couldn't actually see it because his face was down by my neck.

"Success," he murmured, and I felt him untangling us.

I closed my eyes as his breath raised goose bumps on my skin.

"I think I kissed your neck last time, didn't I?" he said, so, so quietly.

"Um," I breathed, unable to form words.

"I'm pretty sure I did," he said, and his mouth was so close to my neck I could feel the vibration of his voice. "And we don't want to mess with the superstition."

"Well, if that's what you remember happening," I managed, fully aware that we both knew that had never happened, "we definitely don't want to mess with the . . ."

I trailed off when his lips touched my skin. There must've been a framework of nerve endings in that very spot, because every cell in my

LYNN PAINTER

body sparked and sizzled at the feel of his mouth on my skin.

"And if I recall," he said, his teeth dragging over the side of my neck, "I might have nibbled a little bit too."

My eyes closed of their own accord and my head fell back. *How the hell does Alec know how to make me feel this way?*

"Yeah, you definitely maybe did that," I said, and my toes curled in my shoes when he laughed a *very* dirty laugh against my throat.

"You like that, Collins?" he very nearly *growled* against my skin.

"Not sure, maybe go again," I said on a breath, and then I gritted my teeth when he did.

Dear *Lord*, I thought as my hands were suddenly on the back of his head and he was doing the most incredible things to my neck with his mouth. Somewhere in my brain an alarm bell was ringing because this was a terrible idea, but it was silenced by the way his body was pressing mine against the lockers.

"We should probably stop," I said, sliding my fingers into his thick hair, definitely not stopping anything.

Not even slowing.

"I mean," I managed, even though I didn't make a move to untangle myself from him, "we don't want the mojo to swing too far the other way."

"Collins," he murmured against my skin before lifting his head to smirk down at me with sleepy-sexy eyes. "Will you stop talking if I kiss you?"

"Only one way to find out," I said, feeling daring all of a sudden.

"Hell, yes, there's my girl," he murmured as his smirk disappeared into something hotter and his lips slid over mine and then he was kissing me, kissing me like he appreciated my boldness, like he was fucking *enthralled* by it, like he wanted to devour every bite of it.

Oh my God, he kisses like he plays hockey.

His mouth was hot and wild as he released my waist and pressed his palms against the lockers on each side of me, caging my body between his and the lockers, leaning into me in a way that made me dizzy.

I gripped his hair, chased his kiss, but then a noise outside the locker room reminded me.

"Also, someone has to be coming soon to lock up the locker room," I said, knowing it was true but unable to move.

"Yeah, you're right," he said against my mouth, and then he pulled back. His dark eyes and dirty grin didn't help with the dizziness, especially when he leaned down and dropped the sweetest kiss on my neck—where it'd all begun—before straightening.

"Um, okay," I mumbled, tucking my hair behind my ears and feeling out of it—*is this what drunk feels like*—as I looked at a spot on the lockers.

"Okay," he said, sounding amused. "Give me five minutes to throw on a shirt and I'll be out."

"Perfect," I said calmly, somehow managing to exit the locker room on legs that were weak and wobbly.

I didn't see another person as I paced in the cold arena, waiting for him, and when he came out, Alec gave me a smile and grabbed my hand.

What the hell are we doing? I thought as I linked my fingers between his.

And yet all I wanted was for him to hold my hand.

• • •

The team dinner was at Alec's house that night. The second I walked in, it felt like coming home, especially seeing Sarah and John in the kitchen with my mom there beside them.

"I didn't know you were going to be here," I said to her as I dropped my coat on the bench.

"Sarah asked me to help and it sounded like fun," she said with a smile.

"Except you forgot to bake a cake," Connor's dad said. Connor was the freshman goalie who never played but seemed very nice.

"Is it someone's birthday?" I asked.

"No, but your mom used to bake all the time in high school. Her German chocolate cake was always the best."

"You baked cakes for people in high school?" I asked, shocked. As far as I knew, my mom didn't bake.

Like, at all.

But now I was picturing high school Hannah with a cake-baking business, like a lemonade stand but with German chocolate cakes.

That couldn't be right, could it?

It seemed far-fetched, but so had a freaking Fricklinhauger Fellowship.

"Sometimes," she said with a shrug, and something in her smile told me it'd mattered to her.

"I'm starving," Alec said, and I felt his big hand on my arm. "We should eat."

"Dani!" Cassie yelled from where everyone was eating in the living room. "Get in here!"

And then Richie yelled, "Yeah, Collins, get your ass in here and bring your oversized man with you!"

324

Mom's face was full of happiness as she laughed, and part of me wondered if this was where she'd always belonged.

In her hometown, in her best friend's kitchen.

Maybe baking.

Guilt suddenly hit me hard, because what would she have become if she hadn't gotten pregnant with me? Apparently she had a genius IQ, in addition to culinary talent, yet she'd spent *eighteen years* being an Air Force wife.

Because of me.

God, how could I even *consider* ruining her brand-new happiness by leaving?

"I need food," Alec said, giving me a playful nudge. "Can we *please* go eat, Collins?"

"Fine," I said, and I let Alec lead me out of the kitchen and into the other room.

And thankfully, the team dinner shook me out of that depressing headspace, as I realized that I *did* feel comfortable on my own with those people. In this town, sitting next to Alec, and stressing about a hockey game I desperately wanted my team to win.

It felt like it was real, and I realized I kind of wanted it to be.

"Okay, listen up!" Coach Osman climbed on top of the kitchen table, and I offhandedly wondered if he'd asked Sarah or John for permission first. "I don't need to remind you what tomorrow is or what it means."

He started talking, and the house was dead quiet as every eye and ear in the place was on him. Including mine. "Southview has wanted the championship for longer than I've been alive," he said. "Yet we've come up short every time. But not this year. This is our fucking year, boys. We've put in the work and done the time, and you *are* the personnel to make it happen. So let's finish our business, okay? Let's show up tomorrow, punch our ticket to the X, and get this history-making started."

I had literal chills as he wrapped it up, because somehow this meant everything to every soul in that house. In that town. They had the chance to change history, to get the trophy that would match the pride of that massive wall mural, and it felt huge.

"You look so *right* here," my mom said when we pulled into my grandpa's driveway afterward. "I know I've been driving you crazy, pushing everything, but it's only because I want your face to look like it did tonight."

She sounded like she might cry, in a good way, which made my throat a little tight too.

She said, "I know I'm annoying—"

"You're not," I interrupted.

"No, I am about this," she admitted as she put the car in park. "But I want you to have friends who care about you. Friends who yell when you walk into the room and are sad when it's time for you to leave. You're only seventeen, so I don't really care about your love life, but if you're going to date, I want it to be someone like Alec, who looks at you like he knows how lucky he is."

I looked at my grandpa's house through the windshield as her words warmed me.

I wish that were true.

When we walked through the kitchen door, Grandpa Mick was running the blender.

"It's about time," he said, giving us a weird look over his shoulder. His eyes were kind of twinkling, like he was up to something.

"Were we supposed to be home earlier, Dad?" my mom asked, giving me side-eye like *What the hell is wrong with your grandpa?* "Did I have a curfew I didn't know about?"

"Shut up and sit down, wiseass," he said.

"Yes, sir," she replied.

"All right," I said, dropping my backpack on the floor and sitting beside my mom at the table. "Is this like a family meeting or something?"

"Okay, don't ruin my moment of wonderfulness by being a little shit, Dani," he said with dancing eyes.

"Your constant ability to *not* censor yourself in front of your granddaughter is always astounding to me," my mom said.

"I didn't censor myself around you, and you turned out okay," he said.

"You didn't always think that," my mom replied.

"Yeah, so maybe I've come around," he said with a shrug. "Maybe now I think you turned out a little okay."

"Gushing praise."

"This lovefest is disgusting," I said.

"So what are we waiting for here, Pop?" my mom asked, trying her best to sound like a smart-ass, but her entire face was just happy.

"Milkshakes." My grandpa turned off the blender, and I wanted to cry.

Milkshakes.

He was giving me a full-on, ear-to-ear Grandpa Mick smile, the smile that had been mine every summer when we visited him.

The smile he'd always saved for his Danigirl.

His Danigirl who'd been *obsessed* with his chocolate milkshakes.

"You made milkshakes?" I very nearly yelled, out-of-my-mind excited about this throwback surprise. "Are you kidding me right now?"

"No, I'm not kidding. You've got a game tomorrow, so I thought we should celebrate."

"You do know I'm just a manager, right?" I asked.

"I do, but the manager is very important. So important that I made milkshakes and bought you a present."

"You bought me a present?" I pretty much *did* scream that time.

"Here," he said, grabbing a box and tossing it onto the table in front of me. "Open it."

"Really?" It was a medium-sized brown box, the same kind of box that usually delivered something boring like a refrigerator filter or a carbon monoxide detector.

I opened the box and pulled out what appeared to be a burgundy article of clothing. But when I lifted it up, it was a Southview hockey jersey.

"It's stupid that you didn't have one before now, so I had to make it right," Grandpa Mick said.

I was speechless for a moment as I caught the emotion in my grandpa's expression, like he was nervous.

"I love it so much," I said, my chest full and warm as I looked down at the heavy fabric, because it occurred to me that Southview kind of felt a little bit like home.

No, no—that wasn't right. "Home" was too strong a word.

It was more that I felt *at home* in Southview.

That Packers bull on the front made me think about my school and the fake friends I had there, fake friends that felt a lot like *actual* friends. It was stupid, the feeling in my chest as I looked at the jersey, but I hadn't felt *at home* anywhere in a very long time.

"Now look at the back," my grandpa said excitedly, and it was obvious he was more in love with this gift than even I was.

My throat was so tight as I looked at Grandpa Mick's stupid grin.

I flipped over the jersey, only to discover that the back was customized.

It had Grandpa Mick's number—nine—stitched on the back, and my last name.

Next to *his* last name.

BOCHE COLLINS.

He still hadn't apologized for what happened after my grandma's funeral, but when I wrapped my arms around him and he hugged me as tightly as he ever had, I knew we'd finally moved on.

It took me hours to fall asleep that night because my brain was so muddled.

It rotated between happiness from the moment with my grandpa, confusion because my friends and Alec also made me happy and I'd never expected that, and terror as I realized that in less than twenty-four hours, the section final would already be over.

I prayed like a monk as I lay there in the dark, praying for hockey players who wanted to win their future, grumpy old guys who I loved with my whole heart, and messed-up shoulders that made strong boys weak.

Please, God.

CHAPTER THIRTY-SIX
Alec

"Al, wake up," Ashton said, and I could feel her scrambling onto my bed.

"Yeah, Al, wake up," I heard Cole say, giggling, and then they both started jumping on the bed.

"Knock it off, you guys," I grumbled into my pillow, slowly rolling over and opening my eyes.

Too bright.

It'd been impossible to sleep last night—I was still awake at three, staring at the ceiling and running through plays in my head—so this early wake-up call was very unwelcome.

But then I heard her laugh.

I looked at the doorway and Dani was standing beside my mom and Hannah, grinning like the sight of me struggling with my siblings was the funniest thing she'd ever seen.

"Why are you here when it's still sleeping time?" I asked, pathetically happy to see her. "Do you want to get hit in the face by a pillow? Do you want to get dumped by the very sexy captain of the Southview Packers? Do you want to see me cry, Collins, do you?"

"Do I want you to stop asking questions? Um, *yes*," she said, making our moms laugh even harder. "We brought you some food, so get your butt out of bed and come downstairs."

"She said 'butt,'" Ash said with a snort.

"She said 'butt,'" Cole repeated, giggling.

I groaned because I didn't want to be up yet.

"I don't like people jumping on the bed, and I don't like breakfast—you know this, *Dan*," I grumbled.

I'd *never* liked breakfast. Aside from a random donut now and again, I didn't get hungry until I'd been up for a couple hours.

"We went to Kriz's, you whiner," she said, "and got you two chocolate crullers. So it's not breakfast; it's donuts."

Okay—huge difference.

"Yeah, you whiner," Ash laughed.

"Whiner," Cole repeated, giggling.

"Now get your butt downstairs before I eat your food," Dani said, and after the twins said the word "butt" like five more times, it was quiet in the doorway.

I got out of bed and stumbled into the bathroom, deep breathing as I thought through the day. I choked down a few ibuprofen, unzipped the hoodie I'd started sleeping in so I didn't have to raise my arms in the morning when that shoulder was too stiff to move, and took a quick shower before heading downstairs.

But almost as if she knew the day was going to be a struggle for me, Dani was sitting at the table with everyone in my family—and her mom—when I walked in the kitchen.

"It's about time, *Al*," she said sarcastically, because she'd always thought it was funny that they called me that.

She'd said it sounded like they were talking to a fifty-year-old shoe salesman.

"I didn't know there was a specific time I needed to get up on game day," I said.

LYNN PAINTER

"Well, if you're going to eat these donuts for breakfast, you need time for the sugar crash and then to pump yourself back up again."

"You think of everything, don't you?"

"I really do," she said with a grin.

A grin that made me think *not today*.

I was growing way too attached to this relationship, and there was zero doubt that it was real to me.

It was.

But she'd *always* been it for me.

The standard.

I hadn't realized it then, but she'd been laying the groundwork during every one of those summers we'd spent together, setting the precedent for what my type was.

Dani Collins—that was my type.

Period.

I just hoped I was *her* type.

But now was not the time to be thinking about the what-the-fucks of my love life.

There was nothing more important than winning tonight.

That needed to be my only focus.

Dani and her mom left before I'd even finished my first donut, and after that I went down to the basement and started watching game film, losing myself in footage of Edina's team. I watched for hours, familiarizing myself with the players I was already familiar with, watching their habits and seeing their vulnerabilities.

And when it was finally time to go to the Doug for warm-ups, I felt ready.

Bring. It. On.

CHAPTER THIRTY-SEVEN

Dani

I was setting up the camera when my dad texted.

Dad: I'm here. Just paid. Is there anywhere in particular I should sit?

What?? I looked up at the stands, my heart racing as I texted: Wait, you're here in Southview? At the hockey game?

No.

No way.

He couldn't actually be *here*, at the game, could he?

Why was he in town at all?!

Panic ballooned in my chest. *This can't be happening. I haven't even had a chance to talk to Mom about Dad yet.* And now he was here. Without telling me he was coming.

No, no, no, no, no.

I glanced in the direction of where the hockey parents were sitting, and I could see my mom next to John, Sarah, and the twins, right in the middle of their row.

I jumped when my phone buzzed, and my heart was beating in my ears when I read: Since it's been nearly impossible to reach you, I decided to fly in so we can talk. I thought I could surprise you!

Nonononononoonoooooooooo!

I texted: I'm going to be busy during the game with manager stuff and it's pretty packed tonight, so maybe we should just meet up afterward. What hotel are you staying at?

Please, please leave.

Dad: I've already bought a ticket, Daniella. I'll watch the game and we can connect afterward.

God, I couldn't believe he was actually here.

I texted: Sounds good.

My hands were shaking and my stomach churned because I was actually going to have to deal with this. There was no more avoiding it, I was going to have to tell my dad the truth.

I want to live here with Mom, but I also want you to move back so we can see each other.

I didn't want to say those words, not to the colonel, but he was my dad. Even though it wasn't his idea of perfect, he'd want to make the sacrifice to spend time with me, right?

I turned back to the camera and hit record just before they started announcing players, deciding any negative thoughts were going to have to wait until after the game.

I needed to focus.

I watched Alec skate toward the bench, his face so serious that it was hard to believe it belonged to him.

He looked mean.

His dark eyes were focused, his mouth a hard line, and I felt queasy *for* him, knowing how badly he wanted this.

How badly they *all* wanted it.

Hell, all you had to do was look around the Doug and you could *feel* the electricity from how badly *everyone in the town* wanted it.

"I'm so nervous!"

I looked away from Alec as Cassie ran up beside me. "Yeah, same."

"Do you realize that if we win, we'll be staying at a downtown hotel in less than a week, missing school to watch hockey boys all day?"

"You can't say *if* we win," I said. "You have to say *when*. Say it again the right way."

"Someone's getting superstitious," she teased with a smile.

We didn't talk as they announced Edina's team (though the student section had a *lot* to say about them), and when the announcer shouted, "Your Southview Packers" and the crowd went wild, Cassie and I were screaming right along with them like insane fangirls.

And we got worse.

We yelled when they announced Richie, we hollered when they announced Vinny, and Cassie whistled with her fingers when they announced Kyle.

But my heart was in my throat when they announced Alec.

The rink was deafening with shouts of "Zeus," and I felt like I was going to have a heart attack as he skated onto the ice. I'd seen multiple reporters around the arena, and according to him, there were probably NHL and college scouts there as well. Part of me was too nervous to be excited—I kind of wanted to throw up—and part of me couldn't look away from him.

And it was a silly thing to be thinking at that pivotal moment, but he looked ridiculously attractive in his game uniform. It was hard to enjoy his . . . *eye candiness*, though, when I knew how stressed he had to be at that moment.

Please win, please win, please, God, let them win.

It felt like I stopped breathing the second the puck dropped.

Edina was freaking *good*, so good that it was giving me heart palpitations. They were pushing us around, playing *very* physical hockey in their stupid green jerseys, but Alec was always in it, slamming people into the boards as he went after the puck.

I was probably biased, but I swear to God we were in it *because* of him. He seemed to always be there to stop them from scoring, and he seemed to always send the puck exactly where it needed to go, where we came *this close* to scoring.

Unfortunately, they had a guy just like Alec.

When I paused filming at the first break, it felt like my blood pressure was at an unhealthy level. We hadn't scored yet, and neither had Edina.

"This is insane," Cassie said. "We have *got* to get control of this game."

I glanced in the direction of the hockey parents and my blood pressure spiked a little higher as I wondered where the colonel was sitting. "Hey, do you care if I go say hi to my dad really quick? He just got to town."

"Of course," she said. "Go. You need to tell him."

I'd told her about the situation with my dad at Bryce's party, when she found me almost in tears after talking to him, but I'd been nervous ever since that she was going to tell someone.

Alec, specifically, and he didn't need the distraction.

"I know, I know," I said, being vague like it wasn't a big deal.

I started walking up the steps, but stopped when I saw him.

My dad was sitting in the very last row, up by the mural, and he was glaring.

At my mom.

He was craning his neck, staring down at where she sat in the very center of the Packer parent section. She looked happy and like she was where she belonged, and he looked utterly disgusted.

It was sad and made my stomach hurt.

I had no idea what to do with myself at that moment, so I did the only thing I could.

I hustled back to my filming spot and hoped for the best.

"That was fast. How'd it go?" Cassie asked as I sat down beside her.

"I chickened out," I said, forcing myself not to look up in their direction. "Didn't even talk to him."

Just then the guys came back out, and the second I saw number seven, I stopped thinking about my dad altogether. Because when the game started back up, it was no less intense than before. Edina scored almost immediately, but a minute later, thank *God*, Richie sent one into the goal and evened the score. I was screaming as I watched Alec's stick go up, and he skated over in celebration.

After that, things got even more physical. Alec totally slammed Edina's number six face-first into the boards and got sent to the penalty box for the hit, but as the Edina fans heckled him through the glass, he grinned like he found them to be adorable.

Dear God, he was cocky in the hottest way.

We scored again—Kyle this time—but Edina followed up with their own goal.

I never would've imagined a hockey game could be this terribly, horribly riveting.

I was losing my voice from all the screaming, especially when Alec scored a goal three seconds before the period ended.

Cassie knocked over the camera when she shot out of her seat, and we started jumping up and down together, hugging and screaming, and I didn't even lean down to pick it up until after I got to see Alec be surrounded by his teammates, and then they did a chest-bump-the-plexiglass thing in front of the rabid student section, and the crowd lost their minds.

My throat was tight, my heart was full—I was in jeopardy of bursting into happy tears as I watched them leave the ice, energized by their sudden lead.

I didn't move from my seat during the intermission this time because I didn't want to see *that*—with my parents—again.

Watching the Zamboni and stressing over the game sounded like a lot more fun.

All thoughts of my parents vanished when the guys came back out. I hit play and focused on Alec—*as always*—watching his face as he got ready for the third and final period.

It took all of thirty-three seconds for Southview to score. Kyle got the rebound on a shot from Richie on a two-on-two breakaway, which meant Cassie and I nearly broke the camera again, jumping and screaming.

After that, I couldn't sit still because the clock seemed to be moving way too slowly. Yes, we were up by one, but Edina was way too good for that to be a comfortable lead. I clapped and yelled random nonsense that no one but me could hear or understand, and then with a minute left in the period, the entire crowd started counting down the seconds until . . . five, four, three, two . . . one!

"Oh my God!" I screamed, leaping to my feet.

"Holy shit!" Cassie shouted, hugging the custodian who was standing beside her.

The buzzer sounded and it was over.

We were going to the X!

"Oh my God!" Cassie yelled in my ear as she hugged me and we freaked out with the rest of the arena. I was screaming and crying and jumping, but my eyes were stuck on Alec and the team.

It was happening—we made the tournament.

I could barely see through the happy tears as the team piled on top of each other in front of the student section, and as I stood there with Cassie, watching the celebration, I knew that nothing was fake. As hard as I'd tried to create a separation, every single thing was real.

This team, Cassie, the Doug, Southview—I was obsessed with everything in this moment, not as a person using them as a backdrop for a ruse, but as a person who truly and genuinely wanted to be a part of all of it.

"You're so happy!" Cassie said as she looked at my teary face, shaking her head. "Look at you!"

And she pulled me into a hug that made me happy-cry even harder.

I glanced up at the bleachers as she hugged me, and I saw my dad standing by the mural, talking to Big John.

Holy shit, he's talking to Big John.

The few times I remembered my dad ever coming with us to Minnesota, quick little trips for weddings and graduations (never the monthlong summer vacation), he'd always been okay with John. I wouldn't say he *liked* him, but they'd always gotten along.

So had they *just* connected that minute, or did my mom already know my dad was there? I quickly checked my phone after Cassie let go of me, and the lack of messaging from my mom—and him—assured me she'd had yet to encounter my father.

But *shit, shit, shit*, it was only a matter of time.

"Girls!"

The trophy came out, and Coach Oz yelled for us to come onto the ice for pictures.

Apparently, team managers really *were* part of the team.

I swallowed and went out with Cassie, laughing with her while something in my chest burned with a warmth that felt like it had to *glow*, it was so intense. Because this photo was going to be in the year-book, maybe on the mural, and my time at Southview was going to be forever *not* left behind.

I followed Cassie onto the ice as some adult yelled instructions, try-ing to get the team to line up for photos, but when my eyes met Alec's, the dark brown eyes of the best friend I was so fucking proud of, it was over.

I ran at him and his big arms caught me, holding me against him in the tightest hug.

"You did it," I said, the tears back yet again. "That was amazing, Barczewski."

"Thanks," he said, and when he pulled back, I loved how huge his grin was. That was the smile of my old friend, the full-on beam of the happiest boy I'd ever known.

"You're going to the tournament," I said, lifting my hand to touch the chain around his neck as I squealed out the words.

"Hell, yes, we fucking are," he said, squeezing my waist and grinning, looking like he wanted to shout again. "You know you're gonna have to reenact the locker room tie-up for the rest of the games, right?"

"Of course I am," I said, feeling almost breathless with joy.

But as I looked at his wide smile and the way it made his eyes squint as he looked down at me, all I could see was the Alec I'd always loved, the nerdy boy I'd kissed in the shed.

There was no Zeus, no fake boyfriend—just *my* Alec.

Holy shit, I love him.

The realization settled over me, shocking and absolutely unsurprising all at once.

"Your face," he said, amusement shining in those brown eyes. "What is that look?"

I met his gaze as my heart raced, and I couldn't stop myself from blurting, "I really, really want this to be real."

CHAPTER THIRTY-EIGHT
Alec

"Wait, what?"

I leaned down closer, but now her eyes were huge and her mouth was closed, like she'd startled herself.

"I'm going to need you to say that again," I said calmly, which was hilarious because I felt like I was having a heart attack. My chest was tight like a fist as I looked down at brown eyes and blond curls. The way she was trying to avoid looking at me while nibbling on that full bottom lip gave me so many thoughts that my head was about to fucking explode.

I needed her to say it. My hopes were way the fuck up and if I was misunderstanding, I needed to know immediately.

"Dani, hon, you should be on this end since Cassie's on the other side," Oz's wife yelled as she stood in front of the team, trying to organize a photo. "And Zeus—you need to be in the back row toward the middle."

"Okay, one sec," I said, my eyes still on Dani's face, waiting.

"We should go line up," she said, glancing nervously at the rest of the team. When she took a step and turned away from me, I couldn't stop myself from grabbing a fistful of the cool-as-fuck custom Southview jersey she was wearing and hauling her back.

She looked up at me, startled, and I repeated, "I need to know what you're saying, Dani."

"We need you over here, Zeus," Coach yelled.

Dani said, "Yeah, let's talk later because—"

"Hang on, okay?" I yelled toward everyone who wasn't Dani. "I just need a minute."

I sighed and looked down at her, trying my damnedest to sound calm when I said, "Spell it out for me, Collins."

"I want this to be real," she said. "Us, that is."

She gave her head a shake and quickly explained, like she was trying to hurry things along, "Everything that I've said is fake feels really real and I want it to be real but I'm also great with it not being real if you want it to stay fake."

I want it to be real.

That heart-attack feeling was back as she kept babbling.

"In fact, it's probably better to stay fake," she continued, her cheeks flushed, "so maybe I should just—"

I cut her off with a kiss.

I couldn't help myself; it felt like I'd collapse if I didn't kiss her that very second.

She kissed me back like the woman she was, grabbing onto the front of my jersey right there on the ice with the team waiting for us and the entire student section still present.

I couldn't seem to stop myself. I couldn't bring myself to pull back.

Because we were real.

I got a little lost in it—yet again—but then I heard the applause and whistles.

I'm not sure who started laughing first, me or Dani, but that made us finally stop.

"Okay," I said, clearing my throat and wondering how she could look so fucking beautiful, beaming up at me in a hockey jersey and glasses. "*Now* I can pose for the damn picture."

If they'd told me not to smile, it would've been impossible. The night was going to go down as one of the best ever. Beating Edina, making it to the tournament, having Dani tell me it was real for her, too—what the fuck else could I want?

Okay, for my shoulder to stop throbbing, but that's starting to feel like an impossible ask.

As soon as the pictures were done, I found my way back over to where she was.

"What are you doing after this?" I asked, really wanting to celebrate with her. "Because you can't just go home."

"I'm not sure," she said, a little crinkle between her eyebrows. "My dad is here, so I'm—"

"No way—the colonel's here?" Another thing I could want: for her dad to *not* be there. Why the hell would he be there? "Why? Did you know he was coming?"

"Um, no," she said, waving a hand like it was no big deal.

"Is he here just to visit you, or . . ." I asked, needing her to be honest.

"Yeah, I don't really know," she said, looking uncomfortable, like she didn't want to talk about it. "I think—"

"Everyone's going to the Cro," we heard from behind us, and when we turned around, it was my parents and Hannah.

"Great game, kid," my dad said, grinning as he pulled me in for a hug and a back slap. "Big-boy hockey right there."

"Thanks," I said, hugging him back.

344

"And you shut down Bodie," my mom said with a smile. "I mean, you might've been a smidge too rough, but it was nice to see."

A smidge too rough that sent me to the penalty box twice. I loved my mom.

"I didn't hate that part," I said, taking a moment to enjoy how happy they looked.

"Do you, um, know where my dad went?" Dani asked, leaning to look behind them.

"He's meeting us at the Cro," my mom said, which made Dani look at her mother like she was worried. She seemed to be . . . processing, like there was something she was trying to work through.

My dad said, "Kendall said they've got a band 'on call' for the win, so by the time everyone gets there, there'll be live music upstairs and the usual downstairs."

"Looks like we're all going to the Cro, then, huh?" I said, dying to be alone with Dani for just five minutes.

I mean, I couldn't wait to celebrate with the guys, but what she'd said to me about everything being real and the way she'd been acting with my friends and the team in general lately, suddenly she felt like an important part of my life.

Not someone occasional, not someone dropped into my world but moving kind of *around* it, but someone who was wholly in the middle of everything.

And I fucking loved it.

"Looks that way," Dani said with a smile, but there was a tiny crease in her forehead that I didn't like.

CHAPTER THIRTY-NINE

Dani

Things were normal between us as we exited the rink, but then Alec went rogue.

"Come on," he muttered, pulling me in the opposite direction from where Burrito was parked. Instead of heading toward his car at the end of the lot, he led me around the side of the building—through the snow—and didn't stop until we were in a dark corner, my back against the side of the Doug.

"What are we doing?" I asked, my voice almost a whisper. The high winter moon let me see the sharp angles of his face as he looked down at me, and I felt almost breathless with how badly I wanted him to be my *real* boyfriend.

"No idea," he said. "All I know is that I need to kiss you."

"Oh," I said, feeling warm as his big body pressed my back against the wall and his big hands came up to slide underneath my hair.

"Have I ever told you how obsessed I am with your hair?" he said, his eyes making me feel drunk with the way they were hot on me, roaming all over.

"I—I don't think so," I managed, my voice barely a breath in the night.

"I cannot look at it without wondering how long it takes to dry after a shower," he said, his fingers slowly twisting around random strands. "Or how wild it looks the minute you open those brown eyes in the morning. The things I would do to get a first look."

His words weren't risqué, but the way he was saying them was, dear *Lord*.

"You said . . . something about a kiss," I said, feeling hypnotized by the slow-motion twirl of his fingers.

"Impatient?" He rubbed his nose over mine, sending a shiver through my body.

"*Yes,*" I breathed, going up on my tiptoes to close the space between us.

"Praise Jesus," he said, and then he was *on* me in a way that nearly made me pass out.

Because it was different when he slanted his mouth against mine and kissed me as my *actual* boyfriend. It felt bigger as he dove in, possessive as he boldly fed me feverish kisses that had me gripping the front of his jacket to keep from melting to the ground in a puddle.

God, he knows how to make me feel.

When he kissed me like that, it felt like I was everything he could ever want, like he was desperate to be closer.

Which was powerful because I felt the exact same way.

I snaked my arms up around his neck to pull him closer and he made a noise of approval in the back of his throat, not lowering the heat in the slightest.

"Zeus!"

I jumped at the sound of Vinny's voice, scrambling to guiltily untangle myself from Alec.

"What do you want, Vin?" Alec said, barely pulling back as he gave me a look that told me he was *not* happy about the interruption.

"You guys headed to the Cro?"

I looked over Alec's shoulder to see Vinny in the back seat of a car I didn't recognize that was pulled up behind the building.

"Yeah." Alec sighed and dropped his hands to his sides. "In just a sec."

"Okay—see you there," he said, and then the car squealed away.

"I guess we should go," Alec said, his voice so deep as he put his mouth next to my ear that a shiver shot down my spine.

He took my hand and started leading me toward the parking lot, only . . . *was that my parents?*

I squinted and yes, holy crap, it was.

My parents—and Grandpa Mick—were standing next to my mom's car, a few spots down.

"—and she shouldn't have to live in *this place* just because you're trying to recapture your youth, Hannah!"

Oh God. They were arguing.

My always composed father is very nearly yelling in a parking lot, I thought as I watched in disbelief, my stomach sinking to my feet as I grabbed Alec's hand and tugged him back so we were between cars, where they couldn't see us.

"That's bullshit and you know it," my grandpa said, pointing at my dad's chest. "If you gave a damn, you'd take any fucking assignment in this country to be closer to her. You'd move to Offutt, even if you hated it, just so you could see her every once in a while. You'd take any little crumb you could get because she's your daughter and she matters to you. But no, you have to be a manipulative dick and convince her that she has to move one more fucking time to be worthy of your love."

Alec grabbed my sleeve and leaned closer. "What is *that* about? Are you going to move again?"

I could see by the way he was watching me that he knew it wasn't good, and I could also see that he fully expected me to tell him what was going on.

But I had no idea how to explain, because I knew he wouldn't understand.

And neither would my mom or my grandpa.

They saw my dad as a huge jerk, which wasn't necessarily wrong, but because of that, they wouldn't get that he was trying, in his bossy colonel way, to be a good father.

To spend more time with me.

He was willing to move somewhere he didn't want to live *just for me*, which was huge.

Yes, he wanted me to leave my mom, which I just couldn't do, but it was because he loved me.

And that meant something.

It kind of meant everything.

My throat felt tight, and I just shook my head and said, "It's complicated, but no."

"Oh, that's rich coming from the man who literally kicked them out of his life for *years*," my dad snapped at my grandpa. "How can you talk about spending time—"

"That's exactly *how* I can talk about it—"

"Let's go," I said, turning and pulling Alec back in the direction we'd come, wanting everything I'd just witnessed to disappear. "Let's take the long way to your car."

"You sure?" Alec asked. "You okay?"

I looked into his dark eyes and nodded. "I will be, once I forget about this and go celebrate."

Suddenly his eyebrow lifted, mischievously, and he pulled out his keys. "Do you wanna blow off the Cro?"

"Do *you*?" I asked, surprised he'd want to miss the party but relieved, because I needed space.

"It's going to be loud and crowded," he said, shrugging. "I'm kind of in the mood for something a little more low-key."

"Where can we go, though?" I asked, looking at him as we crossed the lot to reach Burrito from the other side. "Everyone with a house to go to is *there*."

"True," he agreed.

"Wait—what about the spot?" I asked, because I'd been dying of curiosity about it since the minute we'd gotten out of the moving truck in Southview. "Is it still even standing?"

He looked down at my face like he couldn't believe I was suggesting it. "*Our* spot?"

I loved that he thought of it that way too. "Yeah."

"It actually is," he said, but there was something strangely guarded about the way he said it.

"I'd love to see it! I mean, unless you don't want anyone else to know about it."

"I don't care if Cassie, Lillie, and the guys know, but for the sake of historical preservation, I think we should keep it small."

"Yeah, totally," I agreed, with way too much excitement, but the idea of going back to that spot—tonight of all nights—seemed a little magical. And I needed all the magic I could get to forget about the train wreck that was my dad's sudden appearance.

He pulled out his phone and sent a group text, then put it back in his pocket. "Let's go to the spot."

"This is a great idea," I said, beaming up at him.

He smiled back. "I think *you* might be a great idea, Collins."

CHAPTER FORTY
Alec

"Cass, Liz, and Lillie don't want to leave," Dani said as she looked at her phone, "but Vinny and Richie are on their way. Are you okay with that?"

I was okay with anything that took the worry out of her eyes.

She was still happy, but I could tell that the stuff with the colonel was bothering her.

"As long as you're there, I don't care. But tell them to bring chairs and wood." I held her free hand while I drove, determined to make her forget about anything that wasn't perfection.

Because that night was as close to perfect as any night had ever felt.

Not only had we clinched, but I actually had Dani.

Nine-year-old me would've lost his shit, although to be honest, I felt exactly like nine-year-old me as I drove.

Because I *was* losing my shit over the fact that we were *actually* together.

It was a struggle not to smile like a clown as I followed the road that led to our spot, because talk about full fucking circle. The moon was high in the dark sky when we got out of the car and I grabbed two chairs from the trunk, and when we pushed in the door and stepped inside the shed, I couldn't take my eyes off her as Dani looked around.

"God, it's like a time machine," she said in awe, turning in circles, staring up at the hole in the roof. "It smells the same, it feels the same."

"Wild, right?" I agreed, setting down the chairs.

"Y'know, even with my dad showing up unannounced, I am

incandescently happy right now. His . . . *whatever* can't even ruin this."
She turned back to me, full-on grinning, and said, "By the way, I don't
know if you're interested since you're not a party person anymore, but
I grabbed this just in case."

She pulled a bottle of champagne out of her purse and added, "Even
if we only take one sip and throw it away, I think we should toast the
night that you had."

"The night *we* had," I corrected, because it didn't feel like my night
at all. It was the team's night, it was Southview's night, it was Dani-and-
fucking-Alec's night.

"Yeah," she whispered, her voice going soft. "I want to celebrate us
and forget about everything else."

Her eyes held a hint of sadness, and it was killing me not to ask if she
wanted to talk about her dad and the fight we'd overheard, but I could
tell she was trying to forget.

And I was perfectly fine drowning in ignorance with her.

"Come here, wiseass, and let me toast you."

My heart was in my throat as she took a few steps toward me, looking
so damn pretty with her dancing eyes and fistful of bubbly that Alfie
Jukes's lyrics hummed through my mind.

> *I'm loving you more*
> *Than I have before*
> *To see you with those eyes wide*

I took the bottle from her hand, grabbed the cork with one hand and
the bottle with the other, pointed it away from us, and boom—it popped.

"Holy crap," she said, eyebrows raised as she grinned. "That was
impressive."

I looked at her twinkling eyes and the Packers jersey I could see underneath her coat, and I just wanted to freeze the moment.

"Drink up, Collins," I said, feeling like I was going to explode if I didn't kiss her.

Like, immediately.

Her eyes stayed on mine as she lifted the bottle to her mouth and drank, and dammit—I couldn't wait. I took the bottle from her hand the second she lowered it, dropped it on the ground, and then I was sipping champagne off her lips, sliding my hands up the curves of her face while my tongue got drunk on the taste of her.

She made a noise when I kissed her, it might've been my name or it might've been a sigh, but I felt it crawl up my spine like a shiver. I forgot all about charm and finesse and just kissed the hell out of her, diving into her sweet mouth over and over again as she grabbed both sides of my jacket like she needed something to hold on to.

Yeah, I'll fucking be that for you. Hold on, Collins, and never let go.

It felt like we were trying to absorb each other, like Dani and I were in a race to consume as much of each other as we could in the shortest amount of time.

It was too intense, too good, and I wanted to stop time and stay in this moment.

"They're here," she whispered against my mouth, still kissing me back like she didn't give a shit.

"Boo," I said as I heard voices outside, regretting that we'd told the guys where we were going. A car door slammed, but I didn't care enough to pull back and deny myself the intoxicating slide of her bottom lip against mine.

"Fucking perfect," I breathed, then did it again.

But when the door flew open, it wasn't my friends who were standing at the threshold of the crumbling shed.

No, it was fucking Benji Worthington.

Ben walked in with three St. John's guys: their goalie, Adam; their forward, Cody; and Austin Clark, the coach's son.

I swear to God I heard a roaring in my ears as I watched them enter *our* space.

What the fuck were they doing there?

"Benji?" Dani said, sounding shocked to see him.

The goalie snorted. "Did she just call you Benji?"

What the fuck were they doing there?

"Are you ever going to remember to call me Ben, honey?" Benji said with a smile that made me want to kill him.

What the fuck are they doing here?

"Did you seriously just call me honey?" Dani said, but she didn't sound pissed. She sounded confused, like she didn't know why the little douche had that much nerve.

"What are you guys doing here?" I asked, keeping my cool.

"We happened to see your *unmistakable* car drive by when we were getting gas on Concord, so we thought it'd be entertaining to see what Zeus and the boys were doing to celebrate the win."

"You *followed* us here?" I asked, my cool going from blue to insta-red. "You're such a fucking loser, Worthington. Get a life."

"I have a life," King Douche said. "But I suspected Dani was in your car, and I wanted to make sure she was okay."

"Of course she's okay," I said, wondering where that little fucker got off. That was the second time he'd acted like he needed to check on Dani when she was with me. "What the hell does that even mean?"

It'd been a great day, and I was not in the mood to deal with Benji's bullshit. I needed him to disappear.

"It means you've always been a prick who's prone to violence—"

"Come on, *Benji*," I said, glancing at Dani because that was such bullshit and I didn't want her to listen. "Kicking your ass for being a cocksucker doesn't mean I'm prone to violence. It means I couldn't take your bullshit anymore."

"And look at this—you brought her to a crumbling shack in the woods. That's kind of a red flag, so I'm just making sure my old friend is okay."

"Your *old friend*?" I looked at his ferret face and wanted to pound him. "She was never your friend."

"You guys," Dani said, sounding uncomfortable. "Knock it off."

"Oh, she wasn't?" Benji said. "Then how did I know where this place was?"

"You just said you followed me here, fuckface."

"Dani brought me here a couple years ago," he said, wearing that smug smile he was born with. "We had a nice walk, caught up, and then she showed me the terrible artwork you drew on the wall. Remember that, Dani?"

I wanted to level him as *I* remembered the way he'd gleefully showed me the picture of Dani on his phone that night, the one where she was laughing with him in our spot.

"Benji," Dani said quietly, sounding different, and when I glanced over, I hated how nervous she looked. "Stop."

"Feels like it was yesterday, though," he said, his tone full of innuendo. "*Great* night."

"Fuck right off, Worthington," I said, pushing him with both hands. "Just get the hell out of here."

"Maybe *we* should go, Alec," Dani said, looking more like the girl who'd been unable to deliver her intro speech than my champagne girlfriend of five minutes ago. "Let's go."

"One sec," I said, not willing to go first because I didn't want them to ruin our spot. I'd leave just as soon as I got *them* to take off.

"I was supposed to take her to see *you* at the hospital, if I recall," Ben said, grinning like he thought he was hilarious. "But Dani decided to hang with me instead."

"It wasn't like that and you know it," she said, rolling her eyes.

Apparently I wasn't *completely* over the past, because the red-hot rage I'd felt the night I learned she brought him there was still alive and well.

How could she bring him *here?*

But I needed to keep my cool, so I just stared down at his ugly face and started counting.

Ten. Nine. Eight.

"The plan was to go see your dad, but we never made it."

"Knock it *off*, Benji," she said, and I didn't like the sound of her voice. I shot her a glance, and she looked like she was about to pass out.

Seven. Six. Five.

I said, "Just leave, Worthington."

"Yeah, let's take off," Austin said. "It's fucking freezing, anyway."

Four. Three.

I tried again. "Listen to your friend, *Benji*."

357

"I'm going," he said, shaking his head and grinning like a psycho. "But God, Dani—we spent a *lot* of hours here, remember?"

Two.

"*Stop*, Benji," Dani snapped.

One.

"That's not what you said that night—"

I pulled back my fist and slammed it into his nose.

"Oh my God!" Dani screamed.

But all I could hear was Worthington's ghoulish fucking laugh as his nose gushed, so I tagged his right eye, that little *fuck*. I'd heard of people seeing red when they were angry, but for me it was like I went blind.

Everything else disappeared, and all I could see was Worthington's nasty little face.

He swung at me and grazed my cheek, but my reflexes were faster than his fist.

"Alec!" Dani yelled. "Stop!"

Ben was still smiling, so I shoved him into the wall with both hands. "You *prick*."

I heard Dani shouting, but I couldn't make out her words and I didn't want to.

Because staring down at Ben Worthington just reminded me of the day my dad had been fighting for his life and the cops came to the hospital to arrest me.

It reminded me of my mom's face when they led me out.

Of my guilt when she had to leave my dad's bedside to go to the police station.

And now he was making Dani have a fucking panic attack. I pushed him again, raising my arm to pin that fucker against the wall when—

"Stop it!"

Dani jumped in front of me, popping up between my fists and that piece of shit.

"Dani, move," I said, needing to get at him.

Needing to teach him a fucking lesson.

"No, Alec!" she said, shaking her head and looking up at me with wild eyes. *"Think."*

"Is this seriously where—" Kyle stopped talking as he entered the shed with Vinny, their laid-back smiles immediately changing into looks of confusion.

"Help me!" Dani yelled to them as I waited for her to move.

"What the hell's going on here?" Vinny asked.

"This motherfucker right here," I said, "is about to get his ass handed to him."

"Stop!" Dani yelled, pushing at my chest. "Alec, think about what you're doing!"

"I *am*," I said through clenched teeth, finally seeing her.

"He's trying to piss you off, don't you see that?" She pushed me again and said, "He wants you to do this!"

"Then I'm more than happy to give him exactly what he wants," I said, my eyes back on Worthington.

"Zeus," Vinny said, grabbing my arm and jerking me away from Ben. "Chill the fuck out."

"Call nine-one-one, Austin," Benji said, holding his sleeve up to his bloody nose. "Tell them I was just assaulted by Alec Barczewski."

"Oh, bullshit, Worthington," Vinny said, even though he had no

359

idea what he was talking about because he'd just walked in.

"Just try calling and see what happens," Kyle said with a scowl. "The rest of the team'll be here any second, and you're so fucking outnumbered, dipshit."

"And *he* looks fucking hammered," Vinny said, pointing at the goalie. "The cops are gonna love this shit."

"Ben," Cody said, "let's just get the hell outta here."

"No way," Worthington said. "Barczewski can't pull this crap."

"So call in the morning," Adam said, turning toward the door. "I'm getting out before shit hits the fan."

I jerked my arm away from Vinny, which made Dani step in front of me again.

"Y'know what, that's fine," Ben said with a shrug, holding up the side of his hand to his busted nose. "I'll just call in the morning. I'll still have the evidence on my face and witnesses, so what's another twelve hours?"

"Get gone, asswipe," Kyle said, shaking his head.

I watched Cody kick the shed door open, and as they walked out, Benji said, "I can't wait to see what the Southview townspeople think of their god after tomorrow."

"Bye, *Benji*," I yelled after him.

"See you in the morning, *Zeus*," he yelled back.

CHAPTER FORTY-ONE

Dani

"I still say you need to go to the hospital."

"No, I don't," Alec said, staring out through the windshield in my driveway.

It was dark, but the streetlight made it possible to see his face.

"But your hand is *so* swollen, and the gash on your cheek looks terrible," I said, clueless how to make him listen to me. He'd been angry and quiet since the fight, and I didn't know how to get through it.

"Only because that jackass was wearing a ring," he said dismissively.

"That still doesn't make it any less injured," I countered. "But fine. Sit still."

I raised the peroxide-soaked paper towel and pressed it to his cheek, making him hiss out a breath through his teeth.

"I know," I said, my stomach dipping because that had to sting *so* much. Benji's ring had kind of ripped open Alec's face, and it wasn't pretty, even in the dark. I'd run into Walgreens on the way home after he'd made it clear he was never going to listen to me and go to urgent care.

But his hand was what had me really worried. It was so swollen.

"I'm sorry," I said, dabbing at the wound.

"For what?" he asked, and finally—*finally*—his eyes met mine.

Since the whole thing went down, it felt like he wouldn't even look at me. Like he was mad at me.

"That I'm hurting you, that this happened, that your amazing night was ruined by Benji," I said in the quiet of his dark car.

His jaw clenched at the mention of Benji's name, and I regretted saying it. Everything Benji had implied was a lie, and I was pretty sure Alec knew that, but it still made things between us feel tense.

Why isn't he talking to me?

"Hey," I said. "It's okay. Remember, you're going to the X."

His jaw flexed again, like he was holding it so tight.

And he still didn't say anything.

"Alec." I didn't know if he wanted me to, but I ran my fingers over that rigid jawline, wishing it would relax. "Everything's going to be okay," I said.

"Is it?" he asked, his voice low and kind of raspy.

"Yeah, this will blow over," I said.

"I don't know, Dani," he said, sounding exhausted. "I've done this shit with Ben before and he goes for the jugular. I might've just fucked everything up."

My chest hurt for him when his voice cracked over the *might've*. It sounded like he was holding back so much emotion, and God, it wasn't fair that he had *more* to worry about after they got the win.

"You didn't," I said, putting my left hand on the other side of his face. "Listen to me. Everyone makes mistakes, and it's going to be fine. This is just a guy acting like a jerk—happens all the time."

He put his head back on the headrest and let out his breath. "God, I hope you're right. Because I'm fucking scared."

That hurt my heart, the admission and how anguished he sounded.

"I mean, I could've just fucked up my chance at playing in the tournament. I could've fucked it *all* up if Ben wants to come after me."

"He won't," I said.

"But he will," Alec said, making me feel a little better by leaning into my touch.

And by opening up and not being so quiet.

"He's greasy as hell and you were right," he said, shaking his head in regret. "I did exactly what he wanted me to. I lost my shit on him and now he's got the upper hand."

"Just trust me," I said, glancing over at Benji's house. His car wasn't there, thank God, and all the windows were dark. "It's going to go your way this time, I just know it."

"Is this more wisdom from the Harvard brain?"

"That's right," I said.

Our porch light flipped on, which made me smile in spite of everything.

"I think my grandpa is telling me to come in," I said, but everything with my family rushed back at me as soon as I mentioned him. The only good thing about the nightmare at our spot was that it'd made me forget about the situation with my dad.

"Yeah, you should go," he said. "Sorry I ruined the night."

"Are you kidding me? We're going to the tournament, and you're my new boyfriend. You and Benji together couldn't ruin that."

That made him pull me closer by the front of my jersey.

"It was a pretty perfect night *before*, wasn't it?" he said, leaning in and setting his forehead on mine.

"The perfectest," I agreed, raising my mouth for a kiss.

"This has to be fast before Mick sees," he said, lowering his mouth and giving me the deepest, most thorough three-second kiss that'd ever been delivered.

I got out of the car and walked up the driveway, and even though I was nervous for him, I had a feeling I could fix this. Benji was a jerk who liked showing off in front of his friends, but he'd always been decent enough when it was just the two of us.

Thank God I've always been nice to him.

So first thing in the morning—at like seven o'clock, before the police station was even open—I was going to visit my friend next door.

And beg like I'd never begged before.

CHAPTER FORTY-TWO
Alec

"Before you freak out—"

"Oh my God!" my mom said, her mouth dropping open as I walked into the kitchen the next morning.

"What the hell happened to your face?" asked my dad, looking up from the paper.

"It's just a scratch," I said, going over to the fridge, trying to act casual even though functioning at all was difficult because I'd barely slept. Every time I closed my eyes, I thought of all the things I might've screwed up by hitting Ben.

"That's not an answer," my dad said. "What happened?"

I sighed and grabbed the OJ.

I didn't want to tell them—*God, I so don't want to tell them*—but this was big enough that I had to.

Damage control was probably impossible, but they needed to know.

"I got in a fight," I said, closing the fridge. "With Ben Worthington."

"What?" my mom yelled, her eyes huge.

"You gotta be kidding me," my dad said, throwing the paper down on the table, his eyes narrowing. "Did that guy jump you?"

"What happened?" my mom asked, standing and coming over to get a closer look. "That gash looks terrible."

I sat down at the table, wanting to puke from how shitty I felt.

I'm so sorry I might've destroyed everything.

"It was stupid," I admitted, dragging a hand through my hair. "Worthington showed up and was mouthy to Dani."

"You didn't hit him, did you? Please tell me you didn't—"

"I hit him," I said, swallowing hard because my throat was so damn tight. "Broke his nose."

"Oh no," my mom said, closing her eyes and covering her mouth. "Not again."

I saw the fear in her face and my gut churned.

I can't believe I'm doing this to her again.

"Who threw the first punch?" my dad asked, his face scary serious.

"I did."

My mom gasped.

"What the hell is so hard about this, kid?" my dad bellowed. "Punching is illegal—why can't you remember that?"

"I don't know," I said with a shrug, because I didn't.

I wasn't a hothead and didn't get in fights (aside from hockey).

Only with Worthington, and only about Dani, apparently.

Fuck.

"So what do we need to know?" my dad asked, shaking his head and looking so fucking disappointed in me. "Because you know his ma's gonna come unglued. Tell us everything."

And I did.

I recounted the whole thing, wondering what could be worse than having to look into their disappointed eyes as I shared every detail. And I got emo as shit because I was fucking terrified.

If Ben went to the police, I could get suspended, which meant I wouldn't be able to play in the tournament.

And everyone—scouts included—would know why.

"Don't worry about the scouts," my mom said. "You can't control—"

"How do I not worry about the scouts?" I said, trying to keep it together, but it was all just fucking clawing at me. "Are you kidding? I spend half my life worrying about the scouts because they control our fut—"

"Alec," my dad interrupted, shaking his head. "No. You gotta stop. You're killing yourself with this."

I scratched my forehead. Wished I could. "How, though?"

"Just play," he said. "That's all you have to do."

"You make it sound so easy," I said, my chest tight.

"It is," he said, shrugging. "Just play the game, and the rest will happen the way it's meant to."

I cleared my throat, wishing it were that simple.

"Sometimes I look at you and I can't imagine what it'd be like to have all that talent, right?" he said. "At my athletic best, I was a third-string point guard who didn't have a three-pointer in me, yet here you are, the guy everybody wants on their team."

I looked down at the table, afraid I'd start bawling like a little kid if I looked him in the eye. I was already blinking really fucking fast to hold it all in; eye contact would end me for sure.

"It's great and it's cool," he said, putting a hand on my shoulder, "but we're still talking about a game here, kid. Hockey is a *game*. It isn't life and death, even though sometimes it might feel like it. Work your ass off so you can play the game to your best ability, and then that's it. No one's gonna die if you win, and no one's gonna die if you lose. We will all be fine no matter what happens on the ice, and who gives a shit about the scouts? Let the scouts worry about the scouts."

I did look at him then, because *fuck*—he had a way of making it seem so basic, and all I wanted was to believe him.

"You hitting Ben Worthington was an idiot move, Al, but we're all gonna be okay. We *will*."

I nodded, not trusting that I was able to speak.

I didn't deserve parents this cool, for starters. The way they supported me made me want to kick my own ass for being stupid and bringing more stress their way—like, what the fuck had I been thinking?

But on top of that, I was still so fucking scared of the legalities of what was coming.

"It's going to be okay, Al," my mom said, coming over and wrapping her arms around my neck. "We'll get through whatever happens."

"I'm sorry," I said, feeling like a little kid, and she kissed the top of my head.

"It's okay, kiddo." She tousled my hair and said, "It's okay."

CHAPTER FORTY-THREE

Dani

I was quietly slipping my feet into my boots when my mom came out of her room.

And stopped in her tracks.

"Where are you going at"—she looked down at her watch—"six forty-five in the morning?"

There was no way for me to lie when I was wearing my coat, hat, and gloves, and my hand was literally on the doorknob.

"I, uh, I have to go talk to Benji about something before he leaves for practice," I said, as if that made any sense whatsoever.

"You guys are friends now?" she asked, looking shocked.

"Not really, but it's a whole thing," I said vaguely, wanting her to let it go.

Needing to get out of there quickly.

"Well, I'm glad you're up, because we need to talk about *this whole thing* with your dad," she said, looking more serious than usual.

Which was fair and unsurprising.

"Did you know he was coming, honey?" she asked.

Please not yet.

I needed to deal with one nightmarish situation before moving on to the next.

"Um, no," I said, shaking my head. "Listen, I have to go do this before Benji leaves for practice—can we talk about this when I come back?"

She sighed. "Fine. I have to run to Knowlan's because we're completely out of sugar, but as soon as I get back from the store, we're hashing this out."

"Thank you," I said, throwing open the door and running down all the deck stairs.

It was barely light out as I went around the garage and crept through the bushes that separated our yards. I wasn't exactly excited to wake up Benji's dad as I rang the doorbell, but I was too desperate to let common courtesy stop me.

This was an emergency.

But the door opened almost immediately after I rang, and Benji was standing there, already dressed in a St. John's Academy hoodie and joggers.

Like he was about to leave.

And whoa, his face.

He definitely had a black eye, and his nose did *not* look good. It was swollen and kind of looked like Mr. Potato Head's nose.

My stomach was dippy as I looked at him, and I wasn't sure if it was because his face was kind of gross to look at, or because his face was hard evidence that could be used against Alec.

"Dani?"

Yeah, I'm surprised to be here too.

"Can I talk to you for a second, Ben?" I asked, looking behind him to see if his dad was in the room.

"He's not here," Benji said. "Come on in."

I followed him inside, crossing my arms and having no idea where to start.

"What's up?" he said as he shut the door, but we both knew this had to do with his face and what'd happened the night before.

I took a deep breath, tried to come up with some clever argument, but then just blurted, "Please don't go to the police, Ben."

He opened his mouth, but I held up a hand.

"I know you two hate each other and I'm sure this seems like a good idea. He *shouldn't* have hit you. But he was trying, in his own way, to defend me, so I feel responsible."

I was talking fast, but he just watched me calmly.

I had no idea what he was thinking.

"You didn't deserve to be attacked, but I'm begging you—as a friend I've known my entire life." I looked into his eyes and prayed he'd have a heart about this. "Can you *please* pretend this didn't happen?"

"How exactly would I do that?" he asked, pointing toward his battered face.

"I mean, you're a hockey player," I said. "If you just allude to the fact that you got in a scuffle, no one will—"

"I'm not letting Barczewski off the hook on this, Dani," he said, shaking his head.

"But don't you see that you could ruin his future—"

"*He* did this, not me," he snapped, his eyes narrowing. "And don't *you* see how wrong it is if he's able to behave this way and still get everything he's ever wanted?"

"I mean, I can see how it might feel that way," I forced myself to say, loathing him for being so vindictive.

"No, it is *exactly* that way. I'll be honest—the idea of him flaming out and failing doesn't make me sad. I'd fucking love it. But *I* didn't do

371

anything to make that happen. *He* is the low-class hothead who chose to come after me."

"Please," I said, feeling perilously close to tears. "I am begging, Benji, please don't—"

"Ben," he snapped.

"Ben, come on," I said, fully panicked now. "And trust me, he won't be getting everything he's ever wanted."

"Yes, he will," he said, and it was obvious that was all he cared about.

"What can I do, Ben?" I blinked fast because I didn't want to cry, but I could tell I was failing and that was terrifying. "Please tell me what I can do to convince you."

"There's noth—actually." His eyes narrowed as he looked at me, like a villain hatching a plan before my very eyes. My heart was in my throat when he said, "Oh. You know, I think there *is* something."

"What is it?" I asked, a sense of foreboding settling over me.

"Nothing illegal, relax," he said, smirking like it was funny. "But if you don't want me to file charges, you need to end things with him."

"What?"

I looked at his stupid facial hair and broken face and couldn't believe I'd heard him right.

He couldn't be telling me to break up with Alec.

That . . . wasn't possible, right?

But he nodded and looked happy all of a sudden, like he was excited. "You've only been here a minute, so it's not like I'm asking you to divorce your husband, and he's going to juniors as soon as he graduates, so you won't be together for long anyway."

He really was more of a tool than I'd ever thought he could be.

"But, like, so then why would you want this?" He might've had a crush on me when we were kids, but I could tell he didn't now, so this didn't make any sense.

"Because *you* are actually the one thing he's always wanted," he said with a casual shrug. "It's perfect."

"No, I'm not, and this . . . this is ridiculous," I said, my stomach so heavy I felt nauseous because I could tell he meant it.

He's seriously demanding I break up with Alec.

"It's ridiculously *simple*," he said. "You break up with him, this goes away. If you don't, I'm filing a report."

It felt like my heart was shattering when I looked at that real-life villain, because he was dead serious, and I didn't have a choice.

He really was the asshole Alec had always said he was.

But I'd seen the fear in Alec's eyes when he realized he might've jeopardized his chance to be the anchor for his family—for the whole damn town—and I never wanted to see that look again.

So there was only one thing for me to do.

I had to break up with him.

CHAPTER FORTY-FOUR

Alec

My heart almost stopped when I heard the doorbell.

My parents had taken Ashton and Cole to their eight o'clock basketball game, so I was trying to ignore the world by getting some overdue homework done in my room. I seriously expected to see a police car when I looked out the window, so when I opened the front door and saw Dani, standing there in the bright morning sunlight, I was so fucking relieved.

Relieved it wasn't something bad, and also relieved that she hadn't decided to pretend she'd never met me after everything that'd happened the night before.

There she stood, bundled up in her big coat with her hair in a long, loose braid, and I'd never been so happy to see anyone in my life.

"Is this a new thing, you walking to my house?" I asked, holding the door open so she could come inside.

"Oh, your face," she said, blinking fast and raising a hand like she was going to touch it, her eyebrows scrunched together in concern.

But then she dropped her hand and asked, "How does it feel?"

"Stings like a bitch," I admitted, and then she gave a little nod and walked into the house.

I closed the door and followed her in, realizing as Dani stopped beside the couch but didn't sit that we were home alone.

Interesting.

"Um, how's your hand?" She crossed her arms over her chest and looked nervous. "Still swollen?"

I looked down at it, clenching my fist. "Not too bad."

"Ah. Good." She cleared her throat and nodded again. "And your shoulder?"

"Are you . . . nervous?" I said, stepping closer. "You seem a little jumpy."

"N-no," she said, taking a step back.

Out of my reach.

"You okay?" I asked, suddenly aware of the way her eyes wouldn't meet mine and how she looked fucking sad. "What's the matter?"

"Nothing." She rubbed her lips together, then said, "It's just . . . here's the thing."

What is this?

"I, um, like, this whole thing with my dad is kind of complicated," she said, the words bouncing out like she was working hard at stringing them together. "And I don't know what's going to happen. I might leave again, I might not, but . . . it seems to me that right now, while you've got so much going on in your hockey career and everything with me is up in the air, maybe it's best if we take, like, a break."

A. break.

A break??

"What do you mean?" I said calmly, but what the fuck did that fucking mean?

A break from our less-than-twenty-four-hour-old relationship?

That couldn't be right.

"I mean that, like," she said, "you don't need distractions right now."

"No." I said, shaking my head, needing her to understand. "You're the opposite of a distraction—"

"The fight last night says the opposite," she interrupted, cracking her knuckles.

I've never seen her do that before.

"Yeah, but—"

"Alec," she said, cutting me off again. "It just seems like the timing is off. Maybe we should, like, wait for, like—"

"You've said 'like' like fifteen times now," I said, not meaning to sound impatient but seriously confused. "That's not you, Harvard. What the hell's going on here?"

"Nothing," she said with a shrug, her eyes moving all over the room. "Everything is just too much right now. Between my dad and school and you and hockey, I just need some time—"

"Wait. Are you breaking up with me?"

Her eyes shot to mine, finally, and—holy shit—I could see I was right.

She was.

Breaking up. With me.

She said, "I mean—"

"Cut the shit, Dani, come on," I said, my chest burning as I watched her stammer. This couldn't be happening. "What happened between last night and now?"

"You don't remember?" she said quietly.

"Wait—this has to do with the fight?"

She looked away from me again and said, "I mean, it was a little jarring to see you like that, so angry—"

"Bullshit," I said, because anyone could see she was lying. "You jumped in front of me and yelled in my face. You have *never* been afraid of me in your entire life, Collins, come *on*. Why don't you tell the truth?"

"Well, then," she said, blinking fast like she was looking for another reason since I'd rejected the last one. What the hell was that? She took a deep breath and then said, "You promised."

"What?"

"You promised that I could be the one to end things, on my terms—"

"When it was fake," I said, shaking my head. *What the hell is happening?*

"—and that's what I'm doing. I'm ending it."

I looked at those brown eyes and felt utterly fucking lost, especially when I saw a tear escape.

"But this doesn't make sense," I said, stepping closer, pushing back the long curl that'd fallen out of her braid. Her eyes were filled with tears—*what the hell?*—so I softened my tone and leaned in, my heart skipping a beat as I heard her take a shaky breath. "You looked at me on the ice last night and said the words, honey. *You* said them. Tell me what happened between then and now."

She swiped at her tears and shook her head. "I just—"

"Why are you *crying* if this is what you want?" I asked, because nothing about this made sense. She looked devastated, fucking heartbroken as she attempted to break my heart, and I couldn't wrap my head around it.

I took her face in my hands to reassure her, but she blinked up at me and suddenly I was lowering my mouth, needy, *desperate* to convince her. My lips landed on hers like a dare, challenging her to show me she meant the ridiculous words she was saying.

The lyrics to "Lose Me Like You Mean It" came at me like a fist.

All I need is
For you to look me in the eyes, make me believe it

And *fuck*.

One taste. One taste and she was kissing me back, as frenzied and wild as me while we kissed like neither of us could bear what she was saying. Her hands came up and covered mine, ten trembling fingers pressing my palms against her cheeks as she frantically met me sip for fucking sip, but then she choked out a sob and pushed my hands away.

"*No,*" she cried, shaking her head and stepping away from me. "You're wrong, Alec. I'm only crying because you're my friend and I don't want to hurt you."

"Then *don't,*" I said, struggling to get a good breath as full-on panic screamed through me. "Collins . . ."

I don't want to hurt you.

I trailed off because *fucking wait.*

I don't want to hurt you.

Did she feel *bad* for me? Was she trying to let me down easy—soft little Alec—was that what this was?

"But you promised," she repeated, sounding like she was begging.

Like she was desperate for me to remember her out clause.

And I realized as I looked at her that I had no choice.

If she wanted to be done, we were done.

Because I wasn't going to beg anymore.

If we're going out, we're going up in flames, baby

My gut burned with shame as I looked at her pretty face and realized I'd done it again. Holy shit, I'd fallen head over heels for the only girl I'd ever wanted and the only girl who knew how to fucking destroy me.

"Same old Dani, eh?" I said, grinding my teeth against the pain that was suddenly like a knife in my chest. I took a big step back from her. "Leaving me behind yet again. At least this time there aren't any letters for you to ignore."

"What?"

"How could you do it, by the way?" I asked, angry at the confused look on her face, done with the bullshit. Everything hurt again, and it was because of her again, and suddenly I needed her to answer the damn question that'd haunted me for years. "How could you walk away when I needed you? I wrote you every fucking week, breaking our stupid rules and begging you to be there for me, but you didn't even care enough to send a *screw you* note in response. How—"

"What are you talking about?" she interrupted, looking at me like I was nuts.

And I realized then, as she blinked up at me with her heartbreakingly gorgeous tear-streaked face, that it actually *didn't* matter.

Because Dani Collins was—and forever would be—what she'd been to me my entire life.

The one I wanted who didn't want me back.

"Nothing, forget it," I said, so pissed at myself for being such a chump. So pissed at her for doing this to me again. "Just realizing that the one thing I can always count on is that I can't count on you."

She made a noise in the back of her throat before she said, "Alec."

"No." I shook my head in disbelief—*so fucking stupid*—and looked down at the carpet. I didn't want to see her face, couldn't look at her, because I was in serious danger of losing my shit and begging on my knees.

Or fucking crying.

All I could manage as my chest fucking burned was "I think you need to leave now."

I heard her sniffle. "Alec, I—"

"Just *go.*"

"Okay," she said in almost a whisper, and a few seconds later she was gone.

CHAPTER FORTY-FIVE
Dani

It's for the best.

I kept telling myself that as I walked home in the cold, justifying my behavior in my head, but the words didn't help when I couldn't stop picturing his face.

God, the way he looked at me.

How was I ever going to stop crying when my brain kept showing it to me on repeat? Every time I started to get it together, to stop sniveling as I stumbled in the direction of my house, I pictured the absolute shock and betrayal on his face when he said, *Are you breaking up with me?* and then I was sobbing.

When I got home, I did my best to pull myself together before going inside. Hopefully I could sneak away to my room and lick my wounds before my mom got back from the store.

But when I walked in the door, she was sitting on the couch in the living room, looking worried.

For a second I thought she knew.

But then she said, "Honey, there's been a slight change of plans."

"I don't know what that means," I said, toeing off my boots, too exhausted to even play a guessing game.

"Hey, are you okay?" she asked, her eyes moving all over my blotchy face.

There was no way she couldn't see I'd been crying, but I was too drained to bother with acknowledging it.

"What's the plan change?" I said, not wanting to discuss how very not okay I was.

"Well," she said, her eyebrows furrowed together in worry. "Your dad had to catch an earlier flight, so he wanted me to let you know he'll call you when he gets back to Germany."

She cleared her throat, and the house was deafeningly quiet as that sentence settled over me.

"Why did he have to catch an earlier flight?" I asked, dropping my coat on the bench next to the door, knowing the answer even as I asked it. "Did something happen?"

"I, um, I don't really know the details," she said, shrugging. "I think he just wanted to get a head start; you know how long those international flights are."

I nodded, surprised I could feel this heaviness in my chest again, the massive weight of disappointment. I would've thought that after what had happened at Alec's, I'd be tapped out on emotion.

"Did he say . . ." I almost couldn't bring myself to finish the question, but then I pushed it out because I just needed the confirmation. "He's not taking the Offutt assignment, is he?"

My mom looked like she didn't know how to answer.

"Is he?" I repeated. "Come on, don't sugarcoat it—it's fine."

"He's staying in Germany." She crossed her arms and said, "I'm sorry, honey."

I nodded, the words Grandpa Mick shouted at my dad last night coming back to me as if I'd committed them to memory.

If you gave a damn, you'd take any fucking assignment in this country to be closer to her.

You'd move to Offutt, even if you hated it, just so you could see her every once in a while.

You'd take any little crumb you could get because she's your daughter and she matters to you.

"So he just left," I said, swallowing hard because it felt like there was a marble stuck in my throat. "Without even calling or talking to me first."

He was my dad, and he was the colonel, but that seemed like something a pouty kid would do, leaving without a goodbye after not getting his way.

"C'mere, honey," she said, patting the sofa beside her.

I came over and sat beside her, and it felt so good to have her wrap her arms around me. I was all out of tears, *thank God*, but I closed my eyes and snuggled into her comfort.

"Your dad loves you so much," she said, kissing the top of my head. "And I will never hate him, because he's your dad. I *want* you to have him in your life."

"I know," I said, feeling like such garbage for not telling her about his plans sooner.

"But he was *way* out of line, trying to get you to move away in *that* way. You know that, right?"

"I'm so sorry I didn't tell you," I said, surprised to discover I actually still had more tears left inside me. I swiped them away and told her, "I love living here with you. I think I was so surprised that he was actually trying that I just . . . I don't know, didn't want to shut it down, maybe."

"I can understand that," she said, patting my arm. "But trust me when I tell you that life is easiest when you're honest. It's not always fun, but it's definitely easier."

I nodded but couldn't talk, because that made me picture Alec's face when he said, *Why don't you tell me the truth?*

"*Do* you really love it here, kid?" she asked. "Just because I do doesn't mean you have to, you know."

"No, I really do love it here," I admitted, but suddenly I was crying again.

"Oh, honey, what is it?" my mom asked, putting both her hands on my cheeks and examining my face. "Tell me what's the matter."

I hiccuped out a sob and gave her a very vague *we broke up* story.

"You can't call him and work out whatever this is?" she asked, which was a fair question when I'd left out the important details.

"Nu-uh," I said, blowing my nose.

I ached to do that, to run back to his house and tell him the truth, but that would be selfish. That would be me acting like my father, putting what *I* wanted over everything else, and I wasn't going to do that.

I *couldn't* do that.

When I pictured Alec's scared face last night, when he thought he might've ruined everything, I knew it was for the best.

"It's over for good," I said definitively, like I'd never meant anything more. "And I'm glad."

On Monday morning, I told my mom I was sick. I was pretty sure she knew it was a lie, but she just gave me a look and called the office.

I stayed in my room all day, buried under the covers, watching mindless reality TV shows on repeat. I heard my grandpa moving around downstairs, but it wasn't until the doorbell rang at six o'clock that it even felt like he knew I was there.

"Dani, get down here," he yelled. "Your friends are here."

I gasped and scrambled over to the window, and when I saw Cassie's car, I was equal parts relieved and disappointed not to see Burrito.

Joke's on you, Grandpa—I don't have any friends of my own, I thought. *They're actually his.*

I didn't want to face them, but I supposed it'd be better if they yelled at me here than at school. I didn't even bother looking in the mirror because I knew what I'd see. My hair was a rat's nest and I'd been wearing my pajamas for over twenty-four hours: not pretty at all.

But I didn't care.

I walked down the stairs, my stomach full of dread.

But when I hit the bottom of the steps, I was surprised to see Grandpa Mick smiling.

"—so you did a good job, but she couldn't stop when she had to switch directions."

Cassie was talking about boot hockey, being typical hilarious Cassie, and my grandpa looked charmed.

"Okay, girl," Lillie said, smiling as she looked over at me from where she was sitting beside Liz on the couch. "I thought you might've been playing hooky, but you really do look awful."

Let the roast begin.

"You don't look awful," Cassie said. "You just look . . . *comfortable*."

"I agree with Lillie," Grandpa Mick said. "That's some kinda hair."

"Gee, thanks." *God, I don't want to face them.* I was so nervous to be alone with them, terrified they hated me. Because they no doubt heard that I broke up with Alec and probably wondered what kind of a terrible girlfriend would do such a thing during the state tournament.

They have to hate me.

And that made my heart hurt almost as much as leaving Alec had.

I'd always known it would happen, but the thought of no longer having them as friends made my chest hurt.

"You have to be better by tomorrow," Cassie said, gesturing for me to sit on the other side of her. "I don't care if you're puking your guts out, you're going to be with me on that bus."

"What?" I plopped down between her and Liz. "What bus?"

That made her give me a weird look. "The game is Wednesday, Co-Manager Who Should Know This, but we leave tomorrow."

"You didn't know that?" Grandpa Mick asked, his eyes narrowed.

"I mean, I . . ."

I trailed off, not really knowing what to say, but I was saved by my grandpa's phone ringing.

"I gotta take this," he said, then stood and walked out of the room.

"Okay, you need to talk fast," Cassie murmured, turning to face me and lowering her voice.

"Kyle told us what happened after the game," Lillie said.

"He did?" I asked, wondering what he'd told them.

"I can't believe Zeus kicked Ben Worthington's ass," she said, talking fast and a little too loud. "It's all the guys could talk about. Kyle thinks that since we're playing St. John's Academy on Wednesday, Ben probably pissed him off on purpose to try to make it so Zeus couldn't play."

Wait. We were going to be playing *St. John's* in the quarterfinal game? How had I missed that?

It made even *more* sense now, why Benji wanted me to do it.

God, I hate him so much.

"The weird thing is that nothing happened," Cassie said, grabbing the remote off the coffee table and turning on the TV. "He didn't end up calling the cops."

"Vin thinks it's because the St. John's guys were drunk at the time. All I know is that everybody hates him, so this is the perfect scenario, knowing he got his ass kicked but no one's on the hook for it."

"Yeah," I said, feeling unsettled but relieved to have confirmation that he actually *didn't* call the police.

"According to Kyle, this could've been a really big deal because Zeus is eighteen now. He was a minor when he was arrested the first time, so even though the charges were dropped, it could've shown, like, a pattern or something."

"Wait—Alec got *arrested*?" I repeated.

"It was a long time ago," Cassie assured me, looking like she was worried she'd blabbed a secret.

"How long ago?"

"Back when Z's dad had his accident, so a couple years, I guess. They got in a fight at a party, and the next day the cops showed up at the hospital and arrested him for assault and battery."

"Wait. They arrested him at the *hospital*?" I asked in horror.

"Oh yeah," Cassie said. "Ben's parents eventually dropped the charges. It came out that Ben threw the first punch, but it was scary for a little bit. His mom and her husband are both lawyers, and they did *not* want to let it go."

No wonder Alec hates him so much.

"So it's a miracle that Ben isn't being Ben about this," Lillie said.

Oh, but he is.

"I think it shook Alec up or something, because he isn't talking about it at all. To anyone. If someone mentions it, he tells them to shut the hell up. He's crazy grumpy without you, so you need to get your ass to school tomorrow."

I didn't want to say it *so badly*, but I had to tell them. I cleared my throat and quietly said, "Actually, um, just so you know, we broke up."

"Yeah, that's part of why we're here," Cassie said, pursing her lips and tilting her head. "You okay?"

What?

I nodded, unsure of why they were here and being nice to me if they knew I wasn't with Alec anymore.

"Listen," I said, my voice so thick I sounded like Kermit the Frog. "I know he's your friend, so I totally get it if—"

"So are you," Lillie interrupted.

"Yeah, but he was your friend first so—"

"Who cares?" Liz said, looking at me like I was being ridiculous. "It's not like we're going to take his side because he tagged us first or something."

"I know, but—"

"You are our friend and we're here for you," Cassie said, pointing the remote control at me. "Even though we love Zeus, too."

So . . . this is real?

I looked at them, at my *friends* for real, and felt like crying again.

But happy tears this time.

Because when did this ever happen? I'd never found *this* at the other places I'd lived, as much as I wanted to and as hard as I'd tried.

Have I landed in the place I belong?

I shut that thought down instantly, though, because even if my new friends were actually genuine, that didn't change the fact that I might've ruined everything else.

"And we're going to have so much fun tomorrow that you'll forget all about him," Cassie said with a grin before she left. "My dad said they're giving the team bus a police escort out of Southview—that's how bat-shit wild this is gonna be."

I smiled because *of course* this town would give the hockey team a police escort.

I couldn't be on that bus, though.

I just couldn't.

I'd already done enough.

So when morning came, I told my mom that my stomach still hurt (which wasn't entirely untrue). She called me out of school and I thought I was in the clear, but everything changed when my grandpa knocked on my door after my mom left.

"Kid," I heard from the other side of my bedroom door.

"Yeah?" I asked, sitting up and shoving the gummy bears into my nightstand drawer.

"Can I come in?"

"Hey," I said, sniffling as I opened the door. "What's up?"

He frowned and said, "Get dressed, I'm taking you to school."

"What?"

He couldn't be serious. I put every ounce of illness I could project into my voice when I said, "I can't go to school. I'm sick."

"Liar."

"Grandpa!"

"You made a commitment, and you need to follow through. I don't care if you broke up with your boyfriend or whatever the hell you have going on—you're not a quitter."

"How did you know about—"

"I can still hear when I'm in another room, for God's sake," he said in disgust.

"I can't—"

"Yes, you can, Danigirl," he said, cutting me off yet again.

I shook my head and swallowed hard, because the nickname and the way it sounded like he genuinely wanted me to open up made everything hurt a little more. "I can't."

He frowned harder. "Yes, you can. Now get dressed for school."

I stared at him for a minute, speechless, and I could tell he wasn't going to be moved on this. The man who'd once played an entire game with a broken wrist didn't understand quitting.

I could tell I wasn't going to win, so I went into the bathroom and pulled my hair back into a ponytail.

But as I started thinking about school, I started freaking out. I was going to have to face Alec, who probably hated me by now.

What if he wanted to talk about it? With the way he always managed to read my mind, what if he looked at me and *knew* about my agreement with Benji?

Before I had a chance to even register I was spiraling, I started breathing too fast. My heart was racing and I was sweating and—*oh God*—I couldn't stop it. I put my hands on top of my head and told myself what I always told myself—*this is just your body freaking out, you are fine*—but I couldn't get air.

"Deep breaths, kid, deep breaths," I heard, and when I looked in the mirror, my grandpa was standing in the doorway, watching me.

He gave me a nod and said it again. "In through your nose and count to four. You're fine."

I tried, but it still felt too fast.

It wasn't working.

"Come on," he said, grabbing my hand and pulling me out of the bathroom. I followed behind him, shaking, and was surprised when he pushed open the doors that led out onto the balcony. Frigid air rushed at me in my pajamas and stockinged feet.

"Grandpa, it's freezing!" I said. "I—"

"It helps," he said, cutting me off. "The cold air helps. Focus on how fucking cold it is."

"It *is* fucking cold," I said, which made him raise an eyebrow.

And then he smirked.

He stood out there with me for a long time, not saying a word as I paced around the balcony with my hands on top of my head, telling myself I was okay while freezing my ass off.

"Better?" he finally asked when I stopped pacing.

"Much," I said, clearing my throat. The cold air *had* helped, and I was ridiculously grateful for this giant grump who'd talked me through the attack. "Thank you, Grandpa."

"Now why don't we go inside and you can tell me why you don't want to go to school and the tournament so badly."

CHAPTER FORTY-SIX
Alec

"I can't believe Dani's still sick."

I kept my eyes out the window, turning up the volume in my ears as I tried ignoring the conversation behind me. This was an epic day and I refused to fucking think about *her*.

Not when we were headed to the X.

The team bus was surrounded by the ceremonial Southview police escort, lights flashing as the cruisers led us toward the city limits, and I was trying my damnedest to find a balance between excitement and focus.

"Did you talk to her today, Zeus?" Vinny asked, leaning forward.

He and Kyle were on the seat behind me.

"Nah," I said, shaking my head and refusing to picture her face.

Kyle shot me a look but didn't say a word.

He was the only one who knew.

I'd confided in him (which meant Cass probably knew), but when he suggested we keep it quiet until after the tournament so no one got superstitiously freaked out, I grabbed the bailout with both hands.

Because I had no interest in having any conversations about what had happened.

I fucking couldn't.

I'd gone through the motions yesterday and today, pretending my girlfriend was out sick, but I couldn't think of her without feeling a thousand fucking feelings.

So I'd stopped thinking about her altogether.

Hell, I was glad she was sick.

Her being there would've been too much.

After she left the other morning, I drove myself nuts trying to figure out what the hell had happened to make everything change so fast, because she'd seemed honest when she said it wasn't about the fight.

But if Worthington and the fight had nothing to do with it, how had we gone from fucking perfect to her crying and breaking up with me?

It didn't make any sense.

What the hell changed?

But the bottom line was that I couldn't let it mess with my head. I didn't have the luxury of being a heartbroken little bitch about this, because it was tourney time.

And we were facing St. John's Academy in the quarterfinal.

Between having to play against the guy who could've had me arrested (which would've destroyed my future) but didn't, and having to deal with the emotional bullshit of getting dumped a couple of days before the tournament, it was going to take every bit of mental focus I had to be a hundred percent locked in.

So the only thing I was thinking about was lacing up my skates and sending St. John's home.

Shoving our win down Worthington's throat.

"I'm a little dialed into other things right now," I said, doing my best not to sound like a dick.

"For sure," Vin said, nodding in agreement. He gestured to my headphones with a smirk. "God, I can't even imagine what kind of softass bullshit you're rocking for *this* game, Z."

Everyone roasted me for listening to the opposite of "pump-up" music (aka Zeus's Lady Tunes, Barczewski's Emo Jams, Alec's Pregame Cryfest) when gearing up for games, but I swear to God they had it all wrong. I didn't need music to get me going—fuck, my goddamn brain never slowed when it came to hockey.

No, I needed the calm before the storm.

Which today came in the form of "exile," though the lyrics were hitting a little too close, making the calm a little tougher to settle into than usual.

"Well, what the hell is on *your* playlist at the moment, jackass?" I asked. "What banger is fucking amping you?"

Vinny flashed an unrepentant grin, pointed at me, and said, "This motherfucker right here with the ludicrous question."

"Aw, shit," I said, laughing in spite of myself. "Walked right into it."

Vinny was obsessed with Lady Gaga and had been on a kick all season, torturing us with his playlists whenever he had the opportunity.

"'How Bad Do U Want Me,'" he said, "is fucking *fueling* me, man."

And Vinny proceeded to hold up his phone and crank the volume so the entire bus had no choice but to give in to the Gaga.

And—*God help me*—give in they did.

We all did.

By the time the police escort left our side, the whole damn team was singing along.

When we got to the hotel, we dropped our bags in the conference room. It was reserved for our equipment, so we unloaded our stuff immediately, laying everything out to dry from practice, and then we checked into our rooms. I was staying with Vinny, which was good because he was pretty chill, and Richie and Kyle were in the room next door.

"I can't believe they took our phones," Kyle said when we walked through the lobby an hour later to get back on the bus to go to the banquet.

"Yeah, what the hell am I gonna do tonight to fall asleep?" Richie asked. "Lie down and just close my eyes like a pioneer?"

"Watch TV, dumbass," I said, wishing we could fast-forward to game time tomorrow.

I knew—because my parents had reminded me about a hundred times—that I should soak up everything about the tournament, but it was hard when I just wanted to go.

CHAPTER FORTY-SEVEN

Dani

I almost couldn't watch the game.

Seeing the guys get introduced, watching the fans going crazy, witnessing the place erupt in chants of "Mr. Hockey" when Alec was announced (because, according to my grandpa, he was the favorite to win the award)—everything inside me wanted to be at the sold-out X so badly.

But I was with Grandpa Mick, instead, watching from a distance.

After the panic attack yesterday, I cried like a blubbering baby as I told him about the postcards, the fake dating, the real dating, and then I told him the truth about why I really broke up with Alec (after swearing him to secrecy).

I'd needed to tell *someone*, and, as odd as it sounded, I trusted my grandpa more than almost anyone else.

I expected him to call Benji a little shit or something, but he'd just handed me a box of tissues and told me to blow.

Then he shocked me by saying I didn't have to go to school on game day because I was going with him to Tom Reid's Pub downtown to watch tournament games all day. We showed up at the hockey pub before lunch, and we'd been sitting there ever since.

It'd been kind of fun, watching games with Grandpa and learning hockey until Southview's game started at seven. I was so nervous for Alec and so sad I wasn't there that I couldn't even sit; I had to pace around our table, cracking my knuckles and wringing my hands.

And the game was insane from the second the puck dropped.

Richie scored a goal ninety seconds in, a lucky empty netter that had Grandpa Mick and me yelling and high-fiving everyone around us. Alec played like he always did, somehow managing to be everywhere and everything all at once, doing an amazing job protecting the goalie. He looked faster than usual, if that was even possible, slamming players into the boards while doggedly going after the puck.

I could barely breathe as I watched.

But in the second period, when Kyle tripped Benji and got sent to the penalty box for two minutes, St. John's took advantage of the power play and managed to score not only once, but *twice*.

"No!" I yelled when the second one went in, dragging my hands through my hair and kind of wanting to vomit.

"Cool it," my grandpa said, signaling to the server that he needed another beer. "Plenty of time."

The buzzer sounded, and I wasn't sure I was going to survive another period of this.

My phone vibrated in my pocket—and, God, it was my dad.

Talk about terrible timing.

And somehow my grandpa knew who it was, because when I glanced at him, he said, "Just answer—you need to talk to him, and you're just going to pace through intermission anyway."

"True," I said, feeling somehow more capable of talking to my dad with Grandpa Mick's support.

"Hey, Dad," I said, standing and walking over to the hallway by the restrooms. The pub was packed and noisy, so I was looking for somewhere marginally quieter.

"Hey, honey. Where are you? It's so noisy," he said.

"Why did you leave?" I asked, because hearing his voice *hurt* something inside me. And it make me feel bold. Bolder than before. I deserved answers. "I mean, how could you leave without talking to me first?"

"Oh," he said, sounding surprised that I'd jumped right into it. *I'm a little surprised myself.* "Well, it just seemed like we weren't going to have a fruitful conversation with—"

"'Fruitful conversation'?" I repeated, immediately frustrated. "Did you really think that asking me to pick a parent would result in a fruitful conversation?"

"I wasn't asking you to do that," he snapped, sounding defensive. "I was simply trying to get closer—"

"But I overheard what Grandpa Mick said to you," I said, steeling myself for his reaction. "And he wasn't wrong. Why couldn't you have wanted to get closer to me without asking me to destroy Mom?"

"Now, come on, that's not what I was doing," he said.

"It was, though," I said, wondering if he really even cared. "You know Mom, and you know how close Mom and I are, so you can't just pretend it didn't occur to you that this would be upsetting."

It was scary, being this honest with him, but I didn't want to stop.

"I know we let you down by moving back, and I'm so sorry for that," I said. "But I'm kind of happy here, I think, being in a place that feels permanent for once. I don't want that to hurt you, and I don't want it to make you distance yourself, because I love you."

I took a deep breath, feeling slightly braver than normal.

"Daniella," he said, his voice quiet, and then he sighed. Said, "I'm sorry too."

"You are?"

"I am," he said, sounding . . . more introspective than usual. "I *did* feel like I was losing you when you guys moved back there, and I'm not proud of my knee-jerk reaction. Your grandpa said some things the other night that really hit home."

"Oh," I said, my chest feeling tight as my dad completely surprised me.

"I've made a lot of mistakes over the years when it comes to you, but it was always because I love you—you know that, right?"

"Of course," I said, absolutely confused by the fact that he was admitting to being wrong.

I guess Grandpa really *had* struck a chord with him.

"Wow, what is *that*?" he asked when a random guy walking to the bathroom yelled something as he walked by.

I explained we were watching the tournament game, and he said, "Yeah, were you as shocked as I was to discover Sarah's kid turned into an athlete?"

Sarah's kid. I could tell my dad was trying, so I wasn't going to focus on the fact that he couldn't seem to remember the name of the kid who was all I could talk about for the first, like, twelve years of my life. "For sure," I agreed.

"I had him pegged all wrong. I thought he was kind of a creepy little dork before that, honestly."

"You did?"

"Well, between the way he always followed you around and all the postcards written in another language, who could blame me?"

The postcards. "It wasn't another language, Dad; it was a code we made up."

"Same difference," he said. "All I know is that the guy kept sending them when he was *way* too old for that, so it seemed like a red flag. What well-adjusted boy in high school is still sending coded messages once a week to a girl he knew in grade school?"

"He stopped sending them when I was in middle school, to be fair," I said, remembering *exactly* when he stopped writing, because it was right when everything in my life was at its worst.

"No," he said. "I distinctly remember telling your mother that it was weird that the kid was going into high school and still doing it."

"I don't think that's right, but—"

"No, it is, Daniella—I started tossing them," he said. "*That's* why you don't remember them, because I chucked them with the junk mail."

"Wait." All the sounds around me disappeared as I asked, "You threw them away?"

He threw. Postcards. Away . . . ?

"I mean, as a parent, it's a little concerning when there's a kid who won't stop sending your daughter messages you can't even decipher—"

"I can't believe this," I said, my thoughts racing back to the things Alec had said when I broke up with him, the things that had seemed to make zero sense. *I wrote you every fucking week.* "So . . . he was still sending them?"

"All the time," he said. "Letters, too. And you were struggling to adjust after what had happened in Texas, so it just seemed better to cut that off."

Letters??

"Oh my God," I said in disbelief, the world stopping as the truth of everything hit me. "You threw away his postcards."

Alec had never ghosted me.

"You threw them away," I repeated, totally in shock.

He had kept writing.

Which meant that he hadn't changed at all.

I closed my eyes, because this also meant that when *I* stopped writing, brokenhearted by his abandonment, I was actually ghosting *him*.

Abandoning *him*.

Oh no.

At least this time there aren't any letters for you to ignore.

Now it made sense, the way he'd seemed mad at me from the minute I showed up in Southview.

How could you walk away when I needed you?

He thought I'd ghosted him.

"How could you do that?" I asked, my voice cracking. "How could you just throw them away?"

"Honey," he said, and I could tell by his tone that he was shocked it was a big deal. "I didn't think those little messages meant anything to you."

They actually meant everything.

"I—I have to go," I said, needing to get off the phone and figure out what this meant. Just when I thought my dad and I were moving forward, we were moving two steps back. It was soul-crushing. "We aren't done with this, but I have to hang up now."

"I love you, kiddo," he said, which somehow made it worse and better, all at the same time. "I'm sorry."

"You too. Bye."

I hung up, shaken by the revelation as I left the hallway and went back into the pub. I pushed through the crowded bar, numb, because this changed everything.

But when I got to the table, my grandpa looked over at me with a weird expression.

One I hadn't seen before.

"What?" I asked, glancing up at the big TV.

I expected to see that St. John's Academy had scored again or something, but it looked like the game had stopped.

And then I saw why.

A player was down.

A player wearing the number-seven jersey.

Alec.

My entire body went cold as I saw him lying on the ice, surrounded by his teammates as a stretcher came out.

"Oh my God, what happened?" I asked, unable to look away from the big screen, my heart in my throat.

As if on cue, the TV switched to an instant replay.

It showed Alec going after the puck, his back to the camera, and then he was checked from behind, a blue jersey slamming into him at full speed. *Worthington.* I watched in horror as Alec flew into the boards, headfirst, then went down on the ice.

Oh God, oh God, oh God.

"Grab your coat," Grandpa Mick said, getting out of his chair. "We gotta go."

"What?" I couldn't look away from the screen, paralyzed. "Where?"

He gestured to the guy behind the bar that he wanted to settle his tab and said, "We're going to the hospital."

CHAPTER FORTY-EIGHT
Alec

"So as soon as the doc gets here, we'll get you wheeled down for surgery."

"Thanks," I said, a big fan of the nurse because whatever he'd put in my IV had calmed my shoulder way the hell down.

Also, his name was *Dan*, which I found to be strangely amusing as the meds did their thing.

"Great," my mom said, nodding.

My dad was still at the X, taking videos of the celebration. He'd FaceTimed us with thirty seconds left in the game, so at least I'd been able to *virtually* be there when we got the dub.

As it turned out, karma was a five-minute major. And grounds for a suspension.

Nothing gave me more joy than learning that Worthington's time in the box had allowed us to score two goals during the power play.

Fucking *yes*, holy shit, we were moving on.

It was literally Benji's fault that his team lost, so that was just the sweetest irony, the cherry on top of the quarterfinal-win sundae.

Of course, as soon as time expired I had to put away the phone and go down to X-ray, followed by an immediate surgical consultation, so not *everything* was a win. My collarbone was fractured, and my labrum was shredded (and probably had been for a while).

Hence the surgery.

But the painkillers were providing help in multiple ways. In addition to numbing my shoulder, they were allowing me to *not* freak the fuck out about what this injury meant. Being out for three months, more medical bills—this was a nightmare.

But I was calm about it for the moment.

There was a knock on the door of my ER room, and when I looked over, I saw Mick Boche.

What the fuck?

He was standing there, looking uncomfortable.

Maybe these pain meds are too strong and I'm hallucinating.

"Hi, Mick," my mom said.

"Hi." He stepped into the room and said, "How's the shoulder?"

My mom launched into a medical explanation, thank God, because I didn't feel like it. I didn't want to talk about my shoulder, and I didn't want to talk to him.

He reminded me of *her*, and I didn't want to think about her.

I watched them talk, not really listening to their words, because I was exhausted.

I let my eyes close, and I don't know how much time passed before my mom said, "I'm running to get some coffee, Al—I'll be right back."

"'Mkay," I said, so tired.

I heard the door close behind her, and then I heard, "Barczewski."

My eyes sprang open because, *shit*, Mick was still there. He was standing next to my bed, looking down at me like he had things to say.

"What's up?" I said casually, even though I couldn't even guess what Mick would want to talk to *me* about, especially now.

"I, uh," he said, grabbing the reading glasses out of his shirt pocket

404

and putting them on his nose. He looked down at his phone and said, "I just want to make sure you know that everything's gonna be fine."

"What?"

He glanced at me, put his eyebrows down, then looked at his phone again. "Even though you can't play juniors this summer, this injury's going to heal quickly, and before you know it, you'll be back on the ice. You don't have to worry."

"Oh, okay," I said, wondering if my mom was texting him. Maybe she'd asked him to talk to me, which would be super weird.

But no less weird than if Mick was actually saying these things to me. "Thank you."

"And this won't affect your NHL chances, either," he said in a weird tone, like he was reading instead of talking. "You're still going to have an epic draft and—"

"Did you just say 'epic draft'?"

The drugs are definitely messing with me, because my mom would never text him the word "epic."

"Goddamn it, I did," he said, shaking his head in disgust. "But you get it, right?"

"I get it," I said, even though I actually did not get it.

"Oh yeah." Mick put his phone down and reached into his jacket pocket. "Here."

I watched as he pulled a king-sized Charleston Chew out of his coat.

"What's this?" I asked in disbelief as he held out the candy bar. My *favorite* candy bar.

"I just, uh, thought you might be hungry after the game." He cleared his throat and pointed the Charleston Chew at me like he was dying for me to grab it, like it was burning his hand. "Here."

"What's going on?" I asked, because I had no idea what this could be about.

"What do you mean?"

"Why would you give me this?" I hadn't had a Charleston Chew in years, but it'd been my favorite candy bar the summer after sixth grade, when Dani and I discovered how good they were frozen.

"I don't know, it's a snack," he said, shrugging.

"But why *this* snack?" I asked.

"You don't like it?" he said with a scowl.

"That's not the point," I said. "What made you get it?"

Mick sighed. "For the love of God, can't you just take the damn snack and say thank you?"

"Fine. Thank you," I said, grabbing the Charleston Chew.

"You're welcome," he said with a beleaguered sigh.

His phone chirped, and he made a growling noise in the back of his throat before pulling it out of his pocket.

He looked at the screen and sighed yet again.

"One more thing," he said as he looked at his screen. "Did you tell the doctor about the shoulder troubles you were having before the game?"

"What *is* all this, Mick?" I asked, because something was obviously going on. "Level with me here."

He stared at me for a minute, like he was weighing his options, and then he said, "Oh, for fuck's sake—just look."

He held out his phone, and I could see a string of text messages.

A string that started ten minutes ago.

From Dani.

Dani: Tell him that everything's going to be fine and that even though he can't play juniors, this injury's going to heal quicky and before he knows it, he'll be back on the ice. Make sure he knows he doesn't have to worry.

Mick's response was a simple: Got it.

Dani: Coming from you this will mean a lot. Make sure you tell him that it won't affect his NHL chances, either. Tell him he's going to have an epic draft.

Mick's response: OK

Dani: Don't forget the Charleston Chew

Mick: Christ

Dani: Did you make sure the surgeon knows his shoulder was already messed up?

"What is this?" I didn't understand but suddenly felt wide fucking awake.

He put his phone back in his pocket. "I have no idea what you're talking about. Were you reading over my shoulder?"

"So." A buzz started in my body from head to toe, like I'd just been switched on. "She asked you to come in here and talk to me. Why?"

"Why do you think?" he said as if I was an idiot.

"But she walked away," I said, confused because her texts definitely made it seem like she was worried about me. "She's done."

He shrugged. "Is she?"

Isn't she? "But she said—"

"Sometimes people don't mean what they say," he interrupted. "Did she look like she meant it, dipshit?"

"Geez, Mick, I don't know," I said, offhandedly wondering how the hell this bizarre conversation with Mick Boche could be happening.

And also—no, she *didn't* look like she meant it.

She'd *cried* while she told me she needed a break.

"And sometimes people do things they don't *want* to do. That they feel like they *have* to do."

"Can you stop with the code and just tell me?" I said, because it was obvious Mick knew something that I didn't.

"Maybe you should ask her."

Should I? It seemed like a bad idea.

I should just let it go; I'd already swallowed every bit of my pride when I begged the other day.

I'd be a pathetic moron to open it up again.

Mick's phone chirped again, and he cursed, glaring at me like this was somehow my fault.

"What'd she say?" I asked.

He looked down at the message. "She said, 'What did he say? Does he seem okay?'"

"Where is she?" I asked.

I realized she had to be nearby. "Where is she, Mick?"

"I don't know," he said, but he pointed his head toward the door.

"She's in the hallway?"

The old guy just shrugged.

"Collins!" I yelled. "Get your ass in here!"

Mick looked over at me, and I swear to God he gave me a nod, like he approved.

"Dani Collins!" I hollered even louder.

"It's about damn time," Mick said, almost smiling.

A second later, Dani came running into the room—literally stopping short when she saw Mick, looking bored, and me sitting there with the Charleston Chew in my hand.

"What's the matter?" she asked, looking like she wasn't sure what was going on, which was fair since I'd just screamed bloody murder in a hospital. "Are you okay?"

Her hair was piled on top of her head, that mass of golden curls, but her brown eyes were red and puffy behind those big glasses, her face blotchy like she'd been crying.

"Why did you send him in here?" I asked, my eyes tracking over the sadness on her face, trying to reconcile it with everything else that didn't add up.

I could only come up with one thing that made sense here—*please let Mick be right*—and I wanted it so fucking badly.

"I didn't," she lied, clearing her throat and glancing at her grandpa.

Who shrugged and raised his eyebrows.

"Don't lie to me, Collins," I said, but I wasn't pissed.

At all.

I was . . . on edge.

Suddenly thrumming, on fire, alive.

Again, could be the painkillers.

"I'm not," she lied again.

"Mick, do you think I could talk to your lying granddaughter alone for a minute?" I asked, my eyes staying trained on her as she blinked faster, like she was trying to come up with an escape plan.

"No, Grandp—"

Without a word, Mick walked past her and exited the room.

I was really growing fond of that guy.

"Um, what's up?" she asked quietly, crossing her arms over her chest and gnawing on her lip, looking downright jumpy.

"For starters, would you mind coming closer so everyone outside the door doesn't hear me?"

More fast blinking and a nod. "Sure."

She walked over, turning me on in that fucking Southview jersey and pressing play on ROLE MODEL in my brain, and she stopped beside my bed.

I'm sorry, but I'm deeply still in love

"Now tell me why you made him come talk to me," I said. "And don't lie."

In love with you

Her eyebrows crinkled together and she cleared her throat. Her voice was barely there when she said, "You're my friend, and I knew how stressed you were about everything. So, as your friend, I thought it might help to hear from someone who knows—"

"What about the Charleston Chew?"

I stared her down, trying to read her mind as she avoided meeting my eyes. I could tell she didn't want me to know something, but dammit—I was going to make her tell me.

She shrugged and said, "I mean, you probably haven't eaten since—"

"Can you please just be honest with me?" I said in frustration, *needing* her to open up. "I could die in surgery, Dani, so stop fucking lying."

CHAPTER FORTY-NINE

Dani

"What?"

I looked at him, propped up in the hospital bed wearing a blue gown and his glasses, and the tears were back because what the hell did that mean? I'd been pacing around the ER waiting room for hours, trying not to cry while worrying and missing him and regretting and over-thinking, and now this?

"I thought you were just having shoulder surgery!" I said, aware my voice sounded perilously close to hysterical, but I couldn't help it. My heart started racing and my body was instantly on fire as the best friend I'd ever had watched me react to his news. "Is there something else—"

"No—*shit*—relax," he interrupted, his dark eyes moving all over my face. He looked stunned by my reaction, and then he said, "I was just kidding about the dying thing."

"You were *kidding* about the *dying thing*?" I said (yelled), smacking his forearm as I gritted my teeth and tried containing my anger.

"Hey, you can't hit a patient—"

"You seriously think that's funny? I have been literally falling apart since he made me break up with you and then my dad, my awful, terrible dad, calls tonight and tells me that you *didn't* stop sending postcards but he threw them all away, so I never knew and thought you ghosted me, which means I kind of ghosted you, and just when

I find all of this out, I see your body lying still on the ice like you *are* dead—how can you do this to me? How can you joke about this?"

I wished his collarbone weren't broken because I needed to punch him square in the chest.

"What the *fuck*?" he said under his breath.

Angrily.

I raised my eyes to his face and he said, "Who the hell *made you* break up with me?"

Oh.

Oh no.

Had I said that?

Out *loud*?

"Dani." He looked like hockey Alec as he waited for my answer, his intense eyes flashing as he demanded everything just by saying my name in that tone.

"Wait. *No, no, no*," I said quickly, shaking my head and fake smiling like it was all a funny misunderstanding. "It's not—"

"Tell me what that means, Collins," he said.

"Nothing—I, um," I stammered helplessly. "It's not—"

"Tell me," he said through clenched teeth, his eye contact aggressively intense.

"You don't understand, I have to—"

"*Tell* me, for the love of—"

"Benji, okay?" I yelled, digging my hands in my hair, frustrated and scared and so damn tired. "He said he wouldn't press charges if I broke up with you, but I need you to—"

"He did *what*?" Alec yelled back.

"Listen," I said, holding up a hand as I desperately tried to get him to hear me, to understand that he couldn't go off about this. "I need you to be cool. You can't freak out because—"

"You broke up with me because *Ben Worthington* told you to?" His eyes narrowed and he pinned me in place with his stare. "Are you saying you did it so I wouldn't go to jail?"

"I mean, I highly doubt there would've been jail time—"

"Collins," he snapped impatiently, his eyes all over my face.

"Yeah . . . ?"

He tilted his head, paused for a long moment, and then said, "So if I'd never hit Benji, would you have ended things with me?"

No, never, not in a million years.

"Well, no," I admitted, but quickly added, "But it *did* happen, Alec, and I agreed to—"

"Then we're back together," he said definitively, like he was making an official proclamation. "Starting now."

"What?" He had to be out of his mind or missing the point of what I'd done. "No, we're not. You can't—"

"Yes, we are," he said boldly, looking slightly less angry but just as intense. "Have your feelings for me changed?"

I swallowed, not wanting to answer that. "Alec—"

"Answer the question."

I said, "It's not that simple—"

"Answer the question, Collins," he said. "*Have* your feelings changed for me?"

"No," I snapped, but then I took a deep breath and confessed, "Not one bit."

His jaw flexed and he swallowed.

"Then this *is* that simple," he said, his voice getting quiet. Quiet, yet the only thing I could hear in the world when he said, "We've made everything so fucking complicated since you moved back, but the simple truth is that all I've ever wanted is you—period."

I shook my head, knowing I needed to dissuade him while at the same time wanting to lock those words in a box under my bed so I could reread them every night before falling asleep.

"I wanted you in fourth grade, when you launched me off that water pillow and broke two of my ribs," he said, his eyes narrowed on me behind his glasses like he could still see us at the lake. "I wanted you in sixth grade, when I drove over your foot with my dad's ATV. I wanted you when Mr. Pockets got hit by a car and you cried as hard as I did, I wanted you when you kissed the shit out of me in the shed, and now, God help me, I want you when you shattered my fucking heart to keep me from ruining my own future."

My hands were shaking as he looked so unbelievably . . . *serious*.

Alec Barczewski was never serious.

Not like this.

"Better and worse don't matter with us—they don't—because it's all fucking *better* with you. And what the hell is simpler than that?"

I sucked in a breath, feeling like I was drowning from how badly I wanted to give in, to just let go and fall into the magic of his words.

"But Benji could still—"

"Fuck Benji," he interrupted, his eyes on me as his left hand reached under the bed rail and started moving around, his fingers searching for something. "Benji can't touch us."

"What are you doing?" I asked, watching his hand fumbling all over the rail panel. "Alec."

"Trying to get this damn bed rail to go down," he said. "I know there's a button somewhere because I saw the nurse hit it."

"What?" Maybe the painkillers they'd mentioned were kicking in. "You probably shouldn't—"

"I'm confessing that I've loved you forever, and it doesn't work for me to be confined to a bed and for you to just, like, stand there," he said, "listening and looking at me like I'm crazy."

I bit down on my lip because it was a terrible time to laugh, but suddenly—instantly—I was filled with so much happiness that it didn't want to be contained.

I smacked his hand out of the way, pushing the release latch so the rail went down. "So what *does* work in this scenario?"

"Collins, you fucking goddess," he said, his mouth sliding into that boyish grin I loved. "I was thinking something like this."

I don't know how he did it, but one unexpected hard tug on my shirt with his good hand and I fell forward, closer, half sprawled out on top of him.

"Alec!" I squealed, then got lost in uncontrollable cackling when he used his legs to somehow maneuver me fully onto the bed with him.

"Well, hey there," he said, grinning as I pushed at my out-of-control hair and scrambled into a sitting position. "It feels good being back together, doesn't it?"

"We aren't back together," I replied, giggling. "Not until *I* say we are."

He swallowed and his tone went softer, deeper, when he said, "Then say it, Goldilocks."

"Fine," I replied, a thousand thoughts going through my mind, all of them happy. "We're back together."

"Okay, so listen, I'm gonna need your help," he said, his dark eyes making my stomach weightless as they dropped down to my mouth. "I need to kiss you like . . . two *days* ago, but I can't really move my upper body, so—"

"Enough said," I managed, my heart fluttering as I leaned over him and leaned in, my eyes never leaving his.

But as soon as I got close, he reared up, his lips finding mine as if he couldn't wait another second. He was hands-free, his mouth the only weapon at his disposal, but he didn't need anything else, dear *God*.

I set my hands on his hard jawline, wanting grip because I was under attack.

"Danigirl," he breathed against my lips, licking into me and stealing my breath, delivering white-hot, wide-open kisses that I felt everywhere. The sound of his unsteady breath made my chest burn, and when my fingers found their way to his thick, hockey-mussed hair, I dug in and tugged because what else could I even do?

He grunted—in such a good way—and nipped my bottom lip, sending shocks through my entire body—

"The doctor is in the building so it's time to take you—*ahem*," I heard, and when I jerked back from Alec and turned around, nearly falling off the bed, a nurse was walking into the room.

With Alec's parents beside him.

And my mom.

And my grandpa.

I could die.

"Busted," Alec muttered, and I could hear the smirk in his voice, but

I wasn't *about* to look at him as I *jumped* off that bed.

"Who lowered the bed rail here?" the nurse asked, his eyes narrowed.

"She did, Dan," Alec said, pointing at me and making my mom—and his parents—grin.

And he was full-on smiling, beaming like a happy toddler.

The shit.

"Young lady, he's got pain medication in his IV, so he's a fall risk," the nurse said with a scowl, but he also looked like he was messing with me. "These rails need to be up."

"Yes, but," I said, noticing on his badge that his name was actually Dan, "he told me to do it."

"I'm impaired, though," Alec said, slowly shaking his head like I was the problem. "On account of the aforementioned pain medication."

"You're suddenly a smug little shit, aren't ya, Charleston Chew?" Grandpa Mick said.

"Charleston Chew," I repeated with a snort, falling into unstoppable giggles at the smart-ass nickname.

"No," Alec said, pointing at me.

"If you two are done canoodling," *Dan* said, "we're gonna go get your bones put back together."

Alec mouthed *canoodling* to me with that irrepressible Alec Barczewski smile on his face, and I totally lost it.

"You good now, kid?" Grandpa Mick asked me after they wheeled Alec down to pre-op, tugging on one of the many hairs that'd fallen in my face over the course of the stressful hospital visit.

Was I good? "Good" didn't begin to describe it.

Because on top of everything else, just before they whisked him out

LYNN PAINTER

of the room, I was able to quickly blurt to Alec what I'd learned from my dad about the postcards.

"So I never stopped writing to you, and I'm so sorry I wasn't there when you needed me," I finished in a rush as everyone in the room waited for me to shut up so they could get my boyfriend to surgery.

I expected Alec to look pissed or shocked, because I was still *very* both of those things when I thought of what my father had done, but he *shrugged*.

Alec shrugged—with the most adorably sleepy smile—and said, "Looks like we've got a lot to catch up on when I wake up, honey."

So back to the question. Was I good?

I nodded, wondering how it was possible to be this happy. "Never been better, Grandpa."

DANI'S EPILOGUE
April

"I'm going to get the mail," I said as I walked into the kitchen, my eyes barely open.

"I was starting to think you were gonna sleep all damn day," my grandpa said, stirring a pot of ramen noodles on the stove. "I'm already having lunch."

"Only because you eat too early," I replied, snagging a Red Bull from the fridge.

Although to be fair, it was almost one o'clock. Alec had come over last night and we'd watched TV until like two thirty (when Grandpa kicked him out), so sleeping in had been absolutely necessary.

"Grab *all* the mail," my mom said. "Not just your stuff."

"Fine," I said, setting down the drink. "But I'm not putting on shoes."

"It's a nice morning—you'll be fine."

The second I opened the door, I let out a huge sigh because, God— spring was finally here. The sun was shining and birds were chirping and my feet weren't even cold as I walked down the driveway in my socks.

There was nothing like spring after a long, cold winter.

My phone buzzed, and when I pulled it out of my pocket, I saw it was a text from my dad.

Dad: Are we still on for FaceTime later?

I replied: Yep—14:00 my time, right?

Dad: Sounds good.

My dad and I, after everything blew up, kind of landed in a decent place. He was still the colonel most of the time, but he actually *was* trying. We had a standing FaceTime date, every Saturday at two p.m., and so far, he'd shown up every time.

And as of now he was planning on coming for my graduation.

Weird, right?

I opened the mailbox and grabbed the stack of letters, ignoring all of them as I flipped for what I really wanted, for the piece of mail I received every single Saturday.

There it is.

I grinned as I looked at the picture on the vintage postcard; it was a snapshot of Kriz's Bakery circa 1981.

God, I love him.

I flipped it over, reading the coded message while wondering how I was so lucky.

Collins—

Greetings, girl-whose-mouth-I-like-to-kiss.

1. This morning on the way to school, I almost rear-ended a Subaru because I was distracted by your legs—you've got nice knees, kid.

2. I don't want to teach you to drive anymore—you suck—but I love you, so you

can't be mad.

Counting down the days until summer,

Alec

I giggled—he was *so* not getting out of our driving lessons, and I wondered if any of our neighbors ever looked out their windows and wondered what was up with the girl who laughed at the mailbox every Saturday.

I was walking back up the driveway when I saw it.

Harvard.

There was a large white envelope from Harvard, addressed to me.

Ohhhhhhhh.

They didn't send big envelopes full of paperwork to students *not* getting accepted, right? I stared down at it as my stomach went all light and fizzy, as I realized the final answer was probably inside that very envelope.

I felt like I was going to puke as I held that thick packet in my hands, dying to rip it open but also too scared to dare.

"Hey, Danigirl?"

I tore my gaze from the Harvard mail to see my grandpa and my mom, both standing on the porch.

"Yeah?"

"No one will be mad if you want to go open that big envelope with the Barczewski kid," Grandpa Mick said, grinning.

They knew. They'd seen the envelope in the mailbox, but they'd left it for me to grab.

"Thank you!"

"Just remember to breathe through your nose," he added, making me love him even more since we'd both been working really hard—together—at being proactive with our . . . *issues*.

I shoved the other letters back in the mailbox, clutched Harvard to my chest, and started running down the sidewalk.

"You're not gonna change first?" my mom yelled.

"Or bring us the rest of the mail?" Grandpa Mick asked.

"Nah," I yelled back, jogging.

"You look like a crazy person, kid!" my grandpa yelled, but I could hear the laughter in his voice.

"Takes one to know one!" I yelled back, only interested in getting to Alec.

I ran down the block, not caring that I was wearing my pajamas and hadn't even looked in a mirror yet. I went as fast as my legs would carry me and didn't stop until I was on the Barczewskis' porch, maniacally ringing the doorbell.

"Danigirl!" Big John said when he opened the door. His smile grew a little when he looked at my pajamas and stockinged feet. "Wow. You're a sight this afternoon, kid."

"I know, I know," I panted, holding my side, barely able to talk. "I need Alec."

"Whoa," Alec said, appearing behind his dad. His smile was big as his dark eyes crawled all over me. "What's going on here, Collins?"

"Harvard," I wheezed, holding up the envelope.

"Holy shit. Harvard," he said with his eyebrows raised, coming out onto the porch. "Did you get it? Are you in?"

"Dunno," I managed, shaking my head. "I didn't want to open it without you."

"Wait—did you run all the way here?" he asked, grinning and grabbing my hand, pulling me over to the big porch swing.

I heard John close the front door.

"Yes," I said, still breathing hard. "Now, are we going to talk or open the envelope?"

I settled onto the swing beside him.

"Calm down, you little shit," he said, pulling me closer with his good arm even though his bad one was getting better every day. "Open it."

"I think I need you to do it for me," I said, shaking my head, suddenly so nervous. "I'm too scared."

"Let's do it together," he said, taking the envelope and putting his fingers on one end, then placing mine on the other. "On the count of three."

"Okay," I said with a smile, because it just felt right, doing this *with* him.

"One," he said, dropping a kiss on the top of my head.

"Two," I said, shutting my eyes and hoping with everything I had.

"Hang on for a sec," he interrupted.

"What?" I said with an exasperated giggle, because leave it to him to stop this progress. "Come *on*, Barczewski."

"I just want to say that if for some reason you don't get in, that's bullshit and you're meant for better—you know that, right?"

"Better than *Harvard*?" I said with a face.

"If Harvard doesn't take you, then yes, absolutely there is way fucking better than Harvard."

"Okay," I said, and I actually meant it.

If I didn't get in, I knew I'd be all right.

Because not only did I have Alec, but I felt like I'd finally found my place in the world. Southview, Cassie, Lillie, Liz, living with Grandpa Mick, meat raffles at the PNA . . . I *belonged* here.

Home.

If I didn't get into Harvard, I'd be okay, because I had the support of *home* to make it all better.

"Can we move on to three now?" I asked impatiently, because I still really wanted Harvard. "This is killing me."

"After I kiss you," he said.

"Dude," I complained, "you know I love you, but I'm dying here."

"Here's the thing, though," he said calmly with a finger raised, slowly and with zero sense of urgency. "This is either going to be our last kiss before you're officially a Harvard student, or our first kiss in the new era where you're trying to figure out which other school's offer you're going to accept. I feel like this warrants a moment."

"Okay, now I *have* to kiss you," I said, climbing on his lap, madly in love with this big hockey player who was ridiculously sentimental. "But make it fast."

And, well . . . he didn't.

And I was great with that.

ALEC'S EPILOGUE
June

"Are you going to cry?"

I glanced at Dani, who actually *was* crying, and swallowed. "Fuck, no."

But I wanted to.

As we stood there in the Doug, staring at the new addition to the mural that'd just been unveiled in front of a cheering, packed arena, not crying seemed like the toughest thing I'd ever had to do.

A CHAMPIONSHIP SEASON.

The words were huge, plastered just above the team photo that'd been snapped after we beat Minnetonka to win it all. The guys were grinning, sweaty messes after playing in one of the longest state championship games on record (four fucking overtimes), holding up their fingers in a pile on the ice with all of Southview doing the same in the glass behind them.

Vinny would forever be a god in this town with sixty-five saves that night.

"It's okay if you do," she said. "Kyle's bawling."

"Thanks for that, Collins," Kyle said, and when I glanced over I couldn't *not* smile, because his face was bright red and his eyes were full of tears. "And I'm not *bawling*, for Christ's sake. I'm just . . . *misty*."

"Oh, fuck that, I'd rather *bawl* than be 'misty'—what the hell is that bullshit?" Vinny said in disgust. "Are you an eighty-year-old grandmother? Do you need a crocheted box of tissues for your fucking misty eyes?"

"This is lovely," Cassie said, laughing. "Truly."

"I feel sorry for you if this mural *doesn't* make you misty," Kyle said, and I knew he meant it.

"Oh, will you stop with that word? I'll bawl my fucking eyes out for you if you'll stop saying 'misty.'" Vinny wrapped his arm around Kyle's shoulders and added, "You emo little MVP."

Kyle had played his ass off in that game.

Everyone had played their asses off in that game.

Well, everyone but me.

I'd been there on the bench, with my right arm in its trusty sling, chewing my goddamn fingernails the entire time.

We smiled for the cameras as everyone in town—and the media— lost their shit. It was the last time us seniors would ever put on our Southview jerseys, the last time the first-ever championship team would be out on that ice together.

And that was what was bringing out the "misty" in everyone.

Honestly, I still couldn't believe we were over.

I clenched my jaw as "When We Were Young" added itself to the moment's playlist.

We'd spent our entire season on the hunt for that trophy, each game a step closer to the next game. Week by week, we'd concentrated on scouting reports and strategies, so when the end came, it felt like none of us had even considered the fact that our careers together—as teammates— were suddenly over.

We'd been too focused on the game of hockey to realize that after so many years, our time as a team was finished.

We would never play in the Doug—as Packers—again.

It felt like a loss, like something I'd be grieving for a long-ass time, because my goals and friendships had been tied up with that team for what felt like my entire life.

Let me photograph you in this light in case it is the last time
That we might be exactly like we were—

But "misty" devolved into full-on emo as Mick brought out the trophy and I saw *his* tears.

When we left the ice, I took a second to memorize the way it all felt. I listened to Richie giving Kyle shit to my right, I looked out at the burgundy-and-white crowd behind the glass, I felt the temperature of the rink on my cheeks, and I gazed up at the banners that hung from the Doug's rafters.

I wanted to sear every detail into my brain so I'd never forget.

"You know you'll never top this moment, right?" Richie said as we smiled for all the cameras. "I don't give a shit what happens in Boston—you can't beat this."

"I know," I agreed. "I could walk away right now and be completely happy."

But I wasn't walking away.

I was going to play for Boston College next year.

Before I'd even had a chance to get upset about having to sit out all summer while my shoulder healed, I got an offer from Boston College.

Which had a great hockey program.

427

And NIL money on the table that would make a big fat dent in our medical bills.

So I was going to let my shoulder heal this summer and go away to school in the fall, just like all my friends, and I was going to major in history. I never would've wished to break my collarbone and miss out on juniors, but it kind of felt like a win.

Because now I got to spend the entire summer running around Southview with Dani.

My eyes found hers—they'd *always* been able to find hers—and she winked from where she was standing between Kyle and Cassie. I felt the same kick in my chest that I always felt when I looked at her, the kick I'd never tire of.

The kick I was apparently not going to *have* to tire of.

Because my girl finally got accepted.

Dani was headed to Harvard in the fall, which just happened to be in the very same city where I'd be playing hockey.

It almost felt like it was meant to be.

THE SOUNDTRACK
OF DANI AND ALEC

1. Escorpião | Jão

2. Little League | Conan Gray

3. hell of a good time | Haiden Henderson

4. Come Apart | The Blue Stones

5. Now That We Don't Talk | Taylor Swift

6. girl i've always been | Olivia Rodrigo

7. hate it | chloe moriondo

8. Picasso | Bradley Simpson

9. Pretty Face | Ally Salort

10. Brand New | Hippo Campus

11. undressed | sombr

12. Echoes | Connor Kauffman

13. Anxiety | Doechii

14. sweat | Haiden Henderson

15. ricochet | Aidan Bissett

16. Gateway Drug | Daniel Seavey

17. Famous | Johnny Orlando

18. Want Me | Stephen Dawes

19. The Black Dog | Taylor Swift

20. In the Kitchen | Reneé Rapp

21. Eyes Wide | Alfie Jukes

22. Dopamine | Stephen Dawes

23. No One's Ever Kissed You |
        Winnetka Bowling League

24. Lose Me Like You Mean It | Daniel Seavey

25. exile | Taylor Swift (feat. Bon Iver)

26. How Bad Do U Want Me | Lady Gaga

27. Deeply Still in Love | ROLE MODEL

28. Whatever Forever | Ber

29. When We Were Young | Adele

ACKNOWLEDGMENTS

First and foremost, thank you, God, for giving me this incredible journey that I absolutely can't believe I'm on and definitely don't deserve.

And my mom, Nancy Painter—how did I get lucky enough to have you as a mother? Smart, funny, capable, beautiful—you are EVERYTHING, and words cannot express how much I love you. Thank you for making me fall in love with rom-coms way before I was old enough to even know what a rom-com was.

Thank you, Kim Lionetti, the literary agent who agents better than any agent could ever agent. I'll forever be grateful that you took a chance on me, that I wrote about a tattooed barista named . . . crap, *something* because he definitely had a name . . . who caught your eye. ;) I owe him, because you are so much more than an agent to me.

Thank you, Nicole Ellul, for being the dreamiest of editors. You do it all and somehow manage to always steer my word vomits in better directions. You are a PHENOM. I promise that one of these days, I won't make you work so hard.

And the incredible team at S&S, where do I even begin? Jessi Smith, Anna Elling, Deane Norton, Stephanie Voros, Amy Habayeb, Nicole Benevento, Michelle Leo, Shannon Pender, Nicole Russo, Justin Chanda, Anne Zafian, Amy Lavigne, Kendra Levin, Jon Anderson,

ACKNOWLEDGMENTS

Jonathan Karp, Liz Casal, Sarah Creech—you're all LITERALLY a part of my dream come true, and I'm forever grateful. Ooh—Canada's Natasha and Cayley too. ;) Also thank you to the people I'm forgetting, and please forgive me for being a sketchball.

A huuuuuge thank you to the Kirchners, my incredibly cool MN cousins. Dan, Kris, Liz, Lillie, Andy, Mel, Ashton, Cole, Tawnee, Ed, Bryce, Kylie, Uncle Gary, Auntie Ellen—you all were really cool before, but now you've next-leveled yourselves after letting us bother you all the time with questions and visits where we force you to take us to the Cro and the Moose Lodge for meat raffles and beer.

Random thanks to random people for random joy: Taylor Swift; Samantha Lionetti; Lindsay Grossman; Misty Wilson; my Berklete pals; my faves (taygracie's version); my Frenchie friend Emma; Diana; Sude; Eva; the other Emma; Colleen; Jenn; Joyful Chaos Potato Book Club; Annika; LizWesNation; Diana; Cleo; Clio; Mylla; Becca; Anderson Raccoon Jones; Lori Anderjaska; Aliza; Tiffany Fliedner; Wes Bennett's entourage; Carla; Caryn; Alexis; Ally Bryan; Anna-Marie; Katie Prouty; Jill Kaarlela; Brittany Bunzey; Shaily; Steph Bolan; Marisol Barrera; Abi Griffin; Daniza Jeanne; my Florida girls—Hannah, Elli, Morgan, and Iza; Zurain; Meredith Mincey; the Cro and the PNA in SSP; the SSP Moose Lodge; the MN boys state hockey tournament; Enlightened Soul; Ruby Lynn . . . I could go on forever because I've met so many amazing people on this ride.

And thank you to the places that welcomed me while I wrote this book, places I never expected to go but are now forever a part of who I am: Paris, Berlin, Jena, Madrid, São Paulo, Toronto, Bologna, Venice, Milan, Amsterdam, Ghent, Denver, San Antonio, St. Louis, Chicago,

New York, Atlanta, Orlando, Dallas, and St. Paul. I appreciate you not kicking me out for my picky eating habits.

And of course, thank you to my incredible family for being incredible.

Cassidy, Tyler, Matt, Joey, Kate: you are hands-down the best characters I've ever created. And Terrance, Jordyn, and Emily—so happy you joined our team. ☺

And finally—finally—KEBBIN. Kevin. Kevvvvvv.

If I'd known back when I chased you around like an idiot how great of a husband you'd end up being, I would've chased you even harder, like an even bigger idiot. You make life so . . . *perfect*. Every day with you is a dream. I am so stinking rich with laughter and smiles, and it's all because of you. I love you a real lot. Like . . . more than is probably healthy. Thank you for loving me back.

FALL IN LOVE WITH LYNN PAINTER

Grumpy sunshine and
boy-next-door feels . . .

THE DO-OVER

LYNN PAINTER

NEW YORK TIMES BESTSELLING AUTHOR OF *BETTER THAN THE MOVIES*

A sizzling second-chance
romance

LYNN PAINTER

NEW YORK TIMES BESTSELLING AUTHOR OF *BETTER THAN THE MOVIES*

Coworkers make
a bet on love